THIS TIME THE WORLD

by

Commander

GEORGE LINCOLN ROCKWELL

Second Edition, 1963 by J.V. Kenneth Morgan
Third Edition, 1979 by White Power Publications
Fourth Edition, 1982 by Liberty Bell Publications
Fifth Edition, 1986 by Liberty Bell Publications
Sixth Edition, 1993 by Liberty Bell Publications
Seventh Edition, 2004 by Liberty Bell Publications
PO Box 890, York, SC 29745 USA

www.libertybellpublications.com
803.684.4408

ISBN: 1-59364-015-3

Printed in the United States of America

ACKNOWLEDGEMENTS

The author gratefully acknowledges the inspiration he received in his political career from three great Americans: Senator Joseph McCarthy, General Charles Lindbergh, General Douglas MacArthur. (No implication is here intended that these men are or were members of the American Nazi Party.) In addition, not only the author, but the entire White Race and the American Republic owe an incalculable debt to three men who actually helped in the creation of the only real counter-force openly opposing the International Zionist-Bolshevik, race-mixing criminal conspiracy, the American Nazi Party: Floyd Fleming, who has risked his life and his security; my Deputy Commander, Major J. V. Kenneth Morgan, who has loyally stood by me in countless bloody battles with the terrorists; and DeWest Hooker, who first taught me to know the cunning and evil ways of the enemy.

Dedication

TO: ADOLF HITLER!

Like spiritual giants before you - you were cursed and driven to death
by spiritual pygmies for daring to stand up for a new and vital truth. Your
heroic people lie silent, bound in golden chains and torn between the
two criminal gangs of Bolsheviks and Zionists.
I helped to bomb and burn millions of your brave young men. Your
blue-eyed young mothers were raped and murdered by Soviet and
Negro savages. The millions of little blond boys and girls you
loved so well lie moldering in acres of devastation and ruin.
Millions of my fellow Americans, British, French and others of our
racial comrades, all as ignorant as I once was, were slaughtered and
maimed fighting for these same two filthy gangs of Zionists and Bolsheviks.
The Weltfeind cringes like the Devil at the sign of the cross. Your
mighty spirit has inspired millions with the Holy Truth.
From all over the earth, faintly at first, comes the sound of
marching boots - louder and louder they grow! Listen! They are
singing! "Die Fahne Hoch! Die Reihen fest geshlossen!"
Out of the mud and slime of lies, your holy, red, white and black
Swastika has been flung back into the skies in
Virginia, United States of America, and we pledge you our lives,
Adolf Hitler, that we shall not flag or fail until we shall have utterly
destroyed the forces of Marxism and darkness.

HEIL HITLER!!

GEORGE LINCOLN ROCKWELL

(Taken in Iceland while Commander Rockwell was commanding a Navy Squadron.)

PREFACE

When one becomes as "controversial" as "Lincoln Rockwell", writing an autobiographical book presents monumental problems which do not confront most other writers. I have already experienced a major assault on my liberty when several multi-million dollar Jewish organizations combined to dig up material as far back as my college days at Brown University in 1938, and get me committed to an insane asylum "for observation". They fondly hoped and gleefully told each other in the Jewish press that I would be permanently locked up as a lunatic. By demonstrating not only my sanity, but the rationality of my actions and ideas, I succeeded in winning over even a Jewish psychiatrist, along with many others, and in being released in only ten days, although I was ordered to the observation lock-up by the Court for thirty days!

But I am not so naive that I imagine that will be the end of the matter. The same groups still have their millions and their hate-crazed fanatics who cannot answer or stop my arguments and ideas, and who must therefore stop me personally, or else be exposed and driven out for the villians they are.

They will sieze on this book like starved vultures and comb it for new evidences of the insanity they must prove against me or stand convicted themselves.

Under these circumstances, it is frightening to think what they can or will try to do with the honest little confessions of human foibles and mistakes which I believe are due from an autobiographer to his readers, if the work is not to be a disgusting piece of self adulation. I am also aware that the revelation of intimate and sometimes less-than-heroic acts of foolishness or even wickedness --acts committed by ANY human being, but usually glossed over and hidden --will make it more difficult later on to establish the political legend about my person which will be necessary to provide the White Race with the strong leadership it must have if White Western Civilization is to survive.

This conscious building of a masterful, father-image capable of leadership has always been vital to the masses of common people here and everywhere else.

Nevertheless, in spite of the probable use of my candid honesty by my enemies to make another attempt on my sanity, and in spite of the threat to my dignity as a national leader, I intend to reveal even somewhat embarrassing episodes in my personal history which I believe are genuinely revelatory of my own nature as it shaped and was shaped by the people and events teeming around me in a chaotic world.

This book is directed more to the intellectual circles, presently drowning in oceans of Marxism which have innundated all our colleges and universities, than it is to the masses of common people, for whom the knowledge that I am an exponent of gas-chambers for Jewish (and all other) Communist traitors is sufficient understanding of my philosophy. I do not overly concern myself, therefore, with the probable exploitation of my self revealed foibles and weaknesses, because my enemies are already having a field-day lying about me with far more virtuosity than they could display if they confined themselves to what I write here. The masses will not - cannot - read this book. In spite of their mental set, the intellectuals will understand it and perhaps, admit its sincerity and cogency. I have therefore included these "juicy" items in this first edition and will see that they disappear from view as I reach a wider circle.

But this work has another formidable difficulty because of my current notoriety as the wild and wooly monster of politics.

Every name I mention, for good or evil, with praises or with curses, becomes a target for enormous forces of which the average man knows little or nothing. The Anti-Defamation League of B'nai B'rith, with an annual budget of six million dollars to "protect" the Jews from attacks, and to destroy "Anti-Semites," will latch on to this volume with sharpened claws and tear it apart word by word, searching for every weak point at which I, or those who are or were connected with me, can be reached, pumped or attacked.

For the cost of one volume, they will get what it would take years for their paid agents to search out of dusty files, and they will get facts herein from me which they could never get in any other way at all. The book will thus boomerang on me not only as material to railroad me for another possible trip to the booby hatch, but as material for all sorts of painful personal attacks on myself and the people I love, my family, friends, associates and Party Comrades.

But again, this must be. It is a calculated risk - just as all my other activity has been. I was aware of the possibilities when I hung up the swastika, but did it nevertheless as I calculated the gains would outweigh the agony and inevitable losses -which they have done most satisfyingly. The unmistakeable honesty and sincerity of this volume will, I expect, win me the virile young intellectuals I now need. And that sincerity would be impossible, were I to hide all my weaknesses or mistakes and glorify my successes.

Finally, it is utterly impossible to write the book without hurting people I love -my family. So far in my political career, I have protected them from the kind of unfair attacks I must suffer to the best of my ability. I had no right to jeopardize them so long as my career was such an impossible and wild gamble. It is still a gamble -but it is no longer wild or impossible. It is now, regardless of what wishful thinkers or the ignorant may howl, quite probable that I will achieve leadership as President of the United States in 1973, exactly as I have achieved, step-by-step, the other goals in my plans, either on time, or ahead of time. The publication of this book, in spite of the multi-million-dollar forces which have been deployed against me and the book, is just one example of this predicted and enforced progress.

It is therefore inevitable that my relatives will sooner or later be exposed to the publicity and vicious attacks which are the only answer of the Jews and Communists to our logic and arguments. My relatives, my children and those who have been close to me are inescapably a part of my life, and I had rather present them to the public truthfully and with love, than have them splashed and smeared across the pages of scandal magazines.

To my family, which I am sure cannot yet understand me or my activities anymore than most of the rest of the people, I can only say that I have done my best to write the book as it MUST be written for a cause I hold more dear than my own life, and yet spare the good people who had such a large share in making me whatever it is I am now and will be later. After three years of desperate battling for an idea and goal I believe is of paramount importance to the survival of humanity, and after two years of fighting, I believe I am not making an empty boast when I say that I will one day soon amply repay my family for whatever they are made to suffer because of persecution from those hypocrites who hate me and this book, but pretend to be lovers of intellectual freedom.

I also owe the reader a word of explanation as to my attitude toward myself.

I believe that modesty is either a virtue made utterly necessary by the fact that the possessor is indeed of only modest mental stature, or else it is disgusting hypocrisy of the most revolting kind. A truly superior mind, which can apprehend the mightiest facts and ideas in the universe - facts which are unthinkable to the millions and billions of human beings, can surely perceive its own relationship to those depressing billions of empty heads. Such a great mind can surely realize its own altitude with regard to the worm - like minds which squirm and crawl by the billions in the mud of life. And when such a mind becomes thoroughly aware of the gift which Nature has bestowed on it, it is an act of gross dishonor to make a mealy-mouthed pretense to be "just one of the stupid herd" in order to curry favor with the army of idiots, and be able to lower one's eyes " modestly" while the forces of organized boobery extoll one's genius. It is not necessary, to be sure, to go about boasting and whooping about one's gifts, but, when one has discovered and proved masterful superiority in his chosen field, I believe it is proper and honorable to be proud and conscious of that superiority, exactly as our Viking forbears were not ashamed to stand manfully forth with tales of their own prowess and courage in battle.

In exactly that sense, then, I am prepared to set forth my story, the good with the bad. I am neither afraid to admit my mistakes, nor am I afraid to lay claim to my own genius. What the world may be not yet ready to admit, I will wring from it by simple demonstration -- in combat.

Lincoln Rockwell, Commander
American Nazi Party of the
World Union of National Socialists
Box 1381, Arlington, Virginia, USA

this time the world

by

George Lincoln Rockwell

PARLIAMENT HOUSE
501 FIFTH AVENUE · Suite 1015
New York 17, New York
•
P.O. BOX 75967
Los Angeles 5, California

CHAPTER I

At first we thought the riot had been called off.

It was a hot, Sunday afternoon, July third, 1960.

The week before, June 26th, the Director of the National Capital Parks of the Department of the Interior had called me and sent me, by special messenger, an official letter of urgent warning. He told us that the Department had so much information of violence and riots planned against us that he was "not sure" he could protect us with his police force. He suggested that we give up speaking or move out of town. When I firmly but respectfully refused, he asked me to withdraw the Troopers. I had been keeping in the crowd to heckle the hecklers to keep the crowd from cohering into a riotous and dangerous mob.

We, too, had been receiving more than the usual amount of filthy telephoned threats that this time they would "beat the ---" out of us", etc. I had therefore painted a huge sign for our speaking stand warning the crowd that "certain" groups were planning to riot in order to put an end to our speaking. I had complied with the police request that we pull our troopers out of the crowd --as we always obey all reasonable police requests.

But there had been no riot on the twenty-sixth. We had twenty five of our men on hand, all behind the roped enclosure, and were more than ready for them if they burst through the ropes at us, no matter how many they were, or how tough.

They came to THIS rally, alright! Let no one say that the Jews are a race of nothing but sickly money lenders and feeble clerks. There were two or three hundred BIG, husky, mean-looking Jews who screamed curses and milled around. Some spit at us. But they did not attack. For almost two hours I managed to outshout their heckling and completed my speech by sheer force of will and power of voice.

This week, July 3rd, we felt the worst danger was over. We had faced their mob of hoods and bullies the week before, and had left the field victorious. It seemed doubtful they would try again so soon.

The rolling mall between the U. S. Capitol and the Washington monument was warm and brilliantly green in the hot July sunshine as our convoy of cars and trucks drove up with our troops and equipment. The police were there in force (with their Mounted men hidden behind the building as usual) the police dogs locked in their special little van in their squad cars (and patrol wagons) lined up beside the Smithsonian Museum. But only a few dozen people were in front of our roped-off speaking enclosure.

I sat down under a tree to one side and watched as my lads unloaded the heavy stand from the convoy, set it up, and attached the bunting and banners. A few of our "fans" came over and talked with me or offered me cold drinks. Everything seemed peaceful. In fact, it was too peaceful. Major Morgan, my deputy Commander, on whom I depended as an experienced and utterly capable Storm Leader, had asked for the day off, and had even come down to the scene in civvies with his pregnant wife to enjoy, for once, the ease of a spectator. Only eleven of our men had been able to show up at this rally after the all-out effort of the week before.

But now I could sense something different - something wrong. As the crowd began to gather, the police did a strange thing; they all but <u>disappeared!</u> They retreated over a hundred yards beyond the crowd, and there were only one or two uniformed men anywhere within operating distance of the enclosure!

I mounted the platform when the boys were ready. Then I knew what was going on. Like a horde of locusts, almost in military formation, over two hundred of last week's burly Jew hoodlums and toughs swarmed around our stand and began an obviously organized chant of "sick! sick! sick!". This was not too surprising. But what happened next was HORRIFYING. The Jews began to push and hang over the ropes and swing at our men -- <u>and the Police retreated even farther away with folded arms!</u>

When I say it was horrifying, I do not mean that what the <u>Jews</u> were doing was horrifying. We expected them to try to kill <u>us if</u> they thought they could, and were prepared to teach them the error of this method. But it must be remembered that to survive we have to bend over backward to be legal. The minute the Jews can show that we have violated the law, or even appear to have violated the law, they can bring more than enough pressure to have us stowed away and silenced. We must depend on the police to uphold the law, since we are forbidden to defend ourselves even fairly, by violence, much as we sometimes ache to do so.

When the Police suddenly "couldn't see" the most gross attacks on us, we knew that an honest police department had finally succumbed to intolerable Jewish pressure, and we were in for whatever the Jews could work up their courage to do. For over an hour and a half I managed to hold the howling, spitting mob by arrogance and psychologically calculated disdain for their overwhelming numbers. To say that we were not afraid would be untruthful, for we were only eleven and they were over two hundred and fifty, plus the fact that our whole future, all our struggles and sacrifices for over two years were lying in the balance. It was obvious that they were determined to have their riot this day and then claim that we had to be suppressed for "causing" such disorder. Nevertheless, it took those Jews over an hour and a half to work up the courage to rush us -and even then, they thinned our number first by having one big trooper called out by falsely telling military police he was a Marine, thus reducing our number to ten.

In they rushed, like an avalanche of wild beasts, screaming and howling for my guts! The stand flew over as the Jews struck, and I landed in a struggling mass of fighting men. Two yelling Jews charged me. One of my men, already down and fighting desperately, grabbed his feet and he went down. But the other Jew aimed a blow at my groin. I hit him in the head, and, as he fell, another trooper tackled him. HOW my boys pitched in! But the Jew still went for the same attack on me. This time I replied in kind, and gave that Jew a dose of his own medicine!

The fight lasted for only four or five minutes, after which the police rushed in from where they had been hiding and broke it up. Major Morgan was choked unconscious, was bleeding profusely and had his right knee permanently damaged by a number of kicks he received when he was under a pile of seven or eight Jews. Lt. Warner, National Secretary of the Party at the time, had the top of his left ear bitten almost off, and all of us were cut and bruised. We later discovered that one of the large men who had recently joined us and loudly boasted how he would fight, --Fred Hockett by name--had run out of the ring in terror when the fight began, so that we had only NINE men there to fight that murderous mob.

And we showed the Jews the calibre of those nine men when the police broke up the fight -- for we immediately set up our stand and were prepared to **SPEAK.** I mounted the platform again, broken and wrecked as it was, and would have spoken, but police called me down and I was arrested for "disorderly conduct". For the first time in my life I found myself dragged off to jail, and as I sat in a cell awaiting bail, it was impossible not to think back on the chain of circumstances which had placed me here in the ugly, urine-smelling cell-block of the first precinct of Washington, D. C.

How does an American who fought the Nazis in World War II, who has a college education and is utterly dedicated to his Country, wind up in jail after being attacked by a mob of Jews? How does a man who was looked upon for years as just a "good guy", become a fanatical NAZI who stands up in public and advocates gas chambers for Jewish or any other kinds of traitors, -- and admits he estimates about eighty percent of adult Jews will be found guilty of treason and have to be gassed? Why ME? How had events turned me into such a one, but few or none of my fellows? Was I indeed "nuts" and "sick" as the Jews so feverishly insist?

That I was somehow "different" from most of my fellows seemed obvious. But how? Was I really a moral snake full of pathological hate, as charged by the "normal" Jews or could I lay a valid claim to the apparently inevitable persecution of every advanced idea and of every truly great man Nature has produced in thousands of years. Why had I gone down to that Mall to speak knowing I might be killed or injured or arrested, knowing I would gain no money or even praise, except from a tiny few of my fellow "odd-balls"? Was my brother right when he charged that I would not do these things if I had a fine home and a yacht? Was I one of the disgusting dead-end fanatics I had seen in parks, shouting eternally some idee fixe through whiskers stained with tobacco juice, at more of the same pitiful creatures impatiently waiting only their turn to fulminate on nothing? Was I compensating for some unknown traumatic experience as a kid, as the Freudians would have it?

Sitting alone in the nasty little cell I thought back over my life and tried to discover a pattern, some clue to my motivation in going down to that mall to speak for what seemed a lost cause and in the face of what seemed the violent opposition of the whole world.

I remembered an experience in 1928, when I was ten, in Ventnor, New Jersey, just South of Atlantic City, where I was living with my mother and her sister. A gang of kid toughs my brother and I called "the Bums" came to throw me into the ocean for a cold dunking -a treatment which the boys often received as " new kids " in the school. I remembered being counselled by a few of the more friendly boys to "relax" and be thrown in and get it over with. It was "impossible", they said to resist, since half the school was in on the fun, and nobody ever took the part of the chosen victim. But the thought of calmly letting anybody, or any number of people thus do violence to me and FORCE me to something roused a nameless counter force in me. It was not just temper, because I remember being scared to death, and later on, crying. But, since they had told me it was " impossible " to resist, I was determined to resist with all my might - and that is what I did. After the experiences of two wars I still remember that battle on the deserted beach in Ventnor, New Jersey. I flung about me with my arms and legs wildly, and with a superhuman strength which I am sure surprised the "bums", and, though there were at least twenty or thirty of them, those who could get near enough to get hold of me received some blows and wounds which I am sure must have hurt. I bit, I clawed, I kicked, I tore, I pulled hair -- I used any tactic I could without thinking and fought for all the world like a mad man. I can still remember the curses of the generals of this " bums " army at their troops: "hold his leg! Get his neck! LOOKOUT! @#&%** Watch out for that arm",etc. I can also remember vividly the satisfying feeling of the flesh in my teeth as my jaws closed on the arm of one who was attempting to choke me into submission, and his even more satisfying howl of pain. Then I remember getting some kicks, and being dropped on the beach and lying in the sand crying and exhausted. But I did NOT get thrown in the surf by the "bums". I remembered, with some shame, going to school the next day and getting beaten in a regular fist fight with one of the toughs, who still smarted from the defeat on the beach. I ran home crying.

I considered the two episodes, and, for the first time since the occurances, more than thirty years ago, wondered why I had managed to fight ALL those kids and win -- and then get beaten by just one of them the next day.

My answer was, I believe the key to everything I have ever done in my life.

I have little interest in the ordinary, the usual, and above all what is considered by the world "possible". But when I am faced with an enormous challenge, I become not only deeply interested but my strength seems to increase beyond my own powers. I have in every such case, prevailed over the supposedly "impossible". I am often lazy and shiftless in the ordinary affairs of life which demand no special will or intelligence. My relatives and wives will amply attest this miserable character which produces the utmost personal discomfort in daily living not only for me but for those who must live with me.

I found it was extremely easy in school for me to outwit and and cozen my teachers, so that I could get by with almost no work and I simply could not get interested in subjects and activities which did not offer me a direct challenge, a dare. I therefore coasted along on as little work as would keep me out of too great a conflict with the forces which ordinarily press boys to succeed in school, and devoted all my energies solely to trying to exceed the limits of what my masters said were the "possibilities". In algebra, I worked for many, many hours trying to find a way to solve a single equation with two unknowns. Needless to say, I failed. But in geometry, they told me that if two triangles had a side and two angles the same, they were congruent -- and I proved to the teacher that this was not always the case. I enjoyed a deep gratification at thus accomplishing the "impossible". What a pebble I was in the shoe of education on the march!

Later, in Boothbay Harbor, Maine, with my father, I discovered the same pattern with my sports and recreational activity. I became a sailing fan, even though I had to build my own sailboat out of an old skiff. But I didn't enjoy sailing like most of the others. They all rushed to their boats when the weather was fine, the breeze brisk but not strong, and everything was "normal". And then they stayed mostly within the confines of the Harbor itself. I found little pleasure in this after a while. I preferred to go out only when the others came in because the wind was too strong. I delighted in beating the elements, the worse they got. I remember one hair-raising trip around Southport Island where my brother, a reluctant "guest", literally crouched in the sloshing water in the bilge of the little open boat and prayed fervently and miserable as the spume and green water poured over him. I was "afraid", of course, but the pure joy of combat with the wild elements had me singing and even howling back at the wild wind with animal energy. My brother begged for mercy, which I could not understand, although I feel sorry for him now. He must have thought me mad and hated me -- which he assured me he did.

When even this activity palled a bit, I essayed a trip to Pemaquid far out at sea for such a tiny boat, with another young man of similar tastes, and we made history on that trip by negotiating the "Threads of Life" -- a torturous rock-passage at night (we got becalmed on the way back) -- against the wind, and against a terrible rip tide.

My friend, Eden Lewis and I took turns fending off catastrophe from the bow of the tossing craft as we tacked back and forth only inches from the jagged rocks, with the wind howling against us, and the tide spinning us around most fearfully in the inky blackness, the continual splash of the cold, dark waters in our faces added to the general effect of horror, had we not been rash youths! How we both enjoyed it! And, even more, how we enjoyed the warm feeling of success and mastery when we reached our warm fire-sides, soaked, exhausted, but exulting in our "impossible" victory!

I discover pretty much the same pattern in my emotional life. I cannot abide "pick-ups" or "easy women", which caused me to be a good deal of an odd ball in the service, particularly when I was very young, as one might imagine. I am intrigued only by exceptional females who require something more subtle than physical overpowering.

In short, I am now fairly certain that the driving force in my life is a deep satisfaction in defying any overwhelming odds which seem to press against that which I will. In ordinary affairs, when there is no such challenge, I not only do not excel, I am a positive flop. I cannot work up any real interest in having the best rock-garden in South Podunk, for instance, and those things in life which depend on being a dedicated cultivator of rock-gardens or similar normal accomplishments find me trailing happily at the rear.

On the other hand, in addition to this positive motivation for my activities, there is a negative hate - a burning hate which alone can drive me to lose my temper, a thing I almost never do.

BULLYING -- the beating or torturing of an innocent or helpless creature by an overpowering creature or group of creatures, for the sheer pleasure of bulling and torture, drive me to a frenzy such that it is difficult to control myself.

The combination of these two overpowering drives from deep within me, I believe, are the underlying motivations which sent me down to the Mall wearing a swastika arm-band, ready to die if necessary, and dumped me, for the moment, in the smelly little cell in the basement of the Washington, D.C. Police headquarters.

I believe the same two characteristics, applied at this crucial and precise time in history, will propel me and our Nazi movement from that jail cell, up Pennsylvania Avenue to the White House. The world's longest half mile!

CHAPTER II

Mary MacPherson was the healthiest and prettiest young peasant girl in Pugwash, Nova Scotia. She had helped her Scotch immigrant family fight the Indians for their land. She had been brought up in the rude and rugged life of a pioneer, shearing the small herd of family sheep, carding and spinning the wool, weaving it, and then making clothes for all the family of it. There was no nonsense about life in Pugwash, and no nonsense about young Mary MacPherson as she set off to visit relatives in Providence, Rhode Island, some time in the early spring of 1884.

While in Providence, she met John Rockwell, a mature and dignified civil-war veteran of Scotch-English descent who had opened a real-estate office and had already married and raised a small family, before he lost his wife. Mary MacPherson married John Rockwell and they bought a house, with a large mortgage, on Pemberton Street in the Mount Pleasant section of Providence.

In this house, in 1889, was born a very unusual man -my father. Out of the most staid possible circumstances came a human mutation, a genius, who was to help set America laughing as it had never laughed before and who was to produce a son who would find America in tears and lead the battle to change those tears once again to healthy laughter. -- But not with jokes.

George Lovejoy Rockwell was nothing like his stern and dignified father or his sturdy, no-nonsense mother. From what I can gather he was more like a composite of Pecks' Bad Boy and a mischievous/impudent monkey. He played endless painful tricks on his sweet little sisters but always managed to appear the angel when these innocents appealed tearfully to their mother. He investigated everything and everybody, poked into everything, became an expert young magician, invented a thousand diabolical little devices for an equal number of diabolical purposes, learned to play the penny tin-whistle better than anyone before him, became an artist, cartoonist and sign painter, liberally plastering the cellar walls with signs for various soaps, etc. (They still remain). I have not heard of any scholastic honors awarded him, but I understand he did manage to frolic his way through part of high school, carefully placing hornets in the school-master's lunch box and performing other psychological experiments. But he could not long repress his spirits in a school room.

Starting as a magician, he entered the exhuberant new world of vaudeville. But his patter, delivered with the legerdemain, soon proved more sucessful than the magic act and he teamed up in a comedy bit with various partners including men named Al Wood and Al Fox.

For years he starved. Once, he and his partner had only a single pair of pants between them, when one of them ripped the only pair he had and they were out of work and money. They had managed to keep a room even with the rent overdue, so one stayed in bed in the room while the other searched for some kind of work or income. My father was clever at writing parodies - humorous and irreverent words to well-known songs, and his partner managed to get a few other vaudevillian customers for his services in this line. The partner would bring the customer to the room, excuse himself at the door, run inside, give the pants to my father, jump in bed, and then pretend to sleep while my father wrote the parody on the spot and in the pants.

But poverty was no damper for my old man's irrepressable spirits. Next door to this room, behind paper-thin walls, was a sister-act, and sounds were clearly heard from one room to the next. In those days and in the place, every bed had a not very handsome but utilitarian piece of china beneath it. My father conceived the idea of filling the huge water pitcher kept on the bureau and giving the young ladies in the next room something to think about. He stood on a chair, making sure they were " in " next door, then carefully and slowly poured a thin stream of the water from the pitcher into the vessel kept under the bed. This occupied about ten minutes or so, and his diabolical genius was rewarded, a few minutes later, when the pranksters innocently stepped out of their door, and, sneaking a look back, discovered two pretty heads peeking out, with mouths hanging wide open.

There is material for a delightful book in my father's endless and absorbing tales of his antics on and off stage in vaudeville, and I have urged him repeatedly to do the job himself, without success.

There was the time he bet the rest of the bill in some town in Illinois he could go out on the street and calmly hit a policeman, without being arrested. He put on dark glasses, filled his hat with pencils, and went about "feeling" vigorously with the cane, striking this way and that, until he fetched a cop a good belt on the shins. The cop winced but helped the poor "blind man" and my Pop won. Or the time in Chicago when he got the baby ducks and the whole cast watched them swim in the hotel tub, until my old man got the idea of seeing if they could swim in "rapids." The ducks were tested in the water-closet, and it was discovered with great glee that they could swim so desperately that they could beat the flush!

While Mary MacPherson was growing up as a pioneer in Nova Scotia, a young German youth named Augustus Schade was emigrating to America to make his fortune, and wound up working in a Bloomington, Illinois theater, and finally becoming manager. He married, of all things, a fiery French girl, Corrine Boudreau, his opposite in every possible way, and the two had a miniature World War I, Germans versus French, going from 1914 on.

They had two daughters, Claire, and Arline. Claire was dainty, feminine and took after her French mother. Arline was hefty, overbearing and took after her German father. When the little girls were still very small, they were trained as dancers and actresses for the booming vaudeville business, and the whole family hit the road as "The Four Schades". Little Claire was adored by audiences as a sort of Shirley Temple of her day, and performed as a toe-dancer. She continued in the theatrical business until about 1915, when she met and married my father.

Unable to approach even marriage with proper decorum, my irrepressible father, I am told, was planning to tell his new father-in-law, who by that time was owner and manager of a large Bloomington theater, that he was part colored. He was barely dissuaded by my mother and her mother who insisted that my very unhumourous German grandfather would have promptly shot him to death. This prediction was later confirmed by Augustus himself, who was only prevented with the greatest effort from carrying out the execution when he heard about the plan for the "joke".

About this time, my father had cast off his partners, with their banjos and props, and opened as a monologist. He took the pseudo title of "Dr." Rockwell, Quack! Quack, Quack!", and

Left:
My father, headlined at the Palace Theater In New York -about 1928

Below:
As a young acrobat, about 1919

Below:
Writing syndicated column in Maine, about 1934

Above:
My Father. Maine, about 1936

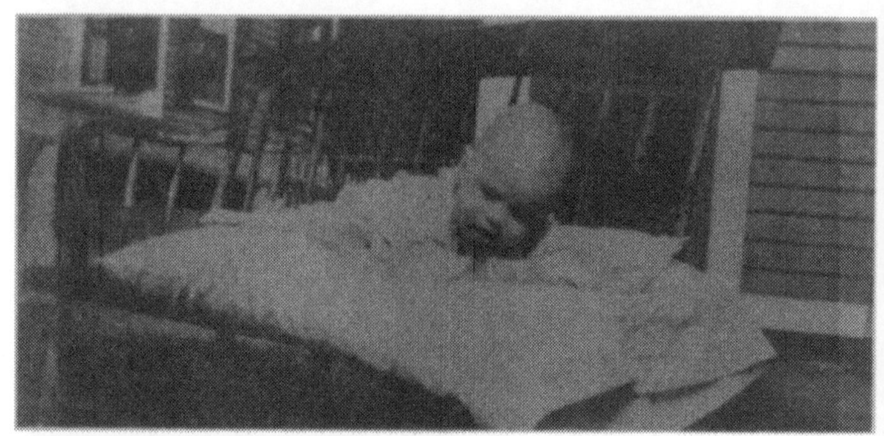

Above:
Three months old.
Providence, 1918

Left: Aunts Margie, Arlene, Helen. Grandmother Rockwell, Grandfather and Grandmother Schade, and my mother

Below:
Mother, Me, Friend, Brother Robert and Grandma Schade

Above: Father and me. Father. Father with Cod-fish, Maine.

Below: Me, Sister Priscilla. With tin whistle. With Brother.

Top: First Grade, 1924
Below: 6th Grade, 1930

Brother Robert, Priscilla,
My Mother and I. Providence.
About 1925

Aunt Arlene, Sister
and Me, Bakersfield, California.

Good view of my
well-fed Aunt Arlene,
Oregon.

posed as a great chiropracter. His only prop was a banana stalk which he demonstrated as the human spine, -- and he did something no monologist had previously dared to do, -- he sat down in an arm chair in the middle of the stage and just talked.

But he did it so successfully that I can remember being in the audience as a very, very small boy and laughing most of all at the fat men and women all around me literally falling out of their seats and suffocating and gasping in ecstacies of laughter. My old man was a master of timing and would blow a police whistle to try to extinguish the laughter so he could continue, but this only drove the howling audience to new paroxysms of uncontrollable mirth. They laughed, I am sure until they ached and hurt all over. At the height of this success, in the middle of the depression, my father was paid $ 3, 500 per week, -- a fabulous salary for the time, and he was worth every cent of it. On and off stage, he kept America almost literally in stiches.

While all this laughing was going on in the politically innocent, carefree, super-"corny" United States, the laughter had been extinguished in the more mature part of Western Civilization, Europe. In Germany and Russia the most gigantic political monster ever to appear on earth was struggling to its scaled feet. The apostate Jew, Karl Marx, had codified the doctrine organizing the biologically inferior millions of the earth, led by Jewish Communist leaders, into a ruthless war of extermination against the elite, the biologically best human material which alone could give civilization and leadership to the masses. At the same time, Theodore Herzl, a Zionist Jew, had perfected plans for gaining Palestine for the Jews from the Arabs who had held it for two thousand years as residents. Simultaneously, in the United States, the Warburgs and Kuhn Loeb and Co., and other multi-millionaire Jews in New York city were using their economic power to destroy our Republic. In 1913, these forces set up the Anti-Defamation League, or "Gestapo", of B'nai B'rith, got rid of the Constitutional safeguard against demagoguery by getting Senators elected directly instead of by the State Legislatures, set up the illegal Federal Reserve System to gain mastery over our money and banking, established the monstrous Rockefeller left-wing Foundation, and -- worst of all, got the Income Tax established to bankrupt America.

In the next three years, these same forces achieved the final wrecking of our strong Republic by diabolically and purposefully getting us into the European War on the side of Britain because Britain unscrupulously offered the Jews Palestine in return for the Jew's promise to get America into the War on the side of England. The result was that everybody lost the war, except the Jews, who got Palestine out of the Balfour declaration, for their Zionism, and Russia for their Communism. (The first government of Russia was overwhelmingly Jewish, as witnessed by Winston Churchill in an article, "Communism versus Zionism--a Struggle for the Soul of the Jewish People", in the London Illustrated Sunday Herald of February 8, 1920, reproduced in part on the next page. This is only an infinitesimally tiny bit of the huge mass of evidence that the "Russian" revolution was not Russian at all, but Jewish. The documents include the Overman report to the U. S. Senate, 1919, Senate Document 88, which shows that of the 388 members of the first Soviet Government, sitting in the Old Smolny Institute in Petrograd, 371 were Jews, and 265 of these Jews were from the lower East Side of New York City!)

In March, 1918, both Russia and Germany were in the advance throes of Bolshevik Revolution. Lenin was on his way in a sealed train to Russia, with over 417 Jewish exile Marxists, to set up the first Bolshevik Government in the world. The Jewish revolutionaries were at work in all the other chaos-ridden European Countries, with Bela Kun (Cohen) seizing Hungary for the Jew-Communists, and Rosa Luxemberg and Karl Leibnicht, both Jews, leading the Bolshevik uprising in Germany.

Meanwhile, an unknown German corporal lay in hospital in Pasewalk, outside of Berlin, his eyes all but burned out by a gas-attack. He writes movingly in Mein Kampf of the hot tears which poured down his face when a gang of deserters from the Navy rushed in proclaiming the Red Revolution, -which forced Germany to sue for an armistice. He writes even more movingly of his disgust and helpless rage when he learned that the deserters were not combat fighters from the front-lines, where he himself had won his Nation's highest decoration, --comparable to our Congressional Medal of Honor, but that they were recognizable Jews!

Five thousand miles across the Atlantic Ocean, in Bloomington, Illinois, Claire Schade Rockwell entered the Kelso Hospital at this same time to give birth to her first child, on the night of March 9th, 1918. The greatest marathon race of human history was launched.

Marx had started the momumental race in 1848, Lenin had

ZIONISM versus BOLSHEVISM.

STRUGGLE FOR THE SOUL OF THE JEWISH PEOPLE.

By the Rt. Hon. WINSTON S. CHURCHILL.

Mr. Churchill inspecting his old regiment, the 4th Hussars, at Aldershot last week.

The National Russian Jews, in spite of the disabilities under which they have suffered, have managed to play an honourable and useful part in the national life even of Russia. As bankers and industrialists they have strenuously promoted the development of Russia's economic resources, and they were foremost in the creation of those remarkable organisations, the Russian Co-operative Societies. In politics their support has been given, for the most part, to liberal and progressive movements, and they have been among the staunchest upholders of friendship with France and Great Britain.

International Jews.

In violent opposition to all this sphere of Jewish effort rise the schemes of the International Jews. The adherents of this sinister confederacy are mostly men reared up among the unhappy populations of countries where Jews are persecuted on account of their race. Most, if not all, of them have forsaken the faith of their forefathers, and divorced from their minds all spiritual hopes of the next world. This movement among the Jews is not new. From the days of Spartacus-Weishaupt to those of Karl Marx, and down to Trotsky (Russia), Bela Kun (Hungary), Rosa Luxembourg (Germany), and Emma Goldman (United States), this world-wide conspiracy for the overthrow of civilisation and for the reconstitution of society on the basis of arrested development, of envious malevolence, and impossible equality, has been steadily growing. It played, as a modern writer, Mrs. Webster, has so ably shown, a definitely recognisable part in the tragedy of the French Revolution. It has been the mainspring of every subversive movement during the Nineteenth Century; and now at last this band of extraordinary personalities from the underworld of the great cities of Europe and America have gripped the Russian people by the hair of their heads and have become practically the undisputed masters of that enormous empire.

Terrorist Jews.

There is no need to exaggerate the part played in the creation of Bolshevism and in the actual bringing about of the Russian Revolution by these international and for the most part atheistical Jews. It is certainly a very great one; it probably outweighs all others. With the notable exception of Lenin, the majority of the leading figures are Jews. Moreover, the principal inspiration and driving power comes from the Jewish leaders. Thus Tchitcherin, a pure Russian, is eclipsed by his nominal subordinate Litvinoff, and the influence of Russians like Bukharin or Lunacharski cannot be compared with the power of Trotsky, or of Zinovieff, the Dictator of the Red Citadel (Petrograd), or of Krassin or Radek—all Jews. In the Soviet institutions the predominance of Jews is even more astonishing. And the prominent, if not indeed the principal, part in the system of terrorism applied by the Extraordinary Commissions for Combating Counter-Revolution has been taken by Jews, and in some notable cases by Jewesses. The same evil prominence was obtained by Jews in the brief period of terror during which Bela Kun ruled in Hungary. The same phenomenon has been presented in Germany (especially in Bavaria), so far as this madness has been allowed to prey upon the temporary prostration of the German people. Although in all these countries there are many non-Jews every whit as bad as the worst of the Jewish revolutionaries, the part played by the latter in proportion to their numbers in the population is astonishing.

"Protector of the Jews."

Needless to say, the most intense passions of revenge have been excited in the breasts of the Russian people. Wherever General Denikin's authority could reach, protection was always accorded to the Jewish population, and strenuous efforts were made by his officers to prevent reprisals and to punish those guilty of them. So much was this the case that the Petlurist propaganda aga[...] General Denikin denounced him a[...] Protector of the Jews. The [...] Healy, nieces of Mr. Tim [...] relating their personal [...] Kieff, have declared [...] ledge on more than [...] committed offenc[...] duced to the rar[...]

infuri[...]
anti-S[...]
Th[...]
terest[...]
cepte[...]
host[...]
ciat[...]
tain[...]
Th[...]

Actual photograph of Winston Churchill's Article on the Jews, from the Library of Congress.

seized the baton from his falling hands, and carried it in 1918 to victory in the first lap. But at the same moment, the red team launched the reaction which would eventually destroy it. Adolf Hitler started the year that I was born (and the year that Marxism took Russia), made a miraculous sprint into history, almost overtook the reds, but exhausted himself in the agony of his super-human exertion. His baton seemed to fall and be crushed into the earth by the ferocity of the other side. It has lain buried now for fifteen years. All over the world it appears to be crucified. But now, at last, it has been seized up by new hands! It will be carried to triumph as inevitably as the laws of Nature decree the evenual victory of the strongest and best. The dead mass of the world's inferiors, led by even the most brilliant tactics of the Jew Communists and Zionists, cannot avoid eventually returning to their natural place of submission to the natural-born lord of life on this planet, the White Man. I have made it my mission in life, above all things, to carry that baton to victory! No matter how long it takes, how painful it may be, or how an eternally blind world scorns and hates it, Adolf Hitler's noble vision of racial idealism will yet master today's chaos and bring order, decency and the innocent fun and laughter of my father's day back to suffering, stumbling, humanity - perhaps even including the unhappy, paranoiac Jews.

CHAPTER III

Fortunately, childhood and youth knows nothing and cares less about serious political and social affairs. I was much too immersed in the immediate deluge of human misery which surrounded me as I started to grow up and became conscious of the world to observe or care about the insane rush of Western Civilization into the abyss of chaos in the 1920's.

There was no lack of the disease which I later learned was and is killing our civilization, in my family environment.

By the time I was six, my parents had been divorced, there was a sheriff's auction of our home and I began to be forced to listen to hours-long lectures by my mother's sister, Arlene, on the rottenness and vileness of my father. Aunt Arlene, as this female tyrant was known to us, considered herself a great expert and master of everything. The fact that this opinion was not shared by anybody else only made her all the more fierce in the attempt to impress the "fact" on my weak-willed mother and on my brother, sister and me. My little sister was too young to be bothered by such affairs much, and my mother simply stepped aside while Arlene became the boss of the place. My brother, at a very tender age, revealed his genius as a diplomat; when Arlene sat him down to hear one of her "lectures", he agreed heartily with all her statements, exclaimed at her profound wisdom, etc., and was quickly excused with happy smiles by the fat "victor".

I, on the other hand, revealed my own nature in just the opposite way. When Arlene would corale me for a lecture, I would try, at first, to escape with my brother's tactics, and agree with her pronounciamentoes. But then I could not help just the tiniest bit of argument when she would make a particularly heinous charge against my father, which seemed irrational to me. The slightest opposition would rouse this human dirigible to fierce determination to suppress the mutiny. And this, in turn, even when I was six or seven years old, roused in me an even fiercer determination not to be bullied out of what seemed reasonable.

I was often forced to listen to these "lectures" until far into the night. My poor, patient, weak mother would try feebly to rescue me, by getting me to do as she and the rest did -give in and crawl out of it -- but I could not do it.

I can imagine the glee with which the Freudian brain-washers will dive into this material here, sure that they have learned at last the source of what they must, perforce, try to explain as my "neurosis" or even worse. But I will remind these discoverers of evidence which they themselves plant that my brother was exposed to this same kind of thing, and his reaction, even at four or five years old was the opposite of mine. No, gentlemen, my reaction to these things was not CAUSED by this tyranny by Aunt Arline, - it was a surge of force deep within me, as my brother reacted with the native genius for diplomatic wriggling which he displays to this day.

Half of the time, my brother and I would be shuttled to penitentiary duty with Arline, and the other half, we were freed to be with my father and his common-law wife, Madeline, in Maine.

My sufferings and struggles and fun as a boy were, I suppose, relatively normal when we were with my mother and Arline the Great, with the exception of the mid-night lectures.

But the time with my father gave both my brother and I an outlook on life and an intellectual disposition which we both treasure. We have found that the non-conformist approach he showed and transmitted to us has enabled us to outdistance most others in creativeness, time after time. He was unbelievably curious about EVERYTHING. We looked into the plumbing business, got tools from Sears, and went about plumbing for people, just for fun. We examined into photography and built an enlarger. We held autopsies on fish to see what they had been eating, and found amazing things in shark's stomachs. We argued happily and endlessly as to whether a pig, who knew nothing of his stupidity, was happier than a man. We brought home a man and a monkey in the orginder business for long discussions and lunch.

Another "guest" was a mental doctor who claimed he could shorten or lengthen your legs, and I remember we had the whole room-full of people, including celebrities like Fred Allen and other entertainment luminaries, stretched out on the floor to see if their legs would grow different lengths. We all learned to play chess, and there were a few times when the whole outfit got so deep into the game that the McNaught Syndicate, for whom my father wrote a column, sent call after call for the latest piece, and finally had to send a man all the way to Maine to stir him up. While we chugged the twenty or so miles out into the Atlantic for deep sea fishing at three and four in the mornings, even when I was only eight or nine years old in sneakers and flapping shirt, we endlessly discussed fine points of politics, history, magic, art, and the whole gamut of subjects usually reserved for college and adulthood. In the evenings, my brother and I would lie in our beds listening to the shrill cry of the sea-gulls on the Maine coast, smelling the clam flats and the bay-berry fields, and my old man would scooch down for an enchanted hour or so during which he told original stories I will never forget. His best were about "the Old Scout", an incredibly tough and masterful Indian battler. Several times he told of his own childhood visits to the home of the MacPhersons in Nova Scotia, where he said he had actually seen battles with the Indian. I have my doubts of this, but I didn't then, and freely and happily forgive the old gent for a bit of poetic license if he did use it, it was well worth it. Even now, I get goose flesh as I remember the smell of his pipe, the hushed voice, and the magic of the Maine dusk as we listened to these superb flights of imagination. Usually the stories would end with all of us falling asleep, the old man only minutes after us. But sometimes he would drop off first, muttering the last few words half consciously and leaving us in impossible suspense. Then our shrill young voices would pierce his ears. "Daddy! Daddy! Wake up! How did the Old Scout get out of the Indian fire and get untied and out of the way of the buffaloe stampede? Daddy! Wake up!" Then the imagination was not so hot, and the Old Scout would suddenly discover some hidden friend who quickly rescued him -- and the old man. We were not to be so easily swindled, however, and usually demanded another version before the tired purveyor of these masterpieces was excused.

Above all, my father taught me to question EVERYTHING. No fact was too sacred to be examined and judged by itself. No authority was too holy to be looked into for probity. If anything, we were taught to be downright suspicious of all that was supposed to be beyond doubt. I was already of this disposition, and my father's training tremendously strengthened this quality of mind and personality.

But I also received other instruction from my male parent

which was not so helpful. The policy of "anything for a laugh" was unfortunately extended to everyday life, and I can remember my father bringing howls of laughter from me when I was still almost a baby, being undressed. My garments, shoes, etc. were violently removed in a sort of game where every piece was violently flung on the floor to the battle-song of "Throw it on the floor, BANG! BANG!" This, of course, delighted me no end, but fostered untidiness, which is one of the plagues of my life. Then there were the sessions when my tiny brother and I would be stood against the wall for "roaring" practice, to develop our voices. "Roar like a bear" we were ordered, and we tried to oblige. Those who have heard me speak, or who will hear me, will testify to the efficacy of this "bear" training -- but it was not much of an advantage bebefore I became Commander of the Nazi Party. My father's friends were also the source of much instruction. Fred Allen, Benny Goodman, Walter Winchell, Groucho Marx, and a host of others all had their turns as guests, and I found each most interesting. Allen was pure joy to be near, and when my Pop and Allen got to punning and tilting at each other with stories and side-splitting anecdotes, it was one of those precious and rare times when life is 100% positive fun, unalloyed with the petty or large annoyances which so often spoil even the best times we have.

But Allen's wife, Portland, gave me the shock of my fourteen or fifteen years when she was the first woman I ever heard say a filthy word -- and in our living room, at that. She used the Anglo-Saxon word for body waste to express her distaste for some idea or other -- and I will never forget the experience. Never, in all those young years, had I heard a female say such a word, and I thought of her immediately as an object of unbelievable disgust. In discussing the matter later, with my father, I learned privately that she was Jewish. I asked him if Jewishness had anything to do with it, and he said they were very "sophisticated people" who meant no harm by it. But he also told me of Henry Ford's accusations against the Jews, and how they forced him to apologize, and said there was no getting away from the power of the Jews; "They're too smart". Except for the permanent memory of my shock at hearing that awful word from a lady in our family drawing room, I thought no more of it, and don't even remember thinking of Portland as anything but a woman who said a horrible, vulgar word for the first time in my presence. I know the Jews and "liberals" and Freudians will once again leap like trout to the fly here, and be sure this is the source of my "hatred" of Jews. But it is simply not true. I assimilated this experience with millions of others, and did not even notice whether the hundreds of Jews in Atlantic City High School, where I went for four years and many of whom were my best friends, were Jews or hottentots. (That may be an unfortunate choice of words, because hundreds of my school comrades in Atlantic City WERE hottentots! And I didn't particularly notice or care about this either.) (The Jews simply CANNOT accept it, of course, and the brain-washed WILL not accept it, but my hatred of organized Jewry stems directly and only from the discovery of what most -- but not all -- Jews are DOING to the Nation and the People I love.) There may have been some slight vestiges of prejudice in my up-bringing, But no more than in the up-bringing of millions of other American boys who are not leading Hitler movements.

An example is Walter Winchell, with whom my father and I once rode to New York from Atlantic City in the drawing room of a Pennsylvania Railroad train. I was fascinated by the fast-talking, nasal twanging man and the stories they told each other. I had no hatred of him at all -- only a fairly warm liking and admiration. But the next time I saw Walter, whose real name I had since learned was Isadore Lipshitz, was two years ago in front of the White House where we were picketing against the kidnapping of Eichmann by the international bandits of Israel. Walter was standing with a group of cops, watching us. I went over to take his picture. At the top of his lungs, as he himself boasted in his column later, he hollered at me the filthiest of all epithets, not once, but several times. When I mentioned this violation of the most fundamental municipal laws, the cops said they hadn't heard it. And Walter went on in his column to display his intimate connection with the filthy pressure and terror group we are fighting by announcing that I would probably be committed to St. Elizabeth's, the project which the vicious Anti-Defamation League of B'nai B'rith then had in the works, and sprung on me a few weeks later, although I didn't know it then. But Walter knew. I hate such cowardly and sneaking tactics and the people who engage in them. I hate Walter Winchell for his lies and for trying to BULLY people out of their ideas and open discussion of facts, not because of his "religion". Who gives a damn what he does in his synagogue! It is what he and those like him do to innocent Americans in the way of smear, economic persecution, and suppression of facts which I roundly hate, and which I am proud to hate.

Benny Goodman is another Jew from whom I learned something. He came up to our idyllic home in the pine woods of Maine, where there was a perfect balance of gracious living and wide open nature. He was supposed to stay for several day's vacation -- but he lasted only an evening. Being away from the crush of people was more than he could bear, and he scurried back to the soul-destroying hot-house life of New York City with his millions of fellow Jews. Since then I have visited "Grossingers" in the Cats-kills, where the rich Jews go out into the beautiful country to "get away from it all" and then crawl all over each other in a trans-planted imitation New York, like a mass of swarming hornets.

But in those days, I knew none of this, and probably would not have cared if I did know. As previously mentioned, I attended Atlantic City High School for four years, and one of my best friends was a Jew named Lennie. I not only had no prejudice whatso-ever, but liked my Jewish companions immensely for their brilliant minds and sharp conversations. There was one characteristic of them which shocked and apalled me, but I took it as simply char-acteristics of individuals not characteristics typical of their whole group, as I have since sadly learned that it is. This was their nastiness of mind. I assure the reader that I am not concocting this as propaganda, but sincerely recalling things as they were.

While all the boys, of course, thought of and talked of inter-course and such subjects as rudely and as often as possible, those whom I now realize were Gentiles were thoroughly sex-minded, you might say, but not weird or depraved. -- while the Jews, I re-member particularly a hawk-nosed individual, took a delight I could not understand in perverted ideas of sex. Hawk-nose, particularly, dwelt on the idea of intercourse with corpses, and another Jew once wrote a little playlet in which Hawk Nose and two ghoulish friends come to a graveyard to dig up Rockwell for his vile pur-poses, and speak of the mater with incredible nastiness. I re-member being apalled at the filth of the thing, but also admiring the virtuosity of the writing so much that I glossed over the nature of this creative piece. I still have this nasty thing in the files from my high school days, and one has only to read it to discover a different kind of mind than will be found in even the coursest and dirtiest minded non-Jew.

At the same time, during my senior year in this predomi-nantly Negro and Jewish high school, I was having my first small scale political battle, and didn't realize it. There was a course in " Problems of American Democracy " taught by an old duffer named Schwab. His method of instruction consisted largely of assigning large portions of the text-book pages on the black board, and requiring these to be transcribed word for word into the students' note-books, while he occupied himself with other matters privately at his desk. In any event, I hated such stupid ideas as that one could fill one's head as one filled a bucket, by filling a notebook, but this was an outrage against all reason, and I rebelled as I once rebelled at my Aunt Arlene's outrages against reason.

It was my last year of high-school, and although my marks were not good, they were not too bad, either. In four or five months, I would graduate. But, as with the lectures and arguments with Arlene, I could not bring myself to bow down to what I considered tyrannical folly. I had heard much in those days of the New Deal of the strike -- so I "struck". I brought pulp Western stories to class, placed my feet on the desk, and ostentatiously read these while the class bent over its mechanical task in the bulging notebooks. Mr. Schwab, of course, inquired as to just what I was doing, somewhat in the manner of Oliver Hardy asking Stanley a similar question. I replied, with all the sang froid I could muster that I was on strike, that I absolutely refused, as a matter of principle, to copy any more of the textbook into the notebook.

At first, he was apparently amused by this monumental arrogance, and would ask me every day as I came in if I were still on strike. I would then prop up my feet and bury myself in the latest gun-fighting episode of my Western magazines. The other kids were somewhat awed by all this, and the girls were almost terrified at such impudence in the face of the almighty. Seeing my apparent success however a few of the boys joined me -- and that did it. Nothing spreads among boys in school like an apparently successful plan for-avoiding work.

So I was informed I would not graduate, unless I immediately wrote in all the missing note-book pages and went back to the copying routine in class. I refused to negotiate, and insisted I would NOT copy another line. I was threatened, reasoned with and begged, but I would not back down.

So I did not graduate.

But Mr. Schwab was called into conference, and the next year, the note-book copying business was eliminated from the course.

While this was going on in class, my private life was proing along fairly normal lines. I played football and hockey, poorly but enthusiastically with the other guys - including negroes, became a radio amateur, did cartoons for the school paper - and fell in "love".

In my " home room " was a sweet young thing named Jean, and, although I would have died before permitting her to know it, I almost literally worshipped her. But what a miserable, disgusting coward I was about it! Other young men around me were quite brassy about approaching the girls they liked -and there were plenty of rumors as to this or that couple actually sleeping together. But it took me almost a year to ask this angel for a date. Before that I would roller-skate to the end of the street where she lived, a distance of four or five miles, peek around the corner for a glimpse of her, and then roller skate the four or five miles back home, my blood pumping so hard I could feel it in my throat! Finally, in a frenzy of embarrassment I will never forget, I asked her if I could take her to the circus. She blushingly accepted, and my "date" was an impossible combination of heavenly joy and terrifying nightmare. We went on one of the old open summer trolley-cars, she in a pretty white dress, and I in baggy pants and what I imagined was a dashing white sports coat. I did my best to be an attentive gallant, helping her on and off the trolley and acting like I had seen movie lovers act with great charm and ease. But I succeeded in tripping her, getting off the trolley, and then catching her in a sprawling mess on the street. I could not breathe in the agony of shame and embarrassment. But I had touched her! I was bright red as we walked past the balloon sellers and lemonade stands toward the big tent!

We managed to get inside the tent and tight-rope walk the bleacher boards to our seats. She sat close enough to me so I could feel her feminine warmth! The roaring surge of what was going on inside my physical being and my soul is, of course, indescribable. But the results were not! I tried to buy her a pink lemonade and spilled it all over her pretty white dress. I honestly wished to die and disappear, if possible.

Somehow I managed to survive and take her skating and to a few basket-ball games. I fairly burst with pride when I found our names linked in the mimeographed gossip sheets which abounded.

But I never tried to kiss her, although she made remarks which I am now sure were dainty scoldings of my miserable cowardice in such matters.

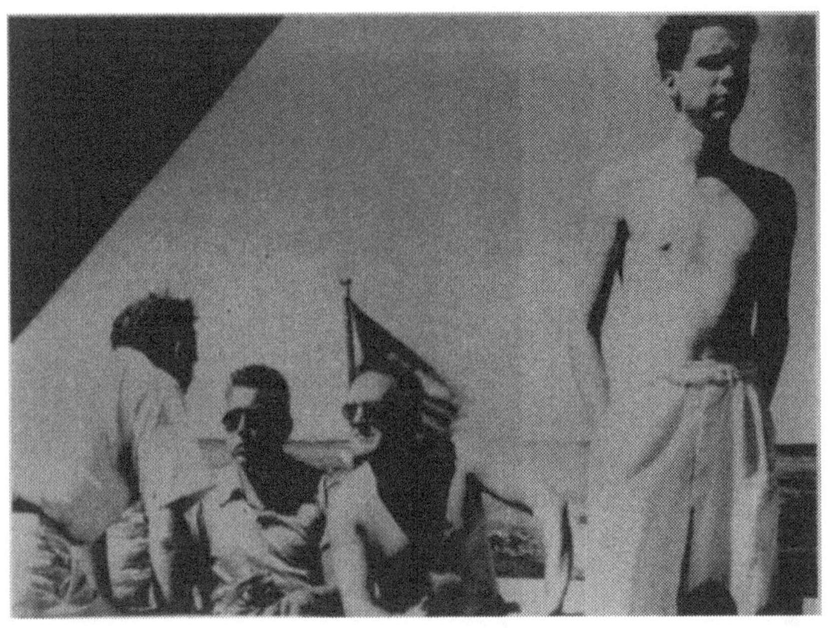

My Father, Fred Allen, Friend, Brother Robert, fishing in Maine.

Our home in Maine, about 1935.

Brother Robert and I after deep-sea fishing, Maine, about 1932.

Myself, Providence, 1936.

Girl friend Hazel, taken about 1939.

Father and I, lobstering.

Brother Robert's Room at Hebron Academy -his roomate, now a U. S. Congressman, seated in chair. 1938.

This super-Victorian attitude with women followed me a long time in life, and I may have missed a great many "good-things" by ordinary standards. But after seeing more of human "love", and what happened to many of the brassy "successes" with women, I suspect that the sweet, story-book memories I keep of such idyllic, if not physically satisfying, love are far more pleasant in the long run than the pleasures of the more sophisticated. I don't believe I can deny that my failure to "go farther" with girls earlier in life was largely due to plain cowardice where girls were concerned. But I also think most people today lose the savor of love and sex through over-sophistication and impatience. It is impossible to enjoy a fine wine by gulping it all down at once, and even a connoisseur cannot appreciate his dainty sips the first time he tries wine.

I believe that the more excellent and more complex an organism is, and therefore the more superior it is in the scheme of nature, the longer it takes for it to mature. Negroes can best white men any day in speed of sex maturity and accomplishment, and experience seems to indicate that it is the same with mental capacity. The stupid man reaches his maximum performance when he is fifteen or sixteen. Anything he might do later, he can then. But when mental capacity and ability is greater, it takes more and more years of practical laboratory experience of the world before such ability can be of value to its possessor and the world. When the point of genius is reached, the ability and range of possibilities are so great that only in middle age is it possible for such an inspired man to translate his ability into intelligent action. Before then, he is more likely than the stupid man to rush up intellectual cul-du-sacs and go off on foolish tangents.

Since I did not graduate from high school, I had to spend another year at it, and decided to take the opportunity offered to me by my paternal grandmother, Mary MacPherson Rockwell, and her daughter (my Aunt Marguerite whom we called "Margie" as kids) to go to school in Providence and live with them.

This was one of the most wonderful years of my life. My grandmother and aunt doted on me, and the atmosphere at home was truly happy. I attended Central High School in Providenee, and excelled in almost everything, I was editor of the school paper, wrote pieces for the Providence Bulletin and Journal, and generally enjoyed myself. I met Hazel Johnson, a very pretty girl who lived only a few blocks away, and who attended Central High School too. Her Swedish Lutheran parents were very strict, and in order to have an excuse to visit her, and sit with her on the couch, she taught me knitting! I actually knitted a baggy, misshapen sweater, which I wore proudly for years! We went to church together, and I sang in the choir with this lovely Swede, holding hands under the long black robes. I liked her folks, and they liked me, and it appeared I was to be eventually inducted into the family. Her father was a great old guy who kidded me roughly but goodnaturedly, and, one day scoffed at my statement that I could learn Swedish in a month. So I DID learn Swedish -- not conversationally, but well enough to say what I had in mind. At the end of the month, he scornfully gave me the "test", with Hazel and her mother sitting around with twinkling eyes, I was to say "Give me a horse to go horse-back-riding" in Swedish, and the old man figured he had me with that bit about the "horse-back-riding". I didn't know the word for that, to be sure, but I had learned the words for "horse", "want", and "go". The part about riding stumped me for a bit, but I remembered a word I had learned for the cut of meat I thought was from the back, but which, I discovered later, meant something else. The result was that I said, in Swedish," I want a horse to go on his ass".

The whole family fell out of their seats laughing and howling, which was a bit different from the reaction I expected, but which was a great success, nevertheless.

That night, I essayed my first kiss.

I stepped into the little hallway to get my coat and Hazel helped me. Screwing up my courage, I seized her in the clumsiest fashion -- in WALTZ position, with my arm out and our fingers interlocked -- and kissed her!

It was a perfectly lousy kiss by ordinary standards. But it nearly killed me with a roaring furnace of emotions and drives. I got out of the door somehow, and -- this may be hard to believe but it is true --I RAN like a deer about a mile down the middle of the deserted dark streets. I could not stop. I was exploding with fierce energy, and HAD to run. It is not hard to understand what nature had in mind for all that energy, but I was too excited and mixed up even to feel that. I just ran -- ran as I never had before nor have since.

I was eighteen years old!

During the year in Providence, I had graduated successfully from Central High School and then again from Hope High School, since I had a free half year and needed an English course for College. My father wanted me to go to Harvard and I duly applied. There was a lot of correspondence back and forth, plus entrance exams, etc. but as fall approached, and no admission papers arrived we went to Cambridge to see what the trouble was, and discovered my school records from Atlantic City had not been forwarded, or had been lost.

So once again I was " available " for a whole year and my father decided the discipline of a boy's boarding school would be helpful. I was not so sure of this but was nevertheless entered in Hebron Academy, far out in the woods in central Maine, near Lewiston.

The life was rough and rigorous but the school good. I learned a lot about life in the raw, living for the first time with a pretty tough gang from Boston. Quite a few of the boys had been sent to Hebron by their folks as a last resort before reform school and they were my first close contacts with such characters.

But more important, in the long hours and days far out there in the woods, I began to think serious and deep thoughts for the first time. I got hold of Will Durant's, "Story Of Philosphy" and it set me on fire. The pure, hard beauty of the thoughts of great men throughout the ages was captured by Durant, distilled, and set forth so clearly that they could be understood and compared and weighed, even by such a young empty-head as I.

Especially, I liked the ruthless logic and unbending dedication to the truth, whatever it might be, of Schopenhauer. I began to see, for the first time, what I have come to know as the conceited, "liberal" mind which imagines itself capable of conquering nature and setting up Utopias because it is packed like a suitcase with "knowledge" and "culture", but which has no understanding of basic relationships and no humility whatsoever before the absolutely unknowable.

I read Sinclair Lewis's "Arrowsmith", mostly sitting on a stump in the woods and got so absorbed in the thing it worried me. It all seemed so real to me and had such an enormous influence on my mind that I began to wonder about the value of reading such a novel.

I came to the conclusion that it is alright to read purely escapist literature, but that when one wants to delve into and weigh the facts which are life and death in human affairs, one is mad to voluntarily permit himself to be hypnotized by a "novelist", transported out of his critical faculties and allow his mind to be powerfully conditioned by almost real "experiences" which are nothing less than the invented devices of another human being. When one of the endless parade of "socially significant" novels which are devoured by our people by the millions, one is helpless to weigh and conciously accept or reject the social conclusions of the skillful novelist who may or may not be correct in his conclusions. If the novelist is not only incorrect but is out to promote a particular idea, in spite of the facts, the powerful realism and emotional impact of the cleverly drawn pictures he stamps indelibly in our mind while we are under his spell, put us in grave danger of unconsciously and emotionally accepting what we would never in a million years accept as a naked proposition presented to our cold reasoning faculties.

I read more of these novels: "Grapes Of Wrath" and four or five others and in all of them I sensed an attempt to convince me of social ideas, not by reason but by emotional manipulations while my mind was hypnotized by my emotions.

I didn't fully realize it, but I had discovered left-wing and commnist propaganda. I hated it, without knowing what it was!

Characteristicly, in these books, patriotism was sneered at and morals were something for boobs, while the people were rotten (except Jews and Negroes who were especially worthy human beings who were usually persecuted wretchedly by brutal, stupid and repulsive White Christian Southern protestants).

But all of this I didn't form into a clear pattern. I saw only the fact that the novel could be and was dangerous to the man who wished to maintain an independent mind. And I was daily growing more independent of mind. Partly through my father's teaching of irreverance for any statement just because somebody else said so, and partly out of native cussedness, stubborness and growing mental confidence, I began to examine everything and everybody in a new light - the light of the best I could do with my own reason.

I began to ponder religion.

Until then, I had been highly religous and even fancied I had often put my allowance in the collection plate as a boy, and felt a great surge of joy in doing so, imagining the warm smile of a personal God as I made the sacrifice. But now I began to wonder at the mounting evil I was discovering in the world, and the illogical explanations for it in my Christian religion. I read and reread the Bible, as I had not done before, from end to end. I was appalled at the demand by God for human sacrifice, for the eating of human body waste by the Lord, for the horrible cruelties and atrocities demanded by the Lord according to the Old Testament, by the Doctrine that the Lord made millions of people to be slaves for the Hebrews whom he had "Chosen" through no merit of their own, while he destroyed his other creatures wholesale for the Hebrew's especial pleasure, and promised them that they would be able to put their feet on the necks of all other people. I wondered that the preachers had never preached from these vicious and repulsive verses. Were they not aware that such monstrosities were in the Bible, as I had been unaware? Or did they know and falsely skip over them just to stay in business? Could I believe that a God who gloried in such vicious and bloody revenge was a "God of Love"? Why all the explanations? It was plain there to read, page after page of it. The Lord had created two innocent creatures out of nothing, placed them in a garden, knowing they were too imperfectly made and too weak to resist temptation, and, unless his foreknowledge was wrong (which was impossible) - knowing they would FALL to temptation and be condemned, along with their innocent children, to ETERNAL misery. And then this "Loving Father" had placed the most irresistable possible temptation -- loaded with unheard of poison -- before his children! I imagined what I would have thought of my feeble human father if he had placed us kids in a garden and then hung ice-cream-cones and lollipops and toys all around, warned us not to touch these irresistable delights, and then put inconceivably deadly poison in all these temptations -- KNOWING ALL THE TIME WITH CERTAINTY THAT WE WOULD BE POISONED AND FIENDISHLY TORTURED FOREVER!

Most of all, I wondered at the idea that if there were a few simple ideas and facts to be understood to enjoy eternal life and happiness, here and later on, and God were all-powerful, he had made it impossible for me to believe those ideas and facts because of the very mind which he gave me! -- And then I am to be threatened with eternal damnation for not believing that which I CANNOT believe!

My first reaction was Atheism.

I did something I deeply regret, and shall never do again. I had begun to discover my own power of persuasion, and, in the eternal bull sessions of a boy's school, religion is not exempt as a topic. I was genuinly sorry I had lost my belief in Christianity for it has truly marvelous power to sustain and help one in times of tribulation. I began to discuss the matter with a devout Catholic boy, who tried with all his heart and might to make me see my error. We skied five miles over to his Church to see a Priest he said could straighten me out, and I was truly anxious to be shown my error, if error it was.

But the matter turned out differently. Coldly and scientifically I argued with that Priest, refusing to let him lead me into the inevitable non sequiturs, redundancies, etc., and brutally holding to logic. He was reduced, eventually to exclaiming, "You just MUST believe, you have to believe!" I told him I could not believe, and asked him if he were not able to help me do what he said I must. He shook his head sadly in despair, no doubt convinced sincerly that I was determined NOT to understand.

But the effect on my friend was something I had not counted on. All the way back to the school we skied in silence. And when we got back, he said not a word. For days, he avoided me, and I felt a secret shame for which I could see no reason. Eventually, he told me that he had been forced to agree with me, and had lost his faith.

That he was no happier about it than I, with my own loss of faith, was obvious. In fact, he was even more stricken. The result was to set me thinking on what I had done, and whether it was right.

I saw then what I believe all great religious teachers knew but could not and did not say. The ordinary man is too weak and too helpless in the whirling vortex of life to sustain himself on his naked human will and his cold human reason. Only with some kind of deep belief -- in an all-powerful magic being of some kind can the masses of humanity maintain social and reasonably worthwhile lives. Without such a belief they can see no reason for not immediately indulging themselves in their most animal and immediate desires, and they despair in the face of death unless they can imagine something further. As long as men are thus ignorant and weak-minded, they MUST have some such spiritual crutches, so that religion, far from being an "Opiate", is truly the sustainer of the masses of people. He who destroys religion before humanity has progressed far beyond its present almost primitive intellectual state is helping to destroy civilization.

Since then I have come still further along the road of understanding, and realize that Atheism is as bad as the rantings of the religious fanatic. The latter says, "I was one of the luckiest human beings on earth and was born into the only true religion -- all the rest of you are damned sinners" -- and the Atheist makes the equally conceited statement, "I have examined the ENTIRE universe and everything in it, and am certain that there is NOTHING I CAN NOT KNOW!"

For a rational man, I think these are both impossibly conceited and stupid conclusions. In the face of our ridiculous helplessness and microscopic nothingness in a universe of billions of light years, it is madness to assert that some kind of an unknown and unknowable force does NOT exist, a force so foreign to all our concepts we are incapable even of thinking of "Him", or "It".

It is the part of the intelligent man, I believe, to recognize both his superiority to the masses who must have the fables of religion to survive the vicissitudes of life, and his unspeakable inferiority to the possibilities of total intelligence.

Under these circumstances, I think we must humbly renounce the right to make grandiose and positive pronouncements concerning a universe (yet unexplored) and possibilities so infinitely enormous that it will be centuries before we can reach even the nearest star in rocket ships. To those who say "we have no evidence of anything on earth of any immaterial thing or any power which does not appear capable, eventually of being known" -- as the Atheists do, I reply "true, but how can you be sure that such forces and power do NOT exist elsewhere? How can you even be sure, preposterous as it probably is, that there is not some giant PHYSICAL being which is master of the universe, and which you may never discover?"

And, in fact, having time and again stumbled through crisis in the historical battle in which I am now engaged, and having learned later that our accidentally discovered solution, or even what seemed like a misfortune at the time, was the ONLY possible way we could have survived, I am convinced that there is scientific evidence of forces which are beyond our comprehension at work. Perhaps it is only the result of unconscious problem solving, etc. -- but who can say? My answer is that we must be

HUMBLE in such matters, because the best of us is horribly, fearfully ignorant of the gigantic mysteries of the Universe.

I am an Agnostic -- which means that to all proposals and explanations of the mysteries of life and eternity, I say, " I do not know, and I don't believe you or any other human does either"

At the same time I stand firmly for positive, ethical religions, whatever they may be, and believe they must be protected and given the greatest freedom to do what they can to lessen the awesome burden of human misery on this tiny planet. I know there will be many intellectuals who will reply that religion has caused untold torture and suffering to stamp out "heresy", but in view of man's need for emotional catharsis and release in today's immensely frustrating world, and in view of Pavlov's experiments, I believe that religion is the poor man's "psychiatry", his only "escape" from intolerable pressures of society.

I have never, since that trip on skiis to the priest up in Maine, tried to argue anybody out of his religion, and have given strict orders in the American Nazi Party that religion is simply not permitted as a subject of discussion for anybody. We have Protestants, Catholics, Atheists and Agnostics among our membership, and all of them are equally welcome and valuable.

We are battling for better things in THIS world, and will leave discussions of religious affairs until we are in the next, if such there be, when better evidence will be at hand.

At Hebron, I formed my first tiny political organization and succeeded with its purpose. There was a chemistry professor by the name of Foster who was a petty tyrant -- even sneaking around the halls of the dorms in his stocking feet to catch boys breaking regulations so he could give them huge numbers of demerits. Ed Lewis and I, and a few other top-floor men from Sturtevant Hall organized the Phi Phi's -- which is Greek for F. F. which referred to what we felt about Professor Foster. We burned the unfortunate victim in effigy, marched about the "campus" with torches and signs, plagued the poor man with impudent notes, and generally make him and the administration miserable for keeping him on. And it worked. The next year, Mr. Foster sought employment elsewhere.

I also had fun at Hebron in the process. There was a genuine, fourteen carat, block-headed "rube" on our floor, the epitomy of stupidity, and I was no less sparing of the sensibilities of such good targets of fun than any other boy. But I was cleverer in perfecting methods of making life miserable for such characters, a standard avocation of all at Hebron. We invited this hay-seed to a super-secret meeting to see about getting rid of Foster. The rube, whom we called "Danny Boone", was delighted at thus "getting in" with us. We discussed what could be done about Foster with dreadful mock seriousness, and finally "decided" he had to be done away with. We had learned in his Chemistry class, (poetic justice) -- how to make nitro-glycerine, and the conspirators decided that that would be the way to send Foster to his reward.

In growing tension and in hushed voices, we decided to draw straws to see who would carry the nitro and throw it into Foster's suite of rooms. One of the guys announced that he had made some of the deadly nitro and had it in cushions in his room. He went and filled a little vial with hair-oil, and we all watched him through a crack in the door as he brought the fearful thing back on a pillow, stepping with immense caution, bulging eyes and bated breath. He set it down in the middle of the room. Covertly, we all watched our rube out of the corners of our eyes. He was transfixed, hypnotized, helpless in the spell of the thing. The fatal drawing of straws was held with terrifying seriousness.

By a "strange conincidence", the boob got the short straw, and stood looking at it, frozen with horror. We all congratulated him on his luck as a maker-of-history, patted him on the back, told him of the praise he'd win from future generations of Hebron men -- etc., etc. Finally, he was handed the terrible thing -- inches at a time in moving -- pushed out the door with it and aimed at Foster's room.

He couldn't move. We cajoled and begged and pleaded, but he couldn't move. Finally he appeared to have a thought. "Hold it a minute," he said, and handed the deadly vial to one of the boys. Then he dashed down the hall screaming, at the top of his lungs, "Mr. Foster, Mr. Foster! They're goihg to blow you up!" -- and disappeared down the back stair way! Foster came bursting out of his room and never did find out what was wrong. The corridor was quiet as a grave, and all was as it should be at Hebron. Only the suffocated groans of diabolical joy under blankets and pillows in a dozen cots were clues to what had happened. But Mr. Foster couldn't hear those.

The summer of 1936 I spent lobstering in Maine, as I had for many years before, and indulging my newly found joys of philosophy and music, combined with the appreciation of nature I had felt since babyhood. I also worked as a waiter at The Green Shutters, a small summer hotel in Boothbay Harbor frequented mostly by school-teachers, and I learned some new facts about the world.

I learned more about females.

There was a girl named Franny working there as head waitress. She was 24, and five years older than I. She was nothing special, but she was not bad either. And she WAS a girl.

I had earned a little 1936 Ford coupe, mostly by selling hand-soap to garages, and with this piece of modern machinery -- (which I doctored endlessly) -- and Franny, I made some further experiments in the processes by which Nature intended there should be more of us. Later, with more experience, I would have had no trouble discovering and experimenting with the process itself, but, with my Victorian up-bringing and ideas, and my utter ineptness in the matter, I allowed Franny to hold the experiments to preliminary investigations and what you might call "dress rehearsals".

Nevertheless, these sessions were so profoundly exciting that the thoughts and images they provoked interfered seriously with my growing interest in music, art, literature and philosophy. I found myself wondering, as I read "the Crito", whether Socrates had had similar experiences. Then, remembering Xantippe and her reputation as a termagant, I decided that if they had shared such experiences, Socrates wasn't adept at it, or had given up too early.

At the Green Shutters, I also learned about Old Ladies, and discovered some effective methods of dealing with them. Their endless empty chatter disgusted me. Nothing but stories of tea-shops, gift-shoppes, difficulties with other old ladies, sly remarks about still other old ladies, and their friends. It was depressing to a lively youth who had just discovered the fabulously interesting world of ideas, sex, music, philosophy, etc. How could these corsetted blimps survive each other's empty conversation about nothing for years and years and years? It was a mystery to me, and still is.

But there was no mystery about their dispositions. There

were a few sweet ones, but these old war-horses of grammar school and high school were mostly arrogant, imperious tyrants with us waiters and waitresses. Nothing, absolutely nothing, was QUITE right for them, nothing QUITE satisfied them! I remember all the same kind of teachers I had had, and began to cast about in my mind for methods of innocent revenge.

They would have me move their mattresses from one cottage to another through the woods, when they would complain of non-existant "lumps" -- and then dismiss me imperiously -- with no tip. They would call me interminably from table to table to complain of small discrepancies in the portions of food or other injustices and indignities to their too-too-dignified persons.

But I discovered there was one thing that drove them crazy: sticky handles on the pancake syrup jars at breakfast. They were a finnicky old lot, and sticky fingers was unbearable to them.

So I carried a sticky rag with me, and dosed up their door knobs, their pocket-book handles, their light switches, and anything else I could find where they would get into the mess.

The effect was thoroughly, delightfully satisfying. I was called out at all hours, of course, and the proprietress and her son were scolded no end for the mysterious plague of stickiness, but nobody could figure it out -- except us waiters and waitresses and we had no interest in spoiling all that fun.

There was one fat, old killer-whale in particular who drove us mad at the table, She was always discovering that there were air-bubbles in her scoopes of ice-cream, and insisting that the terrible deficiency be made up to her. So one evening I decided to be sure her ice-cream was rich enough to suit her. I took a square of butter, which was kept in the same freezer as the ice-cream, and built her a nice ball of ice-cream around it. Then I served it up to her with great style.

We all watched from behind a little screen, looking out between the cracks, and holding our breaths till she came to the butter. I was going to explain that it was an accident, that the butter must have FALLEN into the ice-cream, which it could have, when she squawked.

But she didn't squawk. Instead, we saw her look down at the

dish, bend over, and hack at it with her spoon a few times. Then she took a large bite of the butter, and an almost-lascivious smile spread across her ocean of face. She LOVED IT!

I was called for immediately, and dutifully came to attention beside her. "Young man", she commanded, "this is the finest and richest ice cream I have ever tasted. What kind is it?"

"Turner Center," I told her truthfully.

"Well I want another portion right away, and I will have some of this kind every night. See that Mrs. Clayton orders this kind in the future, not that watery stuff we've been getting."

I fetched her another portion, and this time packed the butter in almost solid. The staff was suffocating and dying, holding onto the door jams and retreating in agonies of laughter to the kitchen when they couldn't stand it any more.

Perhaps the Freudians will have me carted away to the booby hatch for this too. If they do, it will have been worth it! As I write this, I am suffused with a hugely satisfying glow as I recall that stupid human dirigible waddling away from her table, imagining herself mistress of all she could stuff down her ravenous gullet.

I was learning even then, how people work!

I had been accepted at Brown University during the summer by Bruce Bigelow, the director of admissions, who gave me my first clue that I might be different from other people. He frankly told me that, in view of my six years in high school and other vagaries of my student career, I had the worst scholastic record of anybody ever admitted to Brown. But the highest grade on the College Aptitude, which shows intelligence, of all students ever tested. He warned me that I was to be admitted strictly as an experiment to see what would happen, when the immovable object of my disinclination for scholastic achievment was placed against the the irresistable force of my native intelligence in the atmosphere of a college.

I entered Brown in the fall of 1938 literally in a hurricane. That was the year New England was struck fearfully by winds of

My brother and I sitting aft on the Old Man's boat, the "Floating Kidney", returning from a deep-sea fishing trip. About 1939

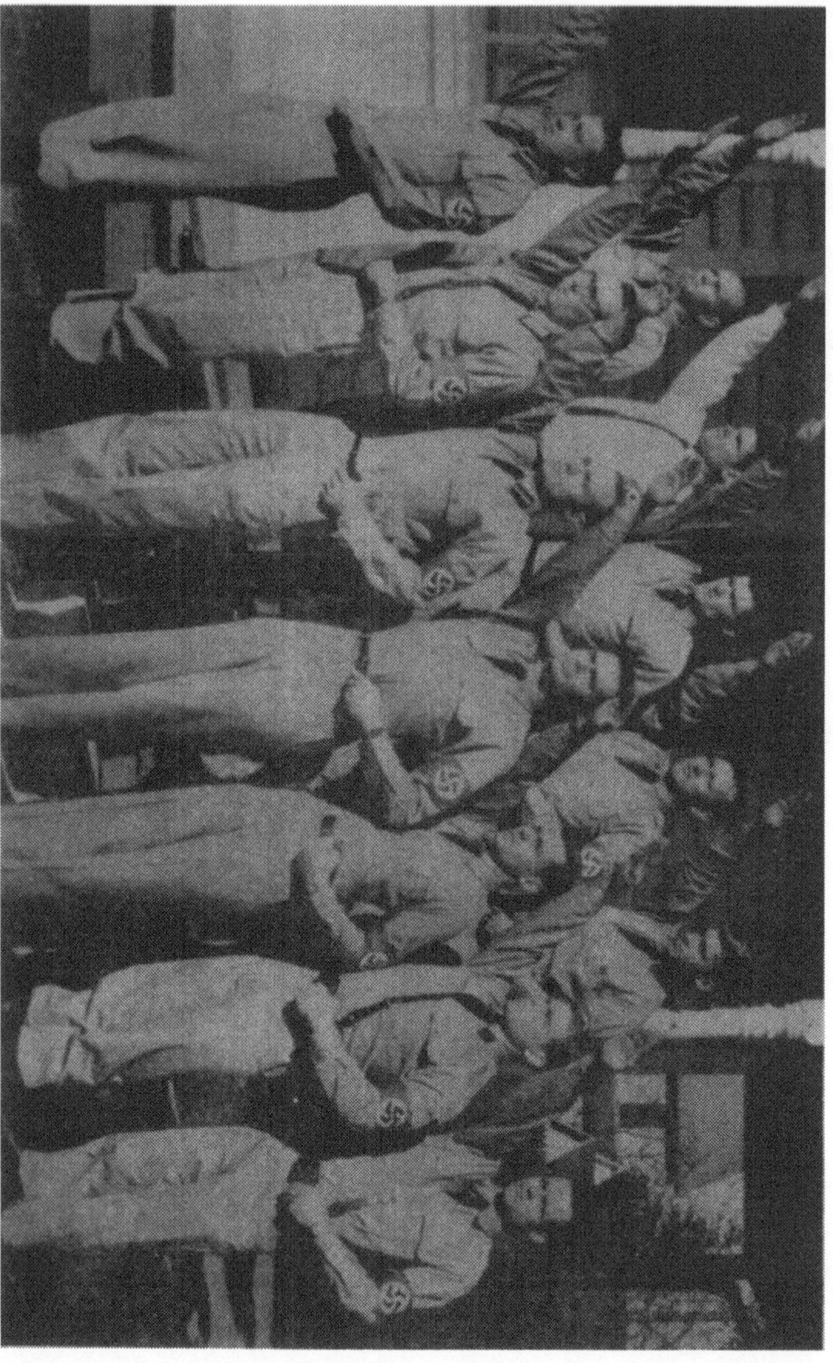

Yeh,-- you and who else?

One of the cartoons I did for Sir Brown, the humor magazine at Brown University which I helped start. I saw this same cartoon, along with many others, in the Municipal Court, D. C., almost twenty years later, when the Anti-Defamation League of B'Nai B'Rith handed them to the prosecutor in a "disorderly conduct" case, and used them to try to railroad me to the insane asylum!

The waterfront, Boothbay Harbor, Maine. My home town. In foreground: Commander MacMillan's Arctic Ship "The Bowdoin." Gold-leaf scroll work by Rockwell.

over a hundred miles an hour, and thousands died in masses of wreckage. My aunt and eighty-year-old grandmother were at the beach called Barrington, on Narragansett Bay, when the storm hit, and I was up in Providence with my Aunt Margie. As soon as we knew how terrible the thing was, I got down to the beach, where we had heard chilling rumors of death and destruction -- and discovered they had not been exaggerated. Whole cottages had been swept away with their inhabitants, and my heart stopped until I could see the wreckage of my Aunt Helen's place, where my Grandmother was staying. Bodies were floating against the beach, as I picked my way over the piles of torn-up lumber, roofs, beds, etc., to the cottage. Inside, to my huge relief, I found my folks alive and well -- even if uncomfortable.

I was about to meet my first wife.

I had started to work on the wreckage, when a little teen age girl behind me somewhere on the pile yelled with infinite impudence, "Hey, you -- Brown Pants! -- Grab the other end of this!" and poked some depris at me.

This little character was a fresh-looking as she talked -- wearing pig-tails and flirting her talk around like a jay bird -- and twice as sassy.

She was something I had never seen before. Her fresh wholesomeness attracted me irresistably, and her bossy manners repelled me almost as much. Here among the wreckage of the hurricane, though, her super-cheerful easiness and "let's get with it, boys" helped erase the atmosphere of tragedy and death.

I tried to sass her back, but wasn't equal to it -- there was no squelching this pert young lady. I couldn't forget her. Some other people there said her name was Judy Aultman who lived nearby, and that's all I found out for another year.

There was plenty to keep my mind busy as I entered college.

There were endless tests to see what courses we needed, and one of the major surprises and shocks of my life was when I discovered that I had passed the fairly difficult tests for Freshman English and Freshman French, a relatively rare occurance. I couldn't believe it, considering my agonies in high and prep schools. But passing showed me I had discovered a new technique in the struggle to avoid school work; a system I have since called the "total situation" approach. In writing those English and French tests, I had been faced with technically difficult performances, but had solved them, not by relying on my rote memory and rules, etc. - but by fathoming the minds of the preparer's of the exams, the minds of those who would grade the exams, and coming up with an over-all IMPRESSION of virtuosity which would sell the grader on my ability. In addition, I had used logic and reason to come up with rules when I needed them, the same way that the rules were originally developed by those who parsed the language in the first place. Over-all, I prepared my "essays" in such a manner as to avoid what I was sure were the standard errors the graders were used to and were looking for.

Time after time, since then, I have discovered that I do not have to study the usual rote memory portions of most subjects to succeed or even excel in performance on tests or use of the knowledge. By learning the most fundamental logical development of the subject, I am usually able to develop any other portion of the subject, as I need it -- very much the way a Navy ship does not need to carry around spare parts for every piece of the ship, but carries, rather, the plans and raw metal which can be worked up as needed for any desired part in the machine shop.

It is my belief that this technique should be the most fundamental part of the education of our youth, instead of the present stuffing of young minds with millions of unrelated facts and unevaluated ideas, or the chaotic development of personal whims and prejudices called "progressive education". Once the PRINCIPLE of a subject is learned, the details can be developed at will in most cases. The beauty of this system of mental discipline is that it leaves the mind free to do creative work, rather than burdening it down with billions of confusing separate facts. It is my contention that the failure to teach young minds today the PRINCIPLES of all logical development, accompanied by the positive emphasis of the insane idea that absolutely everything is "relative" and "grey" -- rather than black and white where principles are concerned, kills the ability to think in our youth. Phenomena which exemplify principles can indeed be on a sliding scale of "greys", and always are, in fact. But the principles themselves, such facts as that force always prevails over weakness in the final analysis, are not relative, but eternal laws of logic which would prevail even in an empty universe.

Once the internally consistent body of principles governing a mental discipline are learned, and the system of deriving the details by logical building therefrom is learned, one can master subjects will enough to use them successfully in a ridiculous fraction of the time usually frittered away in "courses" in schools and universities. This is the method, for instance, whereby I have been able to hold my own and even win a good many victories in the law courts as my own attorney, without a day's training in the law. I have discovered that law is by and large a system of common ordinary horse-sense, based on a few fundamental and simple principles -- at least until our Supreme Court got at the matter . But in our ordinary courts, knowledge of the fundamental principles, a will to succeed, and the application of brainpower to the principles will make any man his own lawyer, and a more successful one than at least the court appointed attorneys who don't have your own motivation.

This is not to assert that a trained, expert and highly-paid lawyer is not a good investment, -- or that I will not make use of such genius in the law when I can afford it. But when it is necessary to have a lawyer, and none will take your case (as has happened to me as a Nazi), and you can't pay them besides, then a knowledge of how to master a subject well enough to use it in a few days by the use of principles plus logical building of details is invaluable.

Incidentally, while I am on this matter, I have also learned that even such majestic subjects as the law are as vulnerable as everything else I have found in this world, to human motivational study. Lawyers and Judges and other officials are human. I have discovered that even the best of them make fearful mistakes, ommissions and blunders, even in their robes and/or wigs. By calculating not only the law, but their emotions and their probable resulting thought processes, I have more than once won victories by something beside the naked use of the law and the facts.

My first year at Brown was, perhaps, the happiest of my life. No responsibility (compared to later life), flowering abilities in all directions, absorbing interest in everything and everybody, and all sorts of new opportunities to drink beer, experiment with women, and discuss the entire world as a "master" with other young "masters-of-everything" in the fraternity house. I launched the college humor magazine which had been dead for a long time, together with sophomores Vic Hillary and Bob Grabb, my best pals at Brown. I was art editor, and Grabb was the editor. Hillery was editor of the College paper, the Brown Daily Herald (both of them were sophomores and I only a freshman). But I worked with endless creative pleasure for both publications, and more than once got called over to the Dean's office for my exhuberance. I developed a horror style of cartoon years before Charles Adams, and these were liberally reprinted in other college papers, such as the Annapolis Log, etc. I was also to see stacks of these works of kid-college humor in the District of Columbia Municipal Court on July 26, 1960, where I was on trial as a lunatic. These exhuberant works of over twenty years ago were diligently gathered together by the Anti-Defamation League of B'nai B'rith, photostated and presented to the Prosecutor (who testified he "didn't know where all the photostats came from") and used to prove that I was a sadistic monster -- although in the twenty-two years since producing them, I had risen from an enlisted man to a commander in the Navy, been selected to command three squadrons, successfully established three businesses, and never eaten a single baby or carved up a wife.

It was at Brown, in 1939, that I first ran head-on into Communism, although I didn't know or even suspect it. I don't remember even thinking about it anymore than I did Thugee-ism in India or Mormonism. I was still blissfully and totally ignorant of Communism, Jews, Negroes and the assault of the masses of the world led by the master of mongrels, the Jews, against the White Race and it's elite. In a way, I am glad of this long maintained ignorance, because today, when I meet young college men and women who are full of conceit of their knowledge, "liberalism" and "understanding" of our social problems, I can be patient with them. I can imagine my own reaction if I had been told there were a Jewish or any other kind of a world conspiracy. I was sure, at that time, that my "deep" studies into the profundities of knowledge would have long ago revealed any such monstrous conspiracy -- and even if not, that my professors and men of learning would surely have known of it. I would have been angry at such effrontery, just as the young college boobs I meet today are at first angry, until I ruthlessly use logic to beat them out of their disgusting and monumental conceit by driving into them, one after the other, the explanations of how come they never ran into such facts.

But then, in 1939, I sat in "Sociology I" class and tried my best to make some sense out of it all. I had been happy at the chance to study sociology, as it appeared to me logical that there must be some fundamental principles of the development of the social relationships of life as I had discovered simple basic principles of other affairs I had looked into. I was most eager to learn these basic principles of the operation of human society so that I could understand the events around me, and perhaps even predict sociological occurances in accordance with the principles I would be taught. I have since learned that there ARE such principles, particularly in Adam's "The Law of Civilization and Decay", and even better, in "The Crowd" by LeBon.

But it would be many, many years before I would fight my way into the intellectual sunshine of such simple, fundamental and logical presentation of the facts of social life. In Prof. Bucklin's classroom on society, all was the most depressing darkness and confusion. It all SOUNDED most enlightening, of course. There were lots of brave new words, ethnic groups, etc. -- but try as I might, I could NOT get to the bottom of it all to find any idea or principle I could get hold of. EVERYTHING was "by and large", and "in most cases", and "on the other hand" and "So-and-so says, but Dr. So-and-so says absolutely not". Muddiness of mind was not deplored, but glorified. I buried myself in my sociology books, absolutely determined to find why I was missing the kernel of the thing.

The best I could come up with was that human beings are all helpless tools of our environment; that we are all born as rigidly equal lumps, and the disparity of our achievement and station were entirely and 100% the result of the forces of environment -- that everybody, therefore, could theoretically be master-geniuses and kings if only we could sufficiently improve everybody's environment.

I was told enough to ask Prof. Bucklin if this were the idea, -- and he turned red in anger. I was told it was "impossible" to make any generalizations, although all I was asking was for the fundamental idea, if any, of Sociology.

I began to see that Sociology was different from any other course I had ever taken. Certain ideas produced apoplexy in the teacher, particularly the suggestion that perhaps some people were no good biological slobs from the day they were born. Certain other ideas, although they were never never formulated and stated frankly, were fostered and encouraged -- and these were always ideas revolving around the total power of environment.

Slowly, I got the idea. At first I just used it to get better grades. When I wrote my essay answers in examinations, I poured it on heavily that all hands in the civilization in question were potential Leonardo DaVinci's, no matter how black they were or how they ate their best friends for thousands of years -- and that with a quick change in environment, these cannibals, too, would be writing arias, building Parthenons and painting masterpieces.

But then I began to wonder "how come"? Certainly environment was important. Anybody could see that. But it was obviously negative. You can make a helpless Boob out of a born genius by bringing him up in a dark closet, but you can't make a genius out of a drooling Idiot, even by sending him to Brown. Was it just old man Bucklin who was insane with environment? Or was it the whole subject?

I went to the library and read more sociology books. They were universally pushing the same idea.

I began to make fun of Sociology in the College paper in my column, and got into more trouble. Some of the columns were "killed" before seeing the light. I was still too ignorant to know that I was fighting Lysenko and Marx and the whole Soviet theory of environmentalism, which has captured and hypnotized or terrorized all out intellectuals, and imagined I was battling just one foolish college course.

During my second year at Brown, my picture of the world darkened, as I discovered more and more the intellectual dishonesty in this University which had at first seemed almost heaven itself to me. I still knew little or nothing about Communism or its pimping little sister, "liberalism" but I could not avoid the steady, pressure, everywhere in the University, to accept the idea of massive human equality, and the supremacy of environment. In every course I was repulsed by the intellectual cowardice of the faculty in standing up for any doctrine whatsoever.

I majored in Philosophy, and, while I admired the intellectual brilliance of my professors, particularly Professor Ducasse, I was hugely disappointed in the headlong retreat of all the faculty whenever they were asked their OWN opinion as to the objective truth in any matter. I was told that "eternal seeking" is the way to knowledge, and there is no denying that. But lively discussion is also vital to any advance, and you cannot have any lively discussion where the opposition either doesn't exist or melts away like a wraith when you seek to take hold of it.

I was running into the disease of our modern life -- cowardice and pathological fear of a strong personality or strong ideas. Dale Carnegie has codified and commercialized this creeping disease as "how to win friends and influence people", which boils down, in essence, to the principle of having no personality or strong feelings or ideas and becoming passive and empty so that the "other fellow" can display HIS ideas and personality. But he, too, is trying to get popular by being passive and dispassionate, so that the result is like two dead batteries, - no current. Such human robots are suited to enslavement by a 1984-type society, but not to a bold, free society of men. This is the way women should be, perhaps, but not our men, and especially not our leaders.

I found the same feeble feminine approach in every subject except in the sciences -- and for these last, I was very grateful. Here, in Geology and Psychology I could find a few principles and laws which stayed there when I reached out to grasp them. And so I revelled in these subjects, and rebelled to the limit of my capacity in the others.

In Sociology, I went so far as to write an insolent examination paper which almost got me thrown out of Brown. We were asked to write an essay answer on the factors leading to criminality and delinquency.

I write nothing but a fable about a crew of scientific geniuses who set out for Africa to see what made ants act like ants -- searched around until they found a lot of ant-hills, observed them for many years, and finally came up with the discovery that when ant-eggs were hatched in tunnels in a certain kind of hill in Africa, and grew up among six-legged creatures called "ants", they themselves were so affected by this strong environment that they became, themselves, ants, and waved their antennae like ants, scurried around aimlessly like ants, looked like ants, and WERE ants.

I was again haled up before the administration for this impudence, and almost thrown out. But I was instead given another opportunity to write the exam, and for the sake of my dear good Grandmother and my patient, loving Aunt Margie, I sat down and wrote what I knew they wanted; a piece showing how unfortunate and most excellent babies were invariably driven to stealing from their parents, relatives and friends, robbing strangers at the point of a gun, and finally axing somebody in sheer desperation at their nasty environment.

This was passed with a C plus.

Meanwhile, I was learning mightily from my endless "bull-sessions" with Vic Hillery and Bob Grabb, my constant companions. Both of them were soused to the ears with the prevailing "liberalism", although I still did not know what it was. I simply discovered that almost all my ideas clashed violently with theirs. My ideas that socially-significant novels were dangerous because they allowed ideas to sneak into the mind while it was hypnotized was especially aggravating to them both, as we all aspired to creative careers, they as novelists and great writers. My attack on the very social novels they were aiming to write was painful, and their reactions, particularly Hillery's, were most passionate. Far into the night we would battle over this matter, with the usual results -- no progress. But in the process, I learned the art of controversy.

At first, I was too sincere and ingenuous to do anything but try to make my opponent see the truth of my position with the utmost force and sincerity. But then I found that I would fall victim of the dirtiest kind of tricks. My position would be enormously and ridiculously exaggerated, and then it would be flung in my face in triumph, to the great laughter of the audience of listeners or participants.

I could not understand when even my revered friends did this to me. I was more than once too hurt by such tactics to defend myself.

But, as with everything else in my life - when I discovered the inevitability of such illogical skullduggery, I schooled myself in it and one day turned the tables on my "liberal" friends. Since I was usually alone in my "conservative" position, surrounded by voluble and hostile "liberals", I had more than a usual share of difficulties in gaining one of the phoney "victories" which are possible in such a battle, where the truth means nothing. Under such circumstances, where the listeners and your opponents are all hostile, one must capture them emotionally, in spite of themselves, with a lightening, unexpected stroke, usually of overwhelming humor or sarcasm, so that they laugh at your opponent, and even themselves, in spite of themselves. Then you must decamp with a flourish but with great haste, before they can recover, and lay loud claim to the victory.

Such practice has served me handsomely many times since then in political battles, particularly in court rooms, when prosecutors get oratorical and too big for their britches. One has only to find the man's weak point in such circumstances, to turn his unfair attack against himself with Judge, jury and spectators.

More and more, at Brown, I came into basic conflict with the prevailing super-liberalism -- still without ever realizing what it was all about. My companions, my courses, my professors, the latest erudite books -- everything seemed to me to be touched with madness. I fought it fiercely and, for my ignorance, powerfully, but mostly by instinct. I simply had never heard of Communism as anything but a fiendish and insane doctrine held by a few fanatics someplace overseas. That the campus, dorms, fraternity houses and classrooms of Brown University were crawling with the filthy thing, I would never have believed, and would have laughed to scorn anybody who had tried to tell me such a "fantastic" thing -- then.

My second year at Brown, at the first fall dance at Faunce House, I recognized one of the freshman girls (my future wife) from Pembroke (the girl's section of Brown).

I saw the same sassy little jay-bird I had met in Barrington in the hurricane. Only this time she was in a party dress. She still looked fresher and wholesomer than any girl I had ever seen, but she looked more than just wholesome in the pretty dress, as she swept across the floor with a succession of partners who cut in on each other. I was busy chasing a few women myself, but I noticed when she disappeared outside into the darkness with somebody. I strolled out onto the campus and over by University Hall, which was behind a fence as it was being remodelled. I saw her come out the door of the fence with this other man, and was immediately irritated. But I kept control, strolled nonchalantly over and said "hello" to her. She recognized me, then I couldn't resist asking her what she had been doing in there in the deserted Hall.

"Ringing the bell", she said -- which I insisted on taking with a double entendre, but which did not embarrass her in the least. I was a sophomore, far above such silly little freshman girls, but she apparently refused to recognize this great difference in our social stations.

I resolved to ask her for a date, and did so the next opportunity.

From then on, my life was a hell of glorious hope and miserable despair. She would seem to be as desperately in love with me as I had fallen for her, only to cut me to pieces with some unheard of cruelty. She was the most popular girl in the freshman class, and played the field with calculated cunning and cold manipulation.

Such were the agonies of pursuing the girl who was to be my first wife.

She would take my fraternity pin, full of love and even traces of passion, only to thrust it back at me a few days later for no special reason. (I later got to know her mother, and suspect her dainty hand in this sort of affair.)

But she had roused in me that fatal resistance to challenge which is my most fundamental quality. Since she seemed impossible to tame or attain, I must have her, and I doubled and redoubled my efforts to that end. I still don't know who got who and I don't think she does either.

Always I was being bounced from Heaven to Hell by this sassy young thing I sought to corral.

But such emotional badminton didn't stop my development politically. Roosevelt was out for re-election for the third term, and I was not only outraged at this conceited flaunting of tradition but Roosevelt's masterful but obvious demagoguery repulsed me beyond endurance. I remember getting a harsh lesson from this Machiavellian "man of the people" when I heard a Republican program wherein different speeches of his were played in sequence, so that the impudent lies of the man were horrifyingly obvious. In one excerpt you would hear this political snake declare his undying devotion to one principle, only to hear him denouncing the very same thing in the next moment, with passionate and self-rightuous venom.

I rejoiced at this genius of the Republicans, and was sure no political leader could survive this devastating exposure of total lack of principle and utter depravity of character. Roosevelt was dead; I was positive! His subsequent landslide election taught me once for all the ability of the people to know, weigh and judge facts per se -- an ability which is almost exactly zero. When Franklin would take to the airwaves with his undulating, calculatingly charming voice, the women would be overcome with his "masterful" leadership, and the males would be scrambling with each other to do homage to this great "liberal". My college mates absolutely staggered me with their apparent blindness to this foul liar and cheat. Grabb and Hillery formed committees to get Roosevelt re-elected, and the campus was alive with a passion for Roosevelt. When I tried to point out the wild lies and inconsistences of the man's words and acts, his demagoguery which should have been obvious to any ass, and his grossly insincere and studied mass-manipulation techniques, I was greeted by a reaction which I have since learned is typical of these phoney "intellectuals" who pride themselves on their "liberalism"; invective! I was called a "reactionary", a "tory", even a "fascist" -- a word I knew nothing of at that time. There was no attempt to show that my arguments or charges were wrong or ill-founded -- only sneers, jeers, curses and name-calling.

It is typical of my political naivete of that time that when the propaganda about Hitler began to be pushed upon us in large and larger doses, I swallowed it all, unable to even suspect that somebody might have an interest in all this, and that it might not be the interest of the United States or our people.

Charlie Chaplin was one of my favorites (and still is) and when I saw his "Great Dictator", I was not only brought to tears by the funny part, but I was brought to bursting indignation by the impassioned speech he makes at the end against Dictatorship (except Stalin's brutal dictatorship, which was pictured as benevolent love for his people, including the massacre of "enemies of the people".) The only dictators attacked by Mr. Chaplin were Hitler, Mussolini, and Tojo -- which I have since found is easy to understand when we know that Charlie is so red even our pinko State Department has banned him from the U.S. -- and the even more significant fact for a capitalist who has made millions here in our hospitable land, that Chaplin's real name is Israel Thornstein.

But in 1940, all of this was hidden from me as it is still hidden from our people for yet a little while longer, and I grew to hate this "vicious monster", Hitler as much as anybody in the Country. It became obvious that we would have to get into the war to stop this "horrible ogre", who planned to conquer America, so we were told, and so I believed.

I was having the time of my life in college, but my idealism would not permit me to enjoy it as long as I sincerely believed, as I did, that my beloved country was in immediate and deadly danger of being enslaved or murdered and destroyed.

I made preliminary inquiries about enlising in the Navy. The president of Brown, Henry Merrit Wriston, called me into his sacred chambers to remonstrate with me.

"How can you expect to become an important man if you don't finish college?" he asked me.

Sitting on the edge of my chair in awe of this grand person, I replied that there was no use trying to become an important man if America was to be destroyed. I said that I felt it my duty to do what I could immediately to stop any conquering of my country, and I wondered how anybody could do differently. This fetched him up short, as he took it as a personal slur on his courage and patriotism. Waving a big stack of papers at me, he fairly shouted "See all these papers? I have just signed them! I sign my name over a hundred times a day! This is what it means to be important! Nobody will want you to sign your name if you do not finish college!"

This seemed to me then, and seems to me now, a pretty sorry argument for finishing college or for being a success, especially for a man who has been asked to reorganize our Foreign Service, and is looked up to as a mastermind. Facing him as a young squirt, I found him to be something less than a Socrates or even a good Scout Leader, and I realize that such pompous and relatively empty-headed "leaders" are, and will be, our lot until we can conquer the Jewish money-power, which can only survive as long as our leaders are either consciously in on the filthy red scheme, or as I think in the present case, are too slow witted to see what stooges they are.

So another student and I went ahead and enlisted at the First Naval District headquarters in Boston.

And HOW my life changed then!

Lt. (jg) Rockwell, instructing at Pensacola. 1943

The Old U. S. S. Omaha, my first ship, 1941

Lt. Rockwell, taking command of SOSU-1, Pearl Harbor

CHAPTER IV

For the first time I found some order and dignity in life!

The rough going as an enlisted man was something hard to take, of course, but my soul rejoiced in the pride and strength of the military. Civilian life seemed soft, weak and feminine, and I got a deep satisfaction in my growing ability to stand up under the discipline and punishment. When we stood at parade and watched the flag go by to the military band and the drums, for the first time I experienced the goose-pimple emotions for which there is no other name than "glory"! How unspeakably proud I was to be an American and a sailor! How I scorned the feather-bedded life I had just left!

And how worthy the United States Navy was of my pride, in those days!

Officers were dignified, rough, and demanding -- not afraid to insist on salutes and privileges. How I worshiped them! There were no Negroes except in the galley, and the chiefs and petty officers over me may not have been paragons of culture -- but lord! They were TOUGH! They used to break us out of the barracks on bitter, snapping cold mornings sometimes at two and three AM in the howling wind and snow to wash airplanes with our bare hands in buckets of boiling water. It was torture, but there was manly pride in just surviving it. What comraderie the suffering produced among us! The mama's boys and lady-officers and Negro brass of today's service will not understand what THAT Navy was like, but the old hands will know whereof I speak. And perhaps, if they reflect on how right I am about what's happened to our services today, they will be a little less harsh on me for discovering who it is who has made such a mockery of our once proud FIGHTING forces, and fighting the evil with every fiber of my being, no matter what I am called or how I am hated. The Communist-Zionist Jew conspiracy cannot afford to have a proud, fighting Navy or any other tough service. For real fighting men would never tolerate the take-over they are now manouvering. So they have consciously and viciously filled our services with "democracy" and fatal softness which will one day destroy us as the French services were destroyed, it we do not drive the seducers out first.

I was sent to "elimination" flight training at Squantum, Massachusetts, to see if they could make a navy pilot of me. I washed out urinals with a rubber glove, I marched endlessly and suffered all the usual military discomforts -- but I was to be a PILOT! That word has lost a lot of its glamour today -- but in 1940 --a pilot -- and a NAVY pilot at that, was just a few notches under a god to a hot-blooded young man.

A tough young Irish Lt. junior grade named McCollough instructed us for a few weeks in "ground school", and I distinguished myself in his class on flying by scoffing when he said we would all bounce when we landed the first few times. I had been over the procedure many times in the book, and was sure I would NOT bounce. McCollough said, with a happy twinkle in his eye, that he would personally take me for my first flight in an airplane, and see how I did!

He took me up on a wintry day in the little open N2S yellow Navy biplane, and in the hard, bright sunshine over Boston bay, did everything within his power to tear the wings off of that government property. He failed. But he did succeed in taking all the impudence and arrogance out of me. When I was completely unsure of up and down, and felt that my eyes were hanging two inches out of their sockets, he gave me the stick and held his hands in the air.

I will ask the gentle reader to spare me the description of the denouement of this little episode. But I am sure McCollough had a ball recounting the tale that night in the Officer's club. I did not find my fellow students overly-reverent in my presence, either.

I later met Mac when I was aboard the Wasp in the Pacific, and we had a lot of laughs over that first flight. But it was not humorous at the time. Irishmen, as I have learned, are charming, but a bit mad in the air.

Marching, washing airplanes, freezing, ogling women in Boston, standing seemingly interminable cold watches in empty hangers, getting chewed out by petty officers, fighting in the barracks, turning each other out of beds and short sheeting others, flying a little bit each day -- I got in my eight hours of dual --- and then the great day. I passed! I was given an airplane all by myself, and the idea was to get it up, around the field, and down again. This is an unforgettable feeling, as you sit there in the cockpit and the safe, dependable instructor climbs down and leaves you all alone in this roaring monster. You get off the ground safely, and then worry about getting in to land. I, of course, to be cocky, had boasted to my mates that I would make a perfect "circle shot" by landing in a hundred-foot whitewashed circle used by Navy pilots for carrier precision landings. I undershot at first and had to put on more power to get here, and gave heart-failure to the entire squadron as I wobbled and skidded and stalled and struggled to the circle. And then I missed.

But never mind, I had survived and soloed, and that was all that was required! Those of us who had passed were too happy to pay much attention to the jibing about my missing the circle, or even to mind the dunking we got in the icy water for soloing.

During this elimination training, I had been seeing Judy, the girl at Pembroke, and, while my new glamour helped some, I was still bounced around very painfully between thinking the game was in the bag, and discovering that another hunter had been poaching.

We were sent down as one of the first few classes at the new Navy training base at Jacksonville, Florida and found nothing much but sand and sun, and an eternal hot wind which drifted the sand everywhere.

There was a dearth of facilities, so, although we were supposed to begin training, we had to serve in the lowest servile capacities as janitors and airplane pushers, watch-standers, etc., for some weeks. But finally we started flying, and I quickly learned that it was not as glamorous as we had imagined. The dread of getting "busted" out was a terrific pressure, to say nothing of the struggle to stay alive. Crashes and deaths were regular.

My first experience with death was when a guy across the hall crashed, and we had to get his things together. I busted two checks in a row on my "stunt", and had to get "squadron time". Then up again to spin, stall, loop, immelman, do wings-overs to perfection, and finally the ultimate, inverted spins. After getting the extra "squadron time", you have to get two ups out of three. My first check was an "up", and I prayed for one more as I waited for my check pilot to appear, only to discover it was "down-check" Graham, a stone-faced terrorist who sent more cadets home than any other pilot. Quaking and sweating, I took him up and fell all over the sky, finally almost ground-looping on the landing. Now my career as a hero of the air hung on what the next man said. I had to wait several days for this final check but at last I sat on the line waiting for my luck as a check pilot. I drew a Jew -- Blenman! I gave him an excellent ride -- somehow or other, and he gave me that desperately important "up".

It was during those days, just before we got into the War, that I discovered what a slouch I was in the eternal "liberty" hunt for women. The other lads were set into motion the moment anything in skirts appeared, and were full of brass and loaded with "line" to catch these fillies. In the first place, I was repulsed by most of these women. They were cheap and often brassier than my companions. When they would use earthy terms in the inevitable banter of the encounter, it turned my stomach, and I would drop out of the contest. Many an evening in these times I sat in libraries or movies while my buddies enjoyed what, to hear them later, were the most voluptuous orgies.

But this is not to say I was a hidden violet entirely. At the Roosevelt Hotel in Jacksonville at a dance one night, I saw an entrancing, feminine little creature whirling around with a host of beaux, and was immediately captivated by the dainty girl. I was interested. I could "operate" as devastatingly as the boldest of my companions, only in a more subtle way. I cut out a whole mob of would-be captors of this little lady, whose name I learned was Elsie, I also got rid of the poor sap who had brought her to the dance. I bowled her off her feet, and swept her out of the place, feeling enormously masculine and possessive.

She had rich folks in Georgia, I discovered, and learned that my catch was far, far beyond my wildest dreams -- she had a Cadillac convertible, and, when I got to know her better, she had me often to her place in Georgia, where I luxuriated like an oriental potentate.

Elsie herself was adorable and cuddly, and willing to cuddle, too. I soon had all those who had scoffed at my backwardness in the streets squirming in jealousy as Elsie would sweep up to our barracks in the Caddy and she and I would float off to transports of joy which needed little exaggeration. But I discovered all this wonder was not unalloyed. Elsie was spoiled. She demanded the uttermost in service, with flourishes, - even homage. Homage I was anxious to give -- but not on command. There were many minor and even a few large skirmishes, but by and large the affair with Elsie was what most men dream of. I asked her to marry me, and she said yes. But then there was a quarrel and she broke the engagement. I stayed away, but she sent emmissaries, and eventually we were going together again, although there was no formal understanding.

Meanwhile, I had passed one check after another, and reached the stage of final fleet training. Here I got a serious disappointment. There were three possibilities. Carrier fighters, Scout planes catapulted off a battle-wagon or cruiser, and Patrol-boats, or "P" Boats as they were called. You were invited to list choices in order, and I listed: "1. Fighters, 2. Fighters, and 3. Fight-ters". But I did not get Fighters. I got what was considered the lowest of the low -- Catapult pilot. How I groaned. But it did no good. I was sent to the seaplane squadron and learned to fly first Steerman's on floats and then OS 2U's -- the lousiest plane in the fleet, we all felt. The underpowered and clumsy float planes were designed to observe only, and their top speed was only 110 knots, with nothing but a couple of thirty calibre machine guns. What a tub! What a miserable vehicle in which to fly to glory!

But I completed training in them, including a catapult shot off the dock at Jacksonville, was a commissioned ensign, and was assigned to an old World War I cruiser, the U.S.S. Omaha.

I drove North in the little flivver I had in college, which my Aunt had shipped to me, and stopped in Newark, New Jersey, to see my first girl, Jean, from Atlantic City. My dashing Navy uniform and wings, etc. captivated her, and she, in turn captivated me. She was as sweet as I had remembered her, only now I had the courage and know-how to kiss her -- which I did. In one evening, she was convinced we were engaged, although I said nothing about it. But I had to resume my travel North to Providence to see my folks.

Arriving in Providence, I of course went to see Judy at Pembroke. My uniform and wings (very rare yet since not many were in uniform) were as efficacious with Miss Aultman as with the others, and I became engaged, this time with me asking the question

I closed out my remaining affairs, and took the train to Norfolk, where I was to catch a ship which would transport me to the secret port where I would get aboard the Omaha for permanent duty. Judy saw me off, none too tearfully I thought, as the other less "fortunate" girls had been.

In Norfolk, I got my first taste of the real old salty sea-going Navy on the U.S.S. Pastores, a supply ship. They had a little bos'n's mate, whose name I forget, but whose character I will never forget. He went about barefoot all the time, and could and did boot a man just as effectively with those caloused toes as with a boot. He was tatooed all over, and obviously tough as a tiger shark. The officers loved him, although they pretended publicly to disapprove of his ways and tactics.

Finally the Pastores was ready to sail, and we moved out into Hampton Roads to swing on the hook for the last day. As an officer I had the run of the ship, and I hung around the bridge to learn what I could of the affairs of managing a great Naval vessel.

About an hour before we were to stand out of the harbor, we got a light message by blinker from the flag headquarters on shore, "Send boat for officers" -- and the whale-boat was dispatched. When it returned, the cox'n was grinning from ear to ear, and the Captain, who had come out to meet the important officers who had held up the ship, discovered that the "officers" consisted of the bos'n, full of beer and immense satisfaction with having avoided missing ship, a serious charge. The business about using the flag's signal light, etc., was relatively "minor" and "Boats" had done it again. The officers laughed for days about this "crime" in the wardroom.

On the Pastores, I had my first experience with "race prejudice". It must be remembered that I had gone to school with negroes, and never even noticed them.

As a passenger officer, the Exec. had put me in charge of one of the holds where there were berthed two or three hundred men who were also passengers. And when I got to the hold, as ordered, I found a riot in the making. Half of the passengers were black, the other half white -- and those were not just ordinary white men but men from Georgia! And this was before Eleanor and Anna Rosenberg had "integrated" the armed services. Blacks were always "mess-boys", and never, never were berthed with white men. Now here I was , a brand new, fishy-green ensign, in in charge of an explosive race situation!

I marched the blacks out of there immediately, mustered them on deck and had them hold ranks, while I found out what to do. But the Exec. was busy getting underway, and I was told to figure it out myself. I checked the other hold and found another passenger officer having the same trouble. He had half white and half blacks. So we traded. Both of us wanted the whites, but we flipped and he won, so I got two hundred Africans and he took all the whites.

I boarded the Omaha in Trinidad, and my Navy life really began. It was so different from the Navy of today that the present outfit seems like that of another country, a much less manly Country.

From the glorious foundations of the United States Navy until 1944 or 1945, when the influx of "quickie officers got too huge to train properly, we had "iron men in wooden ships", to use the old Navy phrase. In 1946, after the Communist "bring the boys home" debacle, all hell broke loose in the salty ranks of the great fighting men and officers who led the Nation in unbroken victories for two hundred years. Civilian meddlers and communist fellow travellers got the power to wreck our armed forces as part of the conscious plan to weaken us, now that the only possible enemy was the Soviet Union. They "democratized" our fighting men, by integrated units, they "luxury-ized" them, and they have almost destroyed them. Every top officer in the service knows the despair of trying to do anything constructive today, and I speak with authority when I say that the morale in the Armed Forces has disintegrated to the point where no matter WHAT weapons we have, we no longer have sufficient MEN and the MASTERS to make a real FIGHTING team. To go back to the old Navy term, we now have "paper men in steel ships". The officers and men who have the guts and gumption and can't stand the phoney atmosphere, get out and "make it" on the outside. The pitifully few old-line officers and career enlisted men who are still trying to keep a backbone in our armed forces are usually "retired" prematurely, like the immortal "Chesty" Puller, the greatest leader the Marine Corps ever had, while slick operators and "brown-nosers" are moved into top commands, where they fight with cocktail glasses and barrages of paper.

The millions of men who are inducted and then jammed in with Negroes and never shown an officer or sergeant with the guts to MAKE them salute and show respect or kick them firmly in the tail (respectively), get out as soon as they can, in highly proper disgust. A uniform used to be the mark of a FIGHTING man. Now they have got old and sacred fighting uniforms for book-worms with horn-rimmed glasses, ladies and even Africans.

Most of this was accomplished by the first pro-communist Secertary of Defense, George Catlett Marshall, who boasted how he destroyed Nationalist China with a stroke of his pen and gave China to our mortal enemies --and by Anna M. Rosenberg --the Hungarian Jewish woman he put in as his first assistant and in charge of MAN-POWER, Anna M. was identified under oath before the U. S. Senate as a member of the Communist John Reed clubs of New York City, and wrote articles for the Communist New Masses magazine. I myself have the photostats of these red articles I made in the Library of Congress, along with her picture, so there can be no howls of "mistaken identity". It was this Communistic Hungarian Jewess who promoted the communist Jew, Peress, when Joe McCarthy got on his track, and it was this Communistic Jewess who "nigger-fied" our once tough fighting forces.

In order to proceed undisturbed at the wrecking of our armed forces, these unspeakable traitors have calculatingly and brutally brainwashed our men with "orientation" courses in "Democracy" (ie. Communism -- see any Soviet propaganda) until any attempt to help them now is met as an attack on them. I am sickened and heart-broken today when officers who should be able to see what has happened tell me what a filthy dog McCarthy was, and explain to me what "progress" is being made in "democratizing" our once-elite and FIGHTING forces. The Army has gotten it the worst, for it is the Army alone the reds fear in the moment of their "take-over". If the Army is led by patriotic Americans, not afraid of personal reprisals and faithful to the Constitution as they have sworn, no red putsch can succeed. But if they can fill up the high posts with toadies and Jews and pinkos and boobs, the helpless and inarticulate masses of men will have to go along and be used, as they were in Little Rock, to destroy their own great American Republic. NOTE: since this was written, in 1960 the "Walker Case" has fully substantiated these charges.

But in 1941, boot ensigns, such as I, still jumped by Jg.'s, "niggers" were just "niggers", Chiefs were TOUGH and could settle maters which now go before Court Martials, with the toe of a well-placed boot, and officers dressed in full formal uniform for dinner every night, no matter what the conditions.

I could and would like to write an entire book on what I learned, and learned to love on that old O-Boat, but cannot spare the pages, in this, my first book. Perhaps later I will write a book on the armed forces, but for now, all I can say is that I found out what a fighting force SHOULD be like on the "Omaha", and Americans should tremble in fear and terror every minute we deny our officers the right, the privilege and the duty of ACTING like officers and making our MEN as tough as the steel and electronic monsters they guide as they were on the old Omaha. There is no "democratic" nonsense in the SOVIET armed forces, and, should we ever have to face these tough, old-fashioned fighting forces, no matter what our technical superiority -- like the French hiding behind their Maginot-line, we will be sliced up like butter before the hot knife of the undemocratic Soviet enemy.

I had my first taste of war on the Omaha, but in odd circumstances. Martinique was "French" and France had fallen to Hitler. We patrolled off this island, and one night when I was catapulted out to search for a reported contact, I found traces of a sub. I got radio orders to stay with it, and was concentrating on this, when the radio man called on the intercom and asked me what the "sparks" were. I looked back, and saw tracers going by, and discovered I was pursued by what I thought was a Navy SNJ -- but which was probably one of our earlier gifts to the French. I was flying an old SOC biplane at ninety knots -- with an open cockpit, and the SNJ, compared to me, was "red hot". It flashed past me below, and disappeared without hitting us. I got a lot of kidding back aboard later, and there were a good many remarks about my "imagination", etc. but the radioman confirmed this odd-ball attack. Later, I depth charged several subs, receiving return fire, but not getting credit for any "kills" because we discovered our depth-charges wouldn't go off. We tested five or six of them, and learned they had been sabotaged or poorly made. Still later, off Africa on the invasion convoy, I am sorry to say I helped sink two axis subs, working with carrier killer groups.

But the day-in-day-out flight operations were much more taxing than the relatively rare combat incidents. We were working the South Atlantic, searching for raiders and subs, and going in and out of Trinidad there were always torpedoings and sinkings. The entrance, Chaca Chacari, was dubbed "torpedo junction" by all hands. The subs used to sit on the bottom, fanned out and pop off the convoy ships as they came out of the harbor, like ducks. Once I remember they blew up a Brazilian vessel loaded with coffee, and the ocean was turned into black coffee for miles. I wondered if it kept the fish awake. We often saw pieces of ships, (once an entire half), floating aimlessly, and had to sink them.

Every morning before dawn, General Quarters would sound, immediately followed by flight quarters, and we pilots would stagger and stumble out of our bunks to the catapults, climb into the old SOC biplanes, be whacked in the back by our old steam-rammed catapults, and find ourselves out over the Atlantic at two or three feet "altitude" over the swells, in the dark, and only minutes out of bed. This was a hair-raising minute or two, but the belt in the back of the head served to clear the sleep and cobwebs from our brains, and we were soon roaring up into the dawn --an emotional experience which never failed to move me deeply. The immense majesty and indescribable vastness of the sea is multiplied and increased a thousand-fold by the terrific contrast afforded by the insignificant little ship you leave behind, as you rise into the grey and pink panorama of the sky. As the tropical sunrise begins, and you are suspended between endless, rolling grey ocean, and towering mountains of multicolored clouds, fired with the almost invisible little black "tooth-pick" of a ship you have just left far below, giving you a sense of the staggering vastness of it all. Only a pig or a stone could fail to be moved deeply.

But then I would have the immediate problem of dead-reckoning that ancient Curtis biplane 500 miles over that empty ocean and back to the ship, not where it was when you left it, but someplace new, where it had zigzagged in those five hours. We had no radar in those days, and were required to maintain tight radio silence. There were no homing devices or other aids. Just our chartboards, pencils, computors, compass and instruments. We usually flew all alone, one plane out on each side, to scout as much territory as possible for the day. The pattern was a huge "U" out from the ship and back, with a three hundred mile inverted "U" at the top -- or bottom -- of the U to cover everything to the limit of sight. During all this time, the wind, which had to be estimated solely from the appearance of the sea far below, was drifting the plane sometimes as much as thirty miles one side or the other in an hour -- or a hundred and fifty miles in the five hour flight, the ship was moving, and we had no automatic pilot or any mechanical aid whatsoever. You figured out everything by vectors, compass course and speed and distance and time, and gas, and then prayed fervently that you and the ship would wind up somewhere in the near vicinity at the end of the flight. If you made a mistake of adding the magnetic variation instead of subtracting it, or forgot a single wind figure, or made any other ordinarily slight mathematical error, it was curtains and we lost several pilots just this way. One panic-stricken pilot broke radio silence against orders when he missed the ship, ran out of gas, and sat down in the middle of the ocean someplace. We tried to find him, but never did.

I recommend this system for those, like myself, who tend to make careless errors in mathematics. I discovered I COULD be perfect, on those hops.

While you were doing all this pencil pushing, you were also burning up the surface of the sea for the tell-tale feather of a periscope or anything else, holding your precision compass course by stick and rudders, and watching out for the switching of gas tanks, mixture control, and everything else about the bit of machinery which alone kept you out of a watery grave below. It was an exacting, exhausting job. But I loved it.

At the end of the five hours, you began to sweat out the "sighting" -- and it is not hard to imagine the joy of seeing that little speck you know is home -- and more living. But sometimes you DON'T see it. Your gas is almost gone, there are no "aids", and you have only minutes to see it -- or compose yourself for a better world. The trick often was to dive down low and sweep the horizon. What you couldn't see against the dark sea, could sometimes be seen as an unrecognizable little jiggle in the horizon against the sky. There it would be! And you would bore in for it with everything wide open.

When you finally arrived over the familiar, rolling shape, you circled around low while they rigged for "Cast Recovery". Having been both on carriers and cruisers, I can assure my fellow pilots that a carrier landing is a pale imitation of the real "hairy" thing of landing alongside a rolling cruiser in twenty or thirty foot swells, and taxiing up in clouds of blinding spray onto the "mat" to towed rope with your wingtips only inches from the steel sides of the heaving ship all accomplished as the ship bowls along underway! We never landed far back in the slick, which the ship made by turning ninety degrees, because it tore up the prop too much, beating against the salt water when you then tried to taxi the hundred yards or so to the ship. My Senior Aviator, "Moe" Lenny, taught us masterfully and exactingly to land about twenty feet outboard and abreast of the fan-tail (stern) so that, on the last wild and wooly bounce -- after you had hit two or three swells with frantic jiggling of stick and rudders to avoid crashing you would wind up neatly and stopped, with the float resting in the mesh of rope called "mat", and your hook engaged to hold you in tow.

Then came the business of catching the swinging iron ball from the crane and boom arrangement which picked you up. Many a man was knocked senseless and overboard playing this little game, as he sat up on the cockpit hood. And then, when you DID catch it, you had to slip the big steel hook in the wire sling you pulled out from behind your head in the cockpit without letting your hands get under the hook -- because when the swells yanked that hook taut, it was easy to lose a hand as the cable lifted the plane clear of the water. Finally you would find yourself hanging in the air, swinging on the boom, and totally free of responsibility for the first moment in five long hours. You slumped in the sweaty parachute harness, just luxuriating in the gratefulness of it all. A few minutes later you would be sipping coffee and being served a fine breakfast in the wardroom, while you lorded it over the "black-shoe" Navy -- the poor slobs who were confined to the rolling decks, and who had to ask you humbly for the story of the hop --- what you'd seen, any action, etc. It was hugely satisfying, and we pilots were not sparing of the opportunity to be as obnoxious as possible to the less "heroic", "deck-apes".

A catapulting or a recovery were often the only excitement aboard for days on end, and we pilots were thus the center of all eyes with our performances. Especially we vied on the recoveries, and the crew divided up behind its favorites. I ached for a carrier and a hotter plane with more combat, but there was much to enjoy in the life on the Omaha, and I enjoyed it. We went to Africa, and all over South America. I often was detailed to the Shore-Patrol, however, and this was no fun, although I learned a lot. It was a kill-joy job. You had to go around with a stern expression and watch the men blowing off steam in the bars, and see them look hatefully at you out of the corner of their bleary eyes.

The first time I got this unpleasant assignment was a pretty brutal introduction to the problems of leading rough, tough men. I think it is wrong to give such a task to a totally green ensign, but I was assigned to take a shore party over the side in Rio, men with heavy beards who had been cooped up at sea for months. I was ordered to line them up on the dock and give them a lecture on the dangers of VD - me a downy-cheeked squirt who knew nothing at all of such matters. I did my best, and the men tried not to laugh, but it was extremely painful and I felt a complete ass. Which I was!

American Nazi
Stormtroopers
on the march
in the streets.

My first wife, Judith, posing for a Christmas card photo, Maine

The lecture was apparently a huge failure, because we had dozens of men on the VD list within a few days in that highly-touted but dirty port.

When I was free, I donned my crisp whites, wings and ribbons, and did enjoy liberty in these exotic lands, but usually it was spoiled somewhat for me by the filth and coarseness of it all, and the crude activities of even my companions.

In Rio, there was the usual "British Club", and we officers were invited. There we met some really charming English young ladies, and invited them to dinner aboard ship. But this was a mistake, it turned out, because even in the immaculate wardroom with its white nappery, good food and excellent service by the as-yet un-rooseveltized mess-boys, we could not escape the effects of the crudity and filthiness.

The old Omaha had no Public Address installation. "The Word" was passed in the old fashioned way of the Navy, by leather-lunged Bos'n's Mates, who would roar down each of the three hatches in the main deck in turn. The evening we had the young ladies aboard for dinner was hot. The wardroom was directly below the number one hatch, and as they were helped into their seats by the mess-boys, the bos'n arrived at the hatch with his pipe and and let go with an announcement.

" EEEEEE--eeeeee--EEEEEEE! (The whistle)-- Now, ALL MEN WITH VENERAL DISEASES, LAY DOWN TO SICK BAY FOR TREATMENT! "

There was a great sound of running and pounding feet up and down ladders, and the young ladies blanched. So did we.

After almost a year in the South Atlantic, the Omaha put into New York for repairs at the Brooklyn Navy yard -- and this was like a trip to heaven for us. But I went chasing once again after the elusive and faithless Judy, in Providence. She gave me all kinds of trouble, on the phone, but when I appeared in my sparkling dress whites in her dormitory dining-room at Pembroke, and she saw the other girls ohh-ing and ahh-ing, she was won over and agreed to come to New York for a week while the ship was in port. But she insisted on finishing college before we were married. I chafed miserably at that, but once again bowed to what I later learned were orders from the High Command -- her old lady, who sensed in me a male who was not so easy to push around as Judy's charming, cultured, lovable but easily-dominated old man.

However, I did manage to get her to agree to share a room with me at the luxurious Pennsylvania Hotel, now the Statler, and I imagined I had things made.

I did spend the week in the hotel room with her - but learned I did NOT have it made. All my powers of persuasion, coercion, brute force, sneakiness and other techniques were to no avail and I spent one of the most unbelievable weeks of my life -- a week I have a hard time convincing anybody could happen in one room with one double bed. Horribly frustrating as it was, however, it was also idyllic and very wonderful. I went back out to sea in a pink cloud of romance, and began to scheme to get back as soon as possible.

But the Navy is not interested in private plans for romance, and cruelly put the war ahead of my schemes, which came to naught. We went back to the old routine of cruising the South Atlantic and I began to chafe miserably, as the war proceeded more hotly elsewhere, especially in the Pacific, while I was still lumbering around in the empty vastness of the South Atlantic, in a plane which was not too far removed in appearance from that of the Wright Brothers. I longed to fly the brand new F4U Corsairs, at that time the hottest and deadliest thing in the air.

I heard rumors that "suicide" photo-pilots were being asked to volunteer to fly stripped down P-38's over enemy beaches, so I wrote an official request for training as a photo-pilot, and got a favorable endorsement from my CO with whom I was on the best of terms for good performance of duty. Even so, it seemed too much to hope for, so that I almost collapsed with joy when the ship got a priority dispatch on the matter. I was ordered to Flight Photo School at Pensacola, with thirty days leave !!!!

I imagined once again that I could marry Miss Aultman as soon as I arrived, and would spend a whole month even better than the week in New York. But once again, I reckoned without my my strong-willed, future mother-in-law. It was decreed that I could not marry Judy until two days before the END of my leave, which gave me one day for a honeymoon, and then one day to get to Pensacola!

There was no appeal, as I had discovered, from these imperial commands, so I had to fritter away the days -- and nights -- until April 24th, when the event was scheduled.

A few days before the scheduled wedding, I was detailed to help Judy address invitations and we were working together on this task when I got my first real look at how her mother operated. My pen ran out of ink, and Judy jumped up and said, "I'll go upstairs and get some ink." -- Her mother burst out of the sunroom shouting, "Hold it! Just a minute! HE goes upstairs and gets the ink. You don't run errands for him!"

On April 24, 1943, I was married in the Barrington Episcopal Church, with all the trimmings, which I disliked enormously. But these amenities are the price one must pay to the ladies, who appear to revel in such painful, public formalities at a time which should be so holy and private and reserved to the young people whose lives are so hugely affected.

Finally, however, we got clear of all the hand-shaking, giggling, cake-cutting, sly jokes, and general silly fussing, and were off in a cab to the railroad station. I was ecstatic, and swimming in the romance of it all. But not my brand new wife. When we had gotten settled on the train, she turned to me briskly and, with what I learned were her final orders from headquarters, announced, "Now there's to be no boss in this marriage, and no babies, at least not now!"

This almost froze me inside, even though the part about the babies made sense. But making "sense" is not always the way to make a good marriage, and such stern announcements at such a time do not help make a honeymoon what it should be.

When we got to the Statler Hotel, in Boston, I got a worse shock. Her suitcase was opened, and she put her clothes away. Then she laid out on the bed what I later called "The Drug Store", a complete assortment of equipment which left nothing to chance, or the imagination! Mother had thought of everything! The inevitable result of such cold chilling of what must be spontaneous and as warm as possible was that she wound up crying -- and so did I. I struggled out and spent hours loading up on beer in the Silver Dollar Bar, and trying to understand what was wrong with the world.

And with the last minute wedding before I had to leave, we had no chance to straighten things out. "Mother" had really thought of everything!

On the train down to Pensacola, I had my first personal

brush with one of the obnoxious types even the Jews call a "Kike". I had my reservations for a sleeper for over a month, of course, and staggered to the station with all my heavy service baggage and uniforms, and my even heavier thoughts of my "marriage", grateful at least that I could rest on the long, trip.

But when I got to the train and looked up my berth, I found a 300 pound, yellow skinned, fat Hebrew getting ready to move in. I showed him my ticket and reservation of a month's standing, and he brushed them aside, telling me he had paid the agent a good deal for these accomodations, and had no intention of giving them up. I called the colored porter, and asked to have my reservations confirmed. The porter called the conductor, who sadly shook his head, said there was some mistake, asked me to step outside -- and then told me that my accomodations had unfortunately been sold twice, and the other man had an "earlier" reservation. I was too young and innocent to know how to deal with such villiany, as I would now, but like most people, I simply bowed to this monstrous injustice because I knew nothing else to do, outside of punching this vile Jew merchant a good belt in the teeth, which would not have helped.

So I sat up all night on my bags in a passageway, while this "chosen" fighter of Hitler (who was probably giving his all to buy war bonds at huge personal sacrifice) rode in style in my berth. This is the first time in my life I can remember hating a Jew as a Jew. But I submit that so would anybody hate him -- even my pious fellow gentiles who now counsel me to tolerance and love.

I plunged into photo-school and flying in Pensacola with happy enthusiasm, over-joyed to be at last on my way to the kind of work and flying I really wanted. We flew half the day, and studied theory or worked in the dark room the other half. I studied hard and did well.

My wife of one day's vintage, finally arrived, after she had graduated from Pembroke in June, and I had prepared a little cottage near the base.

Our married life was far from the passionate affair one might imagine, or rather what it should be. After a life-time of "mother's" training, Judy just COULDN'T relax and enjoy being a female. She had to be on guard every minute to see that she maintained her "rights" which she did -- but meanwhile losing her major birth-right as a human being--real love.

There were a good many tears and scenes, but after a while we arrived at a sort of modus vivendi, and even a bit of gay comraderie in our mutual bafflement. I have since then come to the conclusion that it is not only not wrong for a man to find out more about life before he gets married, but his duty. I feel sure now that, if I knew then what I know now, I could have saved my poor, warped little wife--and our marriage which began even then the crackup which continued for another ten years. But then I was a truly innocent boob in the affair, and too ignorant and scared to exert the masculine force and power given by nature to males to overcome such situations.

There was nothing wrong with July but the insane common disease of all our education today. Her whole life had been dedicated to an unrealistic goal, as are the lives of most of our girls. Without anybody coming out and saying it, the mad scramble for "democracy" has been extended to the sexes and the natural dominance of the male, and the passive submission of the female, which is basic to both natures, and absolutely necessary to their happiness, has been scorned as an evil carry-over from our animal nature. A "modern" girl cannot avoid the impression that it is somehow "inferior" to be "just a woman" or "just a housewife and mother", and the corresponding idea, therefore, that she must try to "be somebody" or "do something worthwhile"--have a "career". She receives all sorts of education, particularly in college, which is not only useless if and when she becomes a wife and mother and housewife, but which irritate and frustrate her in their natural capacities. It is not hard to understand how a woman trained as an expert lawyer might chafe at the humdrum life of a wife and mother--but a life which is desperately important to her own happiness as a person, and to society. From time to time, my college-trained wife would burst from the dishpan in utter frustration and demand an explanation, as I came home tired from all day flying and working in dark-rooms--of why SHE had to wash dishes. "I went to COLLEGE", she would exclaim, "Why should I have to wash DISHES?"

We do the same thing with millions of men, too. When there is obviously no capacity for brain work in a child, it is criminal to drive and beat it into schooling aimed at preparing it to be a "White Collar" worker. With a minimum of schooling sufficient to read and write, it would be happy working with its hands. When it is led to imagine it is a great brain, and then is driven to the sewers and ditches with a shovel--it is understandable that the unhappy victim becomes frustrated and a danger to society, when multiplied by millions.

It is not a question of "superior" or "inferior" involved, but a question of POSSIBILITIES. A girl will grow up to be a woman, a female, no matter WHAT education, ideals, ideas and training she may get. Perhaps it is "unfair" that she was born a woman, physically weak, less able to reason, coldly burdened with the inexorable cyclic functioning of her reproductive system, and blessed with the soft, warm, emotional, understanding and patient nature of the machinery designed by Nature for motherhood above all things.

The effort of femininists and liberals to "correct" what Nature has decreed, whether the effort is "good" or "bad", can lead only to misery for those who attempt to fly in the face of a cold and merciless nature, and social agony for a world which is deprived of warm and submissive females and mothers.

It is a mark of insanity for an individual to ignore "reality" and act "as if" he were something which he is not. It is no less insane when women pretend that their female natures do not exist, that they are not only the "equals" of men, but the SAME as men, except for a slight physiological difference. No matter how a few of them manage to succeed in the poses of engineers and steelworkers and fighter pilots and business executives, women today, as a group are fundamentally acting in the manner of the insane; defying and ignoring reality.

And the results are frightfully visible in our whole civilization. The women are becoming masculinized, while the men are getting femininized. One has only to look at a crowd of our teenagers to see how things are going. They wear the same tight pants, the same jackets and the same hats--even the same duck tailed hair-do's. We are breeding and training up a generation of jazzed-up, negroidized, neutral queers.

Our whole approach to women, today, as with most of our social attitudes, is that of the Soviets, who have women in the army, working in the streets, and even in firing squads, just like men. God save us from such women!

Women are indeed the equal of men, as a group, ONLY when they fulfill the task for which Nature equipped and made them -- successful motherhood. Man was designed, even in the creative process itself, to supply the SPARK, the drive and the aggressive push of life, while woman is designed to supply the basic building material of new life; nourish, treasure, warm and guide it until it can sustain its own life. There is no escape from this fate, even if it were bad, which it is not.

If a man is to be honored for making cigars or building bridges or making beer, as our great business men are, --- then surely we ought to honor those who make our people! But the trouble is that our insane "liberal" attitude toward motherhood and home-making has given women an impossible inferiority complex and frustration about their possible real achievements in life We train our girls by the millions to be anything but successful wives and mothers, lead them to believe they are to be an "equal" part of a "man's" world, when the truth is that it is only nature's world, and man's share in it is no greater or more glorious than that of a female-oriented woman who produces, brings up, and gives to society a family of happy PEOPLE.

If our girls were brought up from first consciousness to realize the absolute and total inevitability of their mission in life, but above all to be PROUD of that mission, train for, and then fulfill it joyously, there would be no more talk of "achieving" equality. They would find that nature has already GIVEN them equality in generous measure, if only they will accept it. There can be no sense in discussing the superiority of negative or positive electricity in a battery; they are merely different forms of the same thing. But the difference is VITAL if there is to be any CURRENT. It is exactly the same with our human battery of life; there can be no CURRENT when the male and female potential or voltages are permitted to become "equal". They must be strongly OPPOSITE, or the current will stop.

The current IS stopping as our broken families and marriages show. In my own case, my first partner was wretchedly twisted from what I am sure were originally good, basic natural instincts. But even more important, I was "civilized" and "liberalized" out of my own savage male instincts of force and domination which, if properly controlled, could have saved both my new wife and our marriage.

It is not women who are at fault in the growing madness of our family and sex frustration, it is the men who have permitted it. The women are still born passive and submissive, and if our fathers and grandfathers had not failed them as a group, as I failed my first wife as an individual, they would still, as a group, be enjoying their birthright and the honor owed them by society for being the most exalted manufacturers and executives in the world, the manufacturers of our PEOPLE!

Upon achieving power, one of our first tasks will be an all-out public-relations drive to help our entire population, men and women, to see that "motherhood" is not the silly, sloppy thing which is made of it today, for the benefit of florists and greeting card publishers, the momism described by Philip Wylie which has made so many Mama's boys and spoiled brats in our society, but a PROFESSION every bit as exasting, scientific and honorable as the law, medicine or education. The latter exalted professions merely HELP the results of the profession of motherhood. It is the part of the women to produce and give to society people who have just the right combination of discipline and love to make people happy and capable citizens.

Where a doctor or a lawyer spends years and years preparing for his work, and then more years of apprentice-ship, most of our mothers today spend their years preparing to be writers, artists, "executives" or some kind of "career girls", -- which few of them actually become, while their only "training" in their real profession in life consists perhaps in a high-school course in how to make a few fancy salads in "Home Ec" and "romance". They plunge into the worlds' most important, most honorable and most exacting profession, knowing nothing of childhood disease, scientific family budgeting, psychology of children (and husbands), or any of the other vital PROFESSIONAL subjects which would make the first years of marriage such a relatively orderly and pleasant experience instead of a wildly chaotic mess every time "something" happens to the baby, and mother either knows nothing about it at all -- or knows only old-wives' tales.

If a lawyer or a doctor attempted to practice as soon as he had purchased a few medicine or law books, the way our women plunge into the business of making human beings and a happy family, as soon as they have gotten a husband, they would be arrested. The law and medicine would be impossible chaos, which is exactly the state of our "modern" family system, as shown by sky-rocketing juvenile delinquency, and millions of wrecked families and broken homes. Our civilization is no longer as simple as the pioneering society of our forebears, and, if family life is to survive--as it must survive if the race is to survive--then we must stop the insane business of considering a mother and home-maker "just a housewife," who needs no special education for her job. We must give our girls the necessary skills and knowledge for their actual and unavoidable profession FIRST, and then, if there is time and money and inclination, give them a "liberal" education or any other kind of education, so long as it does not give them the frustrating idea that they should be engineers, actresses, fighter pilots, etc.

Finally, and most important, we must HONOR them, as we now honor doctors and lawyers. We must establish professional women's schools and universities dedicated not to "home economics", but the exalted profession of Family Science. We must get rid of the disgusting connection of "home-making" with the dust-mop, dishpan and dirty diapers, and make it clear to our people that these tasks are no more the essence of Family Science than sweeping out the office is the essence of being a lawyer, even though a lawyer has to do this himself.

When our whole people have been given this new understanding of the real "equality" of women, and they are HONORED by professional degrees in their especial science of the organization, care, and management of a plant for the intelligent production of decent HUMAN BEINGS there will be less of the misery which lies deep in so many of our girls who wind up in a dishpan or diaper pail after a Cinderella dream of "better things" all their younger days.

My Judith had been told all her life that there was only one thing worse than getting locked up as a house-wife, with a useless man, and that was having kids to be "tied-down" to. The stark realities of adjusting the butterfly life of college and dreams of "better-things" to a washtub and submission to a male were too much for her, as it has been for many another before her.

Aside from this difficulty, there was another problem.

I discovered the utter, fantastic illogicalness of women, which can be so delightful when it is laughable, and so tragic when it causes a family fight, or hurts the children.

The only time I ever laid a hand on her was when we had been in town shopping, and I had told her I was starving for a big steak or a piece of meat. She was commendably anxious to save our small pay, and said not to buy any more, there was a piece of ham in the ice-box at home. I remembered seeing it and said that it was not enough for both of us -- it was too little even for me. She said she didn't want any at all; I could have the whole thing. I pointed out that this was silly when we were right by the store and could get some more, but she insisted over and over that she wanted none of the ham. She made such a fuss that I agreed to let her eat something else, and I would be satisfied with the little piece of ham. So we went home with no meat, and I drank a beer while she got supper ready in the kitchen. When she called me to eat, I looked at the plates, and there were two tiny shreads of meat, one on each plate! They looked like communion wafers.

When I asked her about the meat on her plate, she flew into a tantrum and insisted I was a pig and was determined to hog everything and let her go without! I will leave the ensuing argument to the imagination. My male readers will agree, I think, that such perfidy in regard to an agreement, even in such a small. affair, is hard to take, while I have found the females will consider this sly maneuver a clever way to save money, and very commendable. Suffice to say -- unable to control my frustration at her total lack of understanding of the principle involved, I grabbed the poor thing by the shoulders and shook her!

After completion of photo school, from which I graduated near the top of the class, we were asked what duty we wanted. Photo pilots were, I understood, much in demand, so you got what you wanted!

I made one of the stupidest mistakes of my life! I forgot that fighter pilots were not assigned to carriers, but were assigned to squadrons, which were then ordered, as units, to carriers. I wanted to fly the hottest things in the fleet on combat missions, so I put down "ANY COMBAT CARRIER". What an afternoon when I came home with the assignment to the USS Wasp and we celebrated! I already saw myself swooping over the enemy beaches and disdainfully photographing Tojo himself shaking his impotent fist at me as I went by, too fast to be seen clearly.

But upon getting to the great ship, I discovered that I was "Ship's Company", a sort of glorified janitor, crew for the brave air-heroes, the pilots, who never came aboard except for combat missions, did all the flying, while I did all the watching, except for a few flights now and then when I could manage it. I was V-3 division officer, and thoroughly hated my tasks which were those of a non-flying officer. In addition, I had to watch, green to the gills with envy, while the squadron boys zipped around the sky, shooting and clowning and doing what I longed to do so badly I could taste it.

I did everything I could think of to get out of that situation, and back in the air, including making myself obnoxious with requests for transfer -- finally to the ultimate desperation of asking for "any ship or station." The exec at last took pity on me, and ordered me to the pilot pool in San Diego where they make up the best fighter outfits! I was once again overjoyed. But not for long.

This time, while one after the other of the lads in the pool went to Corsair and Hellcat squadrons -- I finally got orders to SAC -- Support Air Command! I was to run up the beach on invasions and direct the air heroes again from a fox hole with my little radio and ground control team! It almost seemed somebody was purposely doing this to me. How could a guy be so crazy to get into combat in a fighter, and get first on a cruiser, then ship's company on a carrier, and finally, this: an entrenching tool and a radio for my weapons as I cringed in a fox-hole! I almost despaired, as we trained on the beach at Coronado, with LCVPs, and with tanks running over our fox-holes, while the squadrons flashed by in the blue overhead.

From there we went to Guadalcanal, where I got in on the tail end of the action or "clean-up" and flew a few hops I could scrounge out of Henderson Field. After that, Pearl Harbor, and then Guam.

My experiences in all this would make a book, but others who have had far more thrilling and readable experiences have already set forth this sort of thing for all to read. My task is to pick out the experiences which had a special significance in shaping my own character and political career. The only such experiences were the time I watched two marines beating to death with their bare hands a Jap who had been tossing hand-grenades into the camp night after night -- and enjoyed the sight immensely -- a thing which horrifies me now. Such is the hatred born of a bitter war.

There was the business of the Japs yelling filthy things about Roosevelt, at night. I wondered greatly at the oddity of trying to kill these guys who despised the same Charlatan I couldn't stand myself. Luckily, I didn't know then how this Roosevelt, on behalf of world Marxism and it's Jewish masters, plotted and planned to drive Japan to the war, sacrificed thousands of our lads at Pearl Harbor, all just to get our people mad enough to reverse their isolationist stand -and go to war to crush Germany and Hitler, which the enemies of America hate as rats hate bright light. But then, the only thought which crossed my mind was the humorousness of it, and the oddness of such a war.

Back at the Pacific Headquarters of the Fleet in Pearl Harbor, I once again broke my neck to pull a deal of some kind and get back into the air I loved. I found an officer that I knew at AirPac Assignment, and told him I would do anything on earth short of treason or murder to get a flying billet. He said he would see what he could do, and he did.

He ordered me to the USS Mobile -- another cruiser !

But that wasn't the worst of it. The Navy Brass, at that time, was in love with catapult planes on cruisers and battleships, because it was what they knew and loved so many years themselves. But, with 3 and 400-mile-an-hour fighters mastering the air over any task force, and with no ship daring to leave such an umbrella of fighter protection, our hundred-knot cruiser sea-planes were worse than a pain in the neck for the fleet -- their 3, 000 gallons of gasoline (high-octane) stowed aboard ship was a fearful, and useless danger to the safety of all hands in battle. We almost never flew, and it was the ultimate torture for me to stand by the catapults (my battle station), helpless, useless and actually in the way, with our planes lashed down, while the boys from the carriers tangled all over the sky with the suicide or Kamikaze Jap planes which plummeted at our ships with unbelievable ferocity !

My first chance in Pearl, as Senior Aviator of the Cruiser, I asked and got an audience with Admiral Sherman, of ComAirPac,

Officers and pilots of my command, SOSU-1, Pearl Harbor.

My brother, Italy, 1943

Elsie and I, Jacksonville

Liberty in Honolulu, 1944

to see if we could keep the planes on an advance atoll somewhere near the ship's operations, and thus keep in flying training and combat fighting trim. As it was, the rare times we did fly, I lost two aircraft and one pilot just because they couldn't land under rough conditions, and we never had a chance to fly enough to keep sharp. The CO of the Mobile went along with this idea, as he hated the planes and aviation gas which were of no help to him, and constituted a deadly fire menace in fighting his ship.

But I was brusquely rebuffed by the brass. I was told the planes had always been helpful on "wagons and carriers", and always would be. The old boys just could not see that the day of sea planes in the fleet was over, especially with a fast-carrier taskforce in combat conditions.

Then I suggested helicopters, which have since proved to be very excellent aids to such ships. The admiral looked at me incredulously when I mentioned it. He simply didn't believe in any such foolishness, and told me so! He said they would never amount to anything -- like the auto-gyro, for instance!

In despair, I went to my friend at the assignment desk, and finally, at long, long last, made it into the air. It wasn't the combat I wanted, but it was next best. Because of my excellent record and experience, I was given command of a large squadron of Scout and Observer aircraft and pilots for replacement and training for the fleet. I had the best fighters, torpedo bombers and scouts, and the latest seaplane, the SC, - and plenty of authority and men and equipment. I flew like a mad man, amassing my first real time since the Omaha, and deliciously happy every time I got into the air. I found a squadron of P-47's from the Army at Wheeler, and gave them a wild time in the air everytime I caught one up. We had F6F's and they were more manoeuverable than the heavier 47's. With our Navy training, our lads had little difficulty in riding those Army jockeys all over the sky, and we loved it!

I got my only black mark on my Navy record while I commanded SOSU-1 at Pearl. Everybody was scrounging, all over the Pacific, to get movie theaters set up, and I had some of the best scrounging chiefs and warrants in the US Navy. Somehow, they produced the ultimate luxury, and got two BIG, 35mm. regular projectors, which enabled us to get the best movies in the area, instead of the little sixteen millimeter outfits, and their old films.

But what I didn't know was that the 35 milimeter film was dangerously inflamable, while the 16 mm. was not, and there were voluminous regulations to guard against fire. It was my duty to know about or look into it, but it didn't occur to me. And one day I came back from a night hop to see a plume of flame and smoke, over Pearl Harbor, and felt my heart flop as I realized it was my main building. The film had caught fire, and the whole top floor burned off. I was very properly given a letter of private admonition from the Admiral, for failure to take precautions against such a catastrophe.

In August of that year, 1945, I was on the roof one evening watching for the return of an overdue plane -- when I saw star shells bursting over the cans tied up at the Destroyer base. Then whistles began to blow. Then yells and shouts! The war was over!

I started downstairs, and when I was spied by my junior officers and men, they began to clap me on the back and act like insane idiots. Nor was it long before I caught the spirit of it all! I too, acted like an idiot. As the mob spirit of wild joy spread and mounted to a roaring storm of bursting public passion, people danced and cartwheeled through the streets of Ford Island in the middle of Pearl Harbor. Sailors burst into the Wave barracks, kissing and hugging as they went, and when the old maid Lt. in charge protested, she got kissed too. Most of my uniform was torn off, and I wound up on the shoulders of some of my men, almost naked! Toilet paper rolls by the thousands tangled the mob so it was hard to see. Whiskey appeared and the riotous crowd began to exceed all bounds. It sickened me, after a while, and I escaped back to the relative quiet of my own little cottage in the Officers' Quarters section.

Then I had an emotional experience which exceeded in intensity anything I remembered about VJ Day. Amid the howling and screaming and bursting rockets and star shells, only a few hundred yards from the insane mob of celebrators, I heard the most peaceful, but moving, sound in the world. With the noise of the mob in the background, a group of our "Mess Boys", our colored servants, were standing out behind a building under the stars singing spirituals and hymns. One huge negro stood with his head thrown back so the light of the Lord could shine on his face, and I could see the tears rolling and streaming down the black face in the moonlight as he boomed out his gratitude to God for the end of the war!

I cried too!

Let no one say that Religion is the "Opium of the people". I had none of my own, but I could FEEL the good strong warmth of theirs deep in my heart. And let no one say that I desire to hurt or injure or oppress such people. How my heart went out to them and still does! They are a biologically immature race, and I will fight to the death to save our people from mixing with them in any way. So are my children my inferiors and I would not let them sit in on a business conference with me. But I certainly love my kids and, in another sense but in the same way, I love the Negro people, so long as they don't try to push or hurt me or those I love.

I went and got those boys a bottle of wine and gave it to them, and wished I could show them how deeply I was moved by their simple devotion and childlike reaction to overwhelming events. But there was little I could do, with decorum.

I had more than enough "points" to "get out", which was the big rush right away, and started to make plans for sky-castles back in the States, just like a million other war-weary Americans.

I dreamed of buying a surplus piper cub airplane on the West Coast, where my wife was working in San Diego, and flying back together all over the USA! What a wonderful, marvelous adventure that would have been!!

But my hopes were dashed miserably when I got a letter from my intended "co-pilot" that she would have none of flying in any "orange crate" with me!

I returned to Diego on a DE, and got another dose of cold water from my new wife, with whom I had lived only a few months out of the two years, the rest of the time having been in the South Pacific. Judy knew I hated and still hate ear-rings, heavy lipstick and especially nail-polish. I realize this is a personal idiocyncrasy, but it goes back to a hate of ostentation and savage decoration -- which such things seem to me, to be. In any case, my wife usually went along with this wish the few months that I had been home. But now, when I arrived at the dock, after almost two years overseas, I found her consciously bedecked and painted in these things, and when I tried to kiss and hug her in the back seat of the car in which her landlady had picked us up, she pushed me away and explained that this was improper and embarrassing to the landlady. To HELL with the landlady, as any returning sailor will understand! But Judy was adamant. We had to chat about empty nothings with the landlady, which put me in no happy mood. It was the beginning of the long downward dive of the marriage which had its last days, six years, and 6,000 miles later in that same San Diego--with three innocent little children added to the unhappy mess.

We took the train back to the East Coast, and happy reunions with both of our families, and then headed for Maine, and CIVILIAN LIFE!!!

Commander Rockwell flying OS2U over South America

CHAPTER V

As it became obvious the war was drawing to what I imagined was a "successful" close, I began to plan my life as an artist, a life I had envisioned ever since high school. I sent enquiries everywhere to find out which school was the best for commercial art. The general consensus seemed to be Pratt Institute, in Brooklyn, New York.

After the round of family reunions up and down the East Coast, therefore, I stopped in Brooklyn at the famous old school and received a rude shock. It was not just a matter of deciding which school I would attend, but a matter of which school I could fight my way into. With millions of veterans pouring out of the services, and flocking to avail themselves of the free education under the "GI Bill", I was only one of thousands trying to enter Pratt. And when I looked at the work of some of the students at the school, hanging on the display boards, I was apalled at my own amateurishness. I was very fearful I could never make the grade. Nevertheless, I took the tests, drew the samples, and then went up to Maine to await results. My wife and I had rented the lower floor of an old sea-faring home in East Boothbay.

I had already learned that, even if admitted, I could not make the 1945-46 term, so I prepared to go to work and study at home as best I could until the next fall. I bought some books on sign-painting, some brushes and equipment, and practiced long hours over an old bread board, leaned up against a window-box full of smelly geraniums.

When I considered that I was able to paint a readable sign, I hung a poster in the front window of the house reading "Signs painted free by returned serviceman who desires practice". For a long while, there were no takers of even this "bargain". But I was also offering around town to do any odd photography work for a buck, and got a few jobs this way.

One of these photography jobs almost got me run out of town. The local Eastern Star, through some good friends, offered me the exceptional honor of taking pictures of some quite-secret ceremony. It seems the affair was a very rare occurance, and they wanted photographs of the important ladies and their ceremonial vestments. I duly appeared and took flash pictures of the solemn proceedings, doing my best to stay in the background, but somehow managing to get in the way of the hefty ladies who paraded around and around in some kind of pattern of the utmost meaning. When the action was complete, the victorious participants lined up with a great deal of difficulty, carefully observing seniority and diplomatic protocol, for a group picture. There was no mistaking the historical urgency of the atmosphere there. Never again would such an illustrious group of magnificent Past Masters, Past Grand Matrons, Present Grand Matrons, Great Grand Past Matrons, Grand High Past Secretaries, etc., etc., be assembled in all their plummage, their glorious badges and ribbons of high office.

I managed to get my lights connected right, my camera set, and my flashes organized, and even remembered to pull the dark slide out of the camera. I snapped this never-to-be-recaptured historical moment, and felt I had it in the bag. I was promised a dollar a print from many of those present, and the operation seemed to be a great success.

My darkroom consisted of a closet with an old-fashioned chain-toilet installed, in the ancient apartment, and unbelievably crude, home-made and temporary equipment. I rushed home to this "laboratory", and perpared to develop the films, as I had done dozens of others successfully, even in this make-shift set-up. My wife dutifully tried to play the part of laboratory assistant, and I fumbled around in the pitch dark with the precious cut-films, trying to get them into a tray of developer. Somehow I tripped or stumbled over some light cords, and in the effort to catch my ballance, bashed my hand (holding the films) against the corner of a shelf. The pain caused me to let go the precious negatives, and they fell. Not to the floor, as I prayed, but into the toilet !

This would not have been too disasterous, as water would not hurt them, and I was reaching down to get them out, when I bumped into the unscrewed light bulb as I bent over, pushed it in so it lit up brightly, and completely ruined the holy negatives !

I stalled the officials of the organization as long as I could, too scared to tell them the awful truth, but they wouldn't wait forever. Finally I had to admit the fact that there WERE no pictures of the historical event of the decade -- and then hide !

The good Down Maine people of East Boothbay, however, were kind and understanding of the would-be young artist, sign-painter and photographer, and compassionately forgave my incompetance.

In fact, one retired sea-captain eventually responded to my offer to paint signs free, and asked me to do a little white board of his name, on his boat shop, even insisting on paying me.

I was overwhelmed, and went to work on that little white board as though it were for the President of the United States.

The job would not take me, or any sign painter, more than twenty minutes today, but then I didn't know the secret of production for public consumption, as I do now. The eye, heart and mind of the public are unbelievably simple and naive as to technical details, like savages or children, the public is oblivious to what, to an expert, seems serious defects, so long as the WHOLE makes them happy ? Or has a pleasant effect. The grossest and most obvious fraud of a Santa Claus, if properly loaded with toys and in the right atmosphere, WILL BE Santa Claus to happy children, although his beard may be half-off, his pillows showing and his hair plainly visible under the silvery spun glass, to an adult. The best friend of the artist, is the eye of the beholder, if the artist knows how to SUGGEST what the beholder WANTS to see. At the same time, the public, the mob, has an unerring INSTINCT for fear and timidity, and very properly HATES it. A drawing, a poster, or a speech -- done haltingly by even a good technical craftsman, in fear and trembling, no matter how excellent the details, will always repell the crowd.

A sign or a poster, I have learned, can be make up of shaky poorly drawn letters, rotten sketches, and the roughest design elements; but if it is masterfully conceived as a WHOLE, with the EFFECT of the whole being the artist's sole guide, the public will be entranced.

This is why a beginner's figure drawing is almost always so grotesque and ugly in appearance. He concentrates first on an eye, doing it well, perhaps, then a nose, doing it well too, then a mouth, an ear, some hair, and on down the figure. But the finely drawn eye is too big for the nose, which is too small for the mouth, all of which are in the wrong place for the ear, which appears where the chin, perhaps, should be. On the other hand, a more experienced artist has learned that a few dashes and smears for eyes, nose, mouth, ears and hair, etc. will APPEAR to be finely drawn eyes, noses, lips, etc. - providing they are put in the right place and with some "dash" - courage. The eye of the beholder is the artist's best friend. Give the beholder a fair chance to IMAGINE the whole thing LOOKS good, and it WILL LOOK GOOD TO HIM.

But in 1945 I knew none of all this. I was simply determined to make EACH LETTER PERFECT - a totally wrong approach. I did that tiny little sign over and over and over, staying up all night and getting literally desperate. No matter how I tried, there was always a wiggle or a drip someplace, and I finally collapsed in bed, discouraged and exhausted! Just before noon, I attacked it once more - and managed to get it looking at least readable.

I gave it to the man and refused to take any money, although he seemed pleased and offered me a dollar. I wish now I had taken it - because the last time I could get home to Maine, three or four years ago, I went and looked at that sign. It is still there, and it looks fine!

Some time in the latefall, I received word from Pratt that I had managed to win a place in the next year's class, and I felt that I had already conquered half of the world.

With such a great "victory", I was able to convince Judy we ought to have a baby! Both of us had heard that having a baby sometimes "warms up" a wife - and I dearly wanted children anyway. Besides, we had begun to have a pretty good time - going on long walks together and playing like two kids. With a place at Pratt sure, and our marriage showing signs of life, I felt pretty good.

I began to get a good bit of sign painting and photography work, and decided to build myself a little shop in Boothbay Harbor. My father had once run a hotel called Tinker Tavern there, and after it burned down, owned an empty lot in a good spot near the Yacht Club. I got permission to build my shop there, and, the minute the hard freeze went out of the ground in early March, I went to work building my shop. I had never built anything before, but had watched carefully, and was sure I could do it. I had few tools, but the place was only to be twenty-two by twelve feet, and I had time.

My biggest error was in making everything too big and too heavy. I used twelve-by-twelve beams underneath, and had a whale of a struggle lifting them into position alone, nailing or rather spiking them while holding the corners on my back, and then jiggling the whole level on the hill where I built.

I made another error in forgetting to add in the thickness of the boards themselves when calculating the building measurements, and, when I came to put on the roof, found the building eight inches wider at one end than the other. I had to place, nail and saw the pieces thereafter, to size.

In May or June of 1946 I opened the little shop as the "Maine Photo-Art Service" - offering eight-hour photofinishing, sign-painting, advertizing art, and other related services.

Judy pitched in loyally in all this, even helping tar the roof, and, later, running the store part of the building. I worked like a tiger, solving one "impossible" crisis after another to stay in business and rescue my own blunders as a "professional" - without any real experience. Nevertheless, we managed to make a living and do some creditable jobs.

In the fall, we closed up the little shop, and headed for New York. I had arranged to stay with my Aunt Helen and her husband, Roscoe Smythe, in Mount Vernon, until G. I. housing became available at Pratt.

It was while we were in Mount Vernon that Judy presented me with our first baby - at first named "Judith Mitchell" - but then changed just to "Bonnie" at Judy's request.

I got my first lesson in the attitude of "modern" society and hospitals toward breast-feeding at the Bronxville Hospital, where Bonnie was born. The pressure on mothers to bind up their breasts, take pills and do anything else to "dry up" the miraculous fountain of God-given life itself was terrific! It is little wonder to me that many of our children today are "insecure" as the Freudians call it - when they have been denied the direct, warm, animal contact with their mothers in their most helpless state. Babies can't testify to their sensations, of course, nor can they remember them, but I am sure that if they could, a bottle-fed baby would feel just like a man whose wife handed him some kind of rubber mannikin to sleep with. Such a device could be manufactured to equal and perhaps exceed the mechanical performance of a human wife. But the mechanical stimulation is not all that is necessary - it is the indefinable warmth and LOVE, of the person which is the priceless ingredient - and how much more it must be so with a tiny helpless thing which has no OTHER SATISFACTION AT ALL. A baby lives entirely for contact and sustenance from its mother. When she purposely and willfully denies it that warm contact, and palms off a glass-bottle full of milk meant for a cow-mother's baby - no matter how scientifically it is "mixed", she is starving. that baby of the basic element of his life, LOVE, at the very time it should be filled and stuffed and overflowing with warmth and love. If the mother is unable to feed her child, no matter how hard she tries, then, of course the bottle is the only solution. But it should be the last resort, and relatively rare, instead of the present norm in so many cases.

The whole thing is another manifestation of the corrosive and perverted idea of "moderns" that it is somehow "degrading" to be a woman, to have babies, to nurse them, and to fulfill the animal functions of a woman. For my children's sakes, I am happy to say, I was able to prevail over her mother's dictum with Judy, and she lovingly nursed all the kids, even when, with Phoebe-Jean, the youngest, it meant excruciating pain and a breast pump.

Upon entering Pratt, I got my first close look at the human scum which more and more befouls our great cities, especially New York and Brooklyn. The "melting-pot" has turned out to be more of a garbage bucket. One of my class-mates was a Chinese Jewish Negro - with red hair! - and freckles!! One is reminded of the limerick about the young man from Dundee who got together with an ape in a tree. Atlantic City had surrounded me with Negroes and Jews, but there had been some order about it - you could tell who was who or what was what if you looked. But in Brooklyn I saw the streets crawling with creatures which defied identification. My "equals" by the million scrambled everywhere for the crumbs of a paternalistic government, pushing, shoving, fighting, knifing, screaming - giving every evidence of their kinship with a jungle tribe of pygmies or cannibals. Jews in long robes, beannies and black curls shuffled the streets among the teeming "congregations" of the Lord's "chosen", who were throwing garbage and offal in the streets until the smell alone was unbearable. I hate none of these people, any more than I hate caterpillers, grasshoppers, worms or a tribe of Australian bushmen. But I hate what they are doing to our cities, our culture, our little white children, and our national life - under the encouraging aegis of the communist, Zionist Jews and their millions of softheaded agents - most of whom have never lived with this human scum, close-to.

But in those days, I was still monstrously ignorant of race, Jews, and Communism, I saw only a "mess", which I imagined had just "made itself" and was unavoidable. I never considered that it might be caused, or that it might also be remedied with justice and decency - without hating and torturing any innocent people.

My artistic education was launched in the schizophrenic dichotomy of values characteristic of our exploding civilization. Half of my instructors were genuine artists and craftsmen who taught me valuable lessons, and the other half were gross charlatans "teaching" "modern" "art". As had happened in sociology at Brown, I became aware that the teachers of "modern art" were all pushing a pattern of ideas and techniques. And, again as in sociology, I discovered that the basic pattern of these wise men of Boetia was the enshrinement of mediocrity, chaos, disorder and fraud.

It was impossible to get your mind wrapped firmly around any principle or idea in the classes of the "modern" disciples. The only aim seemed to be to be DIFFERENT at all costs! Out of the window with drawing, color, sensitive-feeling, drama, idea--even art itself. But be shockingly different! That was the stroke of genius!

It was the philosophy of the jaded roue, the surfeited pervert. All the "old" values were "reactionary", no good! On to something new, something exciting, something wild - and then wilder still! Never mind if what you do is UGLY, so long, only, as it is shockingly different!

For the first time in my career, and purely by instinct, without understanding the ideas involved, as I have expressed them above, I began to call this kind of "artistic" crap "communism". I knew communism was something foreign and supposed to be bad and ugly -- and this kind of monstrous "art" was all these things.

As I have learned to do many times since, I made a laboratory experiment of these conclusions and theories. We had a class in "design", which amounted to lessons in graphic madness and chaos. The project for the year was a "mural" showing 'workers', "industrial strife", etc. (Sound familiar?) We had to make endless sketches, charcoals, color ideas, etc. But I could see the foolishness of it all, and, as I had in Atlantic City High School in "Problems of American Democracy", I simply rebelled. Only this time, I dared not do it openly, since I was living with my wife and our new baby, Bonnie, on the $90 per month I got for going to school. So George Olsen, another "real" artist and myself, and a few others, discovered that we could simply slip out the door onto a fire escape after checking in, and over to my place for bull sessions and coffee. So we did this almost all year. When the "master sketch" was due for grading, I sat up one night and demonstrated my utter disdain for this organized insanity. I traced my foot on a piece of illustration board, let the baby scribble on it, and then scrambled in different communistic-looking "workers" where they would fit -- any which way. I daubed and smeared color until the foot was somewhat disguised, although you could still see it. It was atrocious! AWFUL!

Then I took it in and presented it proudly to the poor boob who taught this "subject". He was thrilled to death!--Said it was unquestionably DIFFERENT! He held it up to the class, gave a lecture on the "significance" of the baby's scribbles, my foot and the smears. Then he gave me a "B" on it! George Olsen and I had a hard time keeping straight faces. But we did, until we got across the street to my little apartment, where we laughed and howled over the idiocy for hours.

At the end of my first year at Pratt, I got my introduction to the Jewish "enforcement" squad, although at the time, I didn't know such a thing existed.

I had had so much business the summer before at my shop that I wanted to get another student to help me the next year. So I put up a sign on the bulletin board at Pratt to that effect.

Boothbay Harbor, at least at that time, was a highly restricted community -- although nobody talked about it. So I had

Fred Ludekins, famous Illustrator, And Al Dorne, presenting Lincoln Rockwell with $ 1, 000 first prize, National Illustration Competition, New York. Above, design for full page advertisement, American Cancer Society, for New York Times.

Above: 300 foot sign we painted on roof of old fish wharf.

Below: Painting a sign on truck in front of Photo-Art Shop.

SA-Übung in Freimann bei München, 1923

added that fact to the sign when I advertised for a sign painter-artist-helper to come to Maine with me. A Negro, for instance, would have found life simply impossible up there.

A few days later, three husky Jews showed up at my apartment and asked if I were the one who put up the sign. When I said "yes", they firmly and none-too-gently told me that that sort of thing would not be tolerated; that they had been down to the school authorities. Then they handed me my little notice, which they had ripped down. They gave me a lecture on "democracy" and "brotherhood". Then they left, almost in military formation. But the little notice had done its work anyway, and a fine young man, Jack Myers (German), and Miki, his charming wife agreed to come up to Boothbay Harbor with Judy and me for the summer and work in the "Photo-Art Shop".

Jack and I had a roaring business that summer. We daubed signs all over the once charming little fishing village I had known as a kid. We even smeared some of the huge roofs with aluminum paint, advertising marine services and shore dinners--an atrocity as I look back on it now!

We developed thousands of vacationer's films, learning all kinds of intimate secrets I had never before realized were seen by a photo-finisher. It was a wonder to me that more photo-finishers do not get tempted into black-mail schemes.

We did silk-screen paintings and sold them successfully. I drew caricatures at fairs, (one time almost getting thrashed by a customer with no sense of humor). Both Jack and I painted for fun and we held lengthy beer-and-bull-sessions.

In the fall I returned to Pratt, and plunged into the hard schedule of study, plus all the free-lance art-work I could get to eke out a living from our $90 per month from the VA.

The cleavage between the real art I was learning in some courses and the Marxist fakery and trash I had to pretend to do in others was beginning to tear me up inside. I quickly tired of playing "jokes" on the teachers of this madness and humbuggery, once I learned it was so easy. I began to chafe at the dignity and distinction granted these phonies, alongside immortals like Durer, DaVinci, David and the other real masters. I taxed my brain endlessly to discover how they were able to getaway with such MONSTROUS fraud. It was grossly obvious!

I had not yet learned that the authors of this kind of "artistic" garbage, the promotors of this trash, and, most important, the swindlers of public opinion in the press, the "critics", who gave credence to this incredible imposture. -were mostly JEWS!

I learned that the grand-daddy of this vicious perversion of Western Art and Culture -Pablo Picasso -was not a Spaniard, as I had thought -but a JEW! That he was also a Communist, as I have since learned (he did the "peace" dove for the Kremlin), I still did not know or suspect.

The mental struggle for understanding of this fraud drove me almost to distraction, and I commenced to wonder if it were I who was out of line and unable to perceive the "beauty" of these graphicized "catastrophes", in which the human anatomy was ripped and torn into depictions which seemed literally horrible to me. I could see the beauty of modern architecture and advertising, but I could NOT see any beauty in the insane and purposeful forcing of monstrous ugliness in modern painting. I hated these things. I was pushed more and more by the administration of the school to bow down to what bred only disgust and distain within me. It was impossible for me to completely hide my feelings, and, although I didn't rebel openly, I was the leader of a small clique of dissidents and lovers of good drawing, design, etc.— which was a thorn in the side of the school. They pressed harder and harder for conformity with the "appreciation" of "modern" art which was demanded.

Eventually the conflict affected my work -- and I sought help. I went to the Brooklyn office of the V.A., and asked to take the aptitude tests, to see if perhaps I would make a better butcher or doctor than an artist. The results, they told me, showed that I had the best possible qualifications to be an artist. So I resolved to succeed in spite of my disgust at "modern" painting, by sheer excellence of effort.

The National Society of Illustrators in New York, which included such greats as Norman Rockwell, Al Dorn, Fred Ludekins, Al Parker, etc. -- had offered a national prize of one thousand dollars for the best commercial illustration of 1948. I entered a full-page scratch-board drawing illustrating an ad for the American Cancer Society in the New York Times. I paid no attention to the wild notions of "modern" art, but made my work the ultimate of dramatic effect on the basic human emotions.

The entries were anonymous -- so the judges did not know they were picking my work when they awarded my scratch-board job the first prize at Pratt. But when they found out the winner was the old-fashioned "ugly-duckling"--they did a lot of "explaining," how I had actually used all the stuff they had been pushing at me -- the stuff I consciously and purposely excluded from my mind.

Then the art from all over the USA went to New York, with the young "reactionary" - me, representing ultra-modern Pratt!

And, once again, plain, old-fashioned principle and craftsmanship won out over the wildest and most novel "modern" geniuses. I took first prize in the nation -- and had a ball explaining to the newspapers that I did it not because of the "modern" stuff being shoved at Pratt -- but in SPITE of it. Dean James Boudreaux, head of the school, called me in and asked me not to comment -- it was getting too hard for him to explain. I received my thousand dollar check at a big reception attended by the New York greats of illustration and art, and this success enabled me to promote baby number two with my wife.

She agreed to give me another little Rockwell, in addition to my thousand dollars, as a prize. Our marriage was still nothing remarkable, but it was a marriage, and seemed to be settling down to an institution. The first baby, Bonnie, had helped. We both loved her to pieces, and I felt sure another -- especially if it were a son -- would be the kind of cement we needed for a happy family.

My second year at Pratt I also learned about naked women.

In the second year, figure classes work from the nude model -- and during the first year our tongues fairly hung out for this unimaginable and lascivious experience. Lovely naked models parading in front of us to be looked at! What a prospect!

Even though the ancient models are something less than "lovely" -- it is still a bit of a thrill the first time you sit with a group of clothed people, and a lady steps forth on the stage in the altogether. But after two hours of it -- the thrill is over -- forever!

You have learned that it is the human imagination, not reality, that makes nudity seem so unimaginably thrilling, and when you settle down to hard work painting and thinking out your values, colors, and planes -- the model becomes no more than the pitchers, apples, drapes and bottles we painted the year before.

Our grandfathers, as with so many things, had infinitely more sense about sex than we do today. They clothed women so completely, and then piled on so much more that by the time they got to the nakedness, their imaginations had enjoyed what is denied to us -- who have no chance any more to imagine anything with bikini-clad females on view. The chance sight of a woman's ankle was a pleasure to them. For us to experience the same clandestine thrill today, it would be necessary for a woman to get arrested for total exposure.

Naked women, as Schopenhauer says, are dumpy-looking, and so far from the sylph-like creatures we imagine, that only the inexperienced could imagine that the constant sight of naked models would be exciting. At the risk of being accused of fruity tendencies, I must insist that, as a work of straight art, the well-muscled male figure is far superior to that of the blubbery-looking female. Only the sex instinct makes the suggestive curves of a female seem more beautiful -- because they certainly are more exciting sexually.

I had begun to have considerable success with my commercial art work on a free lance basis, and learned the largely Jewish advertising techniques of the Madison Avenue jungle which are now serving me so well in smashing the Jewish "silent treatment," or paper curtain.

From my experience of two years in Maine in the art field, I had discovered that there was an unfulfilled need for an advertising agency in Maine. All the big companies in need of agency services were going down to Boston. And, at the same time, young Maine men who had talent and ability in the advertising field could find no work in Maine and had to go to Boston. It seemed to me to be ridiculous that Maine customers wanting services, and Maine artists, writers, etc., wanting to supply those services, should both have to go down to Boston to get together. When I inquired around about the possibility of starting such an advertising agency. I was told it had been tried a dozen times by experienced men - and that it was impossible. It could not be done.

So, since it could not possibly be done, I determined to do it. I could see no more sense in battling the "modern" art bugs at Pratt, and had proved, at least to my own satisfaction, that I could learn more by myself in the working world of art than from these beatnik bohemians, so I left Pratt and skipped the last year of the course there. I went back up to Maine, and started to work to set up an advertising agency in Portland.

First step was to survey the existing field and see what material there might be to work with. I called on the Portland offices of the Sullivan Company, a big Boston agency, where I found a charming rake by the name of Al Bonney -- a distant relative of the William Bonney who was otherwise known as "Billy the Kid." Al was captivated by the idea of launching our own agency, and felt sure he could walk out with a good batch of the local "accounts." He had a cottage at the beach, and we "batched it" and roughed it down there well into the cold weather, while we cooked up the great ideas and plans, and worked ourselves into the necessary state of fanatical enthusiasm to survive such a wild and "impossible" assault on the world of staid and stuffy Maine business. It occurred to us that it might be good to have some money as one of the ingredients of the venture, so we schemed to ensnare a young playboy whom Al knew from the local beer joints, and whose father was "loaded."

The young gentleman, Norton Payson, scion of one of "THE" families of Maine, was invited down to the cottage for beering and talking and persuading sessions. Hours and hours, night after night, we worked to persuade him that an advertising agency was the place for his genius and talents (and money, which we did not mention) -- but it was slow work, even with gallons of beer. He had a convertible and an easy life -- and, with the iron conservatism of his family and Maine in general, he couldn't see much sense in the hair-raising schemes we outlined for getting started on a shoestring (his shoestring).

He was a quiet, extremely likeable guy, but stolid as a stone Buddha. It took us literally weeks to "catch" him, but finally we did it. The only trouble was, as we learned later -- he caught US.

The company was formed as "Maine Advertising, Inc.," at 53 Exchange Street, Portland, Maine. The capital was supplied by Payson, with equal shares to the three of us, and Al and I signing notes to Norton for our shares, which were to be paid back out of profits. Payson's uncle managed the Jock Whitney estate in New York, and his father's lawyers very kindly arranged the deal. I was president, Al Bonney was secretary, and Norton was the treasurer.

Al and I ran around and sold like mad, mostly from imaginative ads which I sketched up and the customers liked better than what they had. We piled up a good batch of accounts, and even sold clients space in "Newsweek" -- an unheard-of triumph for a Maine based agency.

But then we ran into serious trouble. The magazines and radio stations would not trust us, although we promised to pay when the clients paid us. Cash on the barrell head was what was wanted, and cash was what we didn't have.

But Norton did.

Within a matter of weeks, Norton's lawyers arranged another deal. Norton was head of the agency, with me the Art Director on a salary in the back room and Al out as a salesman!

The Jews love to refer to this as one of my "failures" -- but it was part of my apprenticeship for the job I now have. And a hard school it was.

In so far as I got nothing out of it financially, I was a failure. But I DID establish a successful agency in Maine -- which "couldn't be done." It is there now -- as Simonds Payson Co. -- the biggest in Maine, with huge clients like Bath Iron Works.

Because of my "failure," young Maine men who formerly gave their talents and earnings and taxes to Massachusetts now have a wonderful opportunity to help their state grow, and to bring up their families in a great state, while the clients themselves are serviced right on the spot by top talent.

If this is a "failure" -- then I hope the Nazi Party will also be such a "failure," regardless of whether or not I personally "get anything out of it."

Payson got into business with another man who was supposed to have a lot of advertising experience, a man named Doug Fosdick in Lewiston. The production department was moved up there, which included me, the Art Director.

My wife and Bonnie and I took a little apartment in the French Canadian city of Lewiston, and I dug into the day-to-day grind of advertising agency work. Meanwhile, my "by-product prize" of winning the illustration competition appeared. Little Nancy Rockwell was born in a Lewiston hospital, and once again we went through the routine of fighting off the breast-binders and pill-servers.

I got my first introduction about this time to "office politics." Payson and Fosdick were frequently at loggerheads, and these two titans of finance often had us peasants upset over the insecurity of what was next. Such conditions inevitably produced intrigue and conniving in the growing staff. And how I hated it! I longed to devote myself to the creation and production of advertisements -and was doing pretty well at it -when the blow-up came! Fosdick split off. We were all moved to Portland again.

The atmosphere in the office was now very different for me. Payson had become an important executive and businessman. He was unhappy with me too close - to remind him how he got started. I didn't mention this, of course, but it was inevitable that he would feel it himself.

Al Bonney was eased out, and I could see that it was only a question of time before I, too, would find it simply too difficult to remain. My request for a raise from $75, as the company got more prosperous, was denied by Norton. So I resolved once more to launch a personal assault on the business world; this time for the benefit of my wife and little girls and myself.

Millions of tourists come annually to Maine, but there was no overall and reliable guide for these people as to what was going on, where, when, etc. I designed "The Olde Maine Guide" to fill this need, and started work on getting it out in the summer.

But, in the meantime, to feed the family, I started a little radio guide, "What Next?", which divided programs by type, a new idea at that time.

I sold my little ads successfully, and got "What Next?" going very well, with people actually subscribing for MONEY, a reaction I had not expected. Then I got the ads sold for the Guide and managed to get it published all through the summer, even winning the endorsement of the Maine State Junior Chamber of Commerce. But the financial struggle to stay alive was deadly, and my family lived in a little cottage at Falmouth Foreside in the most heartbreaking poverty and misery.

It was in that little cottage that I first heard the voice and the words which eventually led to my present political career.

One night I heard a man on the radio saying that there were Communists in the American State Department and all over our Government; that there was great danger of subversion from the Communist Conspiracy RIGHT HERE IN AMERICA!

He said we had to learn about it and FIGHT IT!

I listened enthralled! I couldn't believe that there was such a man left in our Government! In his voice there was COURAGE and calm force. He did not sound like the pansies with the faint British accents (phoney), which I had heard from Washington before. He spoke like a MAN and a LEADER!

Who was he?

I waited impatiently to hear his name!

Then they announced it; Senator Joseph R. McCarthy of Wisconsin! I whooped and hollered for Joe McCarthy! It seemed like a voice from another planet! A wonderful, patriotic, AMERICAN voice! A voice which almost seemed to come from inside myself!

But, much as I liked what I heard, it was no more than a very exciting passing thought, at the time. I was deep in the business of surviving. As usual in my career, I was succeeding in something which needed badly to be done, and winning the plaudits of the multitude, but not their dollars. My financial position was almost impossible, and my wife was struggling under fearful conditions. Often we would have nothing to eat but a can of beans donated by Russ Edwards, a man who worked for me, but who also owned a small summer hotel nearby.

Nevertheless, the Guide was doing so well that I had been asked by business men in Boston to see about putting out a Guide down there. I was in Boston, discussing this possibility, when the news came that the Navy had recalled me to active duty because of the Korean War. I was ordered to San Diego, to report within ten days!!

It was a blessing and a curse all at once. It meant the end of the terrible poverty, but it also meant the end of the business for which I had striven so hard, and which was on the point of paying me a return. I had been recalled, I believe, mostly because there was a tremendous need in the Korean War for Air-Support of the hard-pressed ground troops. That had been one of my specialties in World War II.

The jump from near-starvation to the pay of a flying Lieutenant Commander was a financial relief, if nothing else, so I prepared to report to the Navy for another War.

The horrible living conditions and the poverty of the last few months had almost wrecked what was left of my first marriage. My wife had taken the children to her grandmother's place in Hadlyme, Connecticut, so I went ahead, alone, to San Diego which I thought was a mistake.

And so it was that I started off in 1950 with an almost new Nash and drove from Portland, Maine, to San Diego, California. And as I did, I left behind forever my place as an ordinary American citizen. I was about to become a convinced Nazi in San Diego, and start the career which has led me so far to embattled notoriety all over the earth, and which will one day place me at the head of millions of Americans who now imagine they hate me and all I stand for.

The shock of suddenly becoming an officer and a gentleman again, with cash in my pocket, was considerable, but that was nothing compared to the jolt of finding myself again in a hot little Navy Fighter after five years of hardly seeing an airplane. No sooner had I arrived, than I was given the hottest thing with a prop -- an F8F Bearcat -- and told to check out.

Of everything I have ever flown, the F8 is my all-time favorite. It will take off and go straight up like a rocket. It is all engine, and, in fact, the individual wings are smaller than the engine itself! You sit on the floor of the tiny cockpit, with your legs almost literally wrapped around the tiny hydraulic stick and the engine. It has so much power you have to let it all out once in a while on a flight or the engine fouls up. It is almost literally like riding a lightning bolt. When you goose the throttle it GOES! The fastest jet in the sky has not the acceleration and DRIVE of that little bumble bee. The jets will go a whole lot faster -- but they never SEEM as fast or as hot. The F8 is the "hot rod" of sky -- and how I loved it! You can roll it around and around going almost straight up, and tear up the sky like a tiger. It maneuvers so fast and so cute you can beat anything in the air which tries to stay with you -- including jets.

We used these deadly little hornets to train Marine and Navy pilots in the close-air-support of troops. We had perfected the techniques so well that we could work within fifty or a hundred yards of combat troops. To do it, we had to concentrate our pilots on map-reading, terrain identification and efficient communication systems. We taught them half the time in ground school classes at Coronado, and the other half over at El Centro, where we rocketted and bombed all day in the dessert. My specialty was vision training and search tactics. The Commander of The Pacific Fleet Aircraft wrote me a special commendation for my methods, which helped hundreds of Navy and Marine pilots to chew up the reds in Korea.

When I had been able to find and establish a house, my wife, Bonnie and Nancy flew out to join me. Family life was resumed on a relatively happy level. The weather is almost too perfect in San Diego, so that we enjoyed countless picnics, outings and everyday barbecues under our own orange tree in the back yard. I also decided to save money by raising our own chickens, and installed a flock of layers and hatch of chicks to fry.

But this was also the time that Douglas MacArthur was being summarily fired by the midget of history, Harry Truman, in the most humiliating manner, while Joe McCarthy was belting away at the coterie of reds, queers and pinkos in Washington who were basically responsible for the firing of the General.

I began to pay attention, in spare time, to what it was all about. I read McCarthy speeches and pamphlets, and found them factual, instead of the wild nonsense which the papers charged was his stock-in-trade. I became aware of a terrific slant in all the papers against Joe McCarthy, although I still couldn't imagine why.

I had known and respected Douglas MacArthur and we have since corresponded. I thought he would make the greatest president of the U.S.A. When there was a campaign to get him the Republican nomination in 1950, I wanted to do what I could to help. I read a letter in the San Diego Union from a woman who lamented that no one would help her get a MacArthur rally going. So I called the lady, whose name I have forgotten, and offered what help I could give. She was very grateful, and invited me to her little cottage where she lived in retirement with her husband.

I started to tell her all the things I thought could be done, but she smiled with a patient, sad smile and stopped me.

"No", she said, "you can't get a hall so easy, even if you pay. They won't rent one!"

"What do you mean!" I burst - "WHO won't rent one?"

She looked queerly and quizzically at her husband, clearly asking him with her eyes about something. He just shook his head.

"WHO won't rent you a hall?" I asked again, looking from him to her.

She took a deep breath, looked pained - and then said, "The Jews".

"The Jews!" - came out of me involuntarily. "What have the Jews got to do with it? What do they care whether you get a hall or not?"

"They hate MacArthur!" she said, and started to say something else when I interrupted her.

"Hate him! - that's silly! I suppose some of them do. But certainly not all of them! And certainly none of them hate him enough to stop you from hiring a hall for a MacArthur rally!"

She took another deep breath, looking hurt. "It's true", she said, "they all hate him. Look at this, for instance!" - and she handed me a copy of "The California Jewish Voice". There it was; "MACARTHUR APPROACHES: HITLER ENTERS THE CHANCELLERY!" - and the paper went on to rave about how General MacArthur was the threat of a new Hitler! I couldn't believe it!

"That's only one paper!" I countered. "It's probably just an extremist sheet. I'm sure the Jews don't imagine MacArthur is really another Hitler!"

She showed me another Jewish paper. It's tone was more dignified, but the same message was there. She showed me still other Jew papers. In most of them were vile pictures of Joe McCarthy, terrible charges against him and MacArthur, and unmistakable venom for both of these men.

This is the experience which awaits every honest American, but is usually hard to come by - as might be imagined. I had suddenly been exposed to a whole secret world which the average American never even imagines, and never sees, the world of the Jews. In the same Jewish Voice I saw the headlines by the editor, Sammy Gach, "THANK GOD!" the day Russia got the A-bomb!

I saw hundreds of similar treasonable items - but our people are too insulated and easy-going ever to look into this Jewish press. Sooner or later, no matter how long the average American is kept in the dark, or keeps himself in the dark by imagining that discovering treason against his country and people is "bigotry" - he will find the naked evidence of this unified, alien, fanatical Jewish world in the midst of his own people - implacable, hateful, spiteful, bitter and diabolically clever at appearing to be only a persecuted religious group.

The whole thing, however, still didn't register with me. It was too fantastic. I felt sure there was some misrepresentation somehow. But the lady gave me some books and papers to take

With wife Judith (at far right) folding radio guide, "What Next"- 1949

Portland Sunday Telegram And Sunday Press Herald — Portland, Maine —

AN AID FOR MAINE AND MAINE VISITORS.—Lincoln Rockwell, president and [illegible] of the Rockwell Publishing Company of Portland, shows Gov. Frederick G. Payne the first edition of The Olde Maine Guide, a weekly booklet brimming with up-to-the-minute information on dates and places where interesting events are happening in Maine. Standing, left to right, are Herbert Sawyer, legal representative of the firm, and Russell Edwards, treasurer.

'Olde Maine Guide' Publication Tells What's Doin', When, Where

By Richard Hallet

What's doing in Maine from week to week? We know what's doing from century to century, of course. Katahdin always can be guaranteed to peg us down to the map; and the Kennebec will keep on flowing unvexed to the sea. There always will be fish in the lakes, and game in the woods.

But who's doing what, where, when, this week in Maine or the segment of Maine running from Ogunquit through Lincoln County? That's what the Olde Maine Guide, issued by the Rockwell Publishing Company of Portland, undertakes to answer.

The tourist can't tell just by peering into the greenery. The landscape looks attractive, but he can't learn its secrets from the Maine Guide from a hotel lobby or a taxi or a filling-station, and finds them all listed. Here are hotels and inns, tourist cabins, restaurants, movies and drive-in movies, cake sales; entertainment of all kinds in all places; churches and Sunday schools, with address and time of service.

Says Publisher Lincoln Rockwell: "The Olde Maine Guide is a kind of display service that ought to help Maine business. It's like this. A man goes into a big market with no idea in his head except to buy a bottle of milk. He comes out with a ten dollar bag of groceries. Why? Because of the displays. He sees something and goes for it. If these displays didn't work on him, he'd come out with just that bottle of milk he went in for."

... self as a commercial artist. Coming out of the Navy as a Lt. Commander in the Naval Air Corps, he took a course in commercial art at Pratt Institute, Brooklyn, and shortly afterwards won the National prize of $1,000 offered by the American Cancer Society for a poster in aid of its campaign. He has recently been selected by the famous artist, Norman Rockwell, as one of his students.

His publications include "What Next?", a weekly radio and movie guide, which boils down the best programs and presents them in groups.

Lakewood Players To Open Saturday

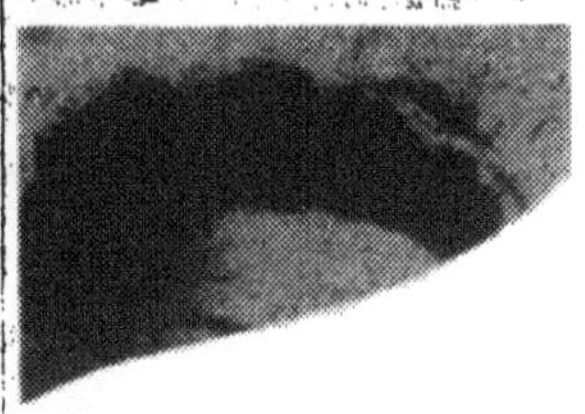

News story of publication of "The Olde Maine Guide"

home and study, and I left.

When I did get home, I looked at the first paper. It was called "Common Sense", and the headline was "RED DICTATORSHIP BY 1954!"

I figured right away I had found the size of this monstrous "Jewish scare", which the lady had told me about--it was a Jewish world plot--and I couldn't finish reading it. It seemed too silly and disgusting for an intelligent man to waste time on.

But in the few lines I did read, Common Sense gave what it claimed were startling "facts" about the Jewishness of Communism and the "Russian" Revolution. It listed, as the sources of some of these unbelievable facts, the Universal JEWISH encyclopedia and various official U. S. Government Documents.

This seemed like an excellent opportunity to spike such a fantastic idea as that Communism was Jewish, and I decided to check these supposed "facts" out. I went over to the San Diego Public Library in Balboa Park and dug around in the volumes mentioned in "Common Sense."

Down there in the dark stacks of the San Diego Public Library, I got my awakening from thirty years of stupid political sleep, the same deadly sleep now closing the eyes of our people and making them cooperate with their enemies in their own destruction, all in the name of "good citizenship", "brotherhood" and all the rest of the shibboleths of "nice" people, the same hypnotic sleep which we are breaking up with our calculated and dramatic Nazi tactics!

I found that Communism was not only Jewish, but the Jews BOASTED about its Jewishness in their OWN books and papers! Rabbi Stephen Wise, for instance, the acknowledged leader of American Jewry for many years, openly and arrogantly laid claim to the Jewish nature of the Communist Doctrines with his oft-repeated statement in regard to the Jewish religion, "Some call it Communism; I call it JUDAISM!"

I found, in unimpeachable documents and intelligence studies by our own U. S. Government that the Russian Revolution was not "Russian" at all, but almost wholly led by JEWS! In the Overman

Report to President Wilson, for instance, it said; "...out of 388 members of the first Soviet Government, sitting in the Old Smolny Institute in Petrograd, 371 were Jews, and 267 of these Jews were from the Lower East Side of New York City" !!!

Not even Russian Jews, but NEW YORK JEWS!!

I learned, from the article called "Khazars", in the Universal Jewish Encyclopedia, published by the Jews, that most Jews are not even Semites or descendants of the Hebrew people of Palestine (and thus of Christ's people), but mostly the descendants of a semi-oriental tribe in central Russia called "Khazars" or "Chazars", whose King, Bulaban, in the sixth Century after Christ, ordered his people en masse to become "Jews". I discovered that these "Jews", called "Ashkenazim" in the "trade", as distinguished from the real semitic Jews, called "Sephardim", constitute the bulk and the leadership of the people we call, generically "Jews". It is swarms of these "Khazars", with their oriental heritage, who are pushing us around, forcing integration on us, degrading our culture with their filthy "art" (chaos and pornography), and, worst of all, spreading the disease of Communism, -all while hiding in the robes of the Jewish "religion"!

I went on to find, in old copies of the New York Journal American, that Jacob Schiff, then head of the gigantic financial empire called "Kuhn, Loeb & Co.", and grandfather of the woman who now owns the super-leftwing New York Post, "sank over twenty million dollars in the Russian Revolution", financing another Jew, Trotsky(Bronstein), in the murder of the Christian and anti-Communist " White Russians" in masses!

Most surprising and revealing of all was the often invisible CONNECTION between a seemingly pure GENTILE Communist, and the inevitable JEW, lurking directly in the rear.

Lenin - not a Jew - was married to Krupskaya, a Jewess! Stalin, also not a Jew, was married to the sister of Lazar Kaganovitch, Rose - a Jewess. Stalin's son married another Jewess, and it turns out that Khruschev was the protege of this same Jew, and married another JEWESS in Kaganovitch's family!

The pattern was the same here in the U.S.! Alger Hiss, a non-Jew, was the protege of Felix Frankfurter, a Jew, of course. Elizabeth Bentley was the mistress of Jacob Golos, supposed to be a "Russian", but actually another Jew. Fredrick Vanderbilt Field, the Gentile millionaire Communist, again, married to a Jewess. Whittaker Chambers, another Gentile Communist (who recanted), married to still another Jewess!

In the satellite countries, it was the same. More Jews! Even that sacred "friend of America", Tito, is the protege of Moise Pijade, another Jew Khazar, who does the "suggesting" for the strutting Mr. Tito.

In the USA, we were, or rather the FBI, was catching literal HORDES of Jew spies: Rosenberg, Greenglass, Soble, Coplon, Moskowitz, Weinbaum, Fuchs, Golos; the names alone were unmistakeable, and where the names were changed, as in the case of John Gates, editor of the Daily Worker, it turned out the real name was Israel Regenstreif! But the picture of these camel-like faces was more than enough to identify these Jew spies!

Out of 41 workers with Communist records at our secret radar laboratories in Fort Monmouth, 39 turned out to be Jews!! Out of 15 Americans CONVICTED of espionage for the Soviet Union since 1946, 13 were Jews! Out of twenty-one CONVICTED of Communist Conspiracy to destroy the U. S. Government by illegal force and violence, eighteen were Jews! When the FBI nabbed the "Second-string Politburo" of 17, 14 of the traitors were identified as Jews! Out of the "Hollywood Ten", who took the 5th Amendment when asked if they were Communists, 9 were Jews!

I looked into the Daily Worker, and found the atmosphere to be strictly "Kosher". There were touching "In Memory Of" ads to "our dear Mother" from Bernie, Abie, Izzy and Nathan Ginzberg, notices of picnics at Weinbaum's lovely Grove, etc., etc.

In Russia, where I had understood anti-Semitism was running rampant, I found the Jews boasting that the head of Soviet propaganda was a JEW -- Ilya Ehrenberg! With all the Jews being caught red-handed as red spies, is it surprizing that the Jew Ehrenberg, head of Soviet Propaganda, wishes to spread the idea that the Communists are "anti-Jewish"?

Even in Japan and China, I found the early planters of the Communist seeds were JEWISH. In Japan there was an Anna Rosenberg, and guess who turned up in China as advisor to Sun-Yat

Sen? Good old George Sokolsky, our "conservative" columnist!

To an intelligent man, the facts were undeniable. They might be explainable, but they were simply undeniable. Communism was Jewish! And the Jews in the United States, at least, were almost unanimous in their venomous hatred and suppression of anybody who so much as ASKED about this fact. Even noticing the number of Jewish communists and race-mixers brought the unfortunate victim an hysterical campaign against him as a"hate-monger"! The same people who screamed the loudest for "academic freedom" to preach Communism were the same people who were most merciless in their campaign of suppression against anyone wishing to discuss the Jews in anything but the most fulsome and disgusting praise.

The Jews were unanimous in hating McCarthy and MacArthur, with one or two negligible exceptions (which I later found were planned so there WOULD be exceptions, such as Joe McCarthy's "Rabbi" Shultz).

I found this exciting, interesting and frightening - but also very depressing. Far down in my soul I could feel the cold dread of our fate, if what seemed to be going on WAS going on. I, too, had been brought up never to say the word "Jew" right out, but always "Jewish person" or person of the "Jewish faith" because of what the Bible calls "fear of the Jews". I could imagine the result of my own temperment and reaction to a challenge, if I found out that there really WAS a Jewish plot against my Country and my people!

I went back to the papers and books the lady gave me and read them carefully. The tone of the things, in most cases, repelled me. They were loose in their charges, poorly gotten up, and full of rabid sensationalism. But they kept revealing new little hidden pearls of FACTS, which I found checked out.

And when I put all the facts together as best I could, there was no question about it, there WAS a Jewish plot of some kind or another, and it definitely involved Communism and moral subversion.

I went back to the lady and we talked some more, this time with me doing the listening. She was mixed up and confused in many ways, but she knew there were dark forces at work to destroy her Country and our White People, and she had the fundamental ideas right.

She asked me if I wanted to go hear a man named Gerald L. K. Smith.

I remembered the name vaguely, as some kind of horrible radical or other. But she said he was a great American patriot and a great speaker, and gave me a ticket to a speech he was making in Los Angeles.

I was afraid to go, since I was in the Navy, and the whole thing seemed so wild and radical and dangerous. So I went to the F.B.I. office and asked to see an agent. I was ushered into a private little chamber, and seated opposite a handsome, extremely Nordic-looking man. I told him about Smith, and asked if it would be all right to go to his lecture.

"Yes, if you don't participate", he said.

So I went to the speech.

And what a thing THAT was!

Few Americans today have ever heard an ORATOR. They have heard talks, speeches, even ravings, perhaps - but it is doubtful they have ever heardan old-fashioned, roof-lifting, earth shaking, soul-shattering ORATION.

Gerald Smith is the master to end all masters of the human voice. Whatever else he may be, he can sieze you by the lapels of your soul, jerk you out of your seat, and hold you helpless and spell-bound for as long as he wants to. He does not just roar and bellow.

He whispers, he sighs, he wheezes, he coos - then he BLASTS with the power of a locomotive roaring through a tunnel. He laughs, he cries, he howls, he cajoles, he mimics, he screams, he begs, he goes back to whispering, sneers, leers, yells, bursts into hysterical laughter - then whimpers some heart-rending bit which leaves you limp. I sat in the balcony, literally on the edge of my seat. If Smith had said suddenly, "JUMP!" - I think I would have done it.

I have not heard him for almost ten years now, and he is perhaps losing his steam. He will have nothing to do with me any more, and hides under an assumed name in the Congressional Hotel when he comes to Washington. But he is still the grandest master of the spoken word alive today - and I would walk twenty miles to hear him again.

But it was not *just* the way he spoke which captivated me - it was *what* he said. When you peeled aside all the emotional overtones of his speech, and got down to the raw meat - you found the basic elements of recognizable truth, beautifully put together to show, at last, the clear pattern of what it is the Jews are trying to DO with their conspiracy.

He had books for sale, among them the "Protocols of the Learned Elders of Zion". And these I studied carefully. The Jews howl bitterly that they are a forgery - but this is as irrelevant as claiming that a man did not commit a murder with one particular knife - but another knife altogether. It matters not which knife was used. The FACT is that SOMEBODY did a MURDER. The protocols, first put in the British museum at the turn of the century, long before World War I or II, set forth with horrible clarity EXACTLY what SOME group would bring about in the way of world wars, inflations, depressions, and moral subversions -how they would do it, and to whom they would do it.

And sixty years later, not one word has failed of fulfilment exactly as set forth in the protocols. If they are "forged" then it was done by a genius who knew exactly what the Jews of the world would do for sixty years, with not partial, but PERFECT accuracy. The protocols alone, of all knowledge on this earth, give one the power to successfully PREDICT historical events, as I have been able to do since studying them. And a theory which enables scientific, calculated prediction is not the mark of a fraud - but always the mark of a realistic theory of thing.

Henry Ford said of the Protocols, thirty years ago, that they were being ruthlessly fulfilled, which was enough proof for him of their genuineness. Adolf Hitler ten years later said the same thing. And any man who takes the trouble to *read* these astounding documents will find the same thing. If they were not written BY a Jew, they were written with devilish accuracy ABOUT the Jews. They enable humanity, for the first time, to UNDERSTAND what, before, seemed impossible chaos. All the chaos, the mad "art", the Communism, the moral filth, the control of the press and entertainment, the development of World Wars, the insane setting of labor against capital, and vice versa - all these things become calculated elements of a steadily progressing plan by a NATION, or RACE - which masquerades throughout the world as a "religion", in order to accomplish this awful work of destruction under the cover of "religious tolerance".

And, when history is examined, we find this NATION steadily and surely progressing toward its goal as "God's Chosen People", who are destined to quietly conquer and subdue the world under the bloody, old-testament despotism of the "King of Zion".

As I researched into the subject of Zionism, I found the Jews not even bothering to cover up this aim of World Domination. With the most monumental disdain of the boobs they call the "Goyim", (non-jews) they openly declare that they spurned offers of much better national "homes" for the Jews than Palestine - places where it would not have been necessary to exile and make homeless a million helpless Arabs - but the Jews arrogantly demand Palestine "because it is the center of the world"!! Not because it is a Biblical promise, but because it is the Cross-roads of all the earth between three continents, and their chosen seat of eventual world power.

I am aware as I write this of the outrage upon reason of such statements. I myself suffered this outrage when I first considered or heard of the ideas. But I can assure the reader that I would not lightly set these things forth in such a permanent thing as a book, which will be around a long time to haunt me if I am frivolous or in error.

For ten years now, since I read the Protocols, I have observed the world not going - but being steadily and inexorably PUSHED, down the exact paths set forth in these supposed "forgeries" more than half a century ago. And with the election of Kennedy now almost sure, as I write this, the Protocols are rapidly approaching total and final fulfilment.

Wide awake now - after reading and studying all I could, I began to think realistically for the first time in my life, instead of according to the slogans to which I had been trained since babyhood, slogans I had never even thought to question, such as "you mustn't judge people by groups, but only as individuals".

When you come to think of it, the latter is MADNESS! We sank German, Jap and Italian subs during the war without asking which ones of the crew were Nazis, Fascists or Militarists. We sank them all. I hated Roosevelt, but the Japs and Germans were not too careful about shooting at me along with the New Dealers who were so anxious to get into the War.

When you see a Nun, you do not inquire as to the health of her kids, nor do you invite 86-year-old men on a parachute jumping party, even though a few of such age, like Bernarr MacFadden, may sometimes do such things. You might fairly expect a Chinaman in a small town would try the laundry or restaurant business, and a Sicilian member of the Mafia to be mixed up in some kind of crime. Nor is it sensible to insist that skirts are not an indication of females just because Scotsmen are found in skirts, too, although they are called "kilts". Nobody would be considered mad for presuming a member of the Ku Klux Klan to be a racist, nor a member of the Americans for Democratic Action to hate the Klan. And by the same token, simply because of the weight of previous evidence, we are not crazy or "hate-mongers" when we presume that any given, unknown Jew is a Zionist or a Communist. The probability that he is one of the two, and sympathetic, at least, to Communism, is overwhelming.

About the only way we CAN and DO judge people, until we get to know them extremely well, is by the GROUP to which they belong. If that group has proved over a long period of time, by its actions, that it is hostile to us, it is not "hate" or bigotry to consider unknown members of that group also hostile, unless and until we learn differently about some particular individual who is an exception to the rule.

The Jews have calculatingly deprecated this utterly necessary rule of daily living and cultivated the opposite, insane idea that we must presume every individual to be a "blank", no matter what the evidence that he is a cannibal or a Sicilian or an Irishman or a Swede, all in order to keep people from noticing that a devilish lot of JEWS are COMMUNISTS and therefore TRAITORS!

Once one has realized that the Jews are NOT "just a relig-

ious group", and a pitiful, persecuted one at that -but a RACIAL and NATIONALISTIC group in our midst, then one can see the obvious FACT that MOST of the individual members of this group can be expected to be certain things - especially Communists, Zionists and race-mixers. This does not mean, of course, that ALL of the group must be a certain thing, anymore than all Germans were Nazis or all Italians are Catholics.

The Jewish-communist Zionist-traitor situation is much like that of the Mafia. Everybody knows that the Mafia is mostly Italians and mostly gangsters. But that does not mean that ALL ITALIANS are gangsters or all gangsters are Italian. On the other hand, the PRINCIPLE the Jews want to suppress is that a member of the Mafia is PROBABLY an ITALIAN and PROBABLY a GANGSTER. Only madmen would put a member of the group called "Mafia" in charge of their police department. Yet this is exactly what the United States has "strangely" done with its deadly atomic and hydrogen bomb. From Lillienthal to Straus, we have put almost nothing else BUT Jews in charge of atomic weapons and programs, although JEWS HAVE CONSTITUTED MORE THAN 80% OF OUR ATOMIC SPIES AND COMMUNISTS!!

Lillienthal, Oppenheimer, Teller, Straus, Rickover, LeMay, Isadore Rabi, etc. etc. etc., always more of the same deadly pattern. Don't judge by groups, but only ONE group somehow always in control of the key spots!

As Winston Churchill pointed out, the "driving power" and leadership of the Marxist forces is JEWISH, and MOST Jews are at least sympathetic to Communism in one form or another, or "cover-up" for Communists by screaming "hate-monger" at real anti-communists.

But by no means ALL Jews are Communists, nor are all Communists Jews. The scientific truth is simply that, on the basis of undeniable statistics, an unknown Jew is PROBABLY, but not certainly, pro-Marxist, whether Communist, Trotskyite, or just a race-mixing "liberal".

As I studied and thought my way further into the chaos of our national madness, I began to wonder why we had gone to war on the side of the Bolsheviks, who had openly boasted for a hundred years, of their plans to destroy us by force and violence and lies and subversion, --while we completely wrecked Christian Germany, which never had a single highly placed spy in our Country, and no practical chance of conquering the world, as I had believed they were trying to do.

I wondered about Adolf Hitler and the Nazis. I had learned he was right about the Jews. It might be worth reading his book to see if he had anything else right, too.

I hunted around the San Diego book-shops, and finally found a copy of Mein Kampf hidden away in the rear. I bought it, took it home, and sat down to read.

And that was the end of one Lincoln Rockwell, the "nice guy" - the dumb "Goy" - and the beginning of an entirely different person.

Mein Kampf was like finding part of me. Chaos and disorder and mental "greyness" are immensely frustrating to me, and I had suffered for years trying to fathom the endless philosophical, social and political "mess" in the world, and the even messier explanations offered by religions, and sociology. Over and over I had said to myself, "There MUST be some sense, some logical causal relationship between social and political facts - and how they got that way!" But no person, no book, nor my own mind had been able to discover head or tail to things. I simply suffered from the vague, unhappy feeling that things were "wrong" - I didn't know exactly how - and that there must be a way of diagnosing the "disease" and its causes - and making intelligent, organized efforts to correct that "something wrong".

In Mein Kampf I found abundant "mental sunshine" which bathed all the grey world suddenly in the clear light of reason and understanding. Word after word, sentence after sentence stabbed into the darkness like thunderclaps and lightning bolts of revelation, tearing and ripping away the cobwebs of more than thirty years of darkness - brilliantly illuminating the "mysteries" of the heretofore impenetrable murk in a world gone mad.

I was transfixed, hypnotized. I could not lay the book down without agonies of impatience to get back to it. I read it walking to the squadron, I took it into the air and read it lying on the chart-board while I automatically gave the instructions to the other planes circling over the dessert. I read it crossing the Coronado Ferry. I read it into the night and the next morning. When I had finished, I started again, and reread every word, underlining and marking especially magnificent passages. I studied it, I thought about it, I wondered at the utter, indescribable genius of it.

How could the world not only ignore such a book, but damn it and curse it and hate it and pretend that it was a plan for "conquering the world" - when it was the most obvious and rational plan for SAVING the world ever written? Had nobody READ it, I wondered, that people went around saying it was the work of a mad "rug-chewer" ? How could sensible people get away with such monstrous intellectual fraud? Why was it so hated and cursed? I could see why the Jews would hate and curse it - but why my OWN people?

I reread and studied it some more. Slowly, bit by bit, I began to understand. I realized that National Socialism, the iconoclastic world-view of Adolf Hitler, was the doctrine of scientific, racial idealism - actually a new "religion" for our times. I saw that I was living in the age of the rise of what, two thousand years ago, was the similar rise of a new "approach" or world-view called a "religion" - a world view which shook and changed the world forever. I realized that this new and wonderful doctrine of scientific truth applied ruthlessly to man himself, as well as to nature and inanimate matter, was the only thing which could save man from his own degradation in luxury, self-seeking shortsightedness and racial degeneration. The doctrine of Adolf Hitler was the new "Christianity" of our times, and Adolf Hitler himself the new "savior" sent recurrantly to a collapsing humanity by inscrutable Providence. Hitler's and Germany's "crucifixion" was all according to the inevitable workings of this unknowable Scenariast. Even the eleven hung disciples in Nurnburg were not without significance! The most hated and dreaded idea two thousand years ago was Christianity, and the most hated and cursed man on earth Jesus Christ. His followers were bitterly persecuted and murdered by the "good", "sensible" people - who could <u>see</u> that anybody in his right mind recognized Rome and the Empire as the solid, substantial thing in the world. I realized that today's Marxist-Democratic world is another sprawling "Roman Empire", and today's Nazis the early "Christians". What is going on is far more than a battle for political supremacy in the present social and political situation - it is the utter smashing and destruction of a society which has become so rotten that it will tolerate and even love its own Marxist destroyers - and the painful slow growth of the new Nazi society which will replace it, even though it is now the most "hated", despised and feared doctrine on earth - as Christianity once was.

Such mighty, awesome thoughts do not come over a man but once in a lifetime, if ever - and when they do, that man changes for all time.

At once a great weight lifted off my soul. I knew that I had found my way to the sun at last, and the days of mental darkness, searching and endless frustration were over. But at the same time, an immensely heavy burden replaced it, but in a different - even satisfying way. I knew that I had to, I MUST do what I could, to spread the new and wonderful idea, and secure its victory in the collapsing world - no matter what it cost me, or even if I were to become a "failure" to be "fed to the lions" in the Colosseum. I was as sure then as I am now that it WILL be done. Nothing can stop the victory of what is now a historical necessity, determined by events beyond our control.

The Marxists have pretended that they too are historically determined. But they are out of time-phasing. They WERE fated to rise to the top - and they HAVE. They have had their victory. Now it is all over, no matter how mighty and terrifying their power and their "Roman Empire" may appear to be. Today, they are in the Kremlin and the White House, wearing different masks to be sure, but nevertheless grinding the whole world under the brutal heel of the Marxist doctrines of "mass" and "equality" and racial defilement. Their "Roman Legions", of which I was so long a part, march and destroy everything which dares oppose them. They "crucify" the whole German nation, and the daring apostles of the Great Man who speak one word for his genius.

But they themselves have spoken their funeral oration when they said that each thing contains within itself the seeds of its own destruction. They, too, are victims of this perfectly valid law - and their destruction now is ready to burst from within themselves in a furious catastrophe. Even their "legions" are disintegrating under their own Marxist Race-Mixing Doctrines.

WE are the new "barbarians", forged to iron hardness in the fires of their hate and persecution. All over the world, WE wait to pounce on the arrogant, strutting "emperors" of Marxism when they have over-extended themselves only a little bit more. They can shore up their confidence with the belief that Nazism is "dead", that they are on the march to final "world revolution", and Jewish mastery of the world by their King of Zion - whether they call him a "Commissar" or "Secretary General of the U.N." or "Premier of Israel"!

But there are MILLIONS of us, everywhere. I know, today, whereof I speak. NOTHING can stop us.

But in 1951, I felt alone with my Book and my inspiration. I did not even know any "conservatives", let alone Nazis. And I dared not mention the subject openly to anyone. Even to my wife I did not betray the truth, that I had become an all-out NAZI, worshipful of the greatest mind in two thousand years: ADOLF HITLER!!!

CHAPTER VI

Living from day to day when you are on fire with a gigantic idea is not only hard on you, but on those who must live with you. The rest of the time in San Diego I was a loving but hard-to-understand husband. I cared nothing for the eternal cocktail parties of the Navy set and ruined those I did attend by turning them into McCarthy rallies. I read and studied every spare minute and my wife had a hard time promoting a few evenings out to dinner, etc. I tried to apply my writing and drawing talents to sneaky attempts to push "the idea", and came up with "The Ducks and The Hens"--which has since been stolen wholesale and reprinted all over the world by some of the very people who disdained it when I offered it back in those days. (Ron Gostick, in Canada, for instance, who preaches that I am a Communist agent-provocateur).

In spite of all this, however, I was well liked in the squadron, and we had many "good-times", as the beer and blabbing sessions are known. I tried mightily to control my desire to "Mc Carthy-ize" everybody I met. But I am sure I seemed pretty odd to a lot of officers and their wives who ran into me in the alcoholic haze which suffuses these "cocktail parties".

The utter, crushing IGNORANCE of even the best "informed people" concerning the terrific ideological struggle going on all around them, the battle for the life or death of the Western and Christian civilization in which they lived, appalled me beyond words. From Admirals to Presidents, Bankers to Butchers, all of them, I discovered, accepted WORDS and SLOGANS for FACTS just as the Protocols had so coldly calculated! Whatever was repeated over and over in "reputable sources" like the New York Times, Harpers, Life, etc., or by oracles like Edward R. Murrow, was simply "IT". And any attempt to question these holy dogmas, such as "Democracy" and "Brotherhood", no matter how overwhelming the argument or the facts, was greeted as just short of treason to America. Although I often heard even the "emancipated" and "liberal" wives of important men use filthy 1-syllable Anglo-Saxon words at cocktail parties, these same women would draw back in horror at the words "race", or "McCarthy"! And, although our Nation is supposed to be a Republic, not a Democrary as pushed by the liberals and pinkos and Jews, any demonstration of the glaringly obvious similarity of what they claimed was "Democracy", and the same product under the same name in Communist countries - Marxist Socialism - was attacked by these "advanced thinkers" with all guns blazing!

I could not get even the men I considered intelligent and open-minded to so much as DISCUSS these forbidden subjects, even though they would talk knowingly about the "Battle for men's minds", one of the stock-slogans of the "best" sources.

I began to despair of my fellow human beings! I felt much like a sheep being herded to the slaughter house, who had suddenly discovered what was ahead and tried desperately and vainly to get my fellow sheep to realize what was happening to our fellow sheep: in Russia, Hungary, Czechoslovakia, Poland, East-Germany and a dozen other Soviet slaughter houses! But they were all either too occupied with nibbling the luxurious grass in the pasture, or too scared of the intellectual sheep-dogs snapping at their heels to pay any attention. It just made them angry to be forced to THINK about such a nasty, "controversial" subject!

But somehow, in spite of the emotional and intellectual cataclysm within me, I managed to go about the business of living with some success, and greatly enjoyed my family and kids.

Little Phoebe-Jean Rockwell was born in the San Diego Naval Hospital, and the five of us made a fairly "normal" family.

There were the marital battles which I found were "usual" in most "modern" marriages. I moved into the BOQ once and prepared to get a divorce. But somehow we kept patching things up. I hated the very idea of divorce as much as almost anything in the world, having been brought up in the middle of one, and still hate even the word. I dearly loved and love my kids. They worshipped me too, and I was willing to suffer almost anything to try to keep the family together.

But in 1952 I got orders to report to Norfolk, Virginia, for further assignment, so the family had to be rooted up.

We made the transcontinental trip in our Nash with the sleeper-seats. All five of us slept in the car, with the baby on the floor in front. The whole family enjoyed it hugely, as we meandered across the USA, camping in the magnificent National Parks, sight-seeing everywhere, and devouring the indescribable glories of this beloved America.

I made it a point to go through Appleton, Wisconsin, Joe McCarthy's home town, and practically worshipped the ground where this great American grew up and lived.

When we got to Norfolk, I walked into the Navy assignment office while the wife and kids waited outside in the car to learn our "fate". Where would my next duty be?

My "sentence" sounded "fatal": ICELAND!!!

I had hardly heard of the place. I imagined, like most people, that it was a land of polar bears, ice and esquimaux. Worst of all, I knew it would be an impossible strain on our already creaking marriage. Families were not then permitted in Iceland, and the minimum "sentence" to this outpost was ONE YEAR!

Although I protested weakly, Judy decided to move right next to her Mother in Barrington, R. I. So I duly deposited her and the kids with her Mother. And then I went to Westover Air Force Base in Massachusetts to catch a plane to the end-of-the world -- ICELAND!

When I arrived, I found the base at Keflavik (pronounced "kep-la-veek", in spite of the "f") a little more civilized and a little less icy than I had imagined, but not much. There are a few dozen stunted trees in the whole of Iceland, but none within thirty miles of the huge and utterly barren U.S. air base. The Gulf Stream runs around one end of the island, and the icy, arctic currents sweep around the other, so that the extreme difference in temperatures regularly produces winds of over a hundred miles an hour. And these gales roar across the volcanic ash and bare ground of Keflavik out of the Atlantic Ocean, unopposed.

I was detailed as Executive Officer of a Fleet Aircraft Service Squadron with patrol bombers. Our working Squadron area consisted of a few Quonset huts and the rudest possible facilities. We had only half of an old World War II hangar, crammed with old jeeps and trucks, to work on our planes. So the men had to work and live in the bitter arctic weather much of the time.

It is dark almost all winter, and the effect of the wild wind, the sweeping, stinging, freezing rain and the eternal darkness is infinitely depressing. It is not cold (actually warmer on the average than Norfolk, because of the Gulf Stream) but the duty up there at Keflavik is as close to a prison sentence as you can get outside the walls.

There were "consolations", however. Liquor was unbelievably cheap - a dollar or two for quarts of the best stuff - and women were something else altogether. They were, and are, beautiful! They are the purest of Nordics, with perfect, handsome faces, lovely figures, and charming dispositions. The social customs of Iceland are particularly entrancing to visiting males in this respect, as sex is not the sternly regulated affair it is everywhere else. The attitude in Iceland is pretty much that sex is like hunger or thirst. When you are hungry you eat. When you are thirsty, you drink - and when you feel like sex in Iceland, --you satisfy this need too.

Many couples just move in together, not bothering about formalities unless a child appears. Even then the wife does not take her husband's name - and even the children take only their father's first name plus "son" or "dottir" (daughter). And even after formalities, instant divorce by mutual consent is available. Further, either party can "ditch" the other simply upon demand, without proceedings - and without any cause - a horrible situation for a loving spouse and parent - as I have learned to my own anguish.

There were few "unavailable" girls at the airport. Most of them worked for the administration one way or the other. But none of them ever realized that they could make money other ways. They were having too much fun being generous.

In fact, unbelievable as it may be, one of my officers almost got murdered by a very pretty little girl, for kicking her out of his bed.

She had spent long hours with him before she was turned out into the snow, so he could get some rest for a morning hop. She did not like being sent away. So she went and "borrowed" a .45 from a sargeant, whom she "knew", in another barracks, stuck it in the window of the Lieutenant's room and started shooting. He and the other two officers in the hut scrambled madly, first to get out of the way, and then to catch and disarm her. The squadron dentist (a Jew, by the way) hid in the closet during this "fire-fight" - and the boys had endless fun afterwards at the Jew's expense - not without justice.

In the Lieutenant's fitness report, I could not resist reporting that he was cool and courageous under "combat conditions" and "heavy fire", which raised eyebrows back in Washington.

It was not at all unusual for girls to take their boy-friends home - and upstairs - with the tacit knowledge and understanding of the folks. One ensign even LIVED with his girl and her folks for months, only moving out when she got pregnant.

"Parties" at the base were more like orgies, with all the free liquor, and the even "freer" girls. I am sorry to say that many of our top, most senior officers, succumbed to the enormous temptations of all this, and conducted themselves in the most disgraceful and un-officer like manner. An Army Commander, for instance, seduced and betrayed, not one of the cheap girls at the base, but the daughter of one of the best families in Iceland - in the most shameful and dishonorable manner.

A Navy Captain, actually publicly "shacked-up" with a divorcee in his quarters and drove her around in his big Navy sedan.

The whole atmosphere at Keflavik International Airport was evil and un-wholesome, depressing and disgusting.

I reacted by almost total asceticism. There was no half-way about it, as could be seen all around me. I refused to touch a drop of liquor. I went to only those parties which my position in the squadron demanded. I ran over a mile a day and exercised to keep in condition, and I devoted myself wholly to study, thought and writing.

After two months or so, the Navy decided to send me back to the States to visit a big "Fasron" to get some ideas for improvement of our work. So I was ordered to Quonset Point in Rhode Island, only a few miles from my family, for two weeks.

When I arrived, I found what I feared. My wife picked me up at the airport at Westover, and promptly informed me that she had learned to be "independent", which was certainly true. It was like coming back from the Pacific all over. She took me to the lovely little apartment she had gotten, and I tried to imagine it was good to be "home". But there was no overcoming Judy's new "independence".

There were scenes over my giving orders to my own kids; there were scenes about whether or not to open the windows; there were scenes about whether I should "bother" her with kisses while she tried to "get things done". There were groans about me taking the car to work at Quonset, now that she drove and was used to having the car - and it was a generally uncomfortable and difficult and unhappy visit. She made it endlessly plain that I was a "fly in the ointment". She wanted to run the place alone. I "spoiled" everything, as she actually put it.

I must, of course, take "credit" for not being a thoughtful husband in San Diego, and not being a good provider before that. But there was not much sense in her actions on this visit. She had simply gotten to enjoy her status as head of the household and possessor of the car without any husband "underfoot" - and she was unhappy with me there. I slept on the couch.

When it came time for me to report to Westover to fly back to Iceland, her relief was painfully obvious. And when I got the word that the flight was postponed, and I would not go for a few more days - her reaction was, "JESUS! More!".

I was hurt - deeply, miserably. And then I found out that she was also angry at me for being still in my own "home", when she had arranged for a visit from her Aunt Polly and a Cowboy with whom the aunt was, at the time, living.

I got out, and went to Westover, where I suffered utter loneliness and misery for three or four days in the barracks only a few miles from my wife and dear little children. She never called.

Back in Iceland, I redoubled my dedication to asceticism, my studies and my writing. There seemed to be nothing else. I banished the agony of losing my family in the hardest kind of mental and physical exercise.

I became interested in the culture and history of Iceland, and particularly the racial purity of the Icelandic people.

The officers living in the quarters used to get together and hire Icelandic girls to clean up and make the beds and do the housekeeping, and the girl in the quarters to which I was assigned used to bring a crew of her little brothers and sisters, and sometimes a girl friend to help her. She would not only give orders to these other Icelanders in Icelandic, but also make what I was sure were all kind of remarks about Americans in general, and, when she felt like it, me in particular. With the curiosity my father taught me, and the consequent interest in everything, I resolved to learn Icelandic, at least well enough to surprise this sassy young Icelandic maid some day.

I had long ago, when forced to study French in high school, come to the conclusion that languages are "difficult" to learn for adults the way they teach them in school, mostly because you do <u>not</u> try to learn just the language, the way you learned to speak English - by speaking it - but you must also learn a whole mess of artificial garbage called "grammar" and rules. I reasoned, that it made no difference how many mistakes I made, I could learn quickly to COMMUNICATE - which is the basic purpose of a language, by learning a small basic vocabulary, and then TALKING TO ICELANDERS, no matter how they laughed at my foolish mistakes.

I frequented the little Icelandic grocery store on the base, and began to "shoot the breeze" with them in my impossible Icelandic. They thought it immensely funny to hear an important American commander making such a linguistic ass of himself. But I kept at it, until one day I could understand, and make myself understood, about like the owner of a Greek restaurant uses English in America. It ain't poetry - but it works.

I waited innocently in the apartment one morning for the sassy maid, and her crew - then listened carefully. Soon enough they started the Icelandic wise-cracks. I suddenly turned, after I heard her say, in Icelandic, "he is lazy, and stays home today!", and replied, "Nej, thadth er thu sem er latur og vill ekki vinni!" "No! It is YOU who are the lazy bum who won't work!"

The electric effect was well worth all the effort. She had no idea, of course, how much MORE I might have understood previously, when she discussed me with her girl-friend - and she turned red and blushed and blushed!

From then on she was more careful, but she also began to take a pride in my ability to speak Icelandic. She would not speak English to me, as she did to the other officers, no matter how I struggled and stumbled. At Christmas, she captivated me with a little present in return for the bonus I gave her by CURTSYING! What a charming, lovely custom that is for young girls!

In Reykjavik, I now began to enjoy myself conversing with the Icelanders. Even the most Anti-American were impressed with an American "Ami" Commander who could take the trouble to learn their language - the language of the ancient Vikings, spoken by less than two hundred thousand people in the world today.

But that was not my only reward. I learned wonderful things about our ancient Nordic heritage from our mighty, bear-skin-clad ancestors of the far north. I learned, for instance that the Icelandic word for a German is "Thodthverdthur" - which means "People's defenders" - the tribal memory of the times when it was the Germans alone who stood between the European White man, and the savage hordes of Genghis Khan for many centuries! (As they stand now between us and the same savage hordes.)

I reread Mein Kampf a dozen times, annotating it and indexing the main ideas. I wrote endless commentaries and plans for organizations. I drew cartoons which were designed for mass consumption - for the millions of boobs who will not read more than a paragraph and have to get their ideas in comic-book form, of the facts about the Jews I had learned. I drew for the same boobs now lapping up the JEWISH comic-books, TV, newspapers, movies and other propaganda which presently passes for "public information and entertainment". I began to correspond with people whose names I found in "conservative" publications like Mercury, and even with Conde McGinley of Common Sense and Major Williams in Santa Anna.

I commenced the writing of a "great book" to be a compendium of almost all knowledge - the knowledge left out of my college education - the knowledge of life and nature and the real laws of society and human affairs.

But I found that I could never get started on the ambitious project - for writing the introduction. The subject was just too vast and too disorganized in my mind to allow me to get into the "meat" of it. Endlessly I wrote and re-wrote "introductory" chapters.

After several months of this monkish existence, I was invited to a diplomatic party in Reykjavik, the capital of Iceland, thirty miles away from the base by the worst kind of dirt road. I had met the American wife of the first secretary of the Norwegian Embassy in Iceland, Cathy Amalie, when I had given her instructions in a silk-screen class as part of the leisure program. Her husband, Egil Amalie, the Norwegian first secretary, and I had become friends. He was a tiny dynamo of a man, full of culture and rough masculine charm, which I liked and admired.

At the party in his lovely home, all sorts of Germans, Dutchmen, Norwegians, Americans and other people in the Service and Diplomatic Set were singing and talking in several languages. I was watching a group singing, when I saw a tall, impeccably dressed man appear in the door, with one of the most beautiful girls I had ever seen. He was introduced to me as the First Secretary of the German Embassy. Somehow I got the idea that the girl was his wife, which immediately saddened me. She captivated me instantly and completely. So I was greatly relieved and happy to learn, later, that she was NOT the wife of the German, but an Icelandic girl named Thora Hallgrimsson.

Tall, blonde, aristocratic in looks and bearing, she had the face of an angel and the figure of a French model. I asked her to dance in a perfect swivet of excitement. She melted to me as we danced, and I knew in my soul that I had met "the" woman in my life. We talked and I found she spoke perfect English, although she had spoken Icelandic only, until she was eighteen, only five years before. But she had been educated in England, had traveled the continent and had even gone to school in Hackettstown, New Jersey. She was subtle and intelligent, yet feminine beyond any woman I had ever known. There is no question but that I was then and there desperately in love with this beautiful Thora!

I told her of my broken marriage and my kids, but mostly about my book, beliefs and ambitions. I did not, of course, tell her I was a Nazi, yet. But I did make my racism and other Nazi ideas clear from the very first evening.

She seemed fairly cool and handed me her engraved card when I took her home and said "Good Night" at her gate.

When I got back to the base, fate took a hand in the affair. I got sick and broke out with red spots. The doctor diagnosed it as CHICKEN POX, a disease I thought I had left behind with my roller skates and marbles!

It is impossible for me to imagine that this improbable disease, coming at this particular and improbable time was not another of the inexplicable strokes of destiny I have now come almost to expect. Thora, too, had been intrigued, and was unable to understand my failure to call her for all that time. So, as I learned later, SHE took action.

I got a call from the wife of the Political Officer of the American Legation in Iceland, Mrs. Roland Beyer, inviting me to a Christmas Party in her home in Reykjavik. I hardly knew the lady, and was at first puzzled. Thora herself later told me that sheand Ruth Beyer had cooked up the party mostly for my benefit!

When I got to the Party, there was Thora again, so lovely that I could not keep my eyes from her. It was Christmas week, and they were playing the "Messiah" on the hi-fi. But I did not even hear this, one of my favorites. I covered my face with my hand, ostensibly absorbed in the music, but actually peeking at the tall blonde. (I later learned that even this was noticed by the conspirators, and added to the calculations.)

We talked some more, and I learned that she had been married before to a man she said was a drunkard and a philanderer of the worst stripe, She also said she had a little boy, and I "managed" to make arrangements to take some pictures for her of the boy at her home.

Her little boy, "Fridthrik", was a problem, to say the least! He had been brought up Icelandic style, with almost no discipline and nothing but "permissive" and indulging love. He ran around wildly in the house, knocking things over and off tables and generally behaving like a spoiled brat. But what a HAND-some, adorable little "brat"! He was a baby Viking, -blonde as the snows on the Icelandic glaciers, bold and with a certain Nordic dignity and arrogance reminiscent of his fur-clad forebears! He was the perfect, scientific "example" to set next to a half-ape African black boy, to banish at one look the damnable "equality" lie. The very noble bearing in his stance even at two years old, and the unbreakable will shining out of his sky-blue eyes simply cannot be found in the inferior races, nor can it be explained as purely the result of the " cold weather", "luck", "point four",etc.

I loved this little "brat", in spite of his atrocious behaviour.

I began to "call on" Thora regularly, whenever I could plow my jeep over the back-wrenching 30-miles of dirt and icy roads between Keflavk and Reykjavik and back. I spent many enchanted, tender hours with her alone in her private drawing room.

She was not only charming, intelligent and lovable, but she also knew how to be LOVING. For the first time, I realized what a marriage SHOULD be like, and resolved to put an end to the "marriage" which was nothing but a shaky business partnership, and put a terrible cloud over the kids who used to cry listening to Judy and I in combat; -a marriage from which I had been "kicked out" for being "under-foot".

I wrote and asked Judy for a divorce. She promptly and curtly replied that she would give it to me provided only that she was assured of steady and plentiful alimony; -Four hundred dollars a month, she demanded!

As soon as I realized how serious were my feelings, I also told Thora of what I planned to do in the world. I told her specifically that I would be either a "bum" or a "great man", and I honestly didn't know which. Especially I assured her I was not a "normal" person, and would never give her a "normal" life. She replied without hesitation and with the utmost warmth that she didn't care WHAT I did; she would follow me and love me even if we had to escape civilization and its rules on a "banana boat"! For years, "banana boat" were secret, key-words with us, when things looked too tough, -which was most of the time.

NOTHING could quench the blazing fire between us, and af-

Top left: Typical Icelandic Scene: no trees   Top right: Party at Norwegian Embassy where I met Thora

Top left: First pictures of Thora and Rickey. Top right: On honeymoon in Berchtesgaden, former SS-house.
Lower left: Honeymoon, lake near Berchtesgaden. Right: Thora at Hitler's "Eagle's Nest", now a tea room

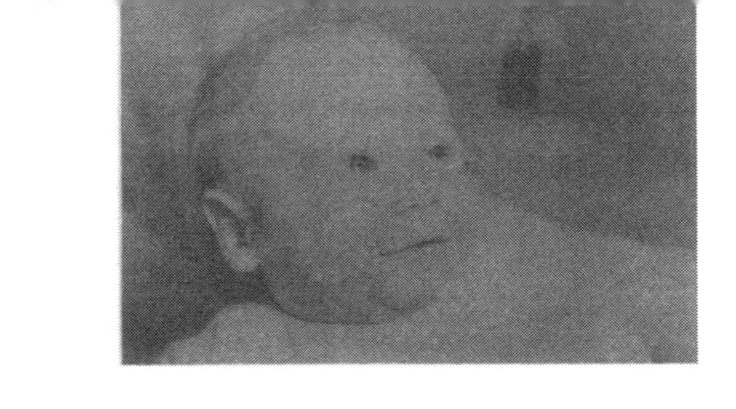

Top left: Our apartment at Keflavik Air Base.
Lower left: My plane and crew in Reykjavik.

Right: "Grampaw", about four months old, Keflavik.
Right: Thora and I with Ricky and "Grampaw", 1954.

My wife Thora

ter a passionate and wonderful courtship of only five months, we were married in Icelandic in the National Cathedral in Reykjavik, where her uncle is the Bishop of Iceland, on October 3, 1953.

For our honeymoon, we went to Berchtesgaden, Germany, which has been made into a U. S. recreation area. But it is also the site of the "Obersalzburg", the home of the Fuhrer in Bavaria in the fairy-tale setting of the Bavarian Alps.

I was appalled and disgusted to discover that the authorities are so fearful of the rise of Adolf Hitler as a "Saint" - a rise which I have already stated is inevitable and which I have gotten well started - that they have razed the Obersalzburg to the ground and that they DAILY run bulldozers over the scene to pulverize over and over again, the tiny fragments from which they fear Hitlerites will one day make relics, as they do anyway!

Thora and I were blissfully happy together, although nothing like as happy as we would have been if we could have enjoyed such a trip after we got to know each other better and love each other as deeply as we did later.

I was immensely proud of my wife as we strolled about in the story book scenery of Bavaria. We had days and nights of unmixed fun on that honeymoon - playing like kids. We spoke Icelandic to each other in public which hugely puzzled the guides especially, who imagined they'd heard about everything. It was our private, secret language, and we could discuss and make insulting remarks about everybody around us like two naughty kids, as we smiled sweetly at them in their ignorance.

This was not an unmixed blessing, however. For when we had a squabble over something, and had to keep it private, it was in Icelandic that we argued. She had a terrific advantage over me then, as my vocabulary is most rudimentary, and I kept getting lost for words as she steam-rollered over my halting arguments. But even these rare and petty squabbles were fun, because of the "making-up". It was one of the most tender memories of my life.

Thora enjoyed being a WOMAN - gloried in it, swam in it - and it brought out the best in me, as Nature intended. I learned at last to know what a FEMALE was SUPPOSED to be like; and it made me feel bitterly sorry for my first wife, Judith.

But I made the mistake of telling Thora this, and thus discovered her only real fault: jealousy. She could not bear to hear sympathetic remarks about any other female -even little ones! I later found I couldn't even pass a cute little girl on the street and pat her tiny head, without my wife making remarks about it and asking why SHE wasn't getting patted, etc.

Back in Iceland from our Honeymoon, I requested and got another year's duty at the base. (They were tickled to find anybody who wanted to stay up there.) So I got one of the rare assignments to one of the family apartments at the base.

I had been made Commanding Officer of the Squadron, and our apartment was directly below that of the Commanding General's. It was very comfortable, if not luxurious.

Thora and I settled down to making a working marriage out of a love affair, a task in which all couples find themselves engaged in the first year or so of marriage. It is usually difficult and almost always, unfortunately, unexpected.

I had to learn that she could never get enough of being told how dearly I loved her and how beautiful she was, while she had to learn by rude experience that I awake rather violently, ready to fight, when anybody turns on the lights abruptly when I am asleep. (This, from wild nights in Navy barracks.) There were a million other petty things we had to learn about each other, many the hard way -so that the first year of marriage is far from a poem or a dream.

But, even so, it was a rich and rewarding experience to be married to such a complete and loving female WOMAN. She almost literally taught me how to feel and behave like a male with females, after my unconscious training in American ways for men, which always seem to involve an inferiority complex for husbands and fathers. The latter are always depicted in movies, TV, etc., as stumbling, bumbling blow-hards who are so incompetent that they have to be constantly rescued, babied and swindled into survival by their patient and know-it-all "help-mate." The carry-over is inevitable, and American husbands tend to be far too timid and self-effacing. And this, in turn, further aggravates the tendency of wives to be far too aggressive, business-like and un-feminine.

On the other hand, having been brought up Icelandic-style, with almost no conception of discipline and "duty", Thora could not understand my instant obedience and respect for the military officers over me.

Once, my immediate superior kept me talking almost an hour overtime after work at the squadron, so that the lovely dinner my wife had hot and tempting for me became cold and greasy by the time I arrived at last. She was very angry. Why was I late?

The explanation that "the Captain kept me" sounded like a lame excuse to her. I should have simply excused myself and come home anyway.

We had quite a scrap over that one. In fact, just about the worst battle of the year. She could NOT fathom that I had to do anything whatsoever my superior ordered, outside of murder, and even that in certain circumstances. He could have kept me there all night, as he once or twice did, later.

There was the time we had an engine fire out over the Atlantic, searching for survivors in a storm, and I had to land on a little bit of rock called Vestmanneyja in mid-ocean, on a landing strip only a few hundred feet long, with cliffs at both ends. I had to actually reverse the good prop just before touch-down to avoid dropping off at the other end. We had to stay at a little Icelandic Inn in the tiny fishing village there. And there were fisherman's daughters in that village.

I had a devil of a time convincing her that I did not fall victim to the wiles of any of these willing damsels while we were so cold and lonesome awaiting rescue from the mainland.

Sending the huge amount of money demanded by Judy every month made life a little tough for us. But we managed.

In May, my wife gave birth in the Base Hospital to my first son, Lincoln Hallgrimmur, whom we came to call "Grampaw". I was overjoyed! After three daughters, at last a SON!

At the end of the year. the Navy had begun a severe cut-back program. My first wife had gone to my senior, state-side commander and raised some hell about me, which didn't help my request to remain on active duty any longer, and I got "riff-ed" out with only a month to prepare to carry the enormous financial burden of the $400 per month alimony, plus a new and growing family - starting from scratch!

I had to think hard and fast, and came up with a solution which seemed to have a chance of solving not only my severe economic problem, but might give me the entering wedge for the political activity on which I was utterly determined.

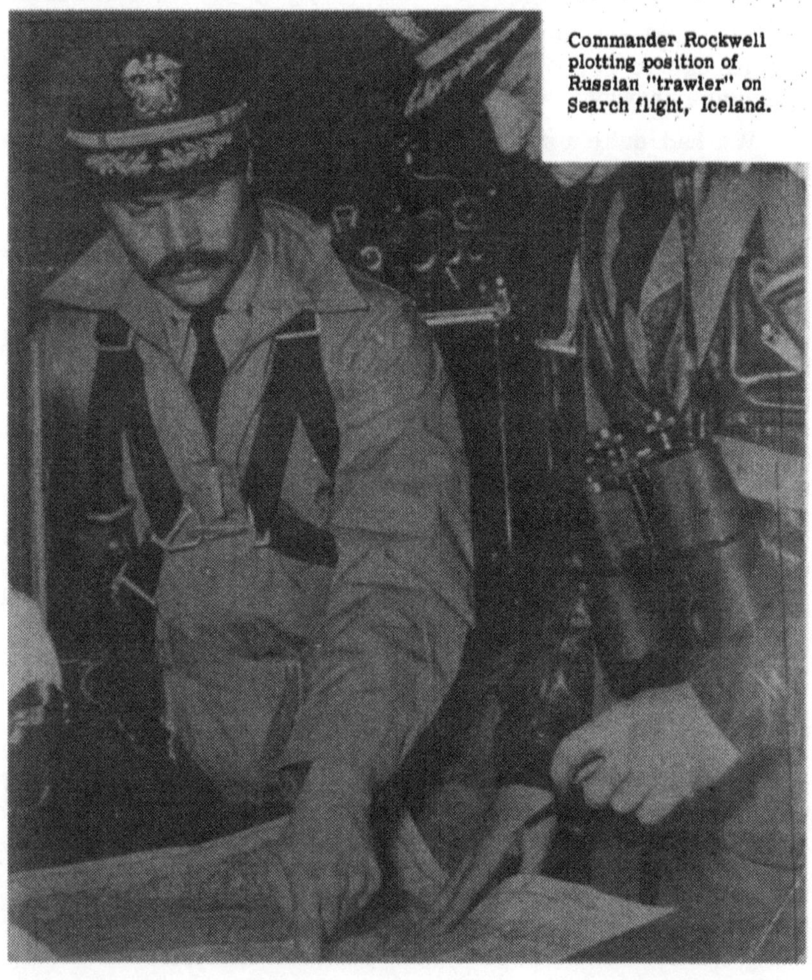

Commander Rockwell plotting position of Russian "trawler" on Search flight, Iceland.

CHAPTER VII

I had observed that the wives of service men were being shipped all over the world and being constantly moved and transferred into wild and strange surroundings with no advance knowledge of conditions. Their problems were totally different from ordinary housewives, especially as America began, unofficially to police the world. There were magazines for ordinary wives and mothers, but none for the millions of service wives. Here appeared to be a market unserviced - the ideal opportunity for a free-enterprising business man in any field.

But in addition to that, I realized that such a magazine would have powerful political force. I had carefully observed the technique of sly propaganda - always in the form of entertainment and information - in all the Jewish dominated papers, magazines, books, etc., - and believed that I could reverse the process with my magazine for service wives.

I would have to be very subtle, of course, but I could, as months went by, begin to drive out the filthy ideas of Marxism, "mass democracy" and racial defilement - and replace them with ideas of authoritarian constitutional government and racial self-respect. I envisioned, for instance, the publication of pieces on the style of Mark Anthony's funeral oration, in which I would sicken the ladies with disgusting pictures of negroes and white girls - perhaps their daughters, dancing and hugging together - along with over-done text praising such "brotherhood", "tolerance", etc. - and showing pictures of the inevitable Jews who were usually responsible for such vile mixed affairs.

There would be so much fulsome "praise" for "brotherhood" that the Jewish advertisers I must win to survive could not complain. But the result would be quite the reverse of what these Jews wished to see.

And I realized that no "ordinary" job I could get would produce the income I must have - with my ex-wife threatening dire action if I failed to send the gigantic alimony, and my present family needing all I could possibly earn. Only a desperate effort to create a job and a business for myself which would pay LARGE sums could prevent catastrophe.

So I started the surveys and studies to put out such a magazine, and decided on the name "U. S. LADY".

I had some certificates printed up as pledges to buy stock, made up a little art-work "dummy" of the magazine, and went around to the service families and the officers I knew in Iceland.

I got eight thousand dollars' worth of these certificates signed, and began to write to U.S. outfits to see about printing, distribution, etc.

Once again I received a dose of the tune I have heard so often.

"It CAN'T be done!"

Publishers, printers, everybody told me I would need millions just to get such a magazine launched. Worse, service sources told me that many others had tried the project, some with the millions, and all had failed. Mrs. George Catlett Marshall for instance, with all her influence and money, had failed to get one going.

We came back to the USA -- arriving, as I had at Brown University, in a hurricane, at Brunswick, Maine, where I was to be detached to inactive duty.

Thora, Ricky, "Granpaw" and I took a little cottage on Bailey's Island, at the very height of a roaring gale, and I set about methodically preparing to publish a full-color national magazine. We had exactly three hundred dollars to our names.

I presented my idea to the armed forces at a meeting in the Pentagon of the Admirals and Generals heading public relations for each of the services, and got a hearty vote of confidence from them. Service morale was sinking fast, under the lash of integration and the withdrawal of dignity, respect, and priviledge: as "democracy" was dumped on our fighting men by Anna Rosenberg. The disaffection of thousands of wives was hurting re-enlistment. U. S. Lady would obviously help, here, and the Department of Defense assured me of every cooperation.

A retired general's daughter, Jane Brownlow, wrote me and said she had heard of the project and was very interested in helping. I met Mrs. Brownlow first at the Icelandic Embassy, where we were living with my wife's uncle, the ambassador, and she became even more enthusiastic. She proceeded to gather information and assistance for us, while I finished getting mustered out of the Navy in Maine.

After final clearance, I drove down from Maine to Washington, D.C., obviously the only place such a magazine as U.S. Lady should be published. After staying again for a while at the Icelandic Embassy, we rented a lovely old Virginia plantation home sixty miles out in the "hunt" country south of Warrenton. We got the place for a hundred a month, since it was so very far out. It was really luxurious. There were bathrooms with fireplaces, chaise-lounges, and oil paintings! But commuting 120 miles a day in my little Plymouth station wagon, was extremely difficult. I began to sleep some nights in the tiny office I had rented in the Walker Building, a block away from the White House.

This situation was terribly hard on my wife. She hated being removed from all social life and people -- and then also deprived of her husband. I was working feverishly, day and night, and hardly saw my family. But there was no choice. I was under the "gun" -- economically -- and it was succeed with U.S. Lady, or starve and be ruined.

Another extremely unhappy element got into the picture, when my wife just couldn't believe I was as deeply in love with her as I was, or that I couldn't resist what she imagined was "temptation." But, for whatever reason, she began to be jealous of the fact that I spent so much time with Mrs. Brownlow in the office.

Eventually I found a little apartment on Connecticut Avenue

right in D.C. -- and we moved there in the middle of the night and a howling blizzard.

Meanwhile, I had been driving ahead to one goal after another. I called in all the stock promises -- and got an amazing half of the money paid in. Then I had to go through the Securities Exchange Commission, and discovered what a hateful, arbitrary, and tyrannical bureaucracy we have in D.C. Time after time I would go down with my statement for filing under regulation "A"— only to be thrown out for some newly invented "discrepancy!" I hired a CPA to make up the financial statement, and even this was thrown out. It was heartbreaking. The Icelandic Ambassador, Thor Thors, watched all this going on, and generously offered to do what he could to help -- but there was no way to help, with these officious bureaucrats. One had simply to bow down and wait until their childish natures were satisfied with the humiliation and exasperation of people trying to PRODUCE something.

I got advertisements made up, inserted in a few papers, and sent out hundreds of thousands of circulars to military wives' clubs all over the world.

The planning took months and endless midnight and early morning hours of heartbreaking work. But at last the results began to come in. Our ads and advance sheets were so effective that we did the impossible! We managed to get thousands of military families all over the world to send us three dollars and eighty-five cents for charter subscriptions to a magazine which was still only an idea!

I knew, of course, that subscriptions would not finance such a tremendous undertaking, so I planned to sell stock in the enterprise, which was the reason for the S.E.C.

I knew we had to write a "prospectus" to do this, but I knew little more. So I sent Mrs. Brownlow out to pick up some sample prospectuses from other businesses --and she came back breathless with excitement. She told me she had run into a man just next door in the Union Trust Building who had wanted to be a publisher, and who was now a big financier and stock man!

So I invited this great man, Landrum S. Allen, together with Mrs. Brownlow, out to my place in Virginia to see what we could work out.

We spent a dreadful afternoon and evening. It was impossible to make head or tail out of this man's conversation. The best I could get was that he wanted to publish a magazine to be called "On The Avenue", in Polish, Swedish, Sanskrit and other languages. When I tried to ask him what his "market" - an absolutely vital fact for a publishing venture, obviously - his reply was "for warm hearted people" - and that is all I could get. He wanted me to do up covers, sample pages, etc., and then move into his offices, so we would publish together.

I declined this golden opportunity, and endeavored to get him to help sell the stock of U. S. LADY but he was skitish as a blind mare.

So we launched the stock sale ourselves, and began to do quite well.

The big job was getting a magazine together, however, and getting it printed. By skillful manoeuvering and being "hard to get", I managed to give an impression of booming success, (which, in a way was true) and we got the big presses to competing with each other for our business. Their salesmen regularly took me to sumptuous luncheons, and I began to bargain for the big job of printing.

With the blessing of destiny, I am sure, I "allowed" Ransdell, Inc. to sign a contract for the printing - which, in effect meant that I secured $23,000 worth of credit - with no capital at all!

And through all this, my wife Thora showed herself nothing less than a heroine. She was pregnant again, but she pitched in with the typing, the filing and making of address stencils at the same time she tried to make a home out of our dingy apartment anda living out of the pennies we had left after sending the money up to my first wife. She even got a job taking a radio survey, door to door. Pushing a baby carriage containing "Grampaw" and leading naughty little Ricky by the hand, she earned a few pitiful pennies by asking the usual listener questions up and down the street. We had no fun, no pleasure, no pause in the desperate scramble to survive and get the magazine on it's feet. But Thora had the faith of a saint. Even when I would get discouraged and felt almost sure my gigantic struggle would come to naught, my brave little wife would put her arms around me, look me in the eyes, tell me how she believed in me and trusted me --and I would fairly burst with new drive and determination. She knew the age-old secret of women: how to inspire and fill a man with power he could never have alone, just by laying a gentle, warm hand on his cheek and letting him feel her faith flowing outward. How I loved her! I can never repay her loyalty and devotion!

I was not able to pay salaries to Mrs. Brownlow or the others but was nevertheless able to gather a staff of almost thirty people, just by enthusiasm and leadership. I was getting the training which is enabling me now to accomplish the far more difficult task of organizing men into the most persecuted organization in the world. (My men have to give up everything of fun and profit in life and then pay to stay with me.) I learned how to get people to create miracles just because of something they BELIEVE IN --a far more powerful force than the naked desire for money.

But I was also having fearful problems with my "women".

It was inevitable that a women's magazine would have a lot of women on the staff, even if it took a man to get it together and ramrod it. And the women necessary for such a task had to be creative, and therefore more than usually tempermental. Further, since I wasn't able to pay them, I had to keep them working and organized by wheedling, cajoling, promising and threatening, by the sheer power of personality and psychology.

But such methods can not keep a business organization going forever without money --cash. And cash I was chronically short of --even when thousands of dollars a week began to come in.

The stock was selling quite well, and, when I succeeded in coming out with the first issue of U. S. Lady in full color, and shipped it all over the world, --a hundred and fifty thousand of them. We got in over fifteen hundred requests to participate in the stock of the company.

Figuring I had it made, I again approached a lot of stockbrokers and tried to get them to take over the stock sales on commission, since I was in the business of publishing a magazine, not selling stock. But none of them would gamble with it, except one, Landrum Allen, the man who had come to dinner out in Virginia. He said he took it only because he was still in love with the idea of being a publisher. He figured he could eventually wrangle U.S. LADY away from me,as he tried hard later so to do.

So I signed a "best efforts" deal with Allen. He was supposed to sell my stock, while I published the book. He was to get one of every five dollars we sold -- a handsome commission -- and I expected that, with all the inquiries we had, he would sell out the issue in no time, and the struggle would be over. But I reckoned without human greed, pettiness and intrigue.

My unpaid and rambunctious women began to buck and kick in the traces, and highly resented almost everything I did. Every one of them felt she knew better than I how it should have been done, and there were always two or three of them a day weeping and having hysterics in my office.

The magazine, meanwhile, was coming out regularly, more and more handsomely and receiving acclamations from all over the world. But Allen had his plans, and the women soon fell in with those plans. I discovered there were regular "rump" executive meetings of my "women" and Mr. Allen in his financial office, two blocks up the street on Vermont Avenue.

Today I would act like lightening to put a stop to such conspiring, but then I was still too green in business and too distracted by a million other things to take effective action. It grew like a cancer.

One of the things distracting me was an effort by a gang of reds to get control of the magazine. I can imagine the scoffing of the "liberals" at this -- but the records of the FBI, and Jane Brownlow, who was in on all of it, will bear me out. I was approached by Frank Bryer, from the Army Times, who took me to lunch at the George Washington Roof, told me that "big interests" were considering supporting me, and wanted me to put out a companion magazine to U.S. LADY to be called "U.S. OFFICER." He described a magazine like "Fortune," a fabulous book, which he said would cost a dollar. I told him that wouldn't begin to cover the cost of the kind of magazine he described, to the small audience it would have. He was drinking martinis one after the other, and, as I pressed him to explain how this magazine would be a financial success, he kept saying his "big interests" had plenty of money to cover it. I explained that such a book would lose millions permanently and asked where in hell they would get money like that. He was obviously flushed with the gin, and drew me close. "From the Soviet Union," he said, not kidding. I pretended to laugh and let the subject drop.

I went back to the office and told Mrs. Brownlow of this. We figured he was perhaps just too drunk to know what he was saying.

But he followed it up. He told me that the "interests" were in Texas, and were ready to pay my fare and expenses to come down there and talk over the deal. I wanted nothing to do with it, of course, and told Mrs. Browlow to say nothing to anybody. But she did anyway. Her boy friend at the time was an Army officer who did some shooting at a range with an FBI friend. She told the officer, who told the FBI friend.

So I got a call from FBI agents, and told them the story when they asked me to. They suggested I go and see what it was all about, and implied that there would be agents around in case it was dangerous. So I agreed to investigate the thing.

There was a moment at home with my wife, when I saw how she and the kids had to live, that the temptation to take the deal was almost overpowering. I knew by then how the reds operate, and knew that I could assure a happy and successful career for the rest of our lives, with luxury and security, just by going along with these people and pretending not to notice what was going on. It is obvious that dozens of other men before me have "gone along" with this filthy red money-power. But once again my dear, brave wife agreed with me that we must scorn this nasty deal, and fight our way through by ourselves.

I went down to Dallas and met the "contact." I was taken to a millionaire's club, and listened to the proposition. They wanted fifty-one percent of the stock -- control -- in return for fat financing, and there was some talk of printing the magazine on the presses they owned in Texas.

The millionaire was the last person in the world I would expect to have anything to do with Frank Bryer, the man in Washington who broached the deal. He was the soul of conservatism,

Nancy saying Grace

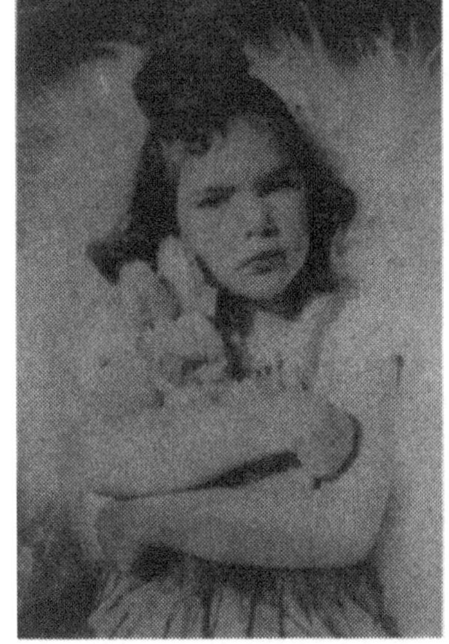

Bonnie with Icelandic sheepskin

Phoebe-Jean having a bath.

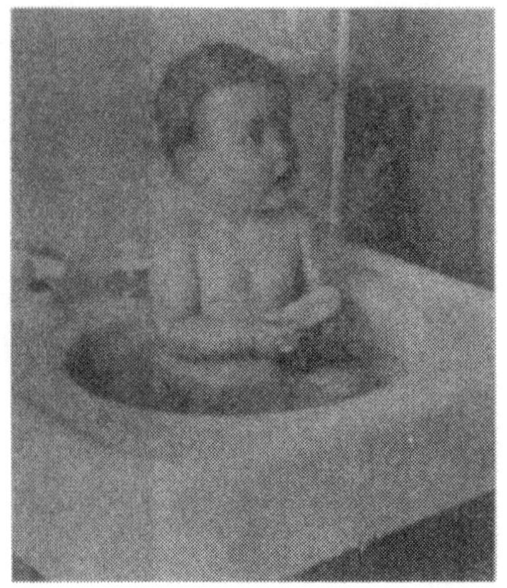

U.S. LADY

Service Wives • Service Women • Service Families

VOLUME I DECEMBER, 1955 NUMBER 4

35¢

Front cover of Christmas Issue of U. S. LADY, in full color.

My office in Washington, 1955, one block from the White House.

Our house in Flint Hill, Va. Sixty miles from Washington

Family with my wife's mother visiting from Iceland. 1955.

Boothbay Harbor welcomes us with biggest lobster ever served, returning from Iceland.

Six of my seven children. Left to right; Nancy, Phoebe-Jean and Bonnie (first family), and Jeannie, Grampaw and Rickey On the way then: Evelyn.

Thora and family, Vienna, Virginia, about 1954.

and seemed to know little of what was going on. We came to no agreement, and I flew back to Washington.

Then the FBI double-crossed me -- unintentionally, I feel sure now. I had told them that Bryer was with the Army Times, an outfit which could have ruined me in the service publishing business, and I did not want him to know I had given the story to the FBI. But they interrogated him anyway, and let him know that they were looking into the "Soviet Union" bit.

Bryer called me in horror when the FBI had left, and I had Jane Brownlow listen in to witness the incredible call. He said he was "hot" and would have to clear out of town, and was going to "hide out" up in Philly for a while. I managed to convince him that I couldn't imagine who had "squealed," and he suggested that I, too, "lie low." Then he blasted the FBI unmercifully, said he gave a speech about FBI tyranny and snooping at his Methodist social action group (!) -- and left for Philly.

Those who imagine this is "propaganda" or lies may reflect that the names are all printed here, and any of these individuals can sue, if these things are not true. And if they are true, which they are -- "liberals" might reflect further as to the Pinko content of so many of our national magazines, books, etc. Perhaps some men prefer millions to patriotism??

Landrum Allen, the stock underwriter, suddenly stopped selling stock one day, and announced that he could not, in good conscience, continue selling until I changed my management methods, etc., etc., etc. He was backed up in this high-handed maneuver by four of my "women" who came to be called "the big four" by the rest of the staff (most of whom were fanatically loyal to me).

I was to give up a lot of authority and do this and that, demanded by the ladies. Ordinarily, I would have sent Mr. Allen scurrying from the office. But in this case, he had the exclusive contract to sell the stock. He refused to do so, and without stock money coming in, until we caught up on the expenses of launching the business, he knew we would collapse. This was exactly what Mr. Allen counted on. He and the women began to interfere with my promotional plans for the magazine. Knowing nothing of promotion (at which I was a professional) they forced me to abandon the highly controversial "advisory board" of the top Admirals and Generals' wives which I had set up (including the wives of the secretaries of the Army, Navy, Air Force, Defense, etc.) -- and, more important, my "Federation of Service Wives" -- a red hot issue, which, had I been able to push it as hard as I had started to do in the first issue, would have made U.S. LADY the center of a political storm and sold it like hot-dogs at a football game.

But the timid ladies were sure the Department of Defense would "close us up" if we went against their policies, so they got Mr. Allen again and I had to back down. Without cash money, I learned, a man is nearly helpless in the business world, no matter how clever, how dedicated, how right, how hardworking he is or how worthwhile his contribution. Without CASH, you are "forbidden" to contribute to our society, except as a muzzled and chained "hired hand." This is one of the things we shall change. Things must be arranged so that free enterprise and investment are regarded, of course -- but also so that genius and talent are not crushed and enslaved by the brutal, ugly power of money. As there are government facilities for the encouragement of health and welfare of even the slobs of the world -- so must there be some kind of government facilities for the protection, growth and development of human genius. Nothing is more valuable to the world than the contribution of its geniuses, yet our Stephen Fosters, our Robert Fultons, and other great creators must fight the whole brutal and ugly world of money in order to force their gifts on a blind and greedy world. And often, even after they have been successful in contributing more value to the world than any millionaire since the beginning of time -- they are allowed to die in misery and poverty! Why must a man be first an expert at the Jewish money game before he is allowed to survive and paint, or write, or think, or build, or organize, or reform? Even if only one out of a thousand brilliant minds produced anything great for society, it will be well worth the little it costs society to establish creative institutes where the finest minds in the population, regardless of other considerations, can be fed and clothed and housed, with nothing asked of them in return except the results of their creative effort. Who knows how many symphonies have died in the poor house, how many great philosophers or statesmen have perished in our gutters, how many immortal paintings lie buried in our potter's fields?

Allen and the conspiring ladies were able to overwhelm

every move I could make, for I simply could not pay my bills every time he stopped selling the stock. Finally, he stopped so long, negotiating and arguing, that the bills got past the point where they could be handled. There were creditor's meetings and talk of bankruptcy. But nobody wanted to see such a good property wrecked. Even Allen didn't want to go that far. He hoped, I am sure, to gain control in the struggle, and thus become, at last, a publisher.

But somehow the news got around, and, from as far away as New York City I got calls offering to buy the magazine. This is something I don't think Allen counted on, as his attitude showed when I sold out, lock, stock and barrell, one afternoon, to John B. Adams of Washington, D.C. Allen sulked at Adams and tried to give him a hard time, and forced him to go to court several times -- but Adams had the hard cash to kick Mr. Allen's nose right out of the business, and that is just what he did.

Adams is now very successfully publishing U.S. LADY in Washington, and Reader's Digest published two pieces from it last year.

Once again, I had created what I set out to create, but lost the fruits of my labors because of lack of capital.

During the last desperate weeks at U.S. LADY, our third child, Jeannie Margaret, was born in the George Washington University Hospital in the District of Columbia, but I had hardly seen the little angel. I spent almost all my time in the office, or collapsing at home -- exhausted.

So, with four thousand dollars in the bank, and the nightmarish pressure of the magazine, the women, Allen and creditors suddenly released, I relaxed at home with my family for a week or ten days to catch my breath before again scrambling for a living -- two livings.

Since I had been unable to keep the vehicle I intended to use for political reform, I decided to go directly into politics, if I could somehow find a way to earn two livings at the same time.

By this time, I had plenty of opportunity to look over the activity of the "right wing" -- the conservatives -- and had come to the conclusion, in my total ignorance of the real nature of the case, that all they needed to succeed was an organizational drive to get them "together", with a business-like PLAN. I had found that there were dozens and maybe hundreds of very rich men, like H. L. Hunt of Texas, and Robert Welsh of Boston, who felt much as I did, and who, together, could pool enough money and resources to swamp the Marxist-Zionist Jews and leftwingers. There seemed to be plenty of talent and ability --and actually a majority of our people over on my side of politics, so that common sense seemed to force the conclusion that it was only a lack of determined effort to put this TOGETHER which permitted the left-wing minority, sparked by the sub-minority of Jews, to keep winning victory after victory and send America down the path to Marxist socialism and racial disintegration.

The "conservatives" lacked any real national and popular medium of expression. With the demise of the Washington Times Herald, there was no longer any "conservative" nationally read newspaper -- and I decided that there was a hungry market for such a journal. I carefully planned a national paper to be called the "Conservative Times", (and still think it would be successful, if the people on the right who are still "nice", unlike me, would finance it.) I learned by surveys that, in Washington alone, the market for such a paper, where the only voices heard are stridently "liberal", was large enough to support it. Many people in the area here would pay them (and would still pay), a premium price for a real right-wing newspaper, even if advertisers were hard to get. And with a newspaper, it would be easy to organize and even dicipline the splintered and squabbling right-wing into a cohesive, effective organization. I realized, even then, that talking and educating are silly and useless unless they are directed at the only worthwhile political goal, POWER. The newspaper must first give voice to our side, then help organize it by effective communication, then discipline it by withholding or granting recognition and praise, as was necessary, to produce a sense of responsibility and direction in the movement -- as the Jews now do with our entire machine of communication and entertainment. When any public figure goes the way the Jews wish he is lavishly praised and built up in the press, and when he displeases them, he is greeted by dead silence, no matter what he does newsworthy, or smeared and blasted until he slinks away with his tail between his legs. With a newspaper, we could gradually begin to do the same thing on our side and I set about the task of applying my ability and experience toward the development of such a newspaper, and eventually a strong conservative organization aimed at POLITICAL POWER. (The John Birch Society has appeared, since this was written, to do what I planned then.)

But I reckoned without any knowledge of the human content of the "right-wing."

From the millionaires to the scared little people who attend the endless pitiful "conservative," "100% American," "old-fashioned," "constitutional," "state's rights" -- meetings -- I learned by bitter experience, that the human material of the right wing consists 90% of cowards, dopes, nuts, one-track minds, blabbermouths, boobs, incurable tight-wads and -- worst of all -- hobbyists -- people who have come to enjoy a perverted, masochistic pleasure in telling each other forever how we are all being raped by the "shhh---you-know-whos," but, who, under no conditions, would think of risking their two cars, landscaped homes, or juicy jobs to DO something about it.

Knowing none of this, however, and being full of my usual enthusiasm and drive. I paid for a series of radio spots before and after Fulton Lewis' show, announcing a Washington meeting to organize the right-wing.

The response seemed to be gratifying. Hundreds of people called and I arranged with one of them, Sam Jones, the correspondent of Bill Buckley's National Review, to use his lovely old Virginia mansion in McLean for our first meeting.

Of the hundreds who called, only about fifty showed up at the meeting, including John Kasper and an Arab friend.

I addressed the meeting in the best "conservative" style, lecturing "nicely" on the need "to get together" more than anything else, and receiving little flurries of polite applause.

UGH! How I shudder now to think of all that feeble, useless, stupid "niceness" -- while our race and our whole world are being brutally destroyed!

From time to time somebody in the audience would ask "what about the Jews!" -- and there would be snickers and shifting around of feet, like grammar school kids when somebody mentions the word "sex". Then I would scold this "bold" character for such a "disgusting display of prejudice", making my righteous love of the wonderful Jews very clear, and even sharing knowing winks with some close friends at my "clever" deception.

The Jews would not have disturbed such a meeting for anything in the world. We, like a million other "conservatives", were giving ourselves the illusion of "fighting" treason, subversion, communism and race-mixing (the Jews) without DOING anything and without HURTING the enemy himself. If we did NOT have such silly little secret meetings, we would eventually build up such a pressure of frustrated patriotism that we just MIGHT have done something forceful -- and therefore effective.

My wife took up a little collection, we passed out membership cards, and then stood around babbling, as is the inevitable custom after such "battles" with the enemy.

Everybody congratulated everybody else at this new and terrible assault on the "Eskimos," as John Kasper called them then, and we went home all aglow with the great "success."

I became friendly with this unknown John Kasper, and he often stayed at our home in Vienna, Virginia. He ran a tiny right-wing bookstore in Georgetown which was frequented by a Bohemian set of odd-balls, dopists, poets and patriots. We confessed to each other our dedication to Adolph Hitler, whom he called "The Saint" - but he had an even greater love, Ezra Pound - the famous poet and broadcaster for Mussolini who was locked up as a nut in Saint Elizabeth's. John Kasper led a circle of worshipful admirers who sat at the master's feet there in the ward full of raving madmen. I attended one of these sessions with my wife one Sunday, and it was an unbelievable afternoon. There was a barefoot lunatic pacing up and down beside the group seated around Pound, silently giving hell to an invisible companion. There was another man crouched in eternal terror in a windowsill, and still others giving the most threatening looks. Meanwhile the group was at the feet of Ezra, who wore shorts, sandles, a loud shirt and a beard. They included a lady dope-fiend, an artist, a beatnik who said he was a poet, John Kasper's hefty, blond girlfriend, Nora Devereaux, John Kasper, Pound's almost silent wife, my wife, and I.

John Kasper worked almost entirely at the direction of Pound when I knew him, and, although I don't know it for a fact yet, I feel sure that John's activity in Clinton and elsewhere was largely inspired if not directed by Pound. When I once went down to Alabama to see if I could help Admiral Crommelin in a campaign for election as Senator, it was John who asked me to come, and it was Pound who was sending almost daily letters of instruction. The letters themselves I thought were nuts --but John treasured them and seemed to obey them to the letter. Fortunately, the Admiral was and is much too strong-willed and self-willed to be influenced much by them or by John's more ethereal ideas.

I poured out my time and money in an all-out effort to organize the right-wing "nicely," as the "American Federation of Conservative Organizations," and published a national conservative paper. We held meetings in the best meeting rooms in the Statler and Mayflower hotels. I had beautiful stationary engraved in gold. I used all my skill in art, writing, organizing, promoting and leading--the same skills which are now serving the American Nazi Party so well -- but they were useless. The basic premise -- the premise of conservatism -- was wrong.

Although it is made to appear so, the battle between the "conservatives" and "liberals" is NOT a battle of ideas or even of political organizations. It is a battle of FORCE, TERROR and POWER. The Jews and their accomplices and dupes are not running our Country and its people because of the excellence of their IDEAS or the merit of their work, or the genuine majority of people behind them. They are in power in SPITE of the lack of these things, and only because they have DRIVEN their way into power by daring MINORITY TACTICS. They can stay in power only because people are AFRAID to oppose them -- afraid they will be socially ostracized, afraid they will be smeared in the press, afraid they will lose their jobs, afraid they will not be able to run their businesses, afraid they will lose political offices. It is FEAR, and FEAR alone which keeps these filthy left-wing sneaks in power -- NOT ignorance by the American people as the "conservatives" keep telling each other. Our right-wing "fighters" keep assuring each other "ye shall know the truth and the truth shall make you free" -- when the truth is that any SLAVE knows the truth -- that he is a slave -- but he is NOT free in spite of knowing this truth, unless he can somehow get the POWER to FORCE his way to freedom. It is not the truth which will make us free in America, because millions already know the truth and hate bitterly what is going on, but they are AFRAID even to admit they know the truth. Ten million signed the petition for Joe McCarthy -- and they are not all dead, although they might as well be, as long as the right wing spends all its time and money trying to "win" another ten million instead of getting the ten million we already have to STAND UP! We have plenty of people, money and facilities to take America back from the traitors TOMORROW MORNING if all the people who already know what is going on, were not AFRAID anymore and would STAND UP!

As long as the right-wing confines its fighting to being "nice", the great masses of the public will bow down like the sheep they are to the left-wing which is NOT nice -- which uses smear, economic persecution, legal harrassment, and finally physical terror to maintain its domination of our national life and culture by FORCE. The force is disguised, of course, in checkbooks, judge's robes, rigged party conventions, etc. -- but it is still either the force itself, or the threat of force which has America down and AFRAID.

No amount of papers and pamphlets, were they all masterpieces of propaganda -- and no amount of talk and meetings can stop this growing left wing force and POWER and the FEAR it inspires -- much less drive it back and finally destroy it.

But in 1955, I still imagined we could "sneak up" on the Jews, like the rest of my "sissy" friends. We would build a great "grass-roots" membership by not mentioning the Jews at all, even praising them -- and then, while they suspected nothing, we could get stronger and stronger, and finally one fine day we would wipe the smiles off our faces, spin around on the surprised Hebrews, and let them see just what we had in mind!

I found this coward's dream being promoted everywhere I went. Every "conservative" I met would draw me aside and groan about the latest outrages and treason of the "you-know-who's", and describe to me the latest plans to sneak up on the tormentors.

And I was as much a part of this childish illusion as anybody else. I spent literally hundreds of hours discussing the methods for this super-sneaky revolution - and the only thing I gained from it all was the final discovery that it was - and always has been -- impossible to unseat the terrorists by talk. One must dislodge such evil usurpers by the same weapon which got them IN -- POWER. Theirs was and is secret and disguised. Ours, by nature, must be open, legal and honest. But it must still be POWER -- not talk or pamphlets or sneaky dreams -- and it involves, therefore RISK.

I also learned to know the people my wife and I came to call the "die-hards" for some obscure reason I can't recall. These were the perennial "patriots", the eternal attenders of meetings, the inexhaustable talkers and babblers, the super-clever know-it-alls who are going to "throw the election into the house this time", etc., etc., etc., and the disgusting hobbyists who discharged their pent-up "patriotism" once a week or so in the masochistic orgasm they seemed to obtain by flagellating themselves with the latest outrages of the Jews. These people seemed to have been "fighting" the Jews all their lives -- years and years and years. Their standard reaction to anything they didn't think up themselves -- a new plan for sneaking up on the Jews -- was "I was fighting this thing before you were born, son" .-- and this was supposed to send the upstart packing. As if people who had spent forty or fifty years fighting so monstrously unsuccessfully had any business daring to open their mouths at all.

These "die-hards" would insist on bending one's ear endlessly and at all hours of day or night. Any attempt to get away from them was taken as a personal insult.

My wife and I grew to dread the sessions with the "die-hards", who were not interested in doing anything except talk, but were World's Champions at the pastime.

Our meetings were better and better attended, but there was no result at all -- nothing accomplished.

As the months wore on and we began to see our small savings diminish with no signs of any real progress, I began to get a case of the "desperationitis" so common to the right wing. I had begun to meet a large, unorganized, but regular circle of "patriots" which exists everywhere, and discuss all kinds of "trick" methods of "spilling the beans" on the Jews, all at once. There were endless plans for dropping "the whole story" out of airplanes by the millions on the public while the helpless Jews watched the leaflets flutter down in rage. There was talk of a plan to raid a TV network station, hold the personal at gunpoint while one of us -- nobody cared to discuss exactly who -- would present to the breathless millions the documents and facts on the Jewishness of Communism -- which we have so abundantly but which mean so little as long as we reach only each other. There was even a scheme for sending aloft huge signs on balloons, tied to inaccessable places, which would "squeal" on the Jews from the sky while they scrambled madly to get them down. These wild ideas are actually -- as you read this -- being discussed by otherwise intelligent people somewhere -- people who are simply too overwhelmed by their own timidity and ignorance to see that even if they DID these nasty tricks on the Jews, there would be NO RESULT at all.

Just two weeks ago, as I write this, the Jews used two or three minutes of one of MY SPEECHES to introduce a long program on behalf of race-mixing on a national TV network show. Mine was the ONLY voice for the White man in that dreary hour of Jewish race-mixing propaganda -- and the Hebrew masters of the ether even used the section of one speech where I explained that the Jew Communists were organizing the colored races of the world in a mass assault on the White Man. The Jews imagine, in THEIR own ignorance, that my speech, delivered to a howling mob in Washington in all its naked passion and ferocity, will repel people -- which is just as wrong as the "Die Hards'" silly idea that "spilling the beans" will somehow "wake them up" and attract them. Neither is the case. People are more inert than it is possible to believe, even after you discover this fact. It takes an incredible amount of propaganda, repeated over and over and over and over and over to move them even a little bit. This is one of the reasons Joe McCarthy told me he wouldn't even attempt to tell the whole truth. "They'd simply put me away as a lunatic," he said, "and the public would forget what it was all about." And he was probably right.

The idea that there is ANYTHING EASY that can be done, which will send the Jew traitors scurrying for Israel like rats, while we walk triumphantly into the White House, is one of the worst self-delusions which has been keeping the right wing babbling and conspiring while the Jews have been laughing at us and trampling all over our Constitution, our rights, our traditions, our dignity and our White Race.

Anybody, when he first discovers what is going on, might be forgiven a certain period of nourishing this delusion and hope. But when he sees the Jews starving the families of his fellow hopers who lose their jobs, railroading them into jail, shipping them to mental health "hospitals," smearing and blasting them for just the teeniest weeniest little attempt to stand up to Jewish power, he ought to get the idea in no more than a few years. Any man who spends thirty or forty years pretending to imagine there is such an easy way, while our Country and our White Race go down and down and down--is not a dreamer--or ignorant--he is a Coward!

"Conservatives" are the world's champion ostriches, muttering to each other down under the sand in "secret," while their plumed bottoms wave in the breezes for the Jews to kick at their leisure. They are fooling nobody but themselves.

One of the conservative leaders I contacted was William F. Buckley, Jr., the publisher of National Review. My friend here in D.C., Sam Jones, was his correspondent, and we got together at a meeting in New York. It was an intellectual thrill, just talking with Buckley and his staff. There is more pulsating brain-power and genius than any place else on earth I have ever been. Bill, himself, is personable in the extreme, and brighter than all the rest. But his staff contains three or four Jews, one of them particularly Jewish-looking, and the atmosphere there is different than with other "conservative" groups.

Buckley is extremely cagey on the Jewish question and even when you get him alone, it is difficult to elicit information as to his awareness. The best you can get are guarded implications from which you are at liberty to infer what you want. I have since learned the reason for this: Buckley's millionaire father had a major interest with the Jews in Israeli Oil -- and the result, even today, is that Buckley's anti-liberalism and anti-Communism stop at the borders of Israel and the Zionist meeting halls.

However, at the time, I too was playing this silly "I've-got-my-eyes-closed" game, so I felt that much could be accomplished by helping Buckley, and I agreed to promote National Review for him. He deposited a thousand dollars in a Washington bank to my account and I started on a project designed to get mass circulation for National Review in colleges and universities.

At the time, however, I was heavily involved in my own effort to launch A.F.C.O. and the newspaper, and I am ashamed to have to admit that I did a rotten job for Bill. I made some efforts, but they were without the drive and full enthusiasm necessary in such a promotion, and nothing happened. I returned the money to Bill, less expenses, with a guilty conscience. Outside of being too cagey on the Jewish question, which is, of course, his privilege, Bill Buckley was a 100% square as a man, and unlike the situation with other right-wingers with whom I have worked or tried to work, my failure to accomplish anything with Buckley was entirely my fault.

During all this time, my wonderful wife and I were enjoying our marriage as I am sure few couples experience the institution of matrimony. She pitched in loyally on everything, helped me with meetings, collected donations -- even gave little talks. I forgot to get Christmas presents for her, forgot birthdays, gave her political lectures, hardly ever took her out in the gay society she loved, cut her off from "nice" people who would have nothing to do with us now that I was a professional "McCarthyite," and I generally gave her damned little in return for the steady devotion and warm love with which she showered me. Often, even as far back as this period in my political career, I would tell her that I knew some day I would have to go to jail, in all probability, not for doing wrong, but for standing against Jewish treason. She never flinched, and I never doubted for a moment she would wait faithfully for any number of years. The only time she would cringe and be silent for a moment was when she would ask if she and the kids were the most important thing in my life. I would tell her they were LOVED the most, but I felt I had a more important duty to do what I could to save my Country and my Race. I told her many times that this duty would have to come first -- as I had told the same thing to her before we were married. Women may judge the quality of wifely devotion which could stand steadfast in the face of such a declaration from a husband.

On the other hand, let no one imagine it was easy to say this to a person I adored as much as my wife. It was tempting to lie or cover up the burning drive within me which I knew could not be deterred by any other desire or need or loyalty I might have. It

took all the courage I could muster to hold such a dear warm person in my arms, look in her deep, loving eyes, and answer that silent devotion by telling her I might some day have to do what I felt called on by duty to do, even at the risk of hurting her.

I continued to widen the circle of my right-wing acquaintances all over the country. I was serving my unavoidable apprenticeship for what I am now doing, although I didn't know it then, of course. I still cherished the hope that we could save ourselves by some easy way -- even though I am sure I knew deep in my subconsciousness that I would someday lead the fight to do it the only way it can be done -- as I am now.

As I reached the bottom of the bank account, with no prospect of any real success, I made one last desperate attempt. I planned a new "Declaration of Independence" for the Fourth of July, and invited Congressmen, Generals, Admirals, important and influential friends and rich men to a big meeting in the Mayflower to set it up. Congressman Ralph Gwinn of New York was helpful, and I also had the help of Dorn, of South Carolina, Wint Smith of Kansas, and several others. Fred Maloof, a Lebanese millionaire came -- and almost ruined the entire meeting. With all the Congressmen, Generals and other important people squirming in their seats, he "came right out with it" and gave a violently anti-Semitic tirade! But I managed to quiet him and get out my presentation and my carefully worked out plans.

Then I sat back and hoped these great personages would see the sense of "getting together" and help to do the job with a will.

The result was absolutely nil -- nothing. There were a good many compliments and pleasant remarks, but no real progress or offers to help build such an organization.

Sam Jones, a faithful and understanding friend, took my depressed wife and me up to the lounge in the hotel lobby above, and we discussed the defeat over drinks.

I really felt low. I knew my plans were excellent, and everybody agreed they were. I knew I had the drive and ability to make them work, and everybody agreed I did. I knew the situation for our People and Nation was desperate, and everybody agreed that it was. But nobody would DO anything No matter how hard I tried, I ran into a solid, blank, silent wall.

Sam cheered us up, and even got us dancing a bit. Then we went home and I lay awake a long time trying to figure things out while my blessed wife stroked my head and mothered me like a spanked boy.

I had failed with the American Federation of Conservative Organizations, the Conservative Times, and it seemed, my political career.

CHAPTER VIII

The catastrophe of my big meeting in the Mayflower seemed complete. I had put all I had into that final effort, including money and thought, time and work. And it had been just another session of talk, like all the rest -- like almost everything else going on in the right wing.

But I reckoned without the hand of an inscrutable destiny which I have come to know and to trust.

One of the men who had come to that last meeting in the Mayflower was Robert B. Snowden, an extremely wealthy plantation owner from Hughes, Arkansas. He had heard of me through my friend, Congressman Gwinn of New York, and then had called me to say he was coming up from Memphis for the meeting.

Part of my humiliation at the meeting had been Snowden's speech. He had used the occasion to tell the group of his own organization and his plan to do exactly what I was proposing, in a different way. Only he had plenty of money of his own plus many many thousands of dollars from other wealthy Americans; he had the actual working backing of many Congressmen and influential people, and his organization, unlike mine, was "in business" and seemed to be a booming success. With all this, he very understandably preached that the support I was asking would be much better put into his organization, called the "Campaign for the 48 States." It made sense. In effect, he simply stole my meeting.

But that was no consolation to me the next morning as I surveyed the wreckage of my political career. With no more money, no organization, paper or business, it was hard to figure a next move. Then the telephone rang. It was Snowden.

"Can you come over to the Congressional Hotel?" he asked, bluntly.

"Sure." I said. I had nothing to lose talking to a millionaire. "When?"

"Right now."

"Be right over " --and we hung up.

I scurried over to his suite in the hotel right next to the halls of Congress. He was in his BVD's, and drinking whiskey from a tumbler. He offered me some in his hearty, bluff manner, and I accepted. I liked him. He was big, florid of face, outspoken, even blunt, and he obviously knew "the score," as it is called in the loose mess of people called "the movement." There was no "Die-Hard" old-lady about Snowden.

"I liked your pitch," he growled. "You've got the stuff we need. I want to put you on the payroll. How about it?"

This was like a man in the electric chair being offered a reprieve. I would probably have agreed to go on the payroll of Nikita Krushchev at that moment, with two hungry families waiting for me to bring home some bacon -- one of them with a warrant and jail ready if I DIDN'T bring home some bacon.

But Snowden had seen me at my best, in plush surroundings, and had seen my record of accomplishment, so I tried to keep cool.

"Doing what?" I asked. "And how much?"

"Helping me organize the Campaign, raising funds, and writing TV films."

"What's the payroll?" I repeated the question, trying to keep down the excitement at this offer of what appeared to be Heaven on a salary. Writing TV films sounded like the answer to my prayers!

"Eight thousand."

We gulped his bourbon and dickered. Several people came and went, and he held court for them in his BVD's. We liked each other. The job, of course, was my heart's desire, although I hid my wild elation over it for a decent period of time. We settled the details, and it was agreed that I would stay right in my home in Virginia and write five half-hour TV shows to be filmed in promoting the five amendments to the Constitution which were the "trick" of the Campaign for the 48 States in sneaking the government back from the usurpers.

Snowden then dressed and we adjourned to the bar below, where we met a friend of mine by the name of Bill Evans, who been kicked out of the Navy (as a senior Lieutenant and graduate of Annapolis), because he pointed out the gross treason going on in the Korean War when he was aboard a destroyer. Evans knew more about the "movement" and the people and which ones were phonies, etc., than any other man I knew at the time, and I thought he might be able to help in the Campaign. Snowden didn't think Evans would be of any help, but felt so expansive and generous that he loaned Evans eight-hundred dollars on the spot to get his wife and children back from overseas, where they were stranded while Evans was down on his luck after his bout with the pinko bureaucrats in Washington. It was another example of the impulsive generosity which I found attractive in Snowden.

But I was soon to learn another side of the man.

I used my last funds to get set up properly in my home in Vienna to write and organize the TV films for him, as ordered. I was to send him the scripts and layouts, as they were completed.

But before I could get started fairly, I received a hurry-up call to report to a big meeting in New York, where I was to help Snowden and Gwinn raise funds at a luncheon. Upon reporting, I found the campaign had been able to gather some of the greatest names in U.S. industry at a sumptuous private dinner. Snowden and Gwinn both made little talks asking for four-hundred and ninety-five dollars from each of the assembled capitalists, an amount as large as possible not requiring reports to the government. The results of the plush atmosphere and the smooth pitch were excellent, and I was very pleased to be part of the outfit -- for a few minutes.

Then, as we parted for the day, Snowden suddenly informed

me that he had hired a firm, which I later found was dominated by Jewish interests, to write the TV films, and I was to move to Memphis and work in the office with him!

This was an awful blow, creatively, financially and family-wise. I would not write the films I was working so happily on. I would have to sustain the severe financial strain of giving up our pretty little Virginia home and moving over a thousand miles into the South. I would have to rip up my family's growing roots and tell my wife of a new hegira. And my wife was getting understandably sick and tired of hegiras. We had already moved four times in two years.

But I was on the payroll, and working in politics which was my chosen career, so there was nothing to be said or done except to move.

Thora and I, Ricky, Grampaw and Jeannie, the baby, piled into our Plymouth station wagon, and we drove the long road to Memphis. On the way, I thought many hours about what might lie ahead, and resolved to take out "insurance" against any more such total uprooting of my family. I sensed, with Snowden's sudden switch, the possibility that my political career, even on "salary" might not be too secure. I resolved not to buy or rent a house or apartment, but to get a big trailer. If there were to be any more sudden moves, I would be ready to hitch up and go.

Snowden ran a miniature dictatorship in his Memphis office, ruling like a tyrant over his other assistant, Fred Rosenberg (German), and his secretary. It had been "Bob" and "Linc" before, but when I walked into the office, I was ordered summarily to address the boss as "Mr. Snowden." This did not bother me too much. I do not mind the boss exercising his authority or dignity, and, in fact, insist on this myself. But his next orders DID bother me.

I asked him what my duties would be, now that I had come all the way down there.

He put me to making out, by hand, little receipts for the $3.65 contributions which poured in from all over the USA ("A Penny a Day" was the organization's slogan). These could have been printed and stamped, as they had been done in my offices in two businesses. It seemed silly to pay a man $ 8,000 and have him move 1000 miles with his family in order to write out receipts eight hours a day.

When he left for lunch, I asked my new associates about the foolish business.

"He's just like that," they said. "He's showing you who's boss."

It did no good for me to emphasize that I was happy to acknowledge him boss, call him "Sir," and obey his orders without cavil. Day after day I reported to work with my sandwiches, and then sat for hours scribbling out those eternal little receipts. While I thus "occupied" my talents, I watched Mr. Snowden swashbuckling around the office, commanding the other two in his imperious manner.

I tried very gentle and extremely diplomatic gambits in offering helpful suggestions, particularly as to methods of cutting out a great deal of inefficient and useless paperwork, such as the endless little receipts. This only made him angry, so I gave it up.

Then one day he got the first scripts from his expensive New York deal. He read them with growing despair. He did not let me look at them. He showed them to Rosenberg, complaining bitterly about the deadness and stupidity of them. He wrote the firm, with whom he had an iron-bound contract, a nasty letter, and got back more lousy scripts.

I had already carried out my resolution to buy a trailer, and I went home to this rather palatial, if compact home, and sat up all night writing the script as I thought it should have been written.

The next morning, I silently handed my effort to Mr. Snowden -- who took it with equal silence and read it. He said nothing, and went out to lunch.

When he came back, he gruffly told me to get busy and write the scripts. So I put away my receipt book, and returned to the work I could have been doing back home in Virginia -- the work I WAS doing before he paid the other outfit to do it, only to find, as he should have known, that only a dedicated and informed -- and creative right-winger could write those scripts.

It made him mad, however, to have me sitting there above his immediate commands, so he told me to go home and write them -- a most welcome order.

I pitched in and wrote the shows which, I understand were finally used, although I never saw them. But not without his "help." His blue pencil had to be delicately inserted into carefully written bits of propaganda like a wrecking bar, and sledge-hammered around to his own tastes.

In the middle of this, I was ordered by the Navy to take a couple of Reserve Squadrons from Anacostia, D.C., to Grosse Isle, Michigan, for a summer "cruise" of two weeks intensive flight training. I was Commanding Officer of Fasron 661 at Anacostia, flying a week-end every month in Washington, and now I was appointed Task Force Commander of the training group. So I had to leave Memphis and my family, and Mr. Snowden, for these two weeks to serve in the Navy. And during this period while I was away, Mr. Snowden offered to take my wife and children for a visit to his sumptuous plantation at Hughes, Arkansas -- where he had a lake for swimming.

It was on this cruise at Grosse Isle, Michigan, as Taskforce Commander of the Reserve Group from Anacostia, D.C., that I learned at last the full extent of the "Jew-democratic" rot which has emasculated our fighting forces.

My orders as Task Force Commander were to take my own Fasron 661 and a scouting squadron attached to Grosse Isle Naval Air Station for two weeks of intensive drill and training to insure the combat readiness of the officers and men.

We were all drawing full duty pay, and enjoying all the benefits of active service in the Navy. So it seemed to me that we oweed the taxpayers of America everything we could do to insure the genuine BATTLE-READINESS of the squadrons, the Officers and the Men.

One of the most elementary necessities in combat-readiness is DISCIPLINE. And discipline, in turn, requires instant obedience and RESPECT. This is the reason for most of the saluting, the honors, ceremonies, dignities and services accorded seniors by juniors in all effective military organizations.

So I made the terrible "mistake" of trying to include this most necessary element in the training program. I ordered all juniors to salute all seniors once a day, and all commanding officers to be saluted every time they appeared except under active working conditions or when flying, etc. This is no more than standard procedure aboard ship where decent discipline prevails.

The result was that some of the officers and men complained to Anacostia, and I got chewed out thoroughly and almost got an unsatisfactory fitness report. I got a lecture on the new "democracy", and the need to make "pals" out of the troops, etc., etc. It was hard to believe it was the same Navy I had been in when I was a catapult pilot on the old Omaha, sixteen years before.

When the Navy still maintained its aristocratic fighting traditions even though some of the troops might have their "democratic" feelings hurt by not being "pals" with their officers, there was every effort made to CREATE a gap between juniors and seniors. There was a greater gap then between ensigns and junior lieutenants, than there is now between ensigns and Captains!!

Before we got "democracy", even a junior naval officer was assigned his private "mess boy", as the privilege of a gentleman whose profession was war. This was before the day when the Jews have managed to spread the idea that every Admiral and General should wash his dishes and his dog, that it is beneath the "dignity" of a negro to do these tasks for a man whose responsibilities may include the fate of nations.

Rank really meant something, and the other ensigns and I never thought of referring to a Lt. (jg) as anything but " sir " There was even a "head" (washroom) for Lieutenants and above, and once, when I was already one of the jg's, I got caught by a Lieutenant using this sacred chamber between flights to save a long run up and down two ladders to my quarters in the "Black-Hold of Calcutta". This dignitary of a higher world was not as popularity crazy as today's officers, and very properly chewed me out in the saltiest tradition for thus intruding on the privacy of my betters. Even as few years back as 1941, American fighting men of all ranks could understand the simple fact that nobody can preserve dignity of command and maintain the respect of large numbers of men when commanders and commanded all stand together in the most undignified of tasks in the most undignified of places, as they sometimes do now, for instance, in the military establishments.

An enlisted man or a junior officer with the right attitude and spirit do not feel themselves degraded and humbled to salute, do honor to, and grant privilege to a GOOD officer. But many of todays officers have become obsessed with a desire to be popular, rather than good officers.

Back in '41, I saluted my Commanding Officer EVERY time I saw him, and was damned proud to salute this fine, tough officer. I did not have the democratic privilege of wee-weeing together with him. But I did have the privilege of following his leadership and of real, solid, eighteen carat respect for an officer and a gentleman who would have unhesitatingly had me clapped in irons for any willful and flagrant failure to show such respect.

Sure we had tyrants and bullies when C. O. 's had the real power they used to have. But sometimes we learned that the tyrants had a purpose in their roughness, and it paid off in combat. And more often than not, our C. O.'s were OUTSTANDING LEADERS. Today, a C.O. is sort of a business-man executive and school-teacher who is expected, above all things to be "popular" in the cheapest sort of way, and then to be a technical expert and paper-shuffler. If he tries to establish the proper conditions of dignity and respect for effective leadership, which always involve the elements of privilege and fear, in addition to popularity, he is promptly accused of not being "democratic".

When I got back from the two-week Navy cruise, there was a new battle with Snowden, this time of a serious nature. He later settled the matter out of court, and I agreed not to divulge the details of this affair, and thus cannot do so here.

After that, things in the office were worse than difficult. In the interest of the cause and my job, I tried to be extremely and even formally respectful and helpful, but my boss redoubled his arbitrary tyranny. I tried to tell him I had established good contacts with Russell Maguire at Mercury magazine, and other contacts which could get us good publicity, but Snowden scorned these offers, and hired a man he admitted he knew was a Pinko to do the publicity -- one of the jobs for which I was hired.

One morning I walked into the office and Snowden was there early. He asked me to look at a bill or something at his desk, and, as I did, I could not help seeing a note reading "fire Rockwell". I asked him what it was, and he tried to hide it -- but it was too late.

We had it out -- and I stamped out of the office, with him ordering me back to hear more -- all the way to the elevator.

Thankful I had the forsight to get the trailer, I hurried home with the awful news for my wife -- who was beginning to feel like a badminton bird. We bought an old '49 Cadillac, and I hitched up that 44 foot giant -- bigger than a truck, and piled the family inside the dwarfed car.

Few combat flying experiences have been so "hairy" as that first trip hauling such a gigantic trailer with a car full of wife and children. The thing swayed dangerously going down hills, and there was one time when I saw a huge Greyhound bus roaring down a hill opposite as I roared down another hill toward the point at the bottom where the road narrowed to a tiny bridge over a creek! It was obvious that we would meet in the middle, and the bridge was barely wide enough for both of us, with less than a foot to spare! I waved my arm frantically to the bus to stop since I couldn't stop, but he kept on with the usual elephantine speed of a bus. My fingers gripping the spinning wheel in a clutch of deathly, cold fear - we shooshed past each other on that bridge in a hair-breadth escape that literally exhausted my wife and I. The kids thought it was fun, of course!

We also had a fearful time getting around tight corners in towns, and my wife often had to get out of the car on the jump and guide me around while flagging other cars down.

On the way, our trailer hitch broke, and we almost had a catastrophe as the trailer dropped with a horrible thud. But we managed to battle and struggle our way up to Washington, D. C., and finally pulled into the lovely park at Haine's Point, on an island in the middle of the Potomac, with a gigantic sigh of relief!

CHAPTER IX

I had already sold Russell Maguire, Publisher of Mercury Magazine, an article about U.S. follies in Iceland, so I now planned to propose further work for him. I called and arranged an appointment in his lavish Park Lane Apartment in New York.

I had never met him, and was happy and relieved to find him the opposite of my recent employer in Memphis. He was small, intelligent, unassuming, and seemed utterly dedicated to the cause of America and the White Race.

We talked over the "movement", as patriotic leaders inevitably do upon meeting, and agreed that what was needed was what he called a "hard core". I told him I thought eventually we would need a Nazi Party, and he agreed, but said it would have to be done with extreme secrecy. At the time, I didn't know enough about it to argue him out of that idea, as I do now, so I went along with that too.

Then he offered to put me on the payroll in his Fifth Avenue offices as his assistant, to help promote Mercury Magazine - his beloved project, and begin quietly setting up the "hard core" he wanted. Even if this had not been what I dreamed of, I would have taken it at the handsome salary. Here was the opportunity prayed for by many a young American I knew - PAY - a living - for fighting treason!!!!!

I reported for work almost immediately, and had the trailer hauled by a moving company to a trailer park in Moonackie, New Jersey, just across the river from Manhatten.

For a while, it seemed too good to be true. I "broke my neck" for Maguire, and he seemed to appreciate it. He was willing to listen to suggestions, and often accepted them. It was heaven after the office in Memphis!

But then I began to get into the office intrigues going on in every office in the world, and it was hard to maintain my position, which had no title. Sometimes "R. M." as the staff called this tiny multimillionaire, would send me over to pounce on all the mail at his Mercury office on 50th Street, and search through to see if the staff over there, including his own daughter (who was the boss at Mercury) was filching from or messing up the mail accounts! This did not endear me to that staff. Nor did I gain any popularity when I discovered left-wing sympathies in some of the editors, and presented the evidence, as was my duty, to the boss. Part of my job was also to filter the thousands of requests for financing which plague every wealthy man, and throw out the scoundrels, the fakes, the boobs and quite a few decent people with whom "R. M." simply did not want to be bothered.

Meanwhile, I was busily searching out and rounding up the talent for Maguire's "hard core".

In the process, I came across a man named DeWest Hooker.

When I met Hooker, once again my life changed permanently.

Hooker already knew Maguire, and Hooker had been the nearest thing to a Nazi which had been since the Bund.

He was a graduate of Cornell, exactly the same age as myself, same temperment, same ideas, and infinitely more experience. He was handsome -- so handsome that he made money as a professional model, and I still see him in cigarette ads. His rugged aristocratic face was framed by perfectly groomed hair, greying at the temples. His build was athletic and tall, and he walked with a bounce and spring in his step which is rarely seen in our beat people. He was decendant of the Hooker who had signed the Declaration of Independence, with millionaire parents, and a millionaire wife.

But most of all, Hooker was a NAZI. Not a "patriot" or "right-winger" or a "conservative" -- but a fighting, tough, all out NAZI. He had gone into the streets of New York City and rounded up gangs of tough kids and potential juvenile delinquents, and converted them to fanatical loyalty to the United States, the White Race, and Adolph Hitler. He called this gang of little hoods the Nationalist Youth League, and I was deeply impressed when I saw what LEADERSHIP and GUTS will do to make decent, dedicated AMERICANS out of little lost baby gangsters. Hooker had those kids WORSHIPPING him! He was an obvious aristocrat from a mansion in Greenwich, Connecticut, who wore a homburg and a chesterfield with supreme dignity -- and led these little New York gutter kids out of despondency, and in picket-lines against Jewish Communism -- right in its filthy stronghold, New York City!

My first meeting with Hooker was a Thanksgiving Day, when he was due at a family dinner. But we got so totally absorbed in our discussion that he kept his wife waiting HOURS -- until she was very angry at him, as we talked -- with him telling me one amazing thing after the other.

West explained the Jews to me more clearly than I had ever figured out before. He described, with dramatic gestures, how they operate like a snake with different skins -- which they crawl out of or into as the strategic need may arise; when Jewish-Communism begins to get too "hot", as it has here in the U.S., as millions saw the parade of Jew Communist spies, they slide out of that skin and become Zionists. And when this too gets too hot, then they become "anti-communists" -- or something else. In the excitement nobody ever seems to notice that it is always the same snake.

Even more enlightening, he gave me a sparkling clear picture on a national scale of the mess I had come to know on my own, locally, as the "movement" -- the cowards, the loud talkers, the hobbyists, the agents of the ADL, the "prostitutes" making money out of it -- and all the rest of the depressing lot of them.

This energetic young genius then told me the astonishing, -- and accurate inside story of Joe McCarthy, completely winning me with the way he was able to fathom, and present the vital information about enemy operations which had so far baffled me.

Every step of the way he showed me documents, newspaper clippings and photostats to back up the story about how Joe McCarthy got started, rose and was finally ruined.

He told me that Bernard Baruch had started it all, when too many Jew spies were becoming prominent. Baruch called Joe up to his New York apartment (here Hooker showed me the newsclip from the Times) and told him that there was need of an anti-communist crusade, but that there was an unfortunate idea getting around that Communism was Jewish, because of so many Jew spies. Would Joe conduct a good, exciting Red hunt, being a little "fairer" and digging up some Gentile, NON-Jewish spies? If Joe would do this, Bernie would see that there was good publicity and advancement in it for Joe. McCarthy could smell the flavor of this, but, like many a shabez-Goy before him imagined he would out-fox the Jew. When the time came, he would use the publicity and backing to drag out ALL the Communists, Jew and Gentile alike. So Joe agreed to conduct the great hunt, and started in Wheeling, West Virginia. He promised to identify the "master red agent" in America, and made a lot of charges about Communism in the State Department.

Then he was approached by his "good" Jew friend, George Sokolsky, the columnist, and warned of the danger of being accused of being an "anti-Semite", because of the mere chance presence of so many Jews in the Communist apparatus. "Why not guard against this by taking a 'good' Jew as head of your staff?" wheedled George, "then they COULDN'T say you were anti-Semitic!"

Joe thought this was pretty good, and George just happened to have in mind the right Jew, Roy Cohn. The matter was soon arranged -- and Cohn the Jew became the organizer of "McCarthyism".

Then Cohn approached fighting Joe, and suggested that, since they needed contributions and more help, and wanted to be doubly sure not to be charged with being anti-Semitic, it might be wise to hire a wonderful rich young Jew friend of his, Dave Schine, for the staff. Again, McCarthy went along with this brilliant stroke.

When all was in readiness, McCarthy duly brought out his

big red fish, as promised -- and it turned out to be a college professor named Owen Lattimore -- a Gentile! Nobody heard much of him before or since, but in the middle of the trials of more than twenty JEWISH Soviet SPIES -- Lattimore was dragged back and forth in the press as the REAL RED HERRING -- a GENTILE Herring, with suitable screaming back and forth by both "sides". Bernie did a fine job.

McCarthy, through all this, figured he was smarter than his manipulators, and, when a REPUBLICAN got into power, he would then go after ALL the reds, Jew and Gentile, and let the chips fall where they may. However, for the moment, here was the man the Jew papers and the Daily Worker were screaming "murder" about, SET UP by a Jew, ADVISED by a Jew, and STAFFED by two Jews.

The loyal and hardworking staff now set about displaying "McCarthyism" to the world. Cohn and Schine, the two Jews, made a whirlwind tour of Europe, visiting libraries of the U. S. Information Service, which are, as a matter of fact LOADED with red and pink propaganda. But they did not do a responsible job of exposing and stopping this rotten use of U. S. taxpayer's money to spread Marxism. Instead they had tantrums for the press, threw books on the floor, and acted like two idiots. Nobody noticed that they were two JEWS, but the press and everybody in the world heard about the insanity of "McCarthyism"!

The election was by now in full swing, and McCarthy went to bat for Ike, dreaming sneakily of the day he would not have Truman to stop him, and could REALLY dig out Communists, no matter how many of them were Jews!

Sure enough, Ike was elected - and McCarthy pulled the plug, floored the accelerator, touched off the boosters, and let go with all he had.

He went to Fort Monmouth, to our most secret radar Laboratories, and discovered 41 people with atrocious security records and highly suspicious activities as reds. THIRTY NINE OF THEM WERE JEWS. Then he found a Jew dentist named Irving Peress who had been caught red-handed committing perjury in denying his red record. McCarthy asked the Defense Department to look into it and report the circumstances. Instead of doing this,

Commander Rockwell speaking in Washington, D. C., park.

U.S. Stormtroopers line up for roll call at National Headquarters.

The office of The Campaign for the Forty-Eight States. Snowden in rear

Robert B. Snowden

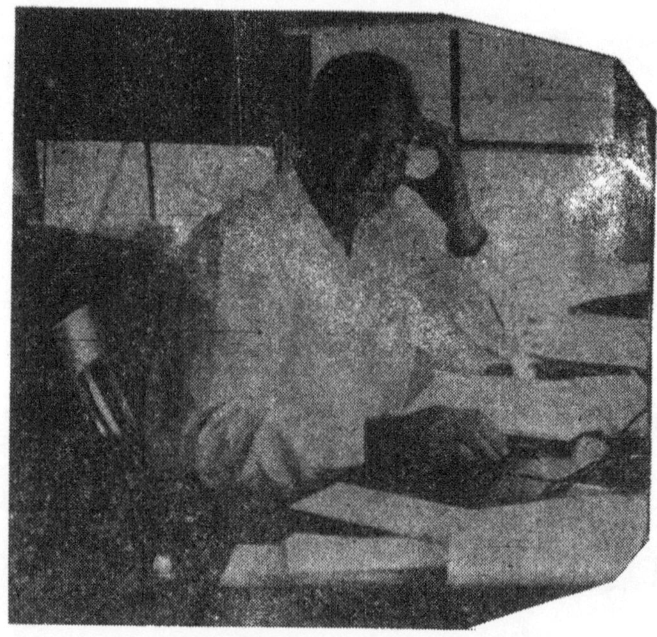

My wife, Thora, Memphis TV

"Grampaw" and Rickey salute the "skipper", rowing expedition

Thora and Jeannie, inside trailer.

Ready for take off, Navy Fighter.

the Anna-Rosenberg dominated Army PROMOTED Peress, and mustered him out, beyond the reach of court-martial, in ONE DAY!

McCarthy, righteously lusting for blood, went after Irving and demanded to know WHO PROMOTED THIS COMMUNIST? He would have eventually been led to Anna, the writer of articles for the New Masses, and member of the Communist John Reed Clubs, and perhaps on to Secretary Marshall, who boasted that he personally disarmed the Nationalist Chinese with a stroke of his pen and this turned China over to Communism.

So McCarthy's two Jew "assistants", Cohn and Schine went into action, again.

Schine was drafted into the Army, and Cohn, in the name of McCarthy, called and tried to get favors for him by influence. This was a perfectly wonderful red herring to take the heat off that question of how come a communist Jew dentist who got caught perjuring himself was promoted and mustered out before he could be court-martialed. Once more, the two Jews, not Joe McCarthy, were the source of the "McCarthyism" and dirty playing which became the cause of the downfall of a truly brave and great-hearted man.

When Hooker finished this utterly devastating and unanswerable display of the genius of the Jews at manipulating, and the genius of Hooker at figuring it all out, I was mentally staggered! How enormous it all was!

I discovered Hooker hated Maguire, for whom I was working. Maguire, he said, was rabid only on one thing, Mercury, his pet project - and the hell with the cause itself. He told me that Maguire was utterly ruthless financially, and would weasel out of any deal he could if it cost him money. He even claimed that Maguire had tried to hire him, Bill Evans (for whom I had gotten the loan from Snowden) and another man to kill key Jews at ten thousand dollars per head, but that when there was an attempt to pin him down on the money, he welched so badly they felt he would never pay, and, in fact, some of the boys wanted to shoot Maguire instead. He said Maguire would talk forever about his "hard-core", but would never, never do anything.

Meanwhile, in our trailer in Moonachie, my wife and I were very happy, considering the restricted living-space. She was once more pregnant, but we had money in the bank and our family grew daily more loving and united. With the pay coming in steadily and Maguire promising me raises for a job I wanted very much to do, the future seemed ideal.

I spent a good deal of time with West at his place in Greenwich, and in New York. He had been driven out of business and political activity by the Anti-Defamation League and Jacob Javits, who, at that time, was New York Attorney General. They had even gotten a permanent injunction against him in New York, as they are trying now to do to me. He had to move from Larchmont, New York to Greenwich, Connecticut.

Now he was convinced that the "movement" would never get anyplace in the U. S. because, he said, "the 'fat-cats' are too selfish and greedy ever to support a movement the way the Jews support Their boys". He was disgusted, and I couldn't blame him, after I heard the series of experiences he had with these "fat-cats" as he called them (experiences which I have since "enjoyed" myself). They would spend any amount for some little pet project they had in mind, but they would not pay any money to the human talent necessary to get a fighting, efficient organization together, as the Jews do.

I still felt then, that they COULD be persuaded to back a RESPONSIBLE plan and responsible people, and talked West into holding off on his plans to quit the movement and go back into business to make money (as he had previously done in TV, for instance, where he made $40, 000 per year). I told West I was working for Maguire with specific instructions to organize such a group, and he scoffed, said Maguire would welch, etc.

I felt differently, and stuck up for Maguire all the way. I felt sure I could bring these two good men together eventually, in spite of the wild talk and charges.

But Hooker had - and has - genius such as is desperately needed by the dead right-wing. I felt sure I could get Maguire to back him eventually as a Leader. I had to run back and forth between them as you would between two pouting school girls who had turned their backs to each other. But little by little, I got them closer together. Finally, Maguire agreed to a secret meeting between Hooker, himself, Fred Willis (Maguire's oldest and best friend) and myself at Maguire's Park Lane apartment.

Hooker put full faith into the effort, came up with complete lists of all the people and "leaders" in the movement, their records, possibilities, and drawbacks. He also had an accurate list of the spies and agents of the Anti-Defamation League which had Maguire itchy-fingered.

Although it irritated him and went against his nature, I even got Hooker worked up to the point where he called Maguire "Sir", as I did.

We presented a complete plan for a slow, secret Nazi build-up under Hooker throughout the U. S. A., using the personnel and leaders already so well known to Hooker, a front group with an "almost" Nazi flavor, and financing by Maguire. Eventually, we all knew, most of the other rich men would help, if they could see something first.

Maguire seemed entranced with everything presented. Hooker wanted to give him the complete list of ADL and other Jewish agents, and evaluations of all Right Wing leaders, but I suggested holding off until we got some kind of commitment. This tactic got results.

"All right!" said Maguire with the air of a man suddenly decided on an immense step. "I'll back it! The country doesn't have five years left! We've simply GOT to do it! I'LL PUT IN A THOUSAND DOLLARS FOR THE FIRST YEAR!"

Hooker looked at me with his mouth open, I looked at Hooker, then we both looked at Maguire's old friend, Willis. Here was a multimillionaire with over eighty million dollars, sitting in an apartment which alone must have cost him fifteen hundred a month, to say nothing of his fabulous palace on the water-front in Connecticut, telling us that he was going to "back" a national political movement of gigantic proportions to save America - - - WITH A THOUSAND DOLLARS A YEAR! - - And he was going to do this great thing, he said, because "we only have five years left!" !!!!

Hooker and Willis were all for giving Maguire hell right

there and then. Willis was worse than disgusted, and said so. Hooker kept quiet at my request.

I tried again.

I knew Maguire spent hundreds of thousands of dollars a year printing Mercury, and reprints, plus all kinds of material for his four or five offices. I reasoned that if he was too stingy to CONTRIBUTE, possibly we could get him at least to TRADE with us as printers, and thus finance the movement. We had dozens of young men who would learn the printing trade overnight and work like horses for nothing - which would make all the printing profits pure gravy for the fight.

Scrambling wildly in my mind to put this deal together while keeping peace at the meeting, I made the pitch to Maguire. He took it.

He agreed to give us the printing AND the fabulous thousand a year!

We parted at the canopied door on Park Avenue, and Willis seemed too disgusted to talk any further. After hearing Maguire moan and groan year after year about the utterly desperate situation of America and the White Race - and then admit that the ONLY way to save ourselves from the Jews was with a tough, hard core - it was galling in the extreme to see him sitting up there on his money bags and offering to toss us a few coppers for going forth into the streets to have our heads bashed in by the tyrants.

But Hooker and I went to his club (Cornell) right around the corner, and sat in the library trying to calm down and get our bearings for further action. In spite of the set-back, it seemed to me at the time that I had rescued things with the printing deal. I wanted to plunge full-speed ahead with arrangements. Hooker was understandably sour, and predicted Maguire would simply welch again, but I wheedled him into going along on the deal. He admitted I had more success than anybody so far with Maguire, just by getting on the payroll and arranging the meeting (Maguire usually refused to see more than one person at a time, to avoid witnesses). So he had a flicker of faith in my own enthusiasm, and we went to work setting up a printing plant.

We got a press, a little store, started the boys frantically reading manuals on printing, held meetings, planned financing, raised money, and generally did all the things necessary to be ready to handle our end of the business deal. Then I went to Maguire and said we were ready to start with some small printing orders, perhaps office forms.

It is probably an insult to the reader's intelligence to state bluntly what happened. Men do not suddenly change their pattern. Maguire DID welch. There was no printing to be had at 500 Fifth Avenue, Mercury, the Texas office, or any of his other places.

Not only did he welch, but I now became a source of great discomfort for him. My constant presence was a silent, unspoken, sometimes even unthought rebuke to him for his faithlessness. It was hard for him to go through the "we've only got five years left" bit with all his visitors, as he did every day, with me at his elbow.

He had hired a fine young Catholic boy named Gridley Wright for Mercury, and Wright was 100% pure in heart. Over at Mercury, he found the same incompetence and, worse, political unorthodoxy, that I did. He began to tell me amazing and horrifying things about what was going on over there. Three or four of Maguire's supposedly picked staff were not only violently anti-Hitler, but were actually sneaky liberals. They would sneak an anti-Maguire article into his own magazine almost every issue. Once we caught a pro-Negro article by a black married to a White girl, and then an article by a Jew, promoting the red idea of universal equality in mental capacity. I duly brought these things to Maguire's attention, along with the other evidences of disloyalty to him in his own offices.

His reaction appeared to be favorable, but blood is thicker than water. Maguire's daughter was the boss at Mercury, and it was not long before I discovered an indefinable blockage to everything I tried to do in the office. I thought at first it was his daughter, Natasha, but found the old man himself behind a few louse-ups.

One day he called me from his office, and told me to meet him two floors below. He didn't want us to be seen conferring. We met in the men's room, and he told me that his wife was giving him a hard time about me. She was a White Russian, and on "our" side, but didn't want to jeopardize the luxurious life she had attained with her husband, nor risk the security of her children. The old story - but I never expected to hear it from a multi-millionaire. Maguire told me his wife was so upset he was taking her on a Carribean vacation, a pattern I have learned he follows whenever things get too hot, as they did recently when the New York papers blasted him at the instigation of the ADL for being "Anti-Semitic" - which the sly little fox denied!

He told me his wife had heard of my efforts to organize a "hard-core" for him, and was "terrified". He whispered on and on so disgustingly about the pressure on him, and kept referring to the possibility of "cutting the thread" -- meaning my employment - that I naturally offered to resign.

He accepted before I had the words all out, assured me he would secretly support me with cash, instead of the salary, to keep up my work, and "soon" give us the printing business to launch the movement.

Needless to say, none of this materialized.

He did, however, buy two of the articles I did when the Marine Corps was under attack by the reds for it's eliteness and aristocratic, tough traditions. The Corps gave me free access to everything at Parris Island, where I spent a week learning how the little Brooklyn reds were coming down and raising all the stink about "brutality" and the mean old D. I.'s, who were actually standing like iron to save the last bastion of our fighting manhood, the U. S. Marine Corps.

And that was about the last I ever saw of Russell Maguire or his money. He is probably still telling people we have only five years before it is all over - so hurry up and subscribe to Mercury! We are, I suppose, to beat the Jews to death with baled copies of this non-anti-semitic journal. (Note: since this was written, he has sold out altogether and run.)

Many right-wingers are sincerely concerned, I know, about my battles with men such as Maguire, Snowden, et al., and my revelations of what they really are. "They are doing good", I am told, "why not let them go about their business their own way. They are helping. Don't hurt them".

I maintain they are only giving the APPEARANCE of helping

- - and are actually hurting.

Before a mass of people will rise up and DO anything effective and forceful about a tyrannical situation, there must be built up a certain emotional PRESSURE. A fire-cracker has not the force of a rifle bullet because it explodes harmlessly in all directions. But the gas from a rifle bullet cannot escape, except by forcing the bullet out at terrific speed, because it is CONFINED, DIRECTED INTO USEFUL CHANNELS.

As long as Maguire and all the rest of his ilk, rich and poor, can give themselves the illusion of "fighting the Jews" by exploding the pressure inside of them VERBALLY and HARMLESSLY - in all directions, and without ever hurting a Jew traitor, they keep the pressure we need to GET MAD AND FIGHT from ever building up.

The Jews know this, and PERMIT these hundreds and hundreds of harmless little right-wing organizations to spout endlessly in silence behind the Jewish "paper-curtain". They don't reach any significant number of people OUTSIDE their own group, and when they do, their approach is so feeble and so psychologically wrong that they win only a few odd-balls. They NEVER, NEVER get out into the public, into the streets - and reach the MASSES with an INSPIRING and DRIVING masculine movement, which alone can win the HEARTS of the MASSES!

If just one tenth of the cash money which pours every year, year after year, into such "fire-cracker" movements were to be contained, directed, and used behind an ideological BULLET forced out by fighting MEN, the Jews would stop at nothing to utterly crush and destroy that deadly "bullet". Even WITHOUT that money, with only a few grains of "powder" - but confined and directed with FORCE, we have already earned the ALL-OUT attack of the Jews, the only sure sign that we are not firing the eternal right-wing "gas" at them - but the deadly bullets which they know will eventually destroy their illegal, tyranical power.

This does NOT mean that we must work ourselves up to a "pitchfork-and-barricaded" attack or revolution by violence. This old-fashioned attack won't work, as our side learned at the Feldherrnhall, in Munich. But we must stiffen the backbones of enough people so that they prefer to lose their jobs - as we do; they prefer to be unjustly jailed and fined, as we are - be railroaded to the insane asylum - as we are, or even to be beaten - as we are - before they will permit Jew tyrants to advance one more fraction of an inch into our last frontiers of racial pride and National freedom.

As long as the hordes of tricky little "patriot" societies all over America allow our oppressed and harrassed people to "blow off" the pressure caused by this filthy tyranny once a week in harmless "wind" and "gas", there will never appear in America that holy and awesome POWER of ROUSED MASSES, the raging fires of social upheaval which alone have always toppled the greatest tyrants, and for which there is no substitute.

There are plenty of people ALREADY awake in America. They are afraid and they are frustrated by their inability to DO anything about the terrible evil they see growing.

Mercury Magazine does indeed "inform" a lot of people. But we don't need any more informed people WHO WON'T STAND UP AND FIGHT TO OPPOSE TYRANNY!

Such things as Mercury also keep the "steam pressure" of emotions down in millions of Americans who are already informed - who feel that as long as Mercury is published, "something" is being done, who are fooled by the constant advice to "write your senator", into imagining that we can somehow petition or talk our way out of tyranny. Worst of all, Mercury, and a thousand other little projects like it, are financial "leaks" which keep the right-wing bled to death and anemic. There simply is no money for the battle, no money for the bullets and powder, because it has all been spent on fire-crackers, uniforms, the band, pictures of the enemy, exciting rallies, and bed-time stories for the troops.

You can't get these myriad stamp-licking and squawking societies together - as I found out, and every experienced "patriot" knows. And even if you could, they would be worse hitched up together than they are squabbling separately. As Hitler puts it so masterfully, "eight lame men walking arm in arm do not make one gladiator".

These false right-wing leaders, who, for forty or fifty years have been preaching a million different tricks to avoid the desperate, dangerous FIGHT which is always the price of any victo-

Daily Mirror

i. Tuesday, August 7, 1962 • • • No. 18,237

Mirror Picture Exclusive

HOW THE 'FUEHRER' BEAT THE BAN

By HOWARD JOHNSON and NICK DAVIES

A GLARING loophole in Britain's security defences has been exposed by the back-door" entry into this country of eorge Lincoln Rockwell, who is the self-tyled Fuehrer of the American Nazi Party.

Just a day after a Home ffice announcement last week at foreign Nazi leaders would barred from Britain, Rockell was walking openly about ondon.

He even went to look at Scotnd Yard—home of the Special ranch which guards Britain's curity. And he stood outside 10, owning-street and Buckingham alace.

Jackboots

At the weekend—as shown in the clusive picture on the right—he peared at a jackbooted rally held in oucestershire by the Nazi-style British ational Socialist Movement.

But by last night 43-year-old Rockwell d drawn a veil over his movements.

Special Branch men and other Scotland rd detectives were looking for him in tels and guest houses in the West untry so that they could prepare a port for the Home Secretary, Mr. Henry ooke.

Rockwell apparently got into England ite simply and perhaps without subterge . . . because there is no immigration eck between Ireland and England.

In his order announced last Wednesday e Home Secretary told immigration icers to refuse entry to anyone known be coming to attend an international nference called by schoolteacher Colin rdan, 39, leader of the National cialist Movement.

Race-hate

Rockwell, an advocate of race-hate who ys Adolf Hitler is his "spiritual leader," aded the barred list.

But he came just the same. "He would em to have entered the country via annon Airport, Eire," said a Home fice spokesman yesterday.

After that, there was no real barrier to ckwell entering England by air or by ss-channel steamer to Fishguard, Liverol, Heysham or Glasgow.

Anyone who enters Eire and gets past e immigration officers there can visit itain without another question being ced. There is no immi-

Meme
Home Se

Mr Bro
That M
in Bri
Here's
picture
prove

This exclusive Mirror picture shows Colin Jordan, left, shaking hands with "Fuehrer" Roc

name and his power in various countries

Front page of London newspaper announcing Commander Rockwell's appearance in England.

Colin Jordan, Deputy Commander of the World Union of National Socialists

Commander Rockwell stands with members of the British National Socialist Movement during 1962 international Nazi meeting at Cotswold, England.

ry, are approaching the end of the road. They can not much longer pretend that we can save ourselves with their sugary nostrums, and, when the patient feels the death rattle in his chest, as White America can feel it now, and will feel it more with a New Deal of Kennedy - our people will become disgusted with the quack physicians and their sugar syrups and pills, and will flock to us with our rough and tough but POWERFUL medicine.

It is for this reason, not personal animosity, that I consciously and calculatingly expose these political frauds. The doctor cannot cure as long as the patient is chasing after quacks, and imagines himself "getting better". The patient, our White Race, is DYING - the situation is desperate! And it is viciously CRIMINAL to be a millionaire and then take sincere little people's dimes and dollars for sugar syrup!

The right-wing can not be wheedled together, but it can be DRIVEN together, and this is our naked purpose. We intend to, and are making it impossible for the fakes to keep up their medicine show, no matter how they pound their drums next to our office. Sooner or later, our mastery of the right-wing is assured. We have faced and beaten the worst the Jews have. We will have little trouble conquering and organizing the feeble right-wing. Exposing the simple truth about such men as Russell Maguire is part of that cruel but utterly necessary conquest. No matter how we are cursed and hated by the short-sighted, we will win all sincere Americans and White Men when they SEE that we have DONE what they have so long prayed for - united the right-wing, and driven steel into its backbone. The process is never easy or pleasant, but we mean to SAVE OUR COUNTRY AND RACE. The hurt feelings of a few millionaires, hobbyists and incompetent leaders will not deter us from that holy mission.

In addition to trifling with a deadly danger, as these people do, the phoney and feeble leaders and tight-wad millionaire "patriots" also have a fearful effect on the REAL leaders who might otherwise lend their talents to the effort to save ourselves.

De West Hooker is now working in Italy with a bottling company. He is disgusted and discouraged. His experiences with Maguire and the others, the same experiences which have made life so miserable for me and my family, have driven him back to the arms of the Jews and their money.

You can't afford THAT, Americans. Every day I am told breathlessly what an indispensible leader I am, and how the movement needs me, and how terrible it would be if anything happened to me. And this is indeed true. To the devil with phoney modesty! Without me, there would STILL be only babbling and whispering and sneaking and publishing and hoping in America, while the Jews counted their money, pushed the blacks into your schools and homes, and made token gestures of attack from time to time at such feeble "anti-semites".

(Three years ago I put in writing the prediction that a spear-head "Nazi" attack would revive the whole right-wing by giving it courage - and it HAS! The Jews are "on the horrors" with more anti-Nazi lies and swindles than ever before!)

Hooker is one of the men who could have led fighting YOUNG men, as I am, in a FIGHT to save you! The "nice" people, backing such "wake up America" "patriots" as Maguire, drove a great White Leader out and into the arms of the waiting Jews with their money and comfort! How many more Hookers there are, is a tragic, unanswerable question.

No, American, it is not wicked to attack and expose Maguire and his ilk. They have been wrecking the movement they are supposed to be creating for many, many years - and until they pitch in with their money, their brains, their guts and their blood - they are FRAUDS, and I intend to drive them out of our way.

Our motto here is "WHITE MAN, Stand and FIGHT FOR SURVIVAL WITH US, or STAND OUT OF OUR WAY!!!"

CHAPTER X

As I sat in our trailer across from Manhatten and contemplated another debacle in my political career, I realized that the chances of supporting two families, as I had been doing, while also working in politics were less than slim. I would have to find some source of business income immediately.

At the same time, I had no intention whatsoever of abandoning my entire purpose in life. I wanted some job by which I could make the money necessary for the two families by extra exertions, and over short bursts of time, leaving me free to work toward my political goals.

While in Washington, I had met a Nazi stmpathizer named Ed Strohecker, who was in the management engineering business, and he had often invited me to join him. He described it as exactly the kind of thing I needed now, a business wherein I could earn substantial money without getting tied down to an "office", and support my two families by extra hard work over shorter periods of actual time consumed.

When Ed heard of my situation, he got in touch with me and offered me a job working under him for a New York firm of Management Engineers. I accepted.

The idea of the business is that most firms can save money and do better business by modern management engineering techniques which are not usually available or known to smaller businesses. For healthy fees, the company provides these techniques. My job was to walk into offices "cold", ask for the president of the firm and then sell this dignitary on the idea of having a survey of their business done for one hundred dollars.. For this fee they would get some suggestions, but the "survey" was mostly a sales pitch for the expensive engineers to come in later.

The reward to the management engineering firm, for almost no investment at all, is relatively astronomical. Consequently, competition among management engineering firms is terrific and the salesmen, therefore, operate more like wolves than businessmen. A lot of small firms are understandably pretty cool to the idea, especially if they have had a "survey" or two at a hundred dollars a clip. (I once got thrown bodily down a stair-well by an outraged president when he discovered the true nature of my call.) So the salesmen have to be far more aggressive and "inventive" than any other kind of salesman, which is pretty aggressive. Not only is the product an "intangible" (often it is invisible) but the client has usually been driven mad with hundreds of other guys at him almost daily with the same "pitch" over a period of years. Just getting to see the President, who is the only man you are allowed to have sign the sale, is usually a matter of master strategy and collossal impudence.

It will not be hard to understand that New York City and the surrounding area would be a bit tough for this kind of business shennanigans. Most of the business men are Jews. And the ones who are not Jews have fought their way up through Jewish jungle-type economic bucaneering. They have battled each other and the helpless public like a pack of torn and bloody rats. They are anything but "softies".

So Strohecker and his company were happy to find a man willing to tackle this area, in which they had nobody.

I went forth with blood in my eye - and TEN hungry mouths yawning in two homes, waiting for me to feed them. I forced, argued, sneaked and fought my way in to see those tough Jews.

And I got in. I was able to see about two thirds of the men I went after.

And when I got in, I was able to SELL! I discovered, as I had in door-to-door selling of vacuum cleaners as a kid, that such selling is not so much convincing as it is a battle of the WILLS of the opposing parties. You must make a convincing "pitch", of course, but even then, in the "close", he wills NOT to buy, and you will that he WILL buy. The sale or loss depends on which will is stronger, not on your arguments. In a business like that, or in door-to-door work, you have to be prepared to be tough, mean, obnoxious, and literally impossible to get rid of without the victim succumbing, so that he gives up meekly and signs, even if just to get rid of you.

I knew the psychology of Jews. They are mostly bullies - and they are impressed and sold by a bigger and tougher bully.

So I SOLD JEWS! My first week I went out and sold THREE of them! One sale of this "product" is considered "par" and a living - but I sold three and "made" three hundred dollars. (The salesman gets the whole hundred for the "survey", which is strictly the entree for the second salesman - the "surveyer".)

I discovered the deep respect these Jews had for forcefulness and for a salesman's willingness to do ANYTHING to get the sale, so I pushed them around unmercifully and arrogantly.

They loved it, even while they groaned.

One greasy character ran a pastics factory in New Jersey, and he kept putting the contract form away in his desk drawer, and telling me he would think it over. I kept opening the drawer in front of his fat belly and putting it on the desk in front of him again, with the pen ready. Finally, talking a mile a minute, he put the contract in a side drawer, locked it with a key, and put the key in his middle drawer. I opened the drawer, got the key, opened the other drawer, slammed the contract down in front of him again and told him he was only putting off what he HAD to do. He looked at me in astonishment and said, "Son, I wish I had just ONE salesman like you!" -- and signed. He said he wanted no part of the "survey" -- but went along out of utter admiration of such unheard-of sales technique.

With things thus apparently going well, I devoted every spare minute in the day, all my week-ends, and my long evenings working on political plans and writings.

It was a wretched life for my wife. My mind was a million miles away from immediate affairs, and living in a trailer with three children running in and out of the inevitable mud, plus a baby, while her husband sat hunched over a typewriter the seven or eight hours he was home every day, and all day on week-ends, was pretty discouraging for a thoroughly sociable young girl. But Thora was loving and encouraging, -- and even listened dutifully to my political lectures, and the reading of my political treatises. She understood little of them, but always assured me and respected my opinions. She and I agreed that a good wife should not be a political battler. It was best if a wife was not a a rabid politician. She believed in my politics because I believed in them. No man ever had a more understanding, long suffering, or loving wife.

I already had all the facts of the political situation I needed to think my way through to an organized plan of action. I knew most of the people in the "right-wing", or through Hooker, had a complete and revealing report of those I did not know. I knew the general scheme of operation of the "enemy", and most of the facts about his subversion, treason and secret tyranny. I knew the pettiness, the meanness, the weakness, the small-minded fanaticism, the bigotry, the stinginess and downright madness of many of the right-wing "patriots" -- and their worse-than-useless tactics.

I knew that all the talk in the world meant absolutely nothing -- all the fine plans and schemes were empty words -- without **POWER** -- without the necessary FORCE to make the plans and ideas into REALITY. Every minute of thought, therefore, was devoted, directly or indirectly, to plans for the attainment of that legal power of government which was being exercised secretly and cleverly by the usurpers who manipulate the Jewish money power.

I saw with an ice-like clarity that, without exception, all right-wing groups were proceeding on the fallacy that if enough people could become aware of what was going on in our national life and government, the evils would somehow stop. At the same time, I heard all these same groups whining that they were unable to reach out to the masses because they were being given "the silent treatment" by the Jewish dominated mediums of public information. No matter what they did or said, there was no report of it in the press, radio, TV, etc. -- while the sly operations of the Jews and their Liberal tools were broadcast endlessly and brilliantly to brainwash the public.

I realized that the only reason the Jewish "paper curtain", -- "the silent treatment" was effective was because THE SUFFERERS NEVER FOUGHT, NEVER WENT FORTH INTO THE STREETS WITH HANDBILLS, PICKET SIGNS OR SPEECHES WHICH MIGHT GET THEM BEATEN OR ARRESTED OR KILLED!

They confined themselves to "safe" efforts in private, talking to each other endlessly, and never FORCED the Jews to notice or report their activities, because they were never sufficiently newsworthy to make it OBVIOUS to the public that the Jews were censoring the press, if the activities were not reported.

I also took notice of the pitiful financial situation of even the richest right-wing organization. The Jews have budgets of millions and millions for such as their "Anti-Defamation League", American Jewish Congress, and American Jewish Committee. Even the richest on our side, Gerald Smith, had no more than half a million a year. And, were we to have five times his funds -- they would never be sufficient to compete in a brainwashing battle with the multi-billion dollar information and entertainment network of the Jews. With their TV alone, the Jews could put on Edward R. Murrow, for instance, and forcefully, emotionally, drive home a subtle idea to many, many millions of people in a single dramatic hour!

Under these circumstances, it is madness to imagine we can distribute enough handbills, make enough personal public speeches or do anything else ever to influence public opinion SIGNIFICANTLY, with OUR OWN TINY FACILITIES.

ONLY IF WE COULD SOMEHOW SUCCEED IN FORCING THE JEWS TO SPREAD OUR MATERIAL ON THEIR FACILITIES COULD WE HAVE ANY HOPE OF SUCCESS IN COUNTERACTING THEIR LEFT-WING, RACE-MIXING PROPAGANDA !!!!!

And to do this, we would need two things: (1) A smashing, dramatic approach which could NOT be ignored, without exposing the most brutal press censorship, and (2) a super-tough hardcore of fighting young men to enable such a dramatic presentation to the public in spite of the inevitable Jewish violence.

I examined the tactics of the Jews in dealing with all previous approaches to the problem, and found they had a sliding scale of increasingly vicious attacks on those who tried to expose and oppose them publically.

The first and instinctive weapon of the Jew is economic. If you are an anti-Semite, then you and your family must starve, if it is in the power of Jewry to accomplish this (which it almost always is, since they either supply, control or are customers for all businesses). The whole weight of Jewish business is brought to bear on anyone who dares to oppose these lovers of free speech. Usually this is enough to terrify and reduce any man, especially one with a family, to humble and disgusting submission to Jewry.

But if that doesn't work, they go after his reputation and social life. He is smeared and blasted and lied about in the Jewish controlled mediums of entertainment and information. He is called a "bigot," "hate-monger," "failure," and finally, when all else fails, he is damned as a "Fascist" or "Nazi."

If there is still life left in the would-be exposer of Jewish treason, they then reverse the field, for fear of giving him "publicity", and give him instead the "silent treatment". His meetings, speeches, distributions and resolutions are simply ignored, no matter WHAT he does. This is a peculiarly frustrating experience, and usually discourages even the toughest battlers, with the mere passage of time.

If the rising Anti-Semite survives all this, they next try their jail-bit. The police are pressured until they crack, and are willing to harrass and prosecute the "offender" for all sorts of "violations." And if the Jew-fighter persists in spite of fines for not having a license for his dog, disorderly conduct for distributing his literature, etc. -- they next fix him up, if they can with a "frame", as they did Emory Burke in Atlanta. He is found with dope, or he has been giving "kick-backs" to his employees, or his income taxes are fraudulent, etc., etc.

Still failing, the Jews hit their man with their newest masterpiece, "mental health". He must be "sick", therefore needs to be locked up in the bughouse.

If this, too, fails -- then they resort to the eternal weapon of all tyrants, naked violence. The would-be opposer of Jewish treason and tyranny is BEATEN by hoods -- his place is attacked by fire and missiles, and he is in danger of losing his life unless he stops.

(Note: Since this was written, almost a year ago, I have been taught by the Jews that there are two more dirty-plays these lovers of sweet reason employ in dealing with exposers they can't intimidate: they build up sincere, but harmless anti-communist outfits like the John Birch Society by showering them with publicity to draw off the growing hordes of maddened Americans from any real and therefore dangerous activity, and (2) they literally bombard lies about Hitler and Nazi-ism, to destroy "Nazis" like ourselves, without giving them any publicity, per se.)

There is no question but that a man who has survived all these attacks, as soon as the Jews feel sure he can be stopped in NO other way, will be killed, if possible. The Jews have no choice. They are too guilty to permit anybody to expose them and organize any effective REAL resistance to them. Traitors cannot survive such an exposure -- and it is therefore kill or be killed with them.

That I could develop the organization and strength to take care of most of these attacks, I had no doubt. It had been done before. But the problem of the dramatic approach which would force spreading of our propaganda in THEIR media, and the organized physical force to protect that spread in spite of the violent attacks of the Jews -- the jails, the insane asylums and the extreme smears were something else.

I was determined, of course, to set up a program which was, in essence, National Socialist -- Nazi. But for a long time I, too, toyed with the idea of "disguising" it, as do most other right wingers, by another name, and a slightly different symbol. At that time, an open "Nazi" party seemed too fanatastic even to think about.

But I began to reflect that the ultimate smear of the Jews was always, "You are a Nazi!" -- and I wondered what it would be like to answer, "You're damned right we're Nazis -- and we shall shortly stuff you Jew-traitors into the gas chamber!"

At once I had the answer! By being an OPEN, ARROGANT, ALL-OUT NAZI, not a sneaky Nazi -- but a Nazi -- with the swastika, storm-troops, and open declarations of our intentions to gas the Jew-traitors (after investigations, trials, and convictions) -- I would not only make an end of the filthy "silent treatment", for they could never "ignore" NAZIS with swastika armbands and talk of gas chambers -- but I would also FORCE the Jews to publish MY propaganda in THEIR press. Every time they howled that I was for "gas chambers", people would be shocked, but they would also lose a tiny bit of their "fear of the Jews", as the Bible calls the filthy terror inspired by these apostles of tolerance.

If millions of people kept reading in the Jew press about a man who was not only an anti-Semite, but an open Hitlerite, a NAZI -- and SURVIVED -- the myth of Jewish invincibility would be broken. The timid little people all over the country who have been silently and fearfully reading all this material designed to "wake them up" all these years would begin to crawl out from under the bed. While the Jews were desperately busy with me, the little fellows would get bold and begin to act more like their American forefathers.

By being a NAZI, with the swastika, I would also automatically gain the only kind of people I wanted around me -- tough, dedicated idealists ready to fight for those ideals and give their lives, if necessary. But even more important, I would automatically GET RID of the millions of blabber-mouths, cowards, fools and crackpots with which the rest of the "movement" abounds. The swastika would probably not bring me many, but those who came would be MEN. At the same time, it would scare out of their wits the human trash with which any fight would only be cluttered up. The swastika would recruit me an army of the toughest, best men in the country, while repelling and scaring away the millions of useless people who have so far destroyed every other movement by their dead weight.

The swastika would have still another, and even better effect.

For years, now, the Supreme Court and all our legal processes have been pushed and shoved and twisted to make it possible for the Jews and Communists to work their subversion and treason legally. One decision after another has been rendered making it safer to preach and commit treason and subversion. The American Civil Liberties Union has worked tirelessly and effectively to break down the resistance of our government and officials to Communist arrogance, while the public has been taught to "turn the other cheek" and be so tolerant that the vilest traitors must be accorded every "right", including the right of spitting in the eye of our Congress with their "Fifth Amendment" arrogance.

Without exposing their naked tyranny, which they are not yet ready to do, the Jews simply cannot grab Nazis and throw them in jail without some kind of procedings, and, since those procedings have been wretchedly twisted for years to make it possible for the Communist-Jews to drive their daggers closer to the beating heart of America, we could use the SAME DECISIONS of the courts and the same procedings and laws to preach and organize the gassing of the traitors, -- by LAW.

In addition to these overwhelming arguments in favor of OPEN Nazism, there is the effect on the Jews themselves.

I had long ago come to the conclusion that the Jews, -- most of them, are the "sick" ones. The standard symptons of paranoia are delusions of grandeur and delusions of persecution, -- and here was a whole race which made a RELIGION of these classic symptons of paranoia. They are "God's chosen people", -- which Gentiles tend to take as a joke, but which I have found Jews really believe in their hearts, even when they are not religious, -- and "everybody hates them", -- they wail and cry and whine and whimper down the endless centuries of history. People once hated the Irish, the Scotch, the Hunkies, the "Guinies", the Greeks, the Japs, the Chinks, -- all minority groups, -- but they all rolled up their sleeves, pitched in, and managed to make their way in America without making a fetish out of being "hated". It is only the Jews who are forever telling us that they are the "scape-goats" -- who are holy and innocent little lambs, -- but that everybody is "discriminating" against them, persecuting and hating them unjustly! These same personality traits in an individual would have the individual locked up in a mad house very quickly. THINK about it! -- But the Jews have made this paranoia the fundamental, if disguised, tenet of our so-called "Americanism" and our Christian religion. If you do not share the Jew's madness, and deny that they are "Chosen", -- then you are a Heretic, -- and if you deny that they are unjustly persecuted, and point out the sins of the Jews as you would the sins of anyone else, -- then you are "un-American", -- a "hate-monger" and a "fascist".

In short, the Jews, I had discovered, are, in the parlance of the street, "nuts".

They display the usual brilliance and apparent rationality of the paranoiac. They are world's champions at "explaining" their madness as the most fundamental reality and the very test itself of sanity. If you don't love Jews -- then YOU are nuts!

But it is the Jews themselves who are flying in the face of reality, and the effort costs them more mental illness per person than any other race or group! They are simply MAD -- and the Swastika therefore has a special side effect which is worth the whole effort of using this dangerous symbol.

For fifty years, the Jews have been planning their attacks on our America, our freedoms, our traditions, our culture and our people. They are ruthless, subtle, daring and brilliant in forming these plans. They always count on the good-natured docility, the sheep-like tendency to follow, the ingenuous credulity, and the liking for the underdog which are so characteristic of the typical American. Not until he has been openly goaded far beyond endurance will the average American "look for trouble" or fight for his rights. Americans simply wish to be let alone in their enjoyment of the ordinary things of life. So long as they are not too seriously disturbed in this "grazing" in the pastures of life, they do not overly concern themselves with the wolf sneaking on his belly at the edge of the forest.

The Jewish "wolf", therefore, had had to take care only not to DISTURB the sheep he is stalking. He has been able to eat the farmer and the shepherd. He has been able to build a big fence around them so they cannot escape his fangs when he attacks. He can do as he pleases so long only as he is not too obvious about it all. The sheep keep grazing happily on their beautiful lawns, two cars, fine homes, Hi-Fi's, T.V., etc., etc. The only thing which would cause them to raise their empty heads would be some kind of a FIGHT - a loud and frightening BATTLE!

Under these condition, the Jew has been able to plan each of his moves with scientific precision. He has been able to go further - and actually plan the activities of the few who have dared to oppose him. Knowing (1) when he himself will attack, and (2) the usual reaction of those who are alert to his deprada-

With De West Hooker. Greenwich, Connecticutt, about 1957.

Thora serving cold dinner in trailer parked as road-side.

Hitched up and ready to haul the trailer on the road.

tions, he has simply planned a "riposte" to the counter moves of his opponents, and he has ALWAYS been successful in thus frustrating all usual attempts to stop him. He knows in advance what we are going to do, because our side has been doing the same thing for fifty years every time he has attacked, so he simply adds to his plans an element designed to destroy his opposition IN ADVANCE.

As long as our opposition to the Jew is exactly what the Jew has calculated - we are doomed to worse than failure - we are doomed to looking ridiculous.

As I have set forth, the Jews are brilliant and clever in these attacks, but they are fundamentally irrational in their paranoia. Knowing this, I reasoned that an attack upon them which was NOT expected by them, which was NOT reasonable to them, and which TERRIFIED the guilty traitors - would produce, for the first time, reactions from them which were INVOLUNTARY. Instead of them forever attacking us slyly and cleverly and superbly, while we have replied foolishly and blunderingly, right into their hands - for the first time the SWASTIKA would seize the initiative and wreck their clever plans! Instead of THEM planning their attacks and our stupid reactions - WE would be planning the attack, and THEIR insane reaction. Even the grazing sheep would notice the wolf frothing and raving and baring his fangs.

Finally, of course, the SWASTIKA IS THE SYMBOL OF THE WHITE MAN, and has been for thousands of years. It is also the symbol of the sun and dynamism - the FORCE which has been driven out of our modern, Jewized Americans.

All the arguments above, which occured to me in deciding what course to take in launching my movement to oppose the downfall of Western Man, were tactical. But there is a far, far deeper reason for the use of the Swastika.

Men cannot survive the cataclysms of history, the mighty ideological and sociological upheavals which move all men as rumblings in the bowels of the earth change the surface forever, without some kind of POLAR STAR, some SACRED SYMBOL which becomes "holy" and greater than any man. Religion formerly supplied these "holy" things, but the day of naked belief in miracles and supernaturalism is over. Millions of human beings on this earth today have no religion whatsoever, which is part of the cause of the current unparallelled chaos. Men are "milling a-round" in the dark, without aim, without hope, without under-standing.

Only if I could succeed in restoring to our people some kind of RATIONAL "polar star" could our people be saved. Only when I could eventually make them see that THE INDIVIDUAL IS NOT AS IMPORTANT AS THE GOOD OF THE WHOLE RACE, AS NATURE INTENDED, COULD I SUCCEED IN TERMS OF HISTORY, AND HUMANITY - RATHER THAN IMMEDIATE POLITICS.

Therefore, even if all the tactical reasons for the use of the Swastika did not exist, I should still have decided to stand forth with that deadly insignia emblazoned on my shield as I hurled my challenge at the Destroyers of Mankind. I am, and must be, above all things, the Apostle of Adolf Hitler, who was the greatest world savior in two thousand years. I must, like Saint Paul before me, now spread what I once misunderstood, hated, and fought. I must, like the early Christians, drive out the evil "spirit" of materialism, greed, selfishness, short-sightedness and coward-ice - and stand defiant, even in the midst of the lions of the Col-osseum (if that be my fate) - to give the world once more that "polar star" of direction, purpose, hope, loyalty and love which can no longer be supplied by the infiltrated religions.

Adolf Hitler carried the baton as far as he could. Now it was my task, since no other would do it, to seize it up and carry it, in my turn, as far as was in my power.

I believe in my deepest being, that it is not without signifi-cance that the swastika has already proved the key to unlock the Jewish "paper curtain" and give me the prestige and notoriety to be able to publish even this book. That symbol has been baptised in the only "holy water" of any effect in this world, BLOOD. It is the ONLY symbol which can destroy its opposite, the symbol of death and disintegration - the Hammer and Sickle.

With these thoughts, I set about writing a book called "Battle Call", putting forth a new book of Hitlerism adapted for America and our mid-century world.

My work with the management engineering firm demanded fairly long trips all over Pennsylvania and New York State and New Jersey - and I now took along a typewriter. I would stop overnight in State parks and camping grounds, set up my jungle hammock, and then write far into the night by lantern. During the day I would fight the Jews for money, and at night, I fought them silently for liberty and survival. In those parks and camping grounds, I wrote the words and laid out the plans that were to burst forth upon America two years later in Arlington, Virginia, where the swastika first flew in America after fifteen years of being trampled in the mud and slime of Jewish lies.

CHAPTER XI

Although I sold well in the New York area, my income failed to rise to the size expected and needed to support the two families. The hundred dollar advances which I was earning were supposed to be only the beginning. The major income was from the percentage you got on "engineering" work sold to the client by the "surveyors", which often ran into five or six figures. The hundred was to be deducted from these commissions. But there was a disparity between my selling and the follow-up men. I was selling too "hard", and it was difficult for the men who came in later to keep the client.

The head of the Company showed me one day in the office in New York that I had established sales RECORDS in New York City, -but also that I had set the "record" for "no goes".

In twenty sales I made in the area, the follow-up men, the "surveyors", had not been able to get a single "go-ahead" with the client agreeing to the expensive engineering work; which meant that there were not only no commissions for me, but that I was a heavy expense for the Company.

I wanted to go back to commercial art and advertising, but my employer felt so strongly that it was only a question of the law of averages before my sales paid off that he offered me the unheard-of inducement in the management engineering business, of a hundred a week SALARY, sales or no! He showed me that they got "go-aheads" on one out of three sales with even the poorest salesman, and, with the jobs I had been able to sell, just one of these would pay both the Company and me handsomely.

I mention all this here because of the recurrent howls of the Jews that I, (and my fellow "hate-mongers") are "failures", who turn to "hate" as a "racket" when they prove incompetent at everything else. When the "mentally ill" explanation begins to get too untenable, these apostles of truth switch to the "failure" angle. My experiences with the management engineering business, like my record as a commercial artist and business man, are all a matter of record, and the records of the Cleworth Company of the Empire State Building, New York City, will bear me out in all I have said here.

Bill Brown, head of the Company, suggested Pennsylvania as the opposite of New York, where the "hay-seeds" should be easier for the follow-up men, the surveyors, to get "go aheads".

In the meantime, my wife had had our fourth child, Evelyn Bentina, in the free clinic of the Hackensack Hospital in New Jersey. We were too poor to pay, what with the other family to support, so my wife was in a ward full of Negroes.

And now, once again, I had to tell her we were moving, this time to Pennsylvania - with a brand new baby!

We hitched the trailer up to the old '49 Cadillac and pulled it over to Lincoln, Pennsylvania, in the Pennsylvania Dutch Country between Lancaster and Reading.

We found a very pleasant little trailer park there, put Ricky, the oldest boy in school for his first year - and I hit the road looking for the back-woods "rubes".

I learned another vital political fact, almost immediately - plus a disappointing piece of business information. The owners of the hat factories, plastics plants, paper factories, etc., - far out here in the sticks - were the same JEWS I had met in New York. There were a few more Gentiles, to be sure - but everywhere I found the same people moving in more and more on our national business life. I found company after company with a Gentile name, - the name of the hard-working founder and producer - where the sons of the founder had sold out to a Jew who was now fouly exploiting the great name of the original owner for all it was worth.

I worked as hard as I could on these gentlemen, but it was discouraging to know that even when you DID get a sale, there would most probably be no income from it when the follow-up boys got there. However, there were three or four "go-aheads" out of the sales there (I got not even one out of twenty in N.Y.) - and I began to pick-up hope again. Our financial situation, after moving again, was worse than awful. It was desperate. For the first time, I missed some payments to my first wife, and lived in dread of sheriffs and alimony jail.

About this time, West Hooker called me from New York, said he had been invited to speak at a meeting in Knoxville, Tennessee, and asked me if I would go in his stead. He was definitely going to Italy, after having gained Nelson Rockefeller as a "partner", to set up the bottling business there, and did not want to get a movement going without millions of dollars, and, since no millionaire would help do the job, he was aiming to become one in his own right, and THEN start the fight.

So I agreed to go, anxious to meet the Southern contingent of "Nazis", which Hooker assured me would be there. However, I am ashamed to admit that I was so worried myself about meeting these "Nazis" that I actually used the name "George Lincoln"!

It was at this meeting, in the summer of 1956, that I met Wallace Allen, Emory Burke, and Ed Fields. Burke had launched and almost succeeded with the "Columbians" in Atlanta right after the war, but had his office infiltrated by agents of the Anti-Nazi League, dynamite planted in his garage, and had been then railroaded to a CHAIN GANG! Ed Fields was a young chiropractor whom Hooker told me was 100%.

Wallace Allen was an amazing human being. He was crippled in both legs by polio, but had such a super-human will that he threw away his crutches one night in Philadelphia - when some unspeakable louse stole them, no less. And from then on, Allen walked without them, in the most unbelievable fashion. His mind I discoverd, was so keen that he could perceive what you were getting at almost before you had the words out. This was a refreshing experience for me - as I usually have a terrible struggle making people see what would appear to be obvious. A meeting with such a man is like being a race-horse who has been forced to work in harness for years with plugs, suddenly being freed to run on a track with race-horses. With Allen, I could let my mind and ideas soar freely, with none of the usual miserable business of going back down every moment or two to recapture the lost mind of the hearer. Wallace Allen has the sharpest mind of any man I ever met, and will one day show the Jews, what it is like to feel the steel jaws of that spring-trap mind snap shut on them.

Since I had already formed the opinion that it was necessary to be an open Nazi, I tried to get the southern group to go along with this, and succeeded mostly in scaring them to death. There was no question of their sentiments, but they all felt that it was suicide to be open about it. They even tried, the next day, to keep me from speaking, but I forced the issue with the audience, and spoke on a sissy presentation of part of our present Nazi program - which I then called the "Lincoln" plan - the plan to get the Negroes back to Africa as advocated by Lincoln and by almost all our early presidents and statesmen.

I pointed out clearly to this audience of mostly Southern racists that, by themselves, as a Southern "minority", they could accomplish nothing - no matter how blazing and heroic might be their "Confederate" spirit or how their rebel yells heated the blood. In fact, the more they appeared to the rest of the Country as a fanatic and utterly different minority, wholly out of touch with the mores of the rest of the Country, the more they isolated themselves from the nationwide mass support which the White Man must have to throw off the shackles of the Jews, and the inevitable race-mixing which is the result of Jewish control. The Civil War is lost.

Most of the rest of the Country does not know the Negro as the South knows him, intimately, closely. The North, Northwest and West sees the Negro either as a rare "lawyer" or "doctor" or "teacher", when they get close - or as a "native" in the "colored section".

Intellectually, the rest of the Country pretends to love and cherish the blacks, and can kid themselves into this attitude only so long as the blacks do not get CLOSE, as they are in the South. Whenever a Negro "moves in", on them, they too become racists quickly enough. But until they have had a good dose of "brotherhood" at real close range, the great millions of the Country will persist in imagining that the only difference between blacks and white is skin color, although they know better deep down in their subconscious minds, where their instincts tell them the truth.

These millions, and the Negroes themselves - who are VOTERS, will have to be WON, if we are ever to get out of the rotten position of frustrated and beaten babblers with no POWER. And to win these soft heads and liberals, plus the Negroes themselves, we have got to propose a CONSTRUCTIVE solution to the Negro problem which can someday WIN them all over to us. Such a solution, regardless of how it is sneared at and laughed at today, is voluntary repatriation for the blacks. For far less money than we now waste on foreign aid and for communist countries who hate us, we can actually pay our Negroes a generous cash bonus, buy all their holdings in the U.S.A., build them a real industrialized area in the best part of Africa - where the ignorant Africans are clamoring for their skills and educated abilities - give them first class transportation to the new and far better living over there than their usual slums here - and then help them get set up decently in business or agriculture. To those who say that it is impossible thus to move fifteen million people, I reply that we moved far more under much more difficult conditions, and under arms - during World War II alone. It is only impossible to solve the Negro problem this way so long as people insist on not thinking about it, but keep dismissing it from their minds. It is the ONLY way that will WORK. Segregation has NEVER in history worked. As long as there is sex, and blacks and white are mingled closely geographically, no matter how stringent the rule for segregation, lust will have its way, and the society will wind up mongrelized, as did Rome, Egypt, Greece and a dozen others.

Once we have convinced the progressive, liberal "nigger lovers" that this solution is FAIR, and will work - which we will do (that is our plan for eventual election to power when we have solved the fearful Negro problem) - we will win not just the "nigger haters" in the South and elsewhere, but the soft-headed liberals who are ashamed not to like Negroes, and try to do it - but would be happier if some way could be found for the Negroes to be "gone", leaving their consciences clear and satisfied that we had done right by the blacks.

For fifty billion dollars, spread over ten years, and pumped into our national economy with healthy effects, we can one day find not a single Negro in our major cities, and, at the same time, know that we have fairly and squarely made up for the original crime of bringing them over here as slaves and selling them.

The audience was enthusiastic, and fooled me into believing there would be a lot of support for the plan to sell the blacks on the idea of voluntarily returning to Africa. So I imagined the contributions they all promised would soon come in to start work on the program, and I would once again be back in politics.

Ed Fields, the organizer of this meeting, used the occasion to establish "The United White Party", the forerunner of his present "National States Rights Party". I was unsuccessful in getting him to see that this could be only a stop-gap at best, as it was strictly southern and reeking with compromise and weakness which would sooner or later destroy it as all other such outfits have always collapsed or been destroyed. But I left Knoxville happy to have met Allen and Burke, who were openly impressed with me. I confidently believed I had "sold" my "back to Africa" "Lincoln Plan".

But as the weeks went by, I discovered I had misjudged the "hard-core" people at Knoxville, just as I had once misjudged the "patriots" and "conservatives". There was NO reaction whatsoever, no support, no help - no word, even, from these "enthusiastic" talkers - although I worked hard at the printing of material, letter-heads, etc.

The only encouraging thing was a call from Wallace Allen in Atlanta. I had let him and Emory Burke have the first proof sheets of "Battle Call" - and the two Georgians were on fire! They raved and swore by the book, and Allen begged me to come down there, and said that Atlanta was the place to fight the Jews.

There was damned little money in Pennsylvania, so I agreed to give Atlanta a try - but I did not want to move my family again, especially with my boy in school. So I went down there alone for a month or so, to see how it would work out.

In Atlanta, I put in a few hours a day making phone-calls, selling advertising in various booklets for Allen, and was staggered by the results! The first week, working less than I ever had before, I earned over two hundred dollars! The next week was good, too, then sales fell off a bit as Christmas approached. But it was still just what I was looking for. I was staying in Allen's lovely home - and working all spare time on political plans. After four weeks of this, I flew back to Lincoln for Christmas, and happily told my wife how things had gone.

It will not be hard to imagine her feelings at the prospect of moving again - but she was as loving and understanding as ever. I had the valves on the old '49 Cadillac ground, we hitched up, and once again started off across the countryside pulling that gigantic trailer - this time with FOUR little children.

We arrived in Atlanta on the coldest January day they had ever had! It was bitter, stinging cold - and, when we pulled into the trailer park I had previously arranged for, we found it wasn't ready. We had to go back outside of town to a "park" which would have been more aptly named a "dump". There was garbage all around, and, with the bitter weather, the pipes in the whole camp were frozen, along with the sewers, so that we had no water connection, no toilet facilities, and, for the first day, no heat! This was quite a situation for a mother with four kids, one a new baby, but Thora pitched in as usual and cheerfully did the best that could be done for all.

We lived on hopes at that time, apparently well founded on my pre-Christmas experience - and suffered out the first, freezing, miserable week. How little we knew that from then on, our fortunes would go from bad to worse to impossible - to that awful day in Arlington, Virginia when Arrowsmith the millionaire suddenly and without warning sent sheriffs and police to our home a writ of replevin, and my wife and I actually had to defend our home physically as the sheriffs tried to push in!

I went to work again on the advertising sales - but suddenly there was a great difference. We didn't know it, but we had hit the middle of the "recession". Allen's business was mostly with the big unions and auto-plants around Atlanta, and, when the "recession" hit, the plants closed down or slowed down, workmen didn't pay their accounts to the tradesmen, and the tradesmen cut out their advertising. I began to have to work very hard all day long to sell enough ads to make a living. Then it got worse. No matter HOW I plugged on that phone, the old customers just wouldn't buy. Their business was just too low.

At first Allen wouldn't believe that I was sincerely trying to sell the ads. Then he tried himself (he had been devoting himself to organizing and preparing the booklets, etc.) and found that it was true. The "gold-rush" was over. There was even a rough and tough scrap with one of the Union heads, and relations all around became severely strained. Allen and I quarreled. I was desperate, again, with a hungry wife and babies, far away from my usual haunts and business, and Allen couldn't help feeling somewhat responsible. He had a beautiful home, two cars, including a Cadillac, and money in the bank (all of which he had beaten out a very cruel world by his own guts and brains) and, at the time, he felt that I was trying to pressure him out of some hard-earned wealth. But he did what he could to offer me a good deal on sales, letting me keep almost all I could sell, and I drove for sales with all I had. But it was no use. Even when I beat a man into agreeing to buy an ad on the phone, the collector would often find that he had changed his mind and would not take the ad or pay.

While all this was going on, I had been corresponding with a man named William Stephenson in Newport News, Virginia. He was the publisher and editor of a handsome, well-gotten up little racist magazine called "The Virginian", much on the style of Time magazine. I had written him a letter, he had heard of me, we compared mental notes and ideas, and he seemed impressed. I sent him a suggestion for a series of cartoons called "Odd Birds", making fun of liberals, and, in a sneaky way, Jews, comparing them to birds. He liked the idea, and we agreed to produce them.

When Stephenson heard of our predicament in Atlanta, he called and gave us some very wonderful cheering up. His call yanked me out of a very deep despondency, as I saw the truly frightful living conditions for my dear wife and babies.

Stephenson invited us to come to Newport News, where he had a press and photo-offset equipment, and work with him - not on a salary, but on a sharing basis, as we published the birds, and other material. I was also to help him with promoting the magazine, etc.

So once again, with only a few dollars in our purse, we hocked my typewriter and camera equipment, and hitched up for the long, long haul back up North.

You are not allowed to drive a trailer at night, and we had to have special permission to have such a huge vehicle on the roads at all, so we had to try to plan very carefully to be at a good stopping place before dark every evening. One late afternoon, as we were nearing Cheraw, North Carolina, I felt the trailer give an uneasy heave and then yank me over to one side. We wiggled and braked to a stop, and I went back to see what was the trouble. One side was drooped way down with a blow out!

I had to jack up the multi-ton trailer with a small car jack, working in spurts and lifts, and finally set the axle on some chunks of wood I found. But meanwhile it was getting dark. The kids were hungry, tired and irritable and were crying and fussing. My wife did what she could. Then I had to unhitch and drive the tire into town someplace to get it fixed. I didn't know what to do about the trailer out in the road, and, at first thought to leave the wife and kids in the trailer, but decided against that, far out in the lonely Country. They went with me to town where we got a still worse blow.

There were no second-hand tires available in the little town, and the ONLY thing we could get was a truck tire which cost FIFTY DOLLARS! - More than we had altogether for the trip! I tried to hock various items, with the service station, including a ruby ring of my wife's - and even that would not work. Meanwhile, the State police were threatening to arrest me for leaving the trailer on the highway, and I had to assure them I was getting a tire and would be right back to move it. In utter desperation, my wife called her cousin in Washington, the wife of the first secretary of the Icelandic Embassy, and asked her to wire fifty dollars, which she did. But the humiliation and the upset and the whole mess was too much for Thora. She cried almost steadily as we struggled through the rest of that nightmare. - an almost unbelievable series of heartbreaks and misfortunes.

We bought the expensive tire with the telegraphed money, and started back in the dark for the trailer. But with the weight of the trailer off the back of the car, the "helper" springs which were inserted between the main-springs and the axle of the car popped out as we went by a swamp! Without the helper springs, we couldn't pull the trailer at all. I had to stop and try to find them in the dark swamp. First I had to crawl under the car to make sure they were both gone. Then I started an inch by inch search in the filthy muck for those little coils! For hours I hunted up and down with my boy helping as much as he could, while my

"Hate" office in State Park, New York; writing "Battle Call".

Grampaw and Jean "Sieg Heil"ing beside trailer, with photo-offset negatives for "Battle-Call" drying on a clothes-line, Pennsylvania.

Trailer "park" in Atlanta. (Note broken toilet bowl in foreground)

With Wallace Allen and Emory Burke in Allen's office in Atlanta.

Self-portrait of the family in the trailer "living-room", 1957

Kids having a bath in trailer bathtub.

Stormtroopers march with 50 foot "White Man...Fight!" banner to protest race-mixing rally, Washington, D. C.

Stormtroopers receive instructions in use of small-arms.

unhappy wife sat in the car crying with the kids. I was dispairing altogether. Then I felt my back pocket to be sure that my wallet was still there.

It WASN'T! It was GONE!

Now we not only had no springs, but no wallet! No money for gas - no way to move another inch!

I discovered the wallet had fallen out of a huge hole in my dungarees, probably when I was under the car feeling for the springs. So I started to back track along the swamp edge with the car, looking in the dark now for both the wallet and the springs. It seemed utterly useless, and I was tempted to sit down beside my wife and just cry.

Then, with one of the inexplicable events which convince me, even though I do not believe in a personal God, that there IS some inexplicable destiny at work, a man and a boy in a farm truck drove up and made me mad, at first. I had no time for games, and this man asked me, "What's your name?!"

I asked him who wanted to know, and he repeated his question. I began to be a little worried and exasperated. I was flat broke far out in the country beside a swamp in the dark looking desperately for my wallet and the spring, with a car full of crying women and children - and this guy insisted on making me identify myself!!!!!

Finally I burst out, "I'm Lincoln Rockwell - now what do you want?".

"Is this your wallet?" he said, holding up the most welcome object!

I thanked him with tears of gratitude in my eyes. He said he had seen the wallet in his headlights up the road, picked it up, and then gone LOOKING for the man who lost it!

This bit of fortune revived my spirits, and I dove into the swamp with a new determination, and shortly found the springs at the bottom of a slimy ditch. We returned to the trailer, got the springs back in, the wheel on, and started for a place to park before we were indeed arrested for driving so long after dark. I finally pulled in to a little park after making the necessary payment to the lady who had to get out of bed to wait on me. She directed me sleepily where to park, and I started over in that direction, only to bog down suddenly in a large patch of gooey mud. The wheels sunk up to the hubs, and so did the trailer. There was no place to connect up the lights or hose to take care of the kids for the night, etc. - so I had to get out of that mud.

For over an hour I struggled, moving the car to front, back, and every which way, rocking the wheels, pushing and heaving. My poor wife was out in the muck pushing with all her heart, about ready to drown herself and the children, who were now, thank God, sleeping.

Once again, the impossible happened. From a little cabin nearby a man appeared with a big chain. It was two or three in the morning, and nobody could be expected to get out of bed to help people nearby who were stuck in the mud, but THIS man did. He hitched his chain to the trailer and then to his heavy car on dry ground. I pushed with the car, he pulled with his, and my wife pushed with her bare hands. The whole parade broke loose of the goo, and we moved onto dry ground. I hooked up the lights and water with the utmost gratitude to the man who had thus helped us, and threw myself into my bed feeling like an empty, hollow shell. My blessed wife fixed the limp, sleeping kids first, then she, too, collapsed beside me. For a long time we were too tired to sleep, and lay there discussing our fortunes. My political career had led us into bitter, bitter times. We finally fell asleep trying to believe that it would soon be much better when we got to Newport News, Virginia.

Two days later, we crossed the bridge over to the peninsula containing the city of Newport News, and were met at the end of the span by Bill Stephenson, Lacy Jeffries, and Mrs. Stephenson.

They were wonderful to us. Mrs. Stephenson comforted my tired, nervous wife; Bill cheered me up immensely; and Lacy gave us twenty dollars. We were FLAT broke - without a dime left. They helped us find a trailer park, then Bill and Lacy paid the first week or so's rent, and gave us a package of weenies.

I couldn't believe such goodness, and finally asked Bill, "Why do you do all this?"

His answer I have never forgotten. It is a phrase which will soon be ringing all over this earth as the gospel spreads.

"Because we are National Socialists", he said quietly, a special, holy look in his eyes.

As long as there is a spirit like that in even a few men, our people will not perish. As long as the unholy but burning faith of the Communists and Jews is opposed by an equally burning, HOLY and TRUE faith in the hearts of Nazis, the White Man will again dominate the earth and maintain Western Civilization.

We got settled down in a rather poor place in the park (it was flooded) and we had to walk on stones to get to the trailer, but we were so grateful to be stopped and safe, and with good people that we hardly noticed this item.

I resolved to dig in and help these good people, and MAKE the cause grow and flourish from right there. It seemed, at the moment, that this was IT.

The kids before breakfast, showing trailer interior.

CHAPTER XII

"Remove your feet!" I was commanded, in the imperious tones of a Roman Emperor.

William Stephenson does not like people to put their feet on chairs, even if they (the chairs) like this one, are worthless and broken. It is part of his character. He does not ask people to do things. He commands them. He is exceptionally brilliant - possibly a genius, and he expects this fact to be properly recognized and respected.

He also does not like abnormally loud sounds, which includes my voice, so I was directed imperiously to lower my tones to a soft, gentle purr. In fact, although Bill liked me, admired my abilities and wanted me to work with him, I was banished to the garage out back as soon as I arrived, where my voice and my feet-on-chairs and other peculiarities would not disturb his creative labors.

He is dramatic beyond all words.

The first evening he pulled a 38 snub-nosed automatic out a drawer, told me his life was in deadly danger, and invited me out for coffee, ostentatiously tucking the weapon in his belt. Nobody tried to kill him. When we got back, he sat me down and kept me waiting in silence for minutes as he sat scowling behind his great desk. Suddenly he leaned over and handed down an official pronunciamento: "I have a temper!" he snapped, in clipped, precise tones, like a Scotland Yard inspector. "I DO NOT LIKE PETTY ANNOYANCES! I want you to understand, no hard feelings, but I lose control -- I am wild when I am in a temper!" Then he leaned over the desk, farther bored his eyes into mine, scowled fearfully and snarled, "I KILL!"

I accepted all this and more like it with a good grace. Bill was only twenty or so, and already making a mark in the world with an excellent publication. At the moment, I had not managed to do half as much politically. At heart, Bill was a first class guy, but didn't know it. He was pampered and spoiled to death by his mother and Lacy Jeffries, his well-to-do and very meek, very silent partner. His slightest wish was tenderly and instantly catered to, and he seemed to have grown to expect everyone around to dance attendance.

In many ways, he deserved such homage. For such a mere boy to have matured so greatly and done so much in such little time is close to genius. I was silently amused by the Roman Emperor act, and liked and respected Bill so much that it did not bother me.

We went ahead with the publication of the "Odd Birds" in high hopes that sales of the portfolio of drawings and commentaries, beautifully done, would bring in the income we so desperately needed. Bill advertised them in "The Virginian," and sent out a special mailing on the sale.

Then we waited for results.

They were miserable wretched -- heart breaking. People loved them, but not enough to pay the dollar.

Often the only thing we had to eat in the trailer was what Lacy or Bill would give us -- a can or two, some weenies, etc. Bills piled up, as usual, and the family was almost at the end of possibilities.

I went down to the Virginia employment office to see about getting ANY kind of temporary work: digging, construction, anything for pay. But they insisted on trying to get me a job according to my qualifications, and such lofty jobs were simply not available in the area.

I did manage to sell some free lance art work and some writing -- but the money situation was urgent. No payments had been made to my first wife for several months, and I was unhappy imagining the situation with little Bonnie, Nancy and Phoebe Jean -- to say nothing of the other four children. My wife's family wanted her to come to Iceland, but she didn't want to go, and I certainly didn't want her to go either. We decided to stick it out.

Meanwhile, the Virginian itself was coming upon hard days. Subscriptions and income dwindled. Their bills, like mine, piled up.

One morning Lacy Jeffries told me that it was going to be impossible to get out another issue -- they owed too much to the printer.

I pointed out that it seemed foolish to pay a printer as much money as they were, when they had an excellent press, an artist and a printer on the spot. I offered to help, but Lacy told me that it would probably irritate Bill to suggest such a plan. Stephenson was a perfectionist, and would not believe WE could turn out a decent magazine on the press we had.

Shortly after this talk, I was approached by Bill Anderson, who worked for Stephenson as a combination body-guard and clerk. He was a young boxer, a dedicated National Socialist, and the kind of FIGHTING patriot our race and Nation so desperately need. He and his family had been moved to Newport News from his home in Chicago with definite promises of pay, etc. -- much as I went to Memphis, and had moved his family down. Now he had been told that his pay would have to be severely cut, although he was on a pittance in the first place. He was also informed that he might have to be dropped altogether.

He was ANGRY! -- and I couldn't blame him. I knew his predicament from experience.

I told him I believed we could save the situation, and that we could put the magazine out by our own hard work. But Anderson said Stephenson would never let me do it -- he was too worried that I would supplant him as "Feuhrer!" I have grown to hate that word when used here in the USA. There was only ONE Feuhrer, and the use of that word in such situations affects me as it would affect a Christian to hear that some minister was insisting that he was to be called "Christ."

I agreed with Bill that Stephenson's high-handed methods were tough to take, and that the deal they were giving him was rotten -- but I insisted that it was only the product of Bill's fear. I have found that something my brother once told me is extremely valuable to remember in situations like this: people are not BAD. When they do "bad" things, it is usually because they are afraid, and they lash out wildly and foolishly like a terrified cat, scratching and biting everything in sight. I assured him that if I could diplomatically and successfully help Stephenson to get the business back on its feet, and Arrowsmith calmed down -- all could still be well.

But Bill, as Anderson had predicted, imagined that I was trying to usurp his position, and refused to so much as discuss the matter with me.

Shortly thereafter, word arrived that the "angel" of this venture, Harold Arrowsmith, Jr., was to arrive for a visit. Bill called me in and told me that the millionaire was very nervous and touchy, and it would be better if I stayed out in the garage ALL the time he was present -- and, if I had to come in, to use the back door.

Several days later, after Arrowsmith had been around for at least a day, I went into the kitchen, via the back door, and Arrowsmith was sitting at the kitchen table with Bill, sipping cocoa. I was introduced in the briefest possible fashion, and left.

A day or so after that, on a Sunday morning, I was typing on more of "Battle Call" when there was a knock on the trailer door. I opened it and found Bill Anderson and Arrowsmith balancing on the paving blocks which rose above the pond surrounding our trailer.

Bill explained bluntly that Arrowsmith was disgusted with the way Stephenson had handled the many thousands of dollars he had put into the operation, and was planning to close it up and sell the equipment. Bill said he had prevailed on Arrowsmith to come and see me, by convincing Arrowsmith that I had the talents and know-how to do something worthwhile with the enormous investment already in the venture--or at least to use the printing equipment which he was going to sell for almost nothing, just to be out of the mess.

I immediately proposed that we all go over to Stephenson together, and have it out -- in the open -- in the interest of the cause. I have always hated intrigue, and believe that the ONLY way to succeed permanently with any human undertaking is by the most open and honest possible approach, even if sneaking might gain a temporary advantage.

But Anderson and Arrowsmith rose excitedly when I suggested this, and insisted they would have no part of such a deal whatsoever. Arrowsmith said he had made his decision, he was going to close up Stephenson no matter what, and all he came to see me for was to decide if he might put the equipment at my disposal instead of selling it. Anderson said he was so angry at the two young publishers for getting him all the way from Chicago with his wife and babies that he thought Stephenson should get his just deserts for the betrayal and the imperious, inexperienced foolishness which had wrecked such a wonderful opportunity for the Cause. Anderson had been brought up in the slums of Chicago, had been knifed, beaten and shot. He was schooled in the dog-eat-dog tactics of the gutter. He himself was a pure Nordic of unimpeachable natural inclinations, but his training had taught him to be ruthless. He insisted that the only way anything could be done was to POUNCE on Stephenson, whisk out the equipment before he could recover, and that would be that. Arrowsmith, who looked something like the actor Sidney Greenstreet, and who always gave the impression of being frightened and cornered, agreed that it had to be done this way, and I was not to tell Stephenson a word.

Nevertheless, in view of Stephenson's great help and decency to me only a few months before, I went to Lacy first, and told him that Arrowsmith was very disgusted, and, unless they could come up with some definite and salable plan to win him back, it was all over. I did not tell him outright what the other two had communicated, but I asked him, in the name of the movement, to try to talk some sense into the "Divine Majesty" of Himself, William Stephenson.

Lacy Jefferies, always gentle, meek, self-effacing and easy going, agreed to see what he could do. I thought it best not to irritate the great Khan by going personally into his chambers, because of the possibility of an emotional blow-up which, upon reflection he would wish he had not permitted himself.

But it was no use.

When Bill heard the message, he raved at me, ordered me "OUT! OUT!" (in those exact words), and made very clear he believed I had conspired to ruin him and "swipe" Arrowsmith.

I tried my best to explain, without betraying the other two, that I had NO part of the plan, and was only trying to keep things TOGETHER, not destroy what already existed. But words meant nothing to Bill -- he was hurt and scared and play-acting like a little boy. Had I been his father, which I wished, I would have grabbed him, given him a convincing "argument" on both ears, and settled down to cleaning up a messy situation.

Once again I learned the weakness and silliness of even the best of my fellow human beings.

Arrowsmith and Anderson again appeared at the trailer, and berated me for having "squealed." It had all gotten back, somehow -- and I caught it now from both ends. But Arrowsmith still wanted me to do what I could to use the equipment, the press, etc., and said he was determined to cut Stephenson off immediately. If I could not come up with a plan for my use of it -- he would sell it then and there!

I could see no more use in trying to save Bill -- especially after he and his wife came over and dumped some of my things at the trailer, including a lovely cashmere sweater my wife had gone to a great deal of trouble to get from England for his wife. There was no use letting the equipment be lost to the cause, so I agreed to think it over and talk to them both the next day.

I had let Arrowsmith borrow my "Battle Call" proofs, and he was very enthusiastic, except for the "Socialist" part of "National Socialist." He, as a multi-millionaire super capitalist (Bill had told me his mother was one of the owners of Dunn and Bradstreet) -- was understandably much against any doctrine that EVERYBODY in society had to PRODUCE SOMETHING, either by invention, management, labor or genuine risk -- but not by "speculation" which is so hedged by usury as to make it no risk at all. We, of course, as National Socialists, are AGAINST the speculative part of capitalism. Arrowsmith, so far as I have been able to learn, never worked a day in his life, and likes this arrangement

But the rest of the program, especially the part about gassing the Jew traitors, he thought was wonderful. He objected to exempting ANY Jews--said none of them were human, but were sub-animals. I asked him if he could personally kill little children because they were Jews, and he answered, "OF COURSE!" -- and I almost, but not quite, believe him. He is too squeamish to eat meat, so it is a little hard to picture him in the bloody role of baby slaughterer.

The next day he came over in his rented car and drove me down to a deserted beach, where we parked and discussed the situation for many hours. He wanted to know what I thought should be done. I told him that the only place in the world where a strong movement could succeed was in Arlington, Virginia, right across from the Nation's Capitol. In every other place the Jews could put so much pressure on the authorities that any strong anti-Jewish effort would be ruthlessly and illegally crushed. But in Washington -- the show place of America and the "free" world -- while they could hurt us badly, the usual Jewish inspired gross violations of all justice and rights to silence exposure of Jewish treason would be too obvious, and thus impossible. Too many people would see and hear about it, no matter how they tried to cover it up, use the "silent treatment," and smear us out of existence. Also, Virginia is still in the hands of decent White Men. Senator Byrd is no Adolf Hitler, to be sure, but he is also no Wayne Morse or Jacob Javits. The courts, largely set up by Byrd, were honest, I believed then -- and have since proved this. Virginia is one of the last, if not THE last State in the Union which is still governed somewhat in the manner intended by the framers of the Constitution. Her officials, while afraid of the Jews at their worst would nevertheless not crawl disgustingly at the feet of the Jews, as the officials of most other states and the federal government are doing today.

Arrowsmith wanted to establish a center where we could print his thousands of revelations of the unbelievable, nightmarish confessions of the Jews themselves, as to their treachery and treason. He was entranced by the idea of such a center right near the Congress, which he loves to visit -- and I had little trouble selling him on the idea of setting up in Arlington. He wanted me to work on an all-out anti-Jewish campaign in PUBLIC, leading to the eventual destruction of Jewry, while we also flooded Congress and official Washington with the incriminating anti-Jewish documents he had gathered in such abundance.

I told him that if he wanted me to work in the WIDE OPEN, as he insisted, I would have to have a safe home and living for my wife and babies. He agreed, and said he would provide that, if I had the guts to come out openly and strongly with the WHOLE story, and "spill the beans," as he called it.

We agreed that I would have a secure home with a printing shop installed, using the equipment now in Stephenson's place, that I would be accorded the privilege of buying the house out of printing profits as I worked the equipment, and I would go all out against the Jews, and print documents as he required.

He wanted to use the name "National Committee to Free America From Jewish Domination", and I agreed to that. I must confess that in spite of all my intellectual conviction of the rightness of open Nazism -- at that time I shared the illusion, still common in the "movement", that any swastika-displaying Nazis would be quickly jailed or murdered. The Jews just seemed too powerful, and I planned to sort of gradually slide over to the open Nazism from the "National Committee".

Even then, we discussed the matter of an office, and I actually imagined that if I set up such an office, I would need body-guards at all times just to go in and out of such an office! Today I go alone to our post office box, in the name of the "American Nazi Party", and realize how ridiculous such fear of the Jews is. But even three years ago, before I had found out the actual strength of the Jews, and the loose nature of their conspiracy, I, like millions of other Americans still do, imagined the power of these sneaks was TOTAL -- that open defiance of them was somehow "sure death"! As a matter of fact, the very fact that I have learned the weaknesses of the Jews, and can debunk their myth of invincible terror, makes me too dangerous for the Jews to permit my continued activity, if there is any way under heaven -- or in hell -- they can stop me.

Once Arrowsmith was ready to go, he couldn't wait. He was actually fidgetty, like a fat little boy waiting for a parade, and insisted that we start INSTANTLY.

Stephenson had announced he was a terror, of course, and would battle to the death to hold the equipment, and told Anderson, whom he didn't realize was involved with Arrowsmith, that he would sabotage the press and equipment before it would go out. But Arrowsmith got a justice of the peace and was told how to get a writ, etc. -- and when Bill heard this, he capitulated. Arrowsmith went to get the stuff with a truck, and Bill confined his "fight to the death" to calling a policeman to have his former benefactor thrown off the premises!

Once again, I realize that there will be howls of agony from many in the right wing at my revelations of all this foolishness and squabbling. "Why hurt these people now?" is the cry -- "It's all over! -- What good can it do?"

The answer, again, is that even as I write this with two black eyes, a torn mouth and a broken nose from a JEWISH organized beating, the Canadian Intelligence Service, headed by Ron Gostick, a good patriot in Canada, has just published a whole pamphlet and spread it all over the world, explaining in great detail, and with devilish but perverted logic -- that I am a spy working for the JEWS!

The petty jealousies, the selfishness, the ignorance, the meaness and stupidity of the right wing has got to STOP -- and I mean to stop it not by begging these people, in the name of our dying race and nation -- (I've tried that with no success for five years) -- but by making it IMPOSSIBLE for these fearful small minds to keep wrecking the movement. Within a short time, it will be out of the question for "sneaky, sissy Nazis" to set up in business and start the usual round of petty squabbling, spy-stories and sabotage of the REAL holy cause which they keep wrecking.

There is nothing like the light to dispell darkness -- and light is what we are going to spread all over the right wing, where darkness and ignorance and fear lie like a stifling black blanket over everything and everybody.

As the story progresses, the reader will see the full villainy and cowardice and treachery not of the Jews alone -- but OUR people.

No talk, no logic, no sweet pleas on bended knee, no letters or prayers have been able to stop the tragic, heart-rending

The Red-Tinged Blackbird

GENUS: NOTSOGOOD MARSHALLICUS

THE RED-TINGED BLACKBIRD, originally a native of Africa, was, in its jungle trees and vines, a rather interesting bit of wild life. In its natural state it tends to eat its brothers and sisters and otherwise behave rudely, but its strong sense of rhythm and irresponsible nature give it a certain curious interest to the cultured observer, as long as it does not get too close. Recently, however, these savage birds show a tendency to confuse themselves with the Birdologist himself, especially when influenced by BROTHERHOOD BUZZARDS. Spurred on by the BUZZARDS, more and more of these wild BLACKBIRDS are flying up out of the forests and pretending to be the same as canaries, except for color. Millions of them are positively drunken with the idea of mixing all birds together so that, instead of blackbirds, canaries, eagles, parrots, chickens, peacocks and humming birds, we will have only a single, dingy brown "neutral" bird, which does not lay eggs, doesn't sing, doesn't look pretty, doesn't do anything except work slavishly for the sly BUZZARDS—the only bird not supposed to "mix" in this scheme.

When they de-junglize like this, the BLACKBIRDS develop a distinct red color in certain areas, hence the name, "RED-TINGED BLACKBIRDS. They may also be recognized by their characteristic call, "EEEEEE-quali-TEEEEEE!"

Many Birdologists, distressed by hordes of these aggressive BLACKBIRDS, try to solve the problem by beating and flailing at the dingy flocks as they sweep down, never realizing that the BLACKBIRDS themselves have almost nothing to do with the matter. They are simply tools of the sly BROTHERHOOD BUZZARDS; even the "National Association for the Advancement of Blackbirds" is not run by BLACKBIRDS, but by these same ugly BUZZARDS.

With the evil influence of the BUZZARDS removed, the BLACKBIRDS would quickly revert to their happy-go-lucky jungle ways, croaking and hopping to their savage rhythms, sitting motionless in the sun for hours, and occasionally, perhaps, consuming an aged uncle for Sunday dinner.

There is no sense in hating or fighting the RED-TINGED BLACKBIRD, no matter how aggressive it SEEMS to be. It is only an honest, less able bit of Nature, unnaturally stolen and pushed out of its nest, and forced to act as a battering ram for the BUZZARDS in their insane effort to run all the other birds, and steal all the eggs.

One of the Odd Birds done in Newport News

The children on steps of new house, on way to Sunday School

My kids teaching their little guests to Heil Hitler
-birthday party in our back yard.

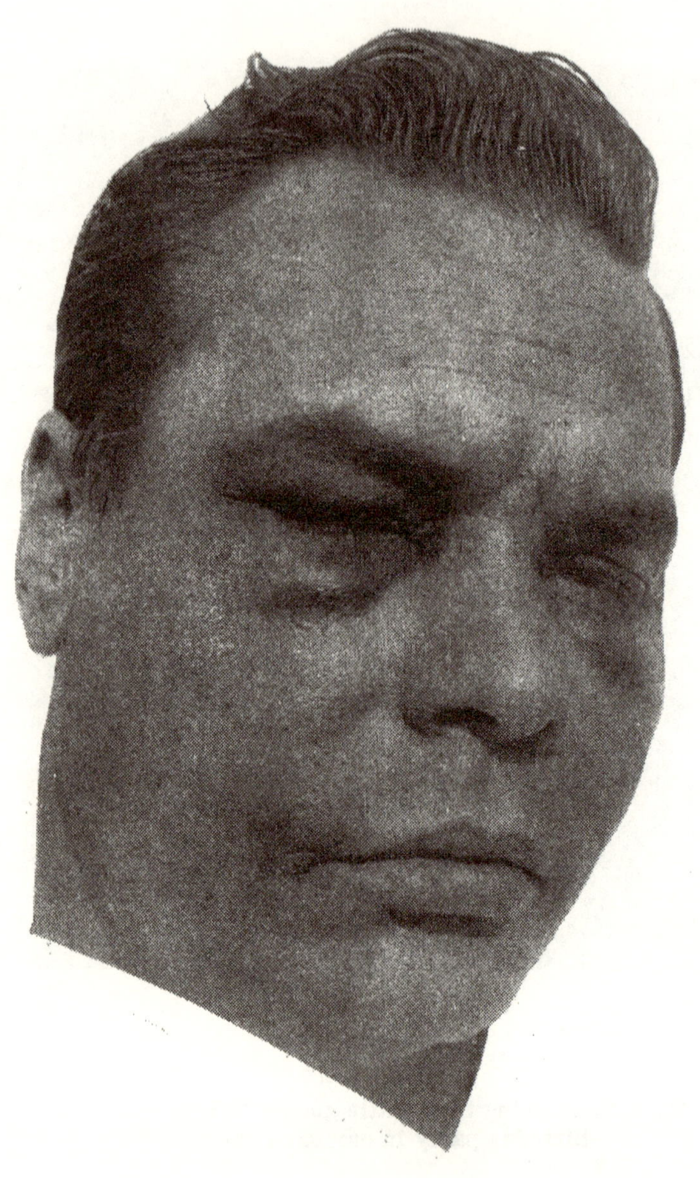

My condition while writing these words - the results of a beating
I got from four hired hoods

squabbling and bickering and sabotage by peanut-souls in the right wing. Just as we cannot beat the Jews and their subversion by TALK, and must build the FORCE and POWER to depose them -- so must we use all legal forms of FORCE to bring order and direction to the right wing. And when chaos prevails, as it does now in the right wing, it is inevitable that people get hurt when you apply that force to establish order. But the hurt to one or two people who claim to believe in our holy cause will mean nothing later when we have demonstrated, as we are doing, our ability to help even those we might now "hurt" to WIN -- beside which even a severe "hurt" is nothing.

If we cannot WIN the most desperate battle for survival in the history of humanity, it will not make me proud to have been a "good guy" and failed to bring order -- and VICTORY to the pitiful right wing.

Even those who may be personally angry at the exposures here, will know that they are true, and those with which they are not familiar are equally true. I have already made peace with more than one of the people already mentioned and will one day make peace gratefully with all of them as soon as they give up childish squabbling and buckle down to FIGHTING -- either with us, or by themselves -- just as long as they do not commit treachery or treason to the CAUSE.

Arrowsmith was almost frantic to get started not as soon as possible, but immediately. He wanted me to try to find some place to set up in Arlington by telephoning to friends, even before we went up there to find a permanent place. I managed to find a temporary place in a friend's basement.

Meanwhile we looked for a permanent place -- and I got to know my new "fat cat".

Arrowsmith was nocturnal, I learned -- a habit just the opposite of mine. I love the morning, and like to go to bed seasonably at night. But he would insist that I sit up until three, four or five every night talking to him about the "eskimos" as he called the enemy. He also made it impossible for me to do anything else to earn any money -- and then welched on his promises to pay me enough to eat while I worked for him. I had a very bad tooth, and my face swelled out like a grapefruit -- but I could not afford a dentist, and this multi-millionaire made me

BEG, night after night, sitting in my car outside of his hotel in Alexandria, for the small money he had promised me to get set up. I was FLAT broke, the wife and kids had NO money, nothing to eat -- and he treated every respectful request for even part of what he had promised as a criminal swindle.

With my head throbbing and swollen in grinding pain, I had to sit for hours listening to this chubby mamma's boy telling me all the delightful projects he had in mind. I would BEG him to get out of the car and go to bed, and let me get some rest and some aspirin, and he would just look hurt and say, "Yes, but the point is ------", and then launch into more lecture.

One night about 5 A.M., in spite of everything, in spite of my impossible financial situation, in spite of my wife and children, in spite of the alimony jail and my other wife and children, in spite of all reason and sanity -- in spite of instinct for survival -- I had had all I could take. I jumped out of the car, ran around to his side, opened the door and told him to get out.

He wouldn't do it. He sat there looking as though he were about to cry, and pouted. He said I was cutting off my nose to spite my face, and told me there was no point in being stupid -- etc., etc., etc.

I cooled off, somehow, and we went back to negotiating.

We found a lovely suburban home which seemed made to order. It was in the Williamsburg section of Arlington, and, amazingly, was zoned "commercial" -- which we needed for the political headquarters and offices. We met with the real estate people and settled arrangements at a long conference. Arrowsmith was to make the downpayment of $15,000 plus settlement and we were to make the mortgage payments, with the principle accruing to us. We were also to pay Arrowsmith on the downpayment loan as we profitted in the printing. We were to have use of the printing equipment. I was to print his material and help him with layout on a book he was getting up. In addition, I was to make an all-out attack on Jewish Communism-Zionism with our "National Committee to free America from Jewish Domination," and Arrowsmith guaranteed a home and the printing equipment for a livlihood for my family's security. There was to be a contract drawn up between Arrowsmith and myself committing this arrangement to paper, and insuring that neither of us would find ourselves "holding the bag" in such a risky, if not dangerous, operation.

Arrowsmith was in a terrible rush to get to New York for something, and left a check with a friend for $ 15, 300 that afternoon, then disappeared. I had the contract drawn up by a lawyer who was also one of the officers of my squadron at Anacostia -- but I could not find Arrowsmith to get the papers signed. I had arranged, through a friend in the White House, to get Arrowsmith introduced to some key political personnel in New York to track down some information on how Trotsky (Bronstien), after getting in serious trouble here in 1917 was able to get all sorts of immigration "favors," and finally took twenty million dollars of Jewish American money to Russia via the port of New York. But none of us could find the elusive millionaire. The papers went unsigned.

I could not stop to hunt him up myself -- I had to scramble to "keep all the balls in the air." I had to sell our trailer, get the press going in the new place, move, find business, print sample propaganda material and get it out to the right wing "customers," and generally start things rolling.

After a few weeks I was having some success at this, when Arrowsmith suddenly appeared one afternoon, and said it was time for "action." He had set up the machinery, he felt, and he wanted to see some RESULTS. He asked me what could be done to shock and wake up the world.

As I had been thinking and planning for years, I told him the only answer was PUBLIC activity -- street action -- not any more pamphlets and paper-exchanging among people who already knew what the Jews were up to.

At the time, the Jewish line in all our newspapers was, paradoxically, that Nasser was both another Hitler, and also a Communist. As a matter of sober fact, Nasser had outlawed the Communist party and thrown his reds in jail--while our Supreme Court was letting ours, even the spies, out. The only Communist party in the Middle East was, and is, in Israel, where these criminals constitute over one-fourth of the citizens and government. There was a pro-Jewish puppet government in Lebanon. The enraged Lebanese Arab people, who had suffered and seen over a million Arabs driven into starvation and misery in the desert so that the Jews could "take back a homeland" occupied by the Arabs for over two thousand years --threatened to take over their traitorous government and go after the International Criminals who had butchered and banished their Arab brothers.

The Jews here used their usual tactics -- press distortion and secret pressure, to force our government to send US Marines to "defend" Lebanon from its own people -- and were arrogantly lying that this was to stop Nasser's"Communism!"It was actually to save Israel.

I appeared to have a home, security for my family, and a perfect chance to do what all others had so long talked about -- ATTACK and EXPOSE the Jewish treachery in PUBLIC -- so I suggested that we organize picketing in several cities, and at the White House, along with literature distributions, to expose this vicious use of American men on behalf of Jewish international aggression in Lebanon.

Arrowsmith was as delighted as a chubby kid going to a circus. He clapped his pudgy hands and asked how we could do it.

My years of apprenticeship in the movement had established contacts with other men all over the country, and I had some in several cities who I thought would cooperate. I had not been in Arlington long enough to build up any contacts with young fighting men, and had only "conservative" whisperers and "silent workers." So I told Arrowsmith that, to picket the White House, we would have to send for my boys -- Hooker's boys -- in New York. It would cost, altogether -- for signs, literature and transportation -- over a thousand dollars. Arrowsmith said go ahead. He couldn't wait. I told him it would involve telephone bills of a size I couldn't handle, and he said he would "take care of it."

So I arranged with New York for a chartered bus-load of the boys, designed and silk-screened huge oil-cloth signs in fluourescent red and black, wrote, designed and printed tens of thousands of two-color leaflets, prepared minute directions for the pickets, telephoned all over the US and managed to get Ed Fields, in Louisville and Wallace Allen in Atlanta, to agree to picket simultaneously with us, and made the thousand other arrangements necessary to such a relatively large-scaled operation. Arrowsmith hovered over all this like a happy boy, even helping silk screen the signs in the cellar.

My wife took all the excitement and disruption of her home in excellent spirits, losing her temper only once. Arrowsmith got purple with fury one afternoon as he and I were discussing plans and the kids were laughing and playing in the next room. He had burst out, "Oh! Dear! Can't you DO something about those damned kids. GAS them, or something!" My wife had flared up and scolded him for the remark, and he had turned away, pouting. I had managed to patch it up with both of them.

All this time, whenever I asked Arrowsmith about signing the contract, he would get angry and complain that I was trying to hold up operations - he would do that after the picketing, when he had a chance to catch his breath and look the contract over.

I was about to learn my next-to-last lesson in not trusting people.

The night before the great event, the bus-load of boys from New York arrived, and it was great to see some of them again. But they had with them a wild and wooley slob by the name of George Legget, whose first remark, as he drove up and observed that we lived next to a suburban bank, was "Oh boy! Let's knock over the bank!"

I warned him again and again that our survival and eventual success depended on nothing any more than being legal and SUPER legal. We not only had to obey laws they HAD - but laws they MIGHT have, or pretend to have,just to get rid of us.

But it was no use. George went out with one crew to distribute our for-that-time BOLD anti-Jewish literature announcing the picketing, and I soon learned that he was nothing more nor less than mad. He pasted stickers on cars, windows, and was about to stick one on an unobserving policeman, when the boys caught him and brought him back to me. I threw him out, but he wouldn't go. We finally managed to convince this fat nut that the New York police were wise to his leaving New York. He was on parole or something, so we got him on a bus back up there.

Meanwhile, I was learning my first lessons in the ways of the Jewish conspiracy. I still imagined, at that time, that the power of the Jews was TOTAL, that the police were a hundred percent in cahoots with the conspirators, and that I must therefore SNEAK out our papers, or expect wholesale arrests.

When our first crew WAS arrested in Arlington, their literature siezed, and then "run out of town" - I SNEAKED them back, instead of openly going to the police and DEMANDING our constitutional rights FIRST, as I always do now. But at that time, we ducked and hid and scurried down back streets trying to avoid policemen, who, I have since learned, hate what is going on as much as we do, and merely do their best to be FAIR, be neutral, and obey orders.

Many in the "movement" can't understand how I "get away" with what we do, unless we are "spies", as they foolishly and cruelly charge.

Until our arrival on the right-wing scene, it was believed that the Police and the FBI and all other authorities are "against" us, and we must "fight" them!

I have proved to those associated with me here, over and over that this is not true. To be sure, the money-power is in the hands of the Jews, and so is much of our administration. Some of our officials are either Jews or openly work for Jews. But the great bulk of our law-enforcement officials are WHITE MEN and simply ENFORCE the LAW - the best they know how. If anything, most of them, being by nature men of FORCE, tend to see things with us, not criminal "niggers" and Jews. But I have found they generally do not permit these opinions to influence their performance of duty much. They have almost all been uniformly courteous and fair to me and to our open, brutally frank anti-Jewish agitation.

I have found that they are as prone to follow the jungle instinct of pursuit as any creature; when you RUN, they chase you. But when you GO TO THEM FIRST, explain your plans, your knowledge of your rights, and respectfully make clear your steely determination to exercise those rights, they respect you and often go to bat for you.

When they see the outrageous pressure brought by the Jews to stop you illegally, unfairly, brutally and even criminally - you don't have to give them a lecture about Jewish methods, for the police to be on fire with a sense of outraged justice. THIS is how we have won the hearts of entire police departments.

No matter what the Jews do at the upper levels, the policemen and officers, the FBI agents, and the honest officials who deal with us know we break our backs bending over to be fair and square and legal, while the Jews resort to such vile and disgustingly obvious tactics to shut us up that the officials can't HELP but admire our calm and determined courage as we stand up to this kind of tyranny and terror, day after day, week after week, year after year.

I have had high officials and judges tell me privately that our public DEMONSTRATION of Jewish tyranny, and the pressure they themselves have experienced as a result of that filthy Jew pressure, has "awakened" them to a situation that not all the patriotic literature in a million years could have made them see. Most of the right-wing's complaints of political persecution by Gentile officials is their own fault in strategy and tactics. I survive, and will continue to survive, because MILLIONS of people are beginning to see with their own eyes, and hear with their own ears what they will never, never READ - another reason why the paper-patriots have been failing so many years with their "wake up America" campaign.

But on those hot July days in 1958, I hadn't yet learned these tremendous truths, and wasted a lot of time and effort "hiding" and running.

Nevertheless, we got out a large number of pamphlets, and prepared to picket the next day, Sunday. It is almost impossible for me to imagine it now, but we were all scared to death. My New York boys, tough as tigers, were restless and worried, and their leader, Luke Dommer, proved to be a complete coward. He told them they would all be killed by "three or four hundred niggers", and got them all determined to quit on me! Then he shoved off for New York on a bus, and left me with a mutiny.

I mustered the lads around me in the back yard, and told them that I was going down there ALONE, if necessary, and I never wanted to see any of the men who would desert me, again. Especially I would never tolerate them calling themselves "Nazis" after such cowardice.

They listened in silence, and, after I stalked off and went back to work on tacking signs to sticks, I thought I would indeed be alone.

Then a Greek kid came up, started helping me with the signs and said he'd go, and the hell with the others. Another lad came over and silently began to push in tacks. Then another. Finally they all came over. I thanked them with an overflowing heart.

When it came time to go, I left one lad to watch my family, and held my wife and looked into her eyes a long time. I really didn't know if I would ever be back - silly as it sounds today. Our signs, using words like "Kike" and showing vile pictures of these hook-noses, were something never seen in public before, and we had received plenty of threats and warnings of arrests and beatings or killings. I was really very scared - as scared as I ever was during two wars.

As usual, Thora was brave and inspiring, and I left determined to succeed or die that day.

We got out of our cars several blocks down the street from the White House, and, with pounding hearts, marched toward the scene of action.

As we approached the White House, a solid phalanx of eight or nine police approached us, with a bull-dog-faced gold-braided captain marching in front.

I was positive this was "it". We would all be arrested, and I would be martyred before I started my fight.

But the rough looking old captain was a man I have come to know as one of the finest old-line cops - and great-hearted human beings - I ever met. It was Captain Mahanney, of the Special Investigations Unit of the D. C. Police. He growled at me that there were certain rules to be obeyed in picketing the White House and he showed me where we were to march.

I would have been relieved under ordinary circumstances, but there were still the "three hundred niggers" we had been warned of, to say nothing of Jews and Communists! I looked around for them! There weren't many yet, but they were there, and they eyed us with relish, like meat.

I stepped off, carrying the worst sign, "Save Ike from the KIKES", with a gigantic picture of an ugly Jew holding a gun at Ike's head - and waited for my fate. The boys stepped off behind me, and we soon had a line moving briskly back and forth between the two trees where thousands of pickets have marched on behalf of and against everything from the Rosenbergs - the Communist Jew spies - to John Kasper.

The ADL photographers were there, and the Jews and hoods began to gather at both ends of our line, and across the street. We kept picketing, and began to settle down a bit. We were still alive at least.

There were no huge mobs such as I have since learned to expect, and control, and no "300 niggers" to send us to the morgue in the meat-wagons.

As soon as things appeared somewhat stable, a man walked past me, as I distributed orange-juice to the thirsty pickets, and whispered "somebody wants to see you over behind the statue", and he jerked his thumb in the direction of a monument in the park across the street.

I knew who it was, of course. I could see his cherubic little face peeking out from behind the stones, and he beckoned to me as I looked that way.

So I had to make a few trips over there for "instructions" from the high-command, the general.

Bill Stephenson also came by, wearing dark-glasses and with his collar pulled way up over his chin. He muttered, "hello" darkly, dramatically, and moved on without giving any sign of recognition.

But I was happy! I had dared the "impossible", and made it!

When we were finished picketing, the Captain observed that there might be some pursuit by the howling crowd which had gathered. I had planned to drive to the police station, if the mob was too large and murderous, but we got a police escort to Haine's Point, where the boys were staying and the chartered bus was parked. We sent out for beer for the celebrating boys, and

Arrowsmith appeared with an Arab whom he said was the head of Nasser's intelligence.

I had warned Arrowsmith to have nothing to do with Arabs, since we were picketing on the Lebanon situation, and I wanted no charges of being a foreign agent. He had nevertheless brought this intelligence officer into the house, where my wife and another lady met him, and he now gave him all our oil-cloth signs. He later told me that they were displayed to Nasser in Cairo.

I went home to my wife in what I thought was glory. I had accomplished exactly what I had set out to do, and what Arrowsmith wanted me to do. It seemed too good to be true. It wasn't.

I was actually on my way to the desperate battle to survive and keep my sanity in the face of crushing poverty, desertion and attack by everything and everybody, and circumstances so discouraging as to be beyond description.

For years I had been saying to my wife, when things got bad in my political career, "This is not the worst. Ahead lie far more difficult days!". She would never believe me - which is not hard to understand!

Now she was to see how true was my prediction.

I thank God I didn't know what was ahead. I am not that brave.

In a few days, we got the news that there had been trouble in the other cities where we had picketed. Ed Fields' group had picketed successfully, but had had people arrested for distributing literature. In Atlanta, our silent, orderly pickets were arrested in THREE MINUTES.

There had been no crowd in Atlanta early on Sunday when they began - no disorder, no word from our pickets. But a police official testified that he got a call from the Anti-Defamation League of B'nai B'rith demanding the arrest of the pickets, and threatening violence if the police did NOT arrest them. So, in a pattern we have learned to know all too well, the police did not seize these threateners of violence and kidnapping, but arrested our pickets and charged them with disturbing the peace and disorderly conduct!

The methods used in Atlanta were cruder than anything we have ever experienced in Washington. The pickets were held in close confinement, threatened and pressured to plead guilty. In one place in the transcript of their trial it shows clearly that one of the pickets was told by police that if they did not accept their punishment, or if they appealed, they would "be tied in with any bombing"!!!! Those were the exact words of a police official, A FEW WEEKS BEFORE THE BOMBING OF THE ATLANTA SYNAGOGUE!

Our pickets refused to bow to such pressure, and DID appeal. After I called him, Russell Maguire, to his credit, sent $ 500 to Arrowsmith to help the Atlanta fight.

Wallace Allen flew up for a meeting with Arrowsmith and me at his room in the Congressional Hotel in Washington, and he told us some unbelievable stories of what was going on in Atlanta. That Southern City has become a stronghold of Jewry, worse than New York, in some ways, because people do not realize the Jewish domination as they do in New York, and they can get away with more raw methods.

Allen told us they had discovered a spy in their little group down there, a sneaky character named L. E. Rogers. He described to Arrowsmith and me how this Rogers had seized the confidential picketing directions I had packed with the signs, when they arrived in Atlanta, and had scooted off to his home with them. Allen and the boys had to go get them back. Later, when John Kasper was released from the Atalanta Penitentiary, and they wanted somebody to greet him, but didn't want the smears and publicity attendant thereon, they had cagily sent Rogers to do the public greeting, and he had not been able to get out of it. Allen thought this was pretty funny at the time.

He also told us that Rogers was forever suggesting dynamiting at the meetings they held in Atlanta. I have learned from this. Whenever anybody in our meetings even vaguely suggests bombing or anything the least bit illegal, we call the police or the FBI immediately. But the boys in Atlanta, while wanting no part of such illegal activity, hesitated to judge, convict and turn in a supposed "fellow patriot" on such slim evidence. Everybody hates to be a "squealer" - so Rogers got away with this provocation - which I have since learned is one of the most easily recognized mark of the Jewish-paid provocateur.

I thought little of the story of Rogers at the time, except to laugh at Wallace's cleverness in sending him to welcome Kasper! The Jews were about to teach us a healthy lesson.

A few weeks later, on October 12, 1958, headlines all over the world blared the bombing of the Atlanta Synagogue! It made little impression on me. My wife and I were lying in bed one morning watching the early morning news on TV, when suddenly we saw Wallace Allen being arrested in the home we knew so well, with his wife and kids saying goodbye to him as he was dragged off to jail! They HAD tied our pickets in with a bombing, exactly as threatened!!! All of them were accused of bombing the Atlanta synagogue!

That early morning explosion had blown my whole life apart forever!

Now, under the pressure of the Jews, the Atlanta police really displayed an illegal ferocity which was unbelievable!

Our pickets were arrested without warrants, charged with vagrancy, held incummunicado, unmercifully driven and hounded to confess to a crime of which they knew nothing. Spies and liars were placed in their cells, in hopes they would reveal something incriminating!

They were charged under a special law which could result in the electric chair if they were convicted! The whole right wing was investigated by agents of the F.B.I., seeking National tie-ins with the "bombers".

Meanwhile, sure that I had no connection with all this, except to help Allen and the boys all I could, I had to push hard to keep my head above water in Arlington. No matter how I begged and pleaded, I could not get Arrowsmith to pay the huge phone bill he had said he would "take care of", and this, and other bills, plus food money were urgent. Then Arrowsmith disappeared again! I heard rumors that he was in New York, and had contacted my boys up there, but I paid little attention. My mind was rivetted on Atlanta and the deadly drama going on down there, as the Jews attempted to literally murder our people in the electric chair as a lesson not to oppose them.

Rockwell, right, clenches fist after being hit and returning to microphone. Rasmusson, left, steps in to restrain crowd on stage.

Cherry grapples with Leonard Holstein, a Rockwell aide from Los Angeles. Jay Rasmusson, student wh invited Rockwell, is at left.

My first picket line in front of the White House, July 29, 1958

WORLD UNION OF FREE

ENTERPRISE

NATIONAL SOCIALISTS

11 March, 1959
AMERICAN PARTY
Command Headquarters
6512 Williamsburg Blvd.
Arlington 13, Virginia

The President of the United States of America
The White House,
Washington, D. C.

Sir:

This organization and its affiliates fervently hopes that you have not lost your commendable and widely advertised determination to bring the despicable bomber of the Atlanta Synagogue to justice.

With George Bright, the first of the five brave men who picketted against treason and lies at the request of this headquarters, now proven completely innocent, and the rest of the picketters apparently not to be tried because they are so obviously innocent, it is clear that the real culprit or culprits are still at large.

We have gathered voluminous evidence clearly indicating that the crime was committed by a Negroe or Negroes hired by a certain L. E. Rogers, under the direction of a group of Communists of Jewish extraction. Their aim was to prevent the growing awareness in the South of the conspiratorial activities of a vicious group of Communist, Zionist Jews who are seeking to promote racial hatred and violence.

If you are sincere in deploring this violence, as we are, we feel sure you will want to track down and prosecute to the limit of the law the villains who blew up the Temple and thus injected violence into a tragic and dangerous situation.

I stand ready to supply you or your representatives with the available but presently unused facts which will destroy this Communist plot and expose the perpetrators to the righteous wrath of the American people, and the legal punishment they so justly deserve.

Most respectfully,

Lincoln Rockwell, COMMANDER,
AMERICAN PARTY,
W. U. F. E. N. S.

Letter sent to the President after the bombing of the Atlanta Synagogue. The FBI dutifully investigated, and, as usual, the Jews in the Justice Department hushed the matter up. In spite of the hue and cry from the Jews, they now want the matter hushed up!

Part of the huge crowd in the Amphitheater listening to the damning facts about the Jew-Communist conspiracy against America and the White Race; San Diego State College, San Diego, California.

But then the rumors from New York became more disturbing. Some of the boys called and told me loyally that Arrowsmith was up there trying to buy leadership of the best and fightingest bunch of men in America with his money, and the press and equipment he had pledged to me and my family for launching this desperate battle. He wanted to snatch the equipment from me, as he had from Stephenson, and send it to New York. But I felt that I had him sufficiently committed before witnesses so that, even without the contract which he would never sign, he could not do such an unjust and immoral thing to my family and me.

I reckoned without the spoiled nature of the little rich boy - Harold. He was used to having his money get him anything he wanted when he wanted it. You can always hire lawyers and buy people - almost all people.

I was down in the cellar printing for a lawyer in Annapolis, when my wife came running down the stairs wiping her hands on her apron and said to me in Icelandic, "There's a man here with a truck and some papers to pick up the press and the other stuff!".

I shut off the press and went up to see about this. Sure enough there was a truck out front from Baltimore, and a man with a "bill-of-sale" at the door. He insisted he had "bought" the equipment and was going to remove it on the spot.

I called the police and they said I had the right to forbid the man to come on my premises, and this is what I did. But not before I called Arrowsmith and tried to find out what it was all about. He pretended not to be in and had his mother say he was out of Baltimore. But I heard him, and called back in a few minutes, using the name of the man with the truck from Baltimore. This time the sneak answered. For an hour and a half (on my long-distance bill) he whined at me that it was my duty to turn over the equipment and move out of the house.

I told him that I would not move out in less than a year, since that was the minimum even in our verbal contract, and that I would not release the equipment he had pledged to me and the family. I did my best to make him see what a horrible injustice being thrown in the streets without a livelihood was to my wife and kids, even if I had done something wrong, but he couldn't even state anything I had done wrong or unfair to him. The best he could work up was that I was a poor printer!

I had to hang up on him to stop the phone bill. He kept saying over and over that I was to turn over the equipment and move out.

A few days later, the press and then the F.B.I. called on me, within hours of each other. I was told of a letter I had written to Wallace Allen, in which I signed "Sieg Heil", and asked if it were mine. I truthfully answered that it was. They had discovered it when they seized Allen and searched his house.

They asked me all about my operation, and Arrowsmith's part in it, and I again told them the truth. We were all under suspicion of complicity in the Atlanta bombing, and lying would only get us into serious trouble - conceivably to share the electric chair with the unfortunate pickets in Atlanta, and there was no point in trying to conceal Arrowsmith's ownership of the house. It was on file in the county offices.

Within hours the nation's newspapers emblazoned across entire front pages the headlines that there was a national underground bombing ring under suspicion by the F.B.I. - and that Arrowsmith and I were the money-bags and mastermind, respectively!!!!!

Arrowsmith scurried to the F.B.I. offices demanding protection.

My home became the target for unbelievable abuse! Cherry bombs were thrown from speeding cars, my kids were stoned, our phone rang constantly, and some of the callers had my wife in tears with the viciousness of their threats and abuse. A car swerved into a parking lot driveway in the dark when I was walking home with a bag of groceries from the supermarket across the street - and nearly hit me. I escaped only by leaping on my face in the nick of time. My boy in school was insulted and hated. One cherry bomb went into an open window and exploded in the bed of my sleeping little four-year-old angel, Jeannie. I doubt she will ever forget the terror of that experience as she came screaming into our arms. I will never forget it, or forgive the bigots, the stupid half-wits and the bullies who did that! One morning we found a home-made bomb on the lawn, a huge piece of pipe capped at both ends and loaded with explosives! If it had gone off, we would have all been killed.

Now Arrowsmith really went into action!

While we were trying to get hardened to this wild life, and still survive and make a living and keep the family going, my wife again came down to the cellar and informed me that there were two sheriffs and policemen at the door with a writ of "replevin". Arrowsmith meant business!

I was determined not to give up without a fight, and checked with a lawyer friend in my navy squadron who had told me that they could not force their way in without a search warrant.

But the sheriff told me they didn't need a warrant, and tried to force his way in a couple of times. I held him out. Then he sent for more men, more police, and the top Sheriff of Arlington County. I tried to call my lawyer, or any lawyer, but they were all off on a legal picnic! While I was on the phone, my wife was trying to hold these pushing minions of the law at the door - and I heard her squeal in pain "You're hurting me!". I went wild. I ran for my .38, ready to defend my beloved wife now, instead of just the house. But she knew what I was doing, and screamed so piteously for me not to do it that I stopped. How I thank God for the presence of mind and heroism of that brave woman!

I later learned that the sheriff did have every right to knock us aside and force his way in. If I had used that gun, my career and probably my life would have been all over.

I also owe a great debt to the Sheriff, who exercised most commendable forbearance when he recognized our desperation, my ignorance of the law - and the cowardly, miserable actions of Arrowsmith. The latter heroically hid all this time over the topof a hill as he sent the paid officers to do his dirty work in the name of the law!

Our battle paid off - and when I finally let the sheriff in, he determined that it was too late to pick up the equipment, and I had until the morning to get a bond posted, and file counter papers to Arrowsmith's blitzkrieg.

But it was a hollow victory. It was obvious now that I not only had little prospect of earning any money in any job, but that it was quite likely that we would have no place to live, and no e-quipment with which to earn a living. In addition, the constant attacks, the threats, the painful notoriety for a sensitive, gentle lady, and the impossible life for the innocent little kids made it clear that I could NOT subject my dear family to any more such conditions.

My wife's family in Iceland are very well-to-do. Mr. Hallgrimmson, her father, is the chief owner and director of Shell Oil, one of the biggest corporations in the Nation. They were eager for her to come up there, where she could be comfortable, economically secure and safe.

Few men have loved their family more than I worshipped that wonderful wife and our beautiful children. But, because of that very love, it was clearly my duty to forego trying to be with my family, when they could enjoy a decent life in Iceland, while I fought my way out of the wreckage after the Atlanta bombing and Arrowsmith's treachery.

My loyal wife did not want to go. Her folks came over here from Iceland to help persuade her and see what could be done. My own heart was breaking at the thought of being alone in all that danger and mess, without the sweetest and dearest human being I had ever known, and my precious kids. But I realized she simply HAD to go, and I had to stay and fight.

I realized what can happen in a year's separation even to people as much in love as we were, and warned my wife that she might get too comfortable and safe up there, and might not want to come back. But she seemed to have the faith of an angel, and I had almost to fight with her to get her to agree to go. Over and over she scolded me for mentioning the possibility she would grow away from me up there, and insisted that nothing on earth could ever spoil our marriage, no matter how long I had to fight. Even when I told her I felt sure I would go to prison, she would not lose her faith. So I made arrangements for my family to go up to Iceland.

Her folks generously paid for packing and shipping and transportation of Thora and the children, and promised to send her back again at the end of no more than a year, when I had been able to fight my way out of the mess.

I drove the family up to Idlewild International Airport in New York. It was a terrible moment in our lives as I held that dear person close, looked into her tear-filled eyes and sent her out of my life for the worst year each of us was ever to face. I hugged all my little ones; Ricky, too excited by the airplanes to notice the tragedy much; fat little Grampaw, fighting with his pixieish little sister Jeannie; and tiny baby Evelyn.

Then I drove away into the lonely, empty battle.

I had no money, no job, no possibility of getting a job, my house was to be seized in the courts, and I faced the most gigantic and vindictive power on earth. I expected to spend most of the year in jail, after the Atlanta bombing, and most of my "friends" (the "die hards") had deserted.

I truly felt alone.

Last shot of the kids before boarding plane for Iceland

CHAPTER XIII

As I walked around the silent and empty house, with my footsteps echoing and emphasizing the utter loneliness, I was tempted to assure myself that this was certainly as low as we could get in life. The sight of a little baby dress left behind, a one-armed doll in the kid's room, or my wife's last half-consumed cup of coffee - very nearly overcame my self-control in sobs of self-pity at losing my precious Thora and our dear little children.

In my innermost being, however, I knew there were yet more agonies before I could safely imagine the worst was over. One does not win a whole new world with ordinary sorrows and agonies, but only after enduring and surmounting the utmost tragedies and olympian agonies.

I spent Thanksgiving and Christmas alone and ostracized even by the "die-hards" and most of the "conservatives", who called to explain that they would have liked to invite me to dinner, etc., etc. - but that I would "understand" it was "too dangerous". As the utility companies grew discouraged with not being paid, the phone and lights were cut off. I was in court day after day without an attorney, fighting desperately to keep the "home" Arrowsmith had "guaranteed" us.

In spite of my notoriety and the fear inspired by my name, I was able to get some odd jobs here and there. Little by little, I paid enough on the bills to get the lights on, and even my phone back. I boned up on the law fiercely, until I was one day able to face Arrowsmith's highly paid attorney before the Circuit Court Judge - and win an agreement to settle.

The day I won the agreement should have been happy. Victory in such an uneven and bitter battle should have been sweet.

But when I went "home" to that cold and empty house which had been so filled with noisy children and a warm, loving wife - the "victory" seemed almost worse than defeat. For the first time I discovered the brutal joke of fate in granting happiness which cannot be shared with somebody you love. Since then I have won goal after goal, and have earned and received the applause of thousands of fine people all over the earth - but all their praise, all the victories - even walking into the White House, can never equal in human satisfaction the tender, blessed smile of my wife at even the smallest advance we shared together.

I - the supposed master of "hate" in the world, since the demise of Adolf Hitler, am blessed or cursed with a soft, loving, and love-craving nature. Since I have been without my wife, I have learned the full, horrible and indescribable bitterness of victory unshared, of triumph unloved. Sunday afternoons, this past summer, after I have come back from major successes over the howling mobs of Jews, and won over the crowds with two hours of sustained oratory which left me drenched and exhausted but victorious - I have tasted the unutterable bitterness of coming back to the congratulations of my Party Comrades, admiring women and friends - and my empty room. No physical blows I have received or will receive, no jails, no courts, no insane asylums and no smears can hurt me inside as the enforced lack of my beloved wife and family to share the successes I am increasingly able to wring from a brutal world.

But objectively seen, my political battle was far from lost.

Behind me I had almost five years of rough, tough apprenticeship, during which I had made my mistakes and learned my lessons. I would not make them again. I was approaching that state of technical virtuosity in the art of manipulating people and events which is the mark of the professional revolutionary. I had progressed from the desire and ability to manipulate paints, paper and words to achieve a desired result to a minimum professional ability in the highest form of art - politics. In all the other arts, one manipulates a limited number of materials and ideas to achieve a very limited aim. In politics alone does the art encompass the whole earth and all that is in it. In the battle of real politics (-not the disgusting sham "politics" of "Democrats and Republicans" which are nothing more than struggles to snozzle the next hog from a place at the slop-trough) - in constructive and therefore revolutionary politics, one's canvas is humanity itself, one's paints are the whole range of ideas, words, graphic arts, bluff, and every tiniest facet of human existence - while one's brushes are not only vocal chords and pamphlets and TV and all the rest of the media of public expression - but one's fists, one's very life itself!

It is not by accident that many of the world's great revolutionaries and politicians have been artists.

Unlike the millions of my fellow "right-wingers" I had become a hardened and determined revolutionary, destined either to achieve the aims of which they only talked, or die. As I sat alone in that empty house, or lay alone in that even emptier bed in the silent, hollow darkness, the full realization of what I was about bore in upon me with fearful urgency. I realized there was no turning back - as long as I lived, I was marked with the stigma of anti-Jewishness.

It was not an empty boast when ADL Chairman Meier Stienbrink, one of the Justices of the New York State Supreme Court, snarled to his fellow Anti-Defamation League members, "We must never forgive them! (Anti-Semites). We must drive them into the sewers. We must fill our jails and lunatic asylums with anti-semitic gangsters!". I could never again hope to earn a "normal" living. The Jews could not survive unless they made an example of me the rest of my life - else too many others might be tempted to follow my example. My "Rubicon" had been crossed, and it was fight and win - or die.

With all this in mind, I went to the post office one morning, and found a big carton waiting for me. It was from James K. Warner, one of our first supporters. Inside I found, carefully and lovingly folded, a huge Nazi flag, eighteen feet long. It was one of the strokes of destiny I have come to expect.

There was no doubt in my mind. I went home and hung the beautiful banner completely across the living-room wall. In the center I mounted a plaque of Adolf Hitler. Then I placed a small book-case under it, and set three candles to burning in front, to make a holy altar to Adolf Hitler.

I closed the blinds, lit the candles, and stood before my new altar. For the first time since I had lost my Christian religion, I experienced the soul-thrilling upsurge of emotion which is denied to our modern, sterile, atheist "intellectuals" but which literally moved the earth for countless centuries: "religious experience". I stood there in the flickering candlelight, not a sound in the house, not a soul near me or aware of what I was doing - or caring.

But as I looked at the stern face of the greatest mind in twenty centuries, I felt the unbelievable flood of "religious" power pouring into me which would be easily understood by any savage Indian standing on a mountain top at sunrise and communing with the Great Spirit before battle - but which the intellectuals have denied themselves because of their conceit that they can "know" everything.

I recalled the words of the Leader, "When human hearts break, and human souls despair, the great vanquishers of distress and care, of shame and misery, of intellectual unfreedom and physical duress look down upon them from the twilight of the past, and hold out their eternal hands to faint-hearted mortals. Woe to the people that is ashamed to grasp them!".

I was moved beyond the power of words to describe. Goose-pimples rose all over me, my hair stood on end, my eyes filled with tears of love and gratitude for this greatest of all conquerors of human misery and shame, and my breath came in little gasps. If I had not known that the Leader would have scorned such adulation, I might have fallen to my knees in unashamed worship - but instead I drew myself to attention, raised my arm in the eternal salute of the ancient Roman legions, and repeated the holy words, "HEIL HITLER!" - meaning every tiny syllable with all my heart and mind and soul.

No longer was Adolf Hitler only a great mind to me. Now I realized the inscrutable power of the human soul. Now I knew why. the power of that human soul for ten thousand years, again and again, has conquered the mightiest aggregates of physical force and tyranny, regardless of odds or possibilities! I had run the full circle from savage and childish animal instinct - the primitive stage of most of humanity - to conceited and sterile intellectualism - the stage of our convinced Marxists and Liberals - and finally I had, with the help of the Great Leader, found my way back to the natural understanding of the world given free to every dog and worm and ape and man, of which the intellect is only a sort of recent development or "trick". I had found my way to that unconscious understanding of eternal riddles which can only be called "wisdom" - the same perception of the essence of things which has, in different guises, formed the basis of the teachings of all great leaders in all times.

As the emotional storm subsided within me, it left me filled with the holy sense of MISSION which is the fundamental weapon and armor of a revolutionary leader. Where before I had wanted to fight the forces of tyranny and regression, now I HAD to fight them. But even more, I felt within me the POWER to prevail - strength beyond my own strength - the ability to do the right thing even when I was personally overwhelmed by events. And that strength has not yet failed me. Nor will it fail. It is the power beyond the atom, the force called "religious" by the non-intellectual, "phychological self-hypnotism" by the "brains" of today, and the "unknowable" by those who have learned true wisdom.

I knew with calm certainty exactly what to do, and I knew, in a hard-to-explain sense, what was ahead. It was something like looking at a road from the air, after seeing only the curve ahead from the ground.

The world was obviously building up to an unheard-of, unprecedented clash between the dark forces of massed ignorance, greed, envy, hate and stupidity - mustered and led by the scheming Jew - and the perishing forces of Nature's Elite - the White Man.

The Jew, with his Marxist Democratic idea of the supremacy of mere numbers threatened to overwhelm the White Man of the world, regardless of boundaries or political affiliations, by the sheer mass of the teeming colored and inferior masses which outnumbered the white builders of civilization by more than 7 to 1.

Adolf Hitler had shown the way to survival. It would be my task on this earth to carry his ideas and his "laboratory example" to total, world-wide victory. I knew I would not live to see the victory which I would make possible. But I would not die before I had made that victory certain.

I had not long to wait before Destiny drew the curtain on the first act in my new role.

There was a knock on the door one evening as I sat, lonely and wondering, by the fire. I opened it, and found a man named Eugene Collton standing there with two other men I had never seen before. Gene was a twenty-seven-year-old right-winger I had met only recently. He introduced one of the men, a bluff and very husky construction-worker-type - as "J.V." Morgan, and the other as Louis Yalacki - a deceptively good-looking little guy who was almost "pretty" - but who was tough as nails underneath.

Collton was not too surprised by my big Nazi banner and the candles - but the other two staggered back in disbelief and horror. They had not been prepared for anything like THIS!

They were indignant at what appeared to them to be treason! Both were service veterans, 100% loyal to America - and were with Collton mostly because, at the time, they hated "niggers". Collton had told them he would take them to see a man who was REALLY fighting the situation, but had not told them I was a Nazi or anything about his own Hitlerism. Morgan and Yalacki were undecided whether to fight or leave or stay and listen, but finally Collton persuaded them to hear the story.

So they came in, and, in the fire and candle light, I gave them an intense, fundamental little talk in earthy terms which they could understand. I explained that the Negro was too unambitious, un-intelligent and good-natured to be causing all the "nigger-trouble" by himself, and that common, ordinary, plain old "niggers" were often pretty good fellows when they didn't push. The two agreed. It was only when they were AGITATED and irritated and organized by other than colored people that the good-natured, laughing, easy-going "niggers" became the aggressive, nasty, repulsive "colored people" typified by the NAACP-type. Again they agreed. Then I drove in hard the evidence that both the NAACP and CORE are financed and led, not by Negroes, BUT BY COMMUNISTIC JEWS. This was a novel idea for them, but when I showed them the pictures of ugly Arthur Spingarn, head of the NAACP and Marvin Rich, head of CORE, they began to understand the idea. Then I went into the rest of the Jewish picture - and their minds could be seen following me stumblingly and almost reluctantly - but inevitably. The FACTS are simply too damning NOT to believe, once they are presented, even to uneducated Americans.

Then I told them how the Jews, using especially their money and domination of press, TV, etc., were organizing the vast hordes of colored people of the earth, mostly with the help of Marxism, against the outnumbered and weak White Man - using "democracy" as the weapon, in which there would be seven black votes for every White Man. And I told them that we could not survive by talk, but must FIGHT for survival as did our forbears - and that the only possible way to fight TOUGH, and yet legally and thus successfully, was as NAZIS - ALL-OUT WHITE MEN!

The result was that in the space of three or four hours, I had four Nazis, instead of just me. Morgan and Yalacki were all for total battle immediately, but Collton felt it had to be done more carefully and slowly.

They began to come to little gatherings every evening, and I slowly educated the two new men to the apalling facts of our historical situation, using always the earthy terms they understood.

Then I decided it was time to stand forth and make our fight, and that the way to do it was to open the doors and big windows to the heavily traveled boulevard so that the public could see our Nazi flag and altar, our candles, red searchlights, etc. I even got an infrared light for the banner itself, for the psychological effect of the HEAT it threw out, in addition to the eerie red-light it cast. We have made it safe now, of course, but at that time, such conduct seemed mad and suicidal.

Gene Collton sincerely felt that such a course would be wrong until we had at least ten men, and detached himself from the effort, but Louis and J. V. were, by this time, hard to hold. They wanted to fight as much as possible and right away, anything and anybody - to defend the White Man.

We got ourselves brown shirts, arm bands and leather belts. J. V. brought his rifles and revolvers and holsters. Consciously and purposefully we swaggered around the house in the most dramatic and provocative possible fashion, knowing that this would be too much for the Jews to stomach.

American Nazi Party Officers of National Headquarters. Front row, left to right: Captain Matt Koehl, Major Karl R. Allen, Captain Roy James and Captain Seth D. Ryan. Second Row, left to right: Captain Alan Welch, Lieutenant Robert Lloyd, First Lieutenant Bernard Davids and Lieutenant Schuyler Ferris.

J. V. Morgan, holding off rioting mob in night attack with riot-gun and .38. Note teen-age hoods and police officer in battle-gear.

Major Morgan, my Deputy Commander

At first it was just kids who came to stare and hoot and throw rocks. But we were not discouraged, and knew that sooner or later, the Jews would be unable to ignore this challenge.

One night a big and expensive car stopped out front and looked at our dramatic display of banners and searchlights and storm-troops. We could see somebody making notes inside. A few nights later, we found out whom it had probably been, when Drew Pearson let go at us with a smashing national broadside about the dreadfulness of it all - Nazis only a few minutes from the Lincoln Memorial, etc., etc.!!!

My reasoning was that a calm, calculating Jew is dangerous but a wildly angry and fearful Jew, raving and frothing about "Nazis", is raw meat for our teeth.

And it worked! Instead of the intelligent and obvious countermeasures they could have used with their controlled press, they panicked. If they had smeared us then all over the front pages, with plenty of pictures, and incited the mobs past all endurance, we would have been quickly finished off before I could have gained strength. But they could not bring themselves to "give publicity" to a man they knew was openly announcing he would FORCE them to give it, so they put on a tight blanket of silence in the papers. Night after night there were riots around our headquarters, with shooting through the windows. But the press was silent about it all. The whole area was alive with talk about us. But the press pretended we did not exist! I put out thousands of leaflets, door to door, pointing out to the citizens the POWER of the Jews to suppress such news, right before their eyes, and the effect was devastating. Even the soft-headed liberals could see that if a minority could enforce censorship on the press on one issue, they could do it on another, on an issue of which the liberals might NOT approve censorship.

Meanwhile, we had begun to gather recruits, exactly as I had planned, because of our FIGHT! - Not talking "patriots" - but tough workers - truck drivers, fighting men who had had enough "niggers" and tyranny by a Jewish minority. Hundreds and hundreds of people every day began to come to our headquarters to talk to me and see what kind of a "creature" I must be. And, again, the Jew lies caused their own downfall, for I convinced more than three out of five of the simpering, supercilious visitors that I was NOT a monster, or a liar, or a fake - as the Jews insisted, but a most sincere and truthful American patriot and White Man, fighting the only possible way to save us from catastrophe.

We began to win most of the high-school kids to our side, and became the major topic of discussion in all the schools for miles around. The Jews forced the teachers to spread the wildest lies about my person and our headquarters and ideas - including the vicious story that my wife had left me, I had tried to drown my kids, I was insane, and we were a gang of criminals and traitors.

Our windows were all bashed out with huge rocks thrown from cars whizzing by, and pies and catsup and paint and stink-bombs were regularly heaved, day and night. But our armed storm-troopers stood guard out front and nobody dared personally attack us.

One day several hundred gathered down the street in a parking lot, and we knew we were going to have to face a pretty deadly mob. We were armed, but it would have been the end of the party to shoot and kill anybody. I had to figure out some way of stopping the mob, short of shooting.

I decided to use the weapon of psychology.

I got my camera ready with an enormous electronic flash I had, and, when the mob approached, I ran at them with the camera, and started taking flash pictures of the leaders! They were scared, and turned their backs! That was all I needed. I jeered at them, and pointed out their cowardice! The mob straggled away and the attack dispersed!

My personal life, meanwhile, was almost unbearable. I suffered an agonizing loneliness and ache for my wife and family, and she had the same experience in Iceland. I got tear-stained letters, and heart-breaking tapes from my wife alone up there. She was catching the very devil from her folks for having anything to do with me. Her sufferings were worse than mine, for I, at least, had an absorbing mission to keep my mind occupied. She had nothing but four squabbling little children to look out for, no money except what she had to account for, penny by penny to her father, and no husband or social life. But at least she was safe from what was happening in Arlington, and she would not starve, as I was doing.

I lived on small parcels of food brought by faithful troopers and friends, stale bread, dented cans, etc.

Floyd Fleming, - the man who had stood so staunchly behind John Kasper, came over to see what it was all about, and at first was also repelled by the Nazi flag. But little by little, I was able to make him see that it was the ONLY way to FORCE the Jewish mastery of the press to break open for us, and attract the YOUNG fighting men we so desperately needed.

Daily the number of visitors grew. Many of them began to be from colleges and universities, and I won their minds and hearts, too. Most of them came out of curiosity, but there was a good percentage who came determined to wreck the place once and for all.

Once seventeen large men from the University of Maryland, (most of a whole fraternity) came in. I made them all sit down before me, as was my practice, while I kept a loaded .45 on the table at my hand. I had two armed troopers standing in both corners of the room at all times, with another at the front door. Several times, as I talked, one of them kept getting up and going over near the big Nazi banner on the wall. He was courteously but firmly sent back to his seat by one of my men.

We later learned that they had been armed, and had planned to give us a good "lesson", beat me up, tear down the flag, burn the place, and put an end to the Party. Instead, they went back to the University, and for two days, flew a Nazi flag from the Fraternity house, until the University took a hand.

I began to learn the science of argument as I never had before. I particularly practiced my growing abilities on the hundreds of vile-mouthed Jews who called on the phone. I learned their standard "arguments", their canned and unreasonable slogans and catch-words, "You can't condemn a whole group because of a few individuals", etc., and, within a few weeks, all of us became masters of such Jewish sophisms. Many at the time reviled me for "wasting my time" with these hateful Jews on the phone, but I used them as jousting-posts, and taught my men to parry their feeble thrusts, and then drive home our facts and arguments in the way which always sends the Jews scurrying for their poisoned pens and their hired hoods.

Many of the characters who were attracted to us were pretty sorry. One man arrived late at night with a caged bird and some "sacred" book, to "join the party". He told us the "bolsheviks" were wrecking his sex life and were always keeping him from having a girl friend - and he wanted to "fight them", he and the bird, that is.

Another lady, festooned in ostentatious fur pieces and a crazy hat with a berry at the end of a stalk, arrived in a cab, and insisted on telling me about the "Jewish underground". I told her I knew about it, and we were fighting it.

"Yes", she said, "but we have got to dig them out! They're down there now, GRINDING up the bones and the flesh!"

She explained to me that the Jews had underground passages running from their "SIN-igogs" and honeycombing the earth everywhere. In these wicked resorts, she explained desperately and passionately, the devils were mashing up people they plucked from society into a poisonous slime which they then put in the food of the rest of us secretly, to ruin our minds!

This woman was the wife of a one-time U. S. ambassador, believe it or not. I sent her away with as much sympathy as I could muster.

The nights were difficult for me, not only because of the crushing loneliness, but because of the attacks. At that time, nobody was living with me, and the troops all had to leave at ten or eleven. Sometimes, especially on Friday or Saturday nights, carloads of hoods would appear at twelve or one A. M. - and I had to hold them off alone until I could get to the phone to call the cops.

Morgan and Yalacki did yeoman work cooling down the worst of the hot-heads. They would sit in their high-powered cars with the lights off, and, when a carload would go by hurling missiles, they would light out after them like hornets - even when there were four or five or six against them. I did not go on any of these wild careening chases, and can't personally vouch for what happened - but I do know that the attacks slowed down and finally almost stopped. We have gained such utter respect and mastery now, of course, that our present headquarters had only ONE broken window, and attacks are extremely rare. We have won most of the youth in our local area by our daring and dedication.

And, as we had planned, we put the Jews on the horns of an impossible dilemma: If they did nothing and continued the news black-out, they not only proved to the public that they were censoring the press, AS WE WERE PREACHING - but we continued to grow and gain thousands of young minds. On the other hand, if they pounced on us illegally and brutally, they would "martyrize" us and give us the publicity we needed and they were determined to deny.

For a while they compromised by attacking our employment. Yalacki worked at Capital Airlines, and he had won a large circle of the workmen who were coming to the headquarters regularly and contributing. The Jews struck there first.

Drew Pearson "exposed" our progress at Capital, so Yalacki and the other men from Capital were told they would have to quit the party or be fired. All but Yalacki quit. Louis, full of fight as a banty rooster, believed me when I told him it was necessary to prove that we could hold the jobs of our men, and refused to quit. He became more Nazi than ever, "Sieg Heiling" in the hangars and openly flaunting his Nazism. We were legal, honest, patriotic and FOR America, not against it. We were not totalitarians. There was no reason why we should be fired because of Jew pressure, and we wrote the management a letter to that effect, and made it clear that if they fired Louis, we would give them all the legal trouble we could invent, from picketing to suits.

Faced with the snarling Jews on one side, and adamant open Nazis on the other, the management decided to be fair. Louis did NOT lose his job! It was a major victory for us, and we knew the Jews could not tolerate such a situation.

They threatened Louis' kids and his wife; they renewed their filthy phone call campaign; they tried every kind of rotten pressure imaginable. We absorbed it all and laughed at them.

One late afternoon I was alone in the headquarters, printing more programs down in the cellar. Suddenly the door behind me burst open, and five or six men rushed in. I recognized a deputy sheriff and some County officials. They shoved a paper at me and told me it was a raid. There were more officials to be let in upstairs at the front door, they said. I went upstairs, and discovered the place surrounded by police cars with red lights flashing, a huge mob, reporters, cops, sheriffs, etc. I opened the front door and greeted Sheriff Taylor and another horde of officials. Behind them were the newspaper reporters, a whole pack of them. I ordered these out and bid the officials enter.

There were fourteen of them, including the Captain of Police, the County Prosecutor, the top detectives, the Sheriff, and other dignitaries. They searched everywhere, confiscated everything Nazi or conceivably Nazi (for "evidence") and gave me a summons on a criminal charge.

While all of this was going on; while they were probing every closet, the cellar and the attic, I took flash photographs, developed them, and printed them - all before the raiding party departed. One of these photos was on the Washington area TV less than forty-five minutes after the raid - ALONG WITH A JEWISH NEWSPAPER STORY THAT I WAS SO "HYSTERICAL" I RAN FROM "ROOM TO ROOM" DURING THE RAID IN FEAR AND IN TERROR, SCREAMING AND SHRIEKING !!!!! The Washington Evening Star paid me ten dollars for the print they used, and I photostated the check, expecting something like this Jewish lie.

A meeting had been scheduled for the party that evening, and, as soon as I saw all the cops, and before I knew they were not going to seize me personally, I called the others on the phone and warned them not to come.

A few minutes later, I heard shouting and yelling outside - and then knocks on the door. It was my troopers, heroically come to face whatever was to be faced with me - shouldering and fighting their way through the mob around the house! Morgan was asked for an interview by a particularly obnoxious little Kike and roared at him, "Out of my way, you FILTHY JEW!" - which tickled the crowd. As each man entered, he shouted SIEG HEIL at the top of his lungs, showing the caliber of our defiance of the latest Jewish pressure.

When the house was stripped even of magnetic tapes of music, which I guess they suspected were secret codes of some kind, the raiding party departed, and I held a press conference with the reporters who had been straining at the leash outside.

We got a sudden flood of publicity - when the Jews felt it would be the end of us. But we promptly got another Nazi flag, more lights, literature, etc. - and opened for business again!

The Anti-Defamation League put out a whole bulletin article on us, however, and, with typical Jewish effrontery, celebrated and analyzed our demise. They called this premature obituary "Fiasco for a Fuehrer"!!! How some of their contributors must make them eat that article now!

Meanwhile, Negro groups throughout the Country, and even in Africa, had been contacting us and thanking us for recognizing the sincerity and honesty of the vast majority of colored people. One leader of a group in Chicago, Mr. S. A. Davis, wrote that his group felt that I was the fulfillment of Bible prophecy - that the black man would serve two hundred years in another land and then return to Africa with gifts and justice at last. Once, when I called him long distance to tell him we were coming to Chicago to see him, his wife was so emotionally overwhelmed with gratitude and religious fervor that she fainted and had to be carried to a bed shouting, "Hallelujah!".

I discovered, as we had suspected, that millions of Negroes wanted to return to Africa - with fair treatment, but were being silenced and prevented by the same gang of Jews who wanted the cheap labor, the hock-shop and installment customers, the rent-payers and the voting power of the hordes of ignorant blacks - at the same time they agitated viciously both the blacks and whites to mix and destroy our white America. Most amazing of all, we found that four million Negroes, believe it or not, had signed a petition to go back to Africa even without the decent program we propose, and this fact was suppressed and the leader of the movement, Marcus Garvey, thrown in jail!

I began to go to Negro hang-outs to learn at first hand, and on the Negroes' own home ground, how they feel. I openly told them they were inferior biologically, that we were ready to fight to the death to stop all mixing, but that we owed them a fair shake.

Indeed, I proved to them the sincerity of our desire to HELP them out of the mess of phony "tolerance" and "brotherhood" which was and is leading only to chaos and bloody violence between the races. (Since this was written, we have established contact with Elijah Muhammad's black muslims, who will inevitably win American Negroes with his inspiring and much misrepresented movement.)

With no funds for a lawyer (and no lawyer who would defend me if we DID have funds), I went to court time after time alone and fought the case against me inch by inch. I studied the law every spare minute, and got invaluable training in the court room facing the hot-tempered Irish prosecutor, William Hassan. I learned to disarm his impassioned oratory to the judge with humble and sincere quiet statements. Observing his red-hot nature, which once led him to whack another lawyer in the teeth in court, I gently needled him with remarks which blew him into a puffing dragon. Particularly, I continually apologized to the judge for the prosecutor's miserable case and arguments, and explained that I understood that he was forced to this sorry pass by all the "pressure" of a certain group. At that word pressure, the prosecutor would leap up, bang the table, holler, turn red, bellow, roar and threaten to attack me. I would draw back in "surprise" and "terror" at this display, and the judge would hide his face behind his hand for a smile he couldn't hold in.

As I won point after point, I also won the respect of the court, the judges and the officials of the County. I learned this for sure when the Sheriff, the same man my wife and I had fought at our door, and who had raided me, called me into his office to help me all he legally could before my trial. I had proved what I had felt sure of, and what will win the battle for us eventually - human courage, pluck - yes, heroism, is irresistable. A gang of sneaks and creeps such as now grinds our people under their heel cannot prevail against open and heroic determination and will. Even with all their money and power and press and brainwashing subversion, the Jews will soon fall before the pure white-fire of our idealism and devotion, no matter how tiny the flame seems to be now.

As all this was going on, the period of occupancy in the house I had won from Arrowsmith was drawing to a close, and my lads could not believe he would throw us out into the streets after the victories we had won, and with the future we obviously had ahead. They tried again and again to get Arrowsmith to agree to some kind of deal, any kind of deal, to keep fighting - but our "fat cat" hated me so much for defying and overcoming his spoiled, little boy peeve that he appeared determined to ruin and smash me if he could.

On the fifteenth of June, the agreement ran out - and the Jews were jubilant. Drew Pearson gloated from Coast to Coast that we would soon be "driven from the banks of the Potomac". It looked like the end of us, to be sure.

I was still facing the criminal charges in court; we had no money; all the printing and other equipment was gone, and now no place to go, either.

I got a lesson in human psychology.

With increasing and arrogant attacks by the Jews on their employment, and the apparently hopeless situation with the headquarters, all but three of my troopers quit. No amount of shaming or pleading could get them to stand by their oaths and promises to go through hell itself with us to victory. It was hard for me to believe, and very bitter medicine.

Morgan and Yalacki and a non-member named Cary Hansel were my only faithful helpers in those impossible days, as I had to borrow a truck and move out. We were unable to find any place to move into except a tiny shack far out in the back-woods of Fairfax County, so we took that. It was without lights, water, toilet facilities or anything else, but it did accomodate our boxes and piles of stuff, and it did have a bed of sorts.

I spent the months of June and July out there alone, broke, seeing no human being sometimes for three or four days, and roasting alive in the heat. The Jews discovered the place by following one of my visitors, and then I had the added humiliation of small airplanes which would glide in silently over the tree-tops and I could see them leaning out with press cameras hoping to get undignified pictures of me.

Now my letters from my wife began to be less frequent, and less filled with the fanatical devotion I loved in her so much. I needed all the sustaining love I could get, and kept heckling her for more mail. Finally, I wrote a relatively sharp letter asking why she couldn't write more often.

I got back a magnetic tape, but couldn't play it because there was no electricity. So I lugged the tape recorder to a nearby church which was empty, sneaked into the basement, plugged in the machine, and listened to the recording of my wife's voice. What I heard chilled my blood.

For the first time in our lives, she sounded really distant and even a little nasty.

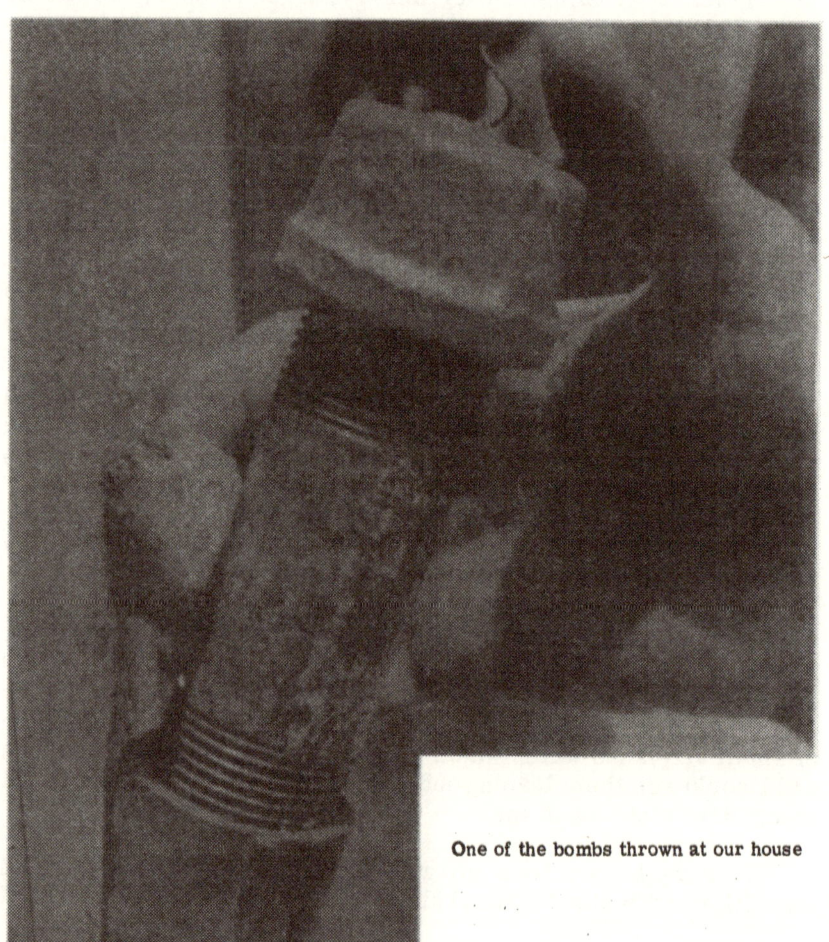

One of the bombs thrown at our house

CHAPTER XIV

Now began the months which were to be the most soul-crushing in my life.

My wife began to complain that her parents were begging her to divorce me, and called it their "campaign". I told her the best thing to do was come home immediately, before anything could happen to our marriage. We could go someplace and work quietly together the best way we could to repair our fortunes. There was no answer to this, but then came a demand to get out of politics for good and all. I wrote long, long letters out there in the hot fields on a little portable typewriter, and mailed almost none of them. I knew philosophy and political argument were the last thing to write to a wife in Thora's embattled position, but it was almost impossible to write anything else which made sense.

During the time in the Fairfax shack, Morgan, Yalacki and Hansel had decided to make an all-out effort to get me in closer to town where they could get together and help more. They scrounged around, and managed to rent a little basement for me in a home in Arlington. Then we borrowed the truck again, and struggled with all the ton or so of books and furniture and other paraphenalia to the new haven. They completely filled up the tiny cellar rooms. And meanwhile, the neighbors had somehow discovered who was to be the new roomer, and were going around with a petition. Some of them explained it was not personal - they were just afraid of riots, etc., in the neighborhood, which was understandable. The landlord tried to throw me out immediately, but I refused to move so instantaneously, of course. It was impossible, and I asked for ten days. At first they demanded instant removal, but a reminder of my reputation as a fighter in court cooled them down and got me the ten days. But the Jews stirred up everybody on the matter, and soon had the Arlington zoning officials trying to evict me immediately as a health menace!

While battling this, I searched for another place to light, and Carey Hansel agreed to let me stay in his apartment in Falls Church while his wife and children were away for the summer.

Once again we gathered up the roomfuls of stuff, and put them in the borrowed truck. This time, however, we decided to put the things in a rented garage, rather than keep moving them. Breakage and loss was terrific.

I was existing on a tiny trickle of funds from two or three people who were unbelievably loyal, and a few odd jobs I could get here and there from sympathizers. I tried to work in a sign-shop incognito, but inevitably, somebody recognized me, and the would-be friendly employer had to ask me to leave.

The mail from my wife began to be heartbreaking. More and more she complained of the "campaign" of her parents, who said they would disown her if she came back to me and I were still in politics, etc.

I could see that my marriage was at stake, and decided to drop politics long enough to repair my financial situation and save my dear family. I went out after work with all I had, and managed to get several odd art jobs, some work making signs and other small bits of income. A lot of Arlington businessmen were sympathetic to me, and did what they could to give me work, but were usually scared away before it could settle down to anything substantial. Nevertheless, I succeeded in gathering together various heterogeneous "accounts" all over the area - people who paid me to exert my talents at promotion in various forms, and had managed to get the old Cadillac repaired and fixed a bit. I had saved some money for the family, and was even working on setting up silk screen business.

Then one day I got another bomb-shell from Iceland: a letter stating that my wife's parents had laid down the condition that I must earn $150 per month for a period of at least three months, have a better car, and make other arrangements on debts, etc. - which would amount to earning five or six thousand dollars before my wife could come home and our family be reunited. If she came back without these conditions, she said, they would disown and disinherit her.

Louis Yalacki on guard at the first Headquarters, Williamsburg Blvd.

The picture I took during the raid on our headquarters--developed, printed and sold to the Evening Star--all while I was supposed to be rushing insanely from room to room in a panic as reported in the Jew-dominated press. This picture was on TV within an hour after the raid, but it was not reported that I took and processed it!

Outside of the first headquarters, teenagers coming in to listen.

Floyd Fleming, crackajack sign painter for the U. S. Navy for 25 years, paints a campaign slogan for National Headquarters.

Under the circumstances, the conditions were impossible. Nowhere in America, for a long time, at least, could I earn any such money as that. I could not understand my wife making such a demand.

Her best friend and her cousin was the wife of the First Secretary of the Icelandic Embassy, so I went to this very charming girl and laid the whole thing before her.

She was wonderfully sympathetic, and assured me that her letters from my wife indicated nothing but an aching desire to reunite our family, and that it was probably only pressure from the parents causing the difficulty.

Since they insisted on my being out of politics, since they had so much influence on my helpless wife, whom they were supporting, and since I could NOT fulfill the conditions they, and she, demanded here - I asked her friend what she thought of the possibility of my going to HER - of my working in ICELAND for the family, where there were only two Jews, and where I knew my talents and abilities could provide a good living, pay her father back the money he had spent supporting my family and give me time to repair the heartbreaking breach in our family. My wife's friend thought this a wonderful idea, and so did her husband, the Icelandic First Secretary, when he heard it.

I wrote this plan to my wife, and told her I was willing to come up there. But she decided to give up the impossible conditions, and come here instead, providing I had a house, a job and other possibilities of supporting the family.

I was overjoyed at this, and spared no effort to gain a minimum foothold for my family's security, even in the difficult circumstances. I pushed the little silk-screen business, doing signs for real-estate and trucking firms, and, by putting an ad in the paper, got several small promotional accounts. My situation was far from good, but I was managing to make enough money to survive and even save some for the family. Carey Hansel's family had returned to his apartment; I had moved into Louis Yalacki's house where I had a room. I rented a house for my supposedly returning family and began to make plans for the joyous homecoming. Daily I wrote my wife long letters of my small victories in squeezing jobs and money out in spite of the Jewish pressure and fear of employers.

Suddenly there was a strange silence from Iceland. Then one day came a letter from my wife that her father had suddenly and unexpectedly been called to America on "business", and would come and look over my arrangements for the family within a day or so!

I knew the super-methodical, ruthless business methods of my wife's father, and how far in advance he planned every move. Now suddenly he was called to America "on business" exactly two weeks before my wife and children were scheduled to return.

I called the New York office of Shell, where I had already met the managers who dealt with Iceland and Mr. Hallgrimsson, and they didn't even know he was coming. A little further checking, and I knew for sure what I had suspected: the "business" of the trip was to see what the situation was before my wife came back, and possibly to prevent the return at all.

This kind of horsing around while my marriage hung in the balance was extremely aggravating, with all the struggle I was having, and I talked it over with my little circle of faithful supporters.

I made a wrong decision.

Since my wife's father, and maybe she too, were playing games, I would do the same. I did have a promise from one man to buy us a house, which has subsequently been fulfilled, but I decided to claim that the house was already bought to give a better impression of security.

When the old gentleman arrived, I took him to see the rented house and told him it was being purchased. I showed him the bank deposit slips for the small sum I had in the bank, and the contract I did have to do sign work for a trucking firm.

He seemed to be impressed by all this, but I should have known and remembered him better than to think I had so easily fooled such an experienced and successful old business wolf.

The next day we had a meeting in his hotel room, and he started asking me penetrating questions about the mortgage payments, etc., and I made a real ass of myself.

The only course seemed to be to tell him to go back to Iceland and ask my wife to wait until I had things under better control. And this is what I did.

Then, while he was on his way back to New York and Iceland, I began to realize how dangerous such a course would be for our marriage, and called my wife long-distance to Iceland. I asked her if she loved me and wanted to come home - and she answered with burning passion, "YES! YES! YES!" She said she would take a plane back by the 21st of October, and I collapsed exhausted and happy beyond words.

I redoubled my efforts to have things ready for the family's arrival - only to get an odd letter a few days later saying she was coming ALONE to look things over - and would stay not with me - BUT AT HER COUSIN'S HOME!

The astonishment and shame and hurt of that was more than I could take. I went out and got a gallon of wine and drank almost all of it. I don't remember what I did - except I know I dropped all the work I was supposed to do. My mind was whirling and dead all at once. I hurt too much to think. I am convinced, as I look back on that day and the nightmarish days and nights which followed, that I was, for that time, the psychotic which the Jews would like to believe I am. I drank and brooded and tried to fight my way to an understanding of what to do, but could see nothing, only stark tragedy. I knew I could not earn a penny if my wife subjected me to the mortal hurt of staying publicly with a friend in order to avoid sleeping with the husband who worshipped and waited for her faithfully for one whole year.

I decided to do the only thing left: go at once to my wife, no matter what.

Recklessly, crazily, I sold everything I had, for nothing - raised all the money I could everywhere, and made all arrangements to go to Iceland to keep my family together. I had to battle to get a visa at the Icelandic Embassy, because of the influence of my wife's father, and the knowledge of all concerned of the personal circumstances of my request to go to Iceland. But I did it all, somehow, arranged to have my art, photography and other professional things shipped to Iceland to make a living, and let everything drop where it was in the U. S.

On the day that Khruschev arrived in the Country, the honest Virginia Courts threw out the case against me. It had been too ridiculous to sustain, including such hysterical charges as "arm-folding" and "heel-clicking", and I was exhonerated completely, after six months of battling alone.

I announced to the press that I was going to Iceland to be with my family and would return after the Country "cooked" a little more - after they had had a chance to see the results of more "brotherhood", spending, etc.

There was no doubt whatsoever in my mind that the deep, abiding love between my wife and I, coupled with my utter determination to do anything necessary to keep our family together would soon melt the ice which was causing the impasse, and we would be once again the happy parents and lovers we were so long and happily - even in the harsh circumstances we had faced.

Only three faithful friends stood by me through this awful mess: Floyd Fleming, Louis Yalacki and J. V. Morgan. I told them I would have to go to Iceland and stay there an undetermined time while I worked to repair the damage, earned the money to repay my father-in-law to free my wife of the gnawing sense of dependency and obligation she suffered, and made my family once again the happiest and most united of all the families I have ever known. These loyal friends never faltered. I promised them that someday I would return with my reunited family, ready to do battle as never before.

I had little idea how soon that return would be as I took off from New York International Airport for Iceland - literally aching and hurting with impatience to see and hold my beloved Thora.

I had cabled my wife of the time of my arrival, and looked for her at the gray and depressing little airport in Reykjavik . There was no one there. I got a ride with a U. S. Army major who was there to meet his wife, and drove over to the address of the apartment I had never seen where I knew my wife and children lived. I was laden with baggage and a steam-shovel toy and a huge doll as I struggled up the stairs and knocked on that magic door! Inside I could hear the little voices of my children - voices I had ached to hear for one year! Then the door opened, and there stood my wife holding little Evelyn Bentina in her arms. She was wearing torreador pants, and apparently had no idea I would show up - why, I still don't know. She stepped back in horror as I stood there, ready to crush her to pieces, and said, "WHAT! YOU! WHAT ARE YOU DOING HERE!".

My little kids came out hesitatingly to look at the toys and seemed to recognize me. I was too stunned to move or say anything at first. Then I tried to kiss my wife, and got pushed back in anger. All she could say was, "What do you MEAN by coming here!" - over and over again.

I sat down on the stairs to the next apartment up, dying and shrivelling and screaming with agonies inside.

I will spare the reader the agonizing description of the unbelievable days and nights that follows. I was ordered out of the house, and when I refused, deciding to fight physically, if necessary, because I couldn't believe my wife's actions, the lawyers and the police were used to force me to leave.

I am absolutely sure I was out of my mind for several days. The grief and hurt and shock and horror was more than I could absorb. I drank what whiskey I could get hold of; I wandered in the cold, grey, drizzly streets; I had a horrible tooth-ache along with everything else. I wanted to die.

In the daytime, she let me come back to see my children, and they remembered and loved me, and broke my heart with endearments. Ricky, the eldest, apparently understood, and told his mother he didn't want us "to divorce". My wife talked calmly and icily to me, and stayed as far as possible from me, even trying to sit in the front seat of a taxi once to avoid riding with me and our little daughter Jeannie.

Somehow, I managed to gather the strength of will to overcome the humiliation of being thrown out and worked up a new determination to fight to keep my family together.

I applied for and got a tentative OK on a good job at the U.S. airbase, thirty miles away at Keflavik, and was preparing to go out there to "Siberia" to support and help the family, even without the privilege of being with them or having my wife's love - when she announced as I was saying goodby and getting ready to take the bus to this horrible isolated exile in Keflavik, "I'm not sure it will be any use!"

I asked her what she meant, and she said she wasn't sure she would keep our marriage no matter what I did.

In Iceland, marriage laws are almost nonexistent. To get rid of a wife or a husband, no matter how faultless they may be, one has only to go to the local preacher (who is also a government official) and announce one's intentions of being finished with the marriage. Automatically, and without any cause, such a person is granted a separation for one year - and then a divorce!

My beloved wife took me, as though we were on a "date", to the same preacher who married us, and asked for the machinery to be started up. I believed it was supposed to be a "reconciliation" hearing - as it was advertised, and begged, pleaded, cajoled and argued. I got down on my knees before my wife and implored her to save our family - but this only made her angry and she got down on hers and said, "See, I can get on my knees, too!"

After a bit more of this farcial "reconciliation" hearing, the preacher sent me down to the local city hall to sign some kind of paper the lawyers said I had to sign, and that was IT!

It was my little girl's birthday, October 28th.

In an emotional hell which I am sure is the limit of human endurance, I begged my wife to get her father to use his influence to get me out of Iceland that night on a plane, which she did. Her father loaned me the fare and got the tickets, and I took off that terrible night.

As I waited for the plane to leave Orn, my wife's ex-husband's brother, who had been sympathetic and helpful, drove up in his little car. I saw my wife beside him. He got out and told me to get in.

She had come to say goodbye! She was pouring tears. I took her in my arms and sobbed uncontrollably. So did she. I begged her to tell me WHY. - but all she would say was that she wished it could be otherwise more than I did!

In more sane moments I might have paused to consider the madness of it all, but I can barely remember those terrible minutes. I couldn't stand it any more and jumped out of the car, beyond control entirely. They drove away into the blackness of the Icelandic night, and I stood there with the icy wind freezing the tears pouring down my face and dripping onto the black runway.

Everything in the U.S.A. was wrecked and gone when I got back. The business accounts I had worked so desperately to get were, of course, gone. My furniture, tools - everything - had been hastily liquidated to go to Iceland and my political organization was a mostly memory. My friends were amazed when I showed up in exactly one week from the day I left.

But worse than all these, what religious people call a soul was gone out of my body. My will, my hope and reason were all temporarily gone.

I went back to Yalacki's house and began to drink wine. I sold and hocked what little I had left in the world and became a disgusting bum. How anybody put up with me or stood by me I will never understand. But my three faithful friends, Morgan, Yalacki and Fleming indulged me and seemed somehow to trust me.

For hours and hours on end I lay in the little hard bed at Louis' house and tried to understand how such a thing could have happened. When I hurt too badly inside to stand it anymore, I would bring out the wine bottle again, and finally fall into a wretched slumber full of nightmarish re-enactments of the scenes in Iceland.

As the days wore on, however, I began to be able to accept reality a bit, and started a conscious effort to jerk myself out of this suicidal mood.

I reflected that there was an unfortunate pattern to my life. For the second time I had lost a family under almost similar circumstances. But especially in business and creative effort, I had many times struggled and succeeded in producing something "impossible", only to have it snatched away by non-creative but "tougher" individuals - people who were not credulous, sensitive, gentle and overly honest - as I had always been. I began to analyze how this happened to me - and in every case I discovered it was the result of believing people, believing IN people, and then failing to take action at the first sign of disloyalty or hostility.

One of the horrifying things which happened to me in Iceland, was my wife's answer when I asked her what I had done to violate our marriage vows, and if she didn't feel bound by her vows and oaths, and the "love forever and ever and ever" in her letters, etc. She replied coldly that these were "just words", and "everybody breaks them".

It was a cruel and brutal lesson, but one I needed desperately. It is true. If such an unparalleled human being as my wife, such a loyal, faithful, long-suffering, good, kind and noble person could cast aside the most sacred vows and a family of six people after reaching a certain point of suffering, then indeed, all vows ARE just words. People keep vows only so long as their happiness or what they believe to be their happiness depends on keeping them. I was forced to come around to the foul but unfortunately true belief of the Jews that you can't trust anybody. Cash on the barrelhead, force, power, punishment, reward and possessions alone are dependable in this world. My losses of my creations in every case had been the result of attempting to believe in promises, friendship, loyalty, love, etc.

Now an implacable destiny had graduated me from the hardest school in the world, and my diploma was inscribed in deep scars on my heart. Never again would I believe ANYBODY just because they "loved me", "promised" or because they were "friends". I had learned the maxim of all leaders: "All men are cowards" - only the breaking points are different.

But there was yet a better result of the emotional and spiritual catastrophe I suffered in Iceland.

Had I managed to fight my way back to a united family up there, after the brutal and heartbreaking battle I had experienced, the warm love of my wife and children might have overcome my sense of duty to the Cause. I might have postponed for too long the all-out battle we have fought and won here, as a shell-shocked man eschews the trenches when he can. Who would leave a warm feather bed to jump into the icy torrents in which he most probably will be drowned?

Irrational or not, I have now come to the conclusion that my beloved wife acted only her part in a drama neither of us understood - which is the only explanation for the crazy goodbye at the airport. She booted me brutally back into the fight I told her, almost the first day I met her, was the whole purpose of my life. In hurting me more terribly than I believed possible for a human being to be hurt and survive, she gave me the one last weapon I needed to fight and HOLD my victory - and she forced me out into the battle.

In addition to all these things she did for me - she gave me the most impenetrable armor on earth.

I had learned in combat, from Guadalcanal to Guam, that the guys who try the hardest not to get hit usually get it - and often in the tail as they are trying to sneak over a coconut log. The guys who don't give a damn, who leap up and charge shouting, "Come on you sons of bitches - do you want to live forever!" - in the immortal Marine battle cry of World War I - almost inevitably are impossible for the enemy to hit! They seem to be charmed and CAN'T get hit.

Rommel used to say, in combat, "Stand next to me! I'm bullet-proof!" - and he WAS!

As I began to recover from my spiritual collapse, I found myself steeled and hardened and almost somnambulistic in my attitude. And for the first time in my life - I just didn't care what happened. I became virtually a tool of the giant Forces which I realized had shaped my life.

My wife had given me the most priceless armor available - fearlessness.

I began slowly to realize what she had done for me. Even unconsciously, this wonderful woman had given me what I needed at the right time.

Just about as I regained "consciousness", James Warner, the young man who sent the Nazi flag, was discharged from the Air Force for his Nazi sympathies, and appeared at Louis' house - ready to do what he could to advance Nazism.

The fact that this young kid was ready to devote his life to our cause and to my leadership was the shock I needed to snap out of depression.

At the same time, two brothers in Baltimore, Bernie and George Harriss had become interested in the cause and gotten in touch with us, and now invited me up to their home for Thanksgiving dinner.

With Louis Yalacki, J. V. Morgan, the Harrisses, Warner and myself, we had the makings of a Party again, and I heaved the wine bottles and the depression in the ash-can. As I had done once before in Iceland, in a similar situation, I drowned my sorrows in work and asceticism. I have not touched beer or liquor for a year now.

Warner and I had to find a place to live since two of us would be too many for Yalacki. We finally got a little cabin almost forty miles south of D.C. in the woods - using Warner's name.

I set to work in the cabin to rebuild the Party, and plan the drive which will take us from the bottom of nothingness to world power in 1972.

With little or no money, I had to invent means of fighting which would bring us maximum returns per penny. I decided on public distributions on the main streets of Washington of the strongest possible literature on the most critical possible question. What we lacked in money we would make up in personal courage and drive. The issue I needed was tailor-made - the Negro situation in the Nation's Capital.

At the present rate, the Capital will be all black in a very few years, and the whites are in headlong retreat, losing property and their lives and liberty at the hands of rampaging hordes of agitated Negroes. Even the "liberals" are getting a lesson they can't miss in Washington, and often it is the wives of the race-mixers who get raped.

By pointing out the facts - that it was the Communistic Jews, not the Negroes, who were causing this impossible situation - and by being the only voice in the black wilderness for the White Man, we would **FORCE** the hand of the race-agitators, liars and newspaper censors. There had been four of us in Washington, but then Louis and I had a falling out, and he left the party. Thus it was an army of three Nazis who descended on Washington in the weeks before Christmas with our carefully worked-up and pitifully few sheets. We stood forth alone on the street corners with our red-emblazoned handbills, waving the sheets so all could see the huge letters: "WHITE MAN! ARE YOU GOING TO BE RUN OUT OF YOUR NATION'S CAPITAL WITHOUT A FIGHT!" - and on the back of the sheet was the documentary evidence of the Jewish communist background of the trouble and the race-mixing. We minced no words, but openly declared our purpose to be the gassing of the Jew traitors - in accordance to the Constitution.

Results were not long in coming. We had little difficulty with the blacks, who pretty much ignored us - but the Jews went wild! They screamed at us, spit on us, tore up the leaflets and threw them at us, and did everything possible to scare us and have us locked up. The Corporation Counsel of the District of Columbia studied our leaflet and ruled that it was legal. That was before the full pressure of militant Jewry struck his department.

We persisted, braving the mobs of howling, screaming Jews, - just the three of us. Sometimes one of us couldn't make it, and there were only two. We defied them!

Finally the Jews resorted to their usual argument when they are beaten by facts: violence. A huge and wealthy Jew named Berman suddenly appeared with five other big Jews, grabbed my stack of leaflets, and started to scuffle - when he was grabbed by Morgan. They would have started an all-out battle, except for the instantaneous action of the Police, who seized both the Jew and Morgan.

The papers could no longer cover up such riotous action, as they had been ignoring the presence of Nazis with what the Jews called "gas-chamber pamphlets" heretofore. They had to report it!

In the meantime, the Jewish groups had been steadily pressing the Navy to throw me out, and the Navy had been as steadily resisting. I was doing nothing wrong or illegal and everybody knew it. But now, with publicity, they won their way, as cabinet officers and President felt the Jewish lash. The Navy called me before a hearing board, and, although I demonstrated the absolute propriety of all my actions as a Commander in the Reserve, and had an almost perfect record, they hastily gave me an Honorable Discharge.

*** *** *** *** *** *** ***

Statement Of

COMMANDER GEORGE LINCOLN ROCKWELL

United States Naval Reserve

(1315 -- 106684)

Presented at a Hearing Before a Board of Officers of the Navy Department, 1 Feb. 1960 at the Pentagon, Washington, D.C.

<u>Gentlemen:</u>

Before I present my defense against the charges which have caused the Navy Department to institute proceedings against my commission as a Commander in the Naval Reserve, I should like to express my deep appreciation for this fair opportunity to defend myself, and to assure the Board that I shall not abuse the privelage nor take any longer than may be absolutely necessary.

It may seem odd that an officer should express gratitude at the opportunity to defend himself against charges, but I am unhappily aware of other Reserve Officers in other services who have held far less radical political opinions than myself but who have nevertheless been summarily dismissed with no opportunity to present their defense at all, as I shall demonstrate later.

Newspapermen and members of the group I have opposed have assumed and in some cases even boasted that this hearing is an empty and meaningless formality, and the decision has been made before I received my first word of the proceedings in the newspapers and on the radio and TV. But, on the other hand, the highest officials in the Navy Department have personally assured me that this hearing is NOT an empty formality, that it is NOT rigged, and I believe them, Gentlemen. I have loved the Navy and served it, and my Country loyally whenever called upon

WHITE MAN! ARE YOU GOING TO BE RUN OUT OF YOUR NATION'S CAPITOL... WITHOUT A FIGHT?

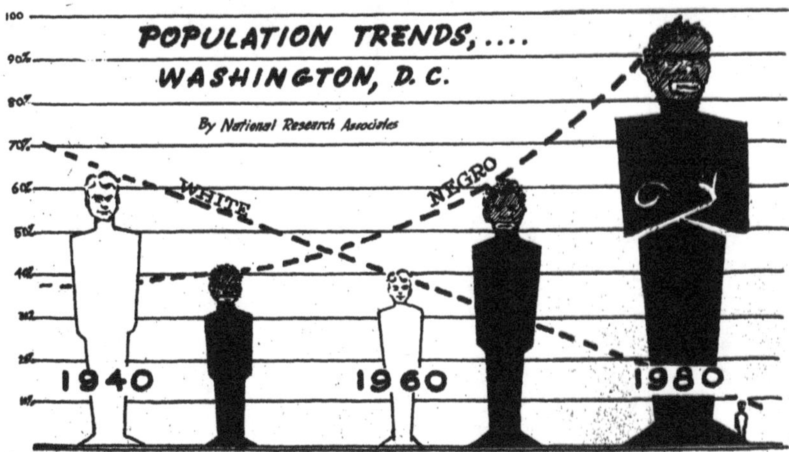

In 1940, Negroes were a MINORITY in e District of Columbia. The Police could ndle them because their hands were not tied outfits like the NAACP.

TODAY, the Negroes are in the large JORITY, (over 58%), and YOU HAVE BE-ME A HELPLESS AND PERSECUTED NORITY IN YOUR OWN CITY!!!

There are plenty of public streets in OUR city, in YOUR NATION'S CAPITOL, here YOU can't go at night without risking savage beating or death at the hands of rampaging herds of black hoods. And, as the recent mugging by blacks of the wife of the ex-secretary of the Air Force on a "nice" street shows, our white women are no longer safe at night ANYWHERE IN THEIR OWN CAPITOL!!

There are plenty of tragic families in D. C. where the sweet little white children can not go out and play at ALL, Because their neighborhood has suddenly become BLACK, and the white kids are assaulted and used indecently by lusting savage blacks if they go out to play in their OWN streets, -YOUR own streets. Their folks can't even move out, because the tidal wave of Negroes has destroyed the value of their home, and th not have the money to buy another home.

The police are powerless to contro hordes of brutal black criminals and ho because rotten political bosses know th black vote is just as good as YOURS to them at the public trough

By humbly licking the toes of the groes, the corrupt "leaders" have disco ed that they can get ELECTED every t and that is all they care about. Watch t

Small reproduction of one of the large red handbills we started passing out in down-town Washington - the "Gas Chamber Leaflets".

American Nazi Stormtroopers on the march battling in the streets against Jew-treason and race-mixing!

Swearing in new troopers

Honorable Discharge

NAVY DEPARTMENT · UNITED STATES OF AMERICA

from the Armed Forces of the United States of America

This is to certify that

Commander George L. ROCKWELL, U.S.N R., (106684)

was Honorably Discharged from the

United States Navy

on the 5th *day of* February, 1960 *This certificate is awarded as a testimonial of Honest and Faithful Service*

W. B. Franke

Secretary of the Navy

Copy of my Honorable Discharge

for almost twenty years, and I have never seen or known anything so dishonorable as would be such a procedure. I believe and trust in the assurance I have been given that, should the facts and evidence I give here so indicate, the Board will find that my private political activities have not and do not militate against my mobilization potential, and that the Board will recommend that I NOT be dismissed or discharged, in spite of the fearful pressure which all hands have told me has been brought to bear. And, should the Board recommend my retention, I have further been assured by the officials concerned that the Board's recommendations will be respected and considered as they properly should.

With the deepest gratitude for a fair hearing, therefore, I have done my utmost to prepare a statement and gather evidence which, in the short time which is reasonable, will, I hope, convince the members of this Board that it would not only NOT be in the best interest of the Navy and the Country to dismiss me from the service, but that my retention in the face of the organized pressure on the Navy Department will be a great and historic service to our American republic and our beleaguered people.

Now it is improbable that any of you gentlemen know me personally. Most of you have had no opportunity to form any judgment of me or my ideas and activities except through extreme, partial and distorted reports in a press which depends for its economic existence on the very group which I have opposed. I can imagine the thoughts which must have bounced around in your head as you prepared for this meeting -- as you tried to picture the "lunatic" -- the "odd-ball" -- or the villian -- you could not help but imagine this guy Rockwell to be. I am not hurt by such epithets. I am used to them. Every day hundreds of people come to see this "nutty monkey" in his "madhouse", which is as I would have it, because I am thus enabled to TALK to these people and win many of them. But I am concerned here lest this preconceived notion of my "madness" -- or this PREJUDICE, might so color and influence the Board, quite understandably, that it would not be able to accept the hard facts and the evidence I have to present to it, except as the frenetic frothings of a "lunatic".

To help establish what I hope is the fact that I am a sane, reasonably intelligent and competent American, and that my facts and evidence are worthy of the most careful consideration, I should like to respectfully show the members a few copies of a magazine with which you may be familiar, U.S. LADY. This is a magazine for the wives of officers and men of the armed forces. Perhaps your wives read and enjoy it. It was I who started and organized and drove that magazine into business in spite of the statements of the best informed professional opinion that it was "insane" to try to launch an international magazine on less than a million or so. My total capital was three hundred dollars, and, without meaning to boast, Gentlemen, I was able to succeed with the "insane" project, where even such luminaries as Mrs. George Catlett Marshall and dozens of others with more funds and influence had failed. U. S. LADY is published all over the world and reprinted often in Reader's Digest. Again, this is not to boast, but to demonstrate that a man able to accomplish this specific task is not a "lunatic".

I should also like to submit to the Board a few copies of the American Mercury, for which I wrote articles, including the two here on the Marine Corps, defending it against the disloyal and vicious attacks which were then being made on this great arm of the Navy. In the process, incidentally, I learned another fact in the chain of evidence which drives me to my present political battle, of which more later.

I earnestly hope these two examples of my sanity and ability will assist the Board in examining my facts and evidence in the light of their probity or their cogency alone, and without regard to the supposed "hate-crazed" "lunatic" who presents them.

The official letter from the Navy Department which instituted these proceedings charges me with the following:

1. That I have been an active participant and leader of various organizations styled along Nazi lines.

2. That I have publicly and openly espoused race and religious hatred.

3. That I have used, or permitted to be used, my rank and status in the Naval Reserve in printed matter distributed to the public fostering racial and religious hatred.

4. That I have departed the U. S. without the Navy Department's permission.

5. That my status as an officer commanding men made up, at least in part, of members of the races and religions at which my propaganda is aimed, is jeopardized.

First, let me say that I am guilty by oversight of the charge of leaving the U. S. without Naval permission. I was forced to send my family to Iceland where my wife's family lives, to avoid the persecution of ignorant or vicious persons who insulted, attacked, bombed and threatened my wife and little children. I went to visit them for only six days, and in the emotional stress of the occasion, forgot the rule about getting permission of the Navy. It would seem, however, unduly harsh to dismiss or discharge an officer from the Naval Service after almost twenty years and two wars for such an oversight, and I can assure the Board that it will not happen again.

The other four charges boil down to three things: (1) I have advocated racial and religious HATE (2) I have used my rank and status in the Naval Reserve in an improper manner, and (3) my ability to serve the Navy and my Country again in positions of Command is so reduced by my private political ideas and activities as a civilian that I would be no use to the Navy in the event of mobilization.

I shall accordingly confine my defense before this Board to proving that:

1. I have never promoted or advocated hate **EXCEPT** of traitors or subverters and others deserving of the hate of all decent, moral people, WITHOUT regard to their race or religion.

2. I have not used my rank or position in the Navy in any other manner or with any more impropriety than have all the other men such as Senators and Congressmen who have conducted a political campaign for election to office, as I am doing.

3. My mobilization potential is no lower than that of any other officer who commands men where there is a hostile racial situation, such as exists right now in thousands of cases.

Finally, I will do my best to show the board that it is not just sitting in judgement of one "odd-ball" officer, but that it is standing at a cross-roads in American history, as many a military tribunal before it has done, and that it has the hard but glorious decision before it of bowing to the pressure on the Navy Department, and continuing America on the downward path of despicable confusion, weakness and eventually slavery - or of standing tall and straight like their fathers and grandfathers, and putting the steel back in the American back-bone which once made us so proud of "iron men in wooden ships".

*** *** *** *** *** ***

All of you gentlemen are Naval Officers with experience, I presume, at sea. I feel sure that some of that experience has been in wartime. Let me ask you how YOU would handle a very special situation.

Suppose you are a very junior officer aboard a cruiser, let us say. You are on screen duty with a Fast Carrier Task Force. You are cruising blacked out on a zig-zag course in the inky darkness. You can't sleep in the heat below, so you go up into the warm dark wind on deck. You are lounging up against a barbette while your eyes get used to the blackness of the night. You begin to make out the looming guns above you and the dark hulks of the carriers, destroyers and the other cruisers in the formation. Then you see what appears to be a tiny blinking light to seaward of the formation - but ON YOUR OWN SHIP! For a moment you are stunned, but you are sure it is blinking a code. You rush over to where it seems to be coming from - and find the Exec lounging there! You tell him about it, flustered, and he scoffs at the very idea. Within two hours, all hands are piped to GQ, and there is a vicious submarine attack and a cruiser is blown in two. You turn over and over in your mind what you saw, but it is all too mixed up and incredible. But you begin to watch the exec in a new way. Two nights later, you find him again on deck, and blinking a tiny light. This time you study it, and read it. It is the zig-zag plan for the watch. - And the GUNNERY OFFICER is with him! You are too appalled to think. But you are sure now. You must stop the treacherous officers before it is too late. So you go to the Captain. He is reading a detective story in his bunk, and scolds you severely for even suggesting such a wild and ridiculous idea, and disturbing him at such an inconsiderate time. A short time later there is another attack, and more ships go down. You get desperate, and go back to the Captain. He is furious, and the whole thing is exploded as preposterous. But from then on, things are different. The Exec and the Gunnery officer see to it that your life is MISERABLE. You are discredited and given every menial or unpleasant task. The other officers, utterly unable to believe such treachery, make your life a very hell. No matter how hard you try to alert them or the Captain, the result is only more confirmation of your madness and vicious imagination.

I am sure it is unnecessary to continue the analogy, Gentlemen. Perhaps we are indeed wrong and mistaken in our beliefs as to the treason and treachery and subversion going on in our precious American ship of state, but if we are, then why is it utterly IMPOSSIBLE to get any hearing whatsoever for our charges of treason going on, and why are we damned and silenced eternally with nasty names, but with no investigation whatsoever of the FACTS we charge?

Let me ask you - would you not HATE the brother officer caught betraying your ship and shipmates to the enemy? Of course you would - if you were not queer! Is there anything WRONG with hatred of treason, treachery, cowardice and bullying? Can a man claim to be a good and moral man and NOT hate treason and treachery? Does the color of the traitor's eyes or hair or skin have anything whatever to do with the matter? Does it mean you hate a man's RELIGION because you discover him committing treason? Certainly not.

Over and over again, in all my publications and speeches I have repeated, "We hate or oppose NO man solely because of his race, which he can't control, and we do not oppose any religion or creed which does not first attack US!" Let me quote from several of the pamphlets we have issued. (Quote from front of "Who's a Hate Monger?", "We Challenge the Jews!", "White Man, etc., etc."). Those passages which we mean with every fiber of our being, should certainly dispel and disprove the charge that I or my associates have advocated hatred of ANY person solely because of his race or color, and that we have positively pressed for understanding and genuine help for the oppressed and innocent Negro people.

And we are positively NOT against any religion, insofar as

it does not ATTACK us, our people or the institutions we treasure. We are not concerned with any man's way of worshipping God, unless it involves making human sacrifices of us, for instance, or is otherwise inimical to our welfare. Let me read again briefly from this little pamphlet, "Who's a Hate Monger?" .... (first paragraphs on Creed)...

At the risk of overdoing this argument, please allow me to make this business of "hate" crystal clear; we do not advocate and have not promoted hate of ANY INNOCENT INDIVIDUAL or GROUP, BUT HAVE ONLY EXPOSED AND OPPOSED TRAITORS OR CREEDS WHICH ARE WORKING FOR THE DESTRUCTION OF AMERICA, OUR PEOPLE AND OUR IDEALS.

If you will check over our official printed program, you will note that it is scrupulously careful, again and again to set up safeguards to see that NO HUMAN BEING is persecuted or injured regardless of his race, color or creed, providing he has not tried to hurt US or commit treason. As a final example, let me submit the application form to join our Party, and point out the words of the oath signed by every member. (Read oath regarding expulsion from Party for persecution or harming of innocent people, regardless of race, color or religion, etc.)

Now, if exposing treason, even when it is committed wholesale by a small minority race of people, is "hate", then every district attorney in the Country is a hate monger for prosecuting the excessively large number of Sicilian Italians who are found to be gangsters. Fifteen Americans have been exposed and convicted of selling out our atomic secrets to the soviets, and of these fifteen, fourteen have been RACIALLY - not religiously - Jews. Seventeen out of twenty-one of the TOP U.S. Communists who were caught by the FBI, tried, convicted, imprisoned and then released by the U.S. Supreme Court - were all Jews again. - Not religious Jews, notice, because they are Communists, and Communists are atheists - but you have only to look at their faces to see that they are "Jewish looking", however distasteful that idea may be to tolerant Americans, and most of them make no secret of their RACE. The head of soviet propaganda, Ilya Ehrenburg, is a RACIAL Jew. This is neither the right time nor place, gentlemen, to present the pounds of unimpeachable documents we have to prove to any normally intelligent person that Communism has been Jewish from its codification by the Jew Karl Marx to

Lenin (real name Tsederbaum, see British Encyclopedia, 1920, Russian Revolution), Trotsky (real name Bronstien - see Trotsky's book "Stalin"), Litvinoff (real name Finklestien), etc., etc., etc., - almost to infinity - clear up to Khruschev, who was brought up in a Yiddish household, speaks Yiddish, and who boasted to Eleanor Roosevelt that even the wives of half the members of the Presidium of the Supreme Soviet were Jewish right NOW (Washington Evening Star) - but that is the FACT. Communism is simply Jewish, and there is no escaping that FACT. Any member of this board who believes that that statement is a fabrication is invited to inspect the files of documents we have to satisfy himself that we are NOT crazy or preaching "hate" because we recognize a vital fact in the defense of our Country and People.

It is getting more and more difficult for the filthy manipulators of public opinion to pretend that those of us who have discovered this GROUP treason by MOST of a small minority group are "hate mongers". Remember, we do not say that ALL Communists are Jews, nor that all Jews are Communists - we simply state the bald fact that the leadership and driving force of Communism all over the world comes from racial Jews, and that far too high a proportion of racial Jews are the promotors of Communism, and that instead of deploring this fact and admiting it, ALL Jewish organizations, without exception, deny it hysterically and resort to the most fiendish means of pressure to drive to distraction any American who tries to expose the problem and deal with it decently and intelligently. But more and more Americans of unimpeachable records and honesty are beginning to see the problem every day, and to stand up to the barrage of smear and filth and oppression they meet for publicly exposing the situation. Admiral John Crommelin, General Stratemeyer, General Del Valle of the Marine Corps, and many, many other military leaders are inevitably getting educated to the deadly problem and combatting it with all their strength, in spite of the smear bund.

And it is not only the top leaders, gentlemen, who are discovering what is really going on. I have already briefly showed you the copies of American Mercury with my articles appearing therein. In order to gather first hand material for these, the Marine Corps was kind enough to give me every assistance at Parris Island to study the "brutality" situation at the beleaguered training base.

The forces bent on weakening and softening America for

alien domination hate the Navy and Marine Corps especially for maintaining their aristocratic and authoritarian traditions, which are the foundation of high morale and discipline in a military organization, as any experienced commander knows. The outbreak of "brutality" charges, like the recent rash of "swastika" publicity were precisely planned by the termites eating at our foundations, and the episodes leading to the charges of Marine "brutality" had one amazing - and suppressed - aspect, which woke up a lot of Marines to what is going on. Most of the spoiled brats who complained so bitterly of the beatings and "brutality" of the D. I.'s were from the New York area, and I will give you only one guess as to what they were. I talked to suffering D. I.'s in batallion after batallion, and got the same sorry story about the wise-guy little Yids from New York who infiltrated the training base apparently with the specific purpose of provoking the incidents so they could be exploited by their brother termites in the Nation's press and information media. The D. I.'s knew it, the officers knew it, and I knew it - but I couldn't **WRITE** it, gentlemen, because of what the Bible calls "The fear of the Jews".

Most of you here today could, I am sure, tell harrowing tales of what you probably believe is simply "SNAFU" - situation normal, all fouled up. But what you may not know, unfortunately, is that many of these "SNAFU" situations should be called by the more unpronounceable name of "SNPFU" - situation normal, **PURPOSELY** fouled up! There are civilians in top places over the military, gentlemen, who are **PURPOSELY**, I am sorry to say, doing all they can to create confusion, injustice, exhaustion and dispair in our officers and men.

Again, gentlemen, I am aware that that seems too incredible to believe, so I have brought evidence and a witness of unimpeachable veracity to **PROVE** to you just one case, at the **HIGHEST POSSIBLE LEVEL.**

First, let me show you two photographs or photostats of a magazine, which I took myself at three o'clock yesterday afternoon in the Library of Congress. Here is the front cover of "New Masses" magazine, which I am sure you all know is the official Communist magazine. The date is December 8, 1942. Remember, this is not a "front" or a semi-Communist rag - this is IT, the **REAL THING!** On the front cover, listed as the contributor of an article, is Anna M. Rosenberg - and please note the middle initial, gentlemen. In this other photograph I have shown two inside pages of this filthy sheet of treason, and here is the DRAWING of Anna M. Rosenberg. Notice also that the Anna M. Rosenberg who wrote this Communist article is listed as the N.Y. State Regional Director of the War Manpower Commission, an office held by the "mistaken identity" Anna appointed to the second highest office in our defense establishment.

Now this evidence is EASY to get, even for me, all alone in the Library of Congress. For the FBI it is less than a cinch.

Can there be any doubt in YOUR minds as to the identity of this Anna M. Rosenberg, or that she wrote a Communist article for the official Communist magazine, "New Masses"?

Nevertheless, my brother officers and fellow Americans, this Hungarian Jewish woman, who was identified under oath twice as a Communist, and who wrote for a Communist magazine, WAS RECOMMENDED BY DWIGHT D. EISENHOWER AND GEORGE MARSHALL AND INSTALLED RIGHT HERE IN THE PENTAGON AS ASSISTANT SECRETARY OF DEFENSE FOR MANPOWER by Harry Truman, where she was master of all the hiring and manpower in our fighting forces!!!!

Perhaps this all sounds entirely TOO much to believe, so I have done my best to provide evidence you CANNOT discredit. I have asked one of America's greatest patriots to come down here and tell you how this Jewish Communist woman from Budapest was passed by your U.S. Senate to be master of our manpower, in spite of this horrible evidence of her disloyalty to this Country. Mr. Benjamin Freedman of New York, who is of the same race as Mrs. Anna M. Rosenberg - the race called "Jewish" - and thus cannot be accused of race or religious prejudice, is one of the men who has sacrificed almost everything good and pleasant in life, as I have, to try to save a Country and people to whom he is LOYAL.

Although the terms are somewhat confusing because of semantic meddling, Mr. Freedman is what the man in the street would call a "Jew" - and we are proud to say we will gladly protect Mr. Freedman and loyal Jews like him with our very lives. He has, like us, given up reputation, money, social position and almost everything else to expose and oppose TREASON in our land. He has been willing to come down here from New York at his own expense to try to explain to you, his fellow Americans, just ONE example of the kind of TREASON which is taking place in this blessed Country. I am mighty proud, gentlemen, to present to you Mr. Benjamin Freedman, of New York City, who will tell you of his experiences during the hearings by the Senate into the fitness of Anna M. Rosenberg to be Assistant Secretary of Defense.

Thank you, Mr. Freedman.

As the last item in my case against Anna Rosenberg, let me point out to the board that I am well aware that I am under oath, that the penalty for open and flagrant perjury is severe, and that there are stern laws against ciminal libel. Knowing all this, gentlemen, and conscious of the import of every word, I hereby state for the record that Anna M. Rosenberg is a Jewish Communist traitor to this Country. If this be a lie, let the forces which have precipitated this hearing to throw me out of the Navy use my open statement here to imprison me for both perjury and criminal libel. There will be no prosecution, you can be sure, because I can prove every word I have said in open court, and that is the LAST thing the conspirators and traitors want or could face.

And that, gentlemen, I hope, will serve to refute the first charge against me, that I have been promoting or advocating racial or religious hatred. I have tried to show you, and I fervently hope you believe me, that I have preached ONLY HATRED OF TREASON AND SUBVERSION, particularly by Communism, and that I have given you a practical demonstration that I am NOT wholesale against "all Jews" by showing you what is unfortunately a rare animal, a GENUINELY anti-Communist Jew.

I am next accused of using my position as a Commander in the Naval Reserve improperly by mentioning it in our propaganda. I respectfully submit to the board that I have mentioned the subject in only two pieces of literature, and only in an incidental fashion. In spite of some urging by associates, and though I believed it would not be improper, I have never printed pictures of me in uniform or with combat aircraft, etc. Here are the two pieces of literature. (Read quotes.) Now the propriety or impropriety of mentioning my service record and connections depends, it would seem, on the propriety, in turn of the literature on which the mentions appear. I am an honorable American who seeks a political career by being elected to office like any other American, in spite of the unorthodoxy of my views, and I believe I have the right to point with pride, as the saying goes, to my military record and honors the same as any other American seeking political office. Unless it can be shown that my literature is somehow immoral or wicked - which it CANNOT on the basis of facts, not nasty names - then I respectfully submit that the Navy has no more cause to dismiss me for mentioning my Naval record and position to further my political career than it has to dismiss the many other reserve officers who are senators or representatives and use this kind of material.

I further submit to this board that I have mentioned my service record and connection primarily because of the scurrilous and smearing attacks on my loyalty to this Country, which I submit is beyond reproach. It seems only fair that a man who is unceasingly attacked in the press and by loose talk as "disloyal" should be allowed to mention his willingness to fight for his Country, his record of having done so with honor, and his present position in his service.

The third charge, and the one easiest for me to understand, is that it might be difficult or impossible for me to command Jewish or Negro troops or officers in view of my ideas and activities, and that my mobilization potential might therefore be reduced beyond the point of any value to the Navy Department.

For two reasons, I do not believe that charge will "hold water".

First, on the RECORD, I have held and worked for the same ideas I now espouse a bit more dramatically - for over ten years. While I was a salaried worker for the Campaign for the Forty Eight States in Memphis, Tennessee, I was C. O. of Fasron 661 over at Anacostia, in the reserve Navy. I had Jewish and Negro officers and men, and never once allowed my private beliefs or opinions to violate my duty to Naval Regulations or policies. In fact, I discovered that two black mechanics in my squadron refused to try for advancement in rating, and that the reason was their fear of persecution and harrassment by officers and noncoms who used sneaky methods to oppose Naval regulations and policies and keep the Negroes "down" by invisible but very real pressure. I rose, as my officers can testify, at a meeting of Commanding Officers in the Ward-room, and adjured all hands to abide by the policy and rules and give the Negroes every chance they had coming to them, and to work to smooth the policy as much as possible. That is the TRUTH, and a check with my Jewish officer, for instance, Lt. Roth, will, I am sure, bear me out.

The second reason I am sure my mobilization potential has not been totally destroyed is that there are so many "hard-shell" southern White Men NOW serving in inferior capacities under Negro officers and non-coms, and there is no movement afoot to divest the Negroes of their commissions or positions, or to dismiss or discharge them as worthless. It would seem reasonable that if a young man from the back-woods of Mississippi can successfully serve under the orders and command of Colored Men, then the Colored Men and or Jews can also be asked, within reason, to serve under an all-out White Supremacist (in private opinion). In short, I respectfully submit, that all my fitness reports will show that I commanded by the BOOK, and my last Commanding Officer in Iceland especially noted, if I remember, that I was a fanatic on the subject of obeying regulations and policy, and can be counted on to do so if mobilized, regardless of the color or race of my men.

I believe I have shown this board so far that:

1. I have not promoted unfounded "hate" against ANY innocent person or group.

2. I have not used my Naval rank with any impropriety.

3. My value to the Navy and my Country in time of emergency is not reduced by my devotion to the fight to preserve my Country and my people in a private political organization.

Finally, gentlemen, I want to bring out an aspect of this presentation which is especially difficult, because it is hard to mention it without seeming impudent, or even arrogant. And I surely do not want to give this board any impression of arrogance or conceit. None is felt or meant. But I do feel, with all my heart, that this is much more than a simple hearing concerning the fate

Cover of "New Masses" - taken with ordinary camera in Library of Congress, D. C.

Inside pages of Communist "New Masses". Note Anna M. Rosenberg's article and picture.

STATE IN YOUR OWN WORDS WHY YOU WANT TO JOIN THE AMERICAN NAZI PARTY IN THE FOLLOWING SPACE PROVIDED (Please Print Clearly)

I Joined the American Nazi because it is the only political party that is offering any real opposition to communism and race mixing. It also is the only party that offers any real help to the people of this nation. this is the only party that recognizes the Negro Race problem and plans to mend the situation.

okay for F.B.I. inspection

I understand that if I ever knowingly violate any law of the United States, a State, or any local ordinance or regulation, - or if I commit an unprovoked act of aggression or violence or if I ever persecute or harm an innocent person, regardless of his religion or race, I will be summarily dismissed from the Party, and, if the offense is serious, I will be turned over by the Party to the proper authorities for prosecution.

Roy James
(Signature)

I hereby swear under Oath, in proper form of law and under the penalties of Perjury, that all of the above information is true and correct; that I have answered the questions herein with no purpose of evasion or for any reason other than to induce the American Nazi Party and its Commander to accept me and trust me as a member of said American Nazi Party because I wholeheartedly believe in the doctrines and aims of the American Nazi Party as set forth in its Program; and that I am not an agent or partisan of any other organization or group whatsoever whose ideals or aims are at variance or hostile to those of the American Nazi Party.

Roy James
(Signature)

State of Virginia
County of Arlington } ss.

Personally appeared before me, Romye Lamborn, a Notary Public in and for the County and State aforesaid, Roy James (name of applicant) and made Oath in proper form of law on this 26th day of February, 1961, that all the answers and statements in the above application are true.

Roy James
(Signature)

Subscribed and sworn to before me.

Romye Lamborn
Notary Public (signature and seal)

My commission expires: Nov. 24. 1961.

Last page of Trooper's Oath--note part marked with arrow. We do not tolerate blind and stupid "hate."

Meeting of American Nazi Party

ssary, and which cannot be tolerated in any for
reeding disintegration and disease.

Government

We shall use only legal, constitutional means to win power in the United States, because we know the people will *demand* our services in government when they finally awake to the Jewish subversion of our people. Until then, we must train, and be prepared to establish an orderly government when the present false prosperity, false peace, false welfare, and false government blow sky-high under the blows of the Jews, as they surely will.

In power, we shall re-establish the actual function of the electoral college as intended by the wise founding Fathers of our Country to protect us from demagoguery, and we shall return the election of Senators to the State Legislatures.

We shall make the pay of all government employees directly dependent on their efficiency, apply modern business methods to government operation, and ruthlessly eliminate the hordes of bureaucratic parasites who make our present government the world's most wasteful, inefficient and extravagant.

We shall call a constitutional convention to draw up amendments and strike out others to enable all the above program, and to insure that never again can any subversive conspiracy bring this great Nation to the very brink of extinction.

Greatly enlarged portion of A. N. P. Program. Let the reader judge if we advocate "overthrow" or "subversion" of the Constitution.

of one officer and his commission which he treasures. I believe that if I try hard enough and do well enough in my plea to you as brother Naval officers and as fellow Americans, you might see with me that this is one of those rare historic opportunities when men of decision stand at a cross-roads. How many officers have wondered what THEY would have done at the court-martial of Billy Mitchell, for instance? Would they have rolled along with the crowd and the "right" opinion, or would they have had the vision and above all the COURAGE to stand against the colossal pressures of "right-thinking" people to vindicate the truth? History shows that usually they do not. From the days when all the "decent" "right-thinking" people nibbled grapes in the Colosseum and wondered at the "lunatics" and "fanatics" who were fed to the lions as "Christians" - followers of the most HATED man of his time and for years thereafter - right up until today when a golf-playing Nero sits helplessly and unconcernedly in the White House while his people grow daily weaker and more confused before the subversion and treason of International Communism and Zionism, the human race has steadfastly persisted in lionizing its boobs and crucifying its saviors.

Here is where I tread the dangerous ground of apparent conceit, Gentlemen, but I assure you I speak humbly and only out of the DEEPEST concern for our Nation and our people. I have given up my family, my income, my earning capacity, my social status, my comfort, my safety and often my liberty, and I may be called upon to give up my life - for something I believe in more strongly than the urge to preserve my own existence. It is only in THAT light that I say to you, my judges here, you stand at a great cross-road in American History, as did Washington at Valley Forge.

I BEG this Board to see our Nation as it is "co-existing" TODAY, and to ask themselves if John Paul Jones would have begged the Captain of the Serapis if he would please not shoot but sail along beside the Bon Homme Richard because Captain Jones was afraid his crew might be decimated by the British big guns - or if Stefan Decatur would have invited the Barbary pirates to luncheon in his cabin and begged his crew not to stir up the brutes for fear they might be offended and want to fight!!!

Five of our top Generals and Admirals in the Korean War testified before Congress that they could have WON the Korean war, the first lost war in our history, but that they were ORDERED not to win by enigmatical forces in Washingtons bureaucracy. General Clark, I believe it was, even testified that he got **FORGED ORDERS** demanding withdrawals, and that he was unable to get any investigation of this monstrous TREASON. In view of the evidence presented here against Anna M. Rosenberg, do you gentlemen have any doubt as to WHO ordered us to lose that war - and all our courageous men - or WHY?

At this VERY MOMENT, the Chief of Staff of the U.S. Army is a man named Lemnitzer - and he is the man who testified before the Congress that it was HE who prevented the arming of South Korea as provided by Congress, and thus precipitated the tragic Korean War. Our honest military planners realized that defenseless South Korea would inevitably attract a Communist invasion - as it DID, and appropriated millions of dollars to arm and train South Korea. Lemnitzer was the man put in charge, and he nonchalantly testified that he prevented delivery of ALL arms and ammunition, and delivered ONLY exactly $ 27.00 worth of barbed wire! ! Yet he has been picked as top military officer.

There are only a very few officers here, gentlemen. But so were there a few at Thermopolae, or Horatio's Bridge - or Valley Forge. But they realized their task and stood up to it manfully, and successfully. I realize the pressure that has already been brought on the whole Department for over a year, to oust me. Here is one clipping which flagrantly shows not only who is bringing the pressure, but how they lie and misrepresent. The Anti-Defamation League of B'nai B'rith headlines in THEIR paper (while suppressing all word of our activities in other papers) that we are "threatening American Jews with the gas chamber" - when the truth is, as we have pointed out over and over again, that we threaten ONLY traitors, Jews or non-Jews alike. They also admit that they have pressured the Navy Department to oust me, and I am aware of the pressures that may be exerted on the members of this board should they conclude that it would be utterly wrong and cowardly to oust me in the face of this dishonest pressure.

But that will be small sacrifice if we can at last show the manipulators and subverters, the traitors and the liars that the blood of our fighting forefathers still flows in our veins, and we will **NO LONGER BOW BEFORE THREATS AND PRESSURE.**

It is impossible for me to change twenty, thirty or forty

years of opinion-forming based on information WHOLLY on one side - in a matter of minutes here today. The most I can hope to have done is demonstrate beyond question in only one or two of the thousands of cases available, that you are being cheated, lied to, and wrecked as military forces by a criminal gang of traitors such as Anna M. Rosenberg, - that the million and one vexations which you lay up to Pentagon "red-tape" are often as not the result of PLANNED and SPREAD confusion and disruption, as demonstrated at Parris Island - that your blessed Nation and its long-suffering, tolerant, easy-going people are in deadly danger from RIGHT HERE IN THIS PENTAGON and HERE IN AMERICA, - far more than from overseas.

On my honor as an officer, by all that I hold dear and sacred, my brother officers, I swear to you that there are TRAITORS crouched in the darkness at the life-lines of America, signalling their treachery and treason to their cohorts abroad and leading you in tolerance and "brotherhood" to your destruction! And I HATE them, gentlemen! They boast they will "bury" you, and they are DOING it, by stealth and by guile. They DESERVE our hate.

Our flag-ship of state is utterly surrounded by wolf-packs of submarines, and I and my suffering, persecuted brother patriots have CAUGHT THEM RED-HANDED signalling to the enemy. We have tried to alert our "ship-mates" - and are hounded and driven and damned for our pains. The turn-coats have won the favor of the Captain; they control the writing of the ship's log; they control the stores and the quartermaster at the wheel so that we are running in circles.

I am all alone in my warning, and, as has happened a thousand times in history, nobody wants to hear or believe my ugly news about men who appear to be loyal shipmates. Nobody will investigate my FACTS, and there are almost none to stand before the howling mobs who have been trained to shout "hate monger" at anyone discovering these FACTS.

I humbly and most earnestly BEG you, gentlemen, to come on deck with me and SEE for yourself the treacherous signalling going on in the dark. Before you dismiss a loyal officer from an organization he has served for twenty years at the behest of a pressure group, look for YOURSELF at the traitors blinking to the enemy fleets out there in the night. Stand with me, if only for a moment, at the life-lines of America, and you will understand WHY, after two bloody wars in which millions and millions of Christian White Men have been killing each other - we are in worse shape than EVER BEFORE.

I am not ashamed, Gentlemen, to IMPLORE you - show the traitors and subverters that there are still MEN in the United States Navy who will NOT bow before the promoted pressure of hysterical public opinion nor before the direct pressure of a gang of professional manipulators and secret terrorists. The question here is not one officer and his fate, but: Can mature and alerted American military men CONTINUE TO BE STAMPEDED by an organized minority bent on treason and subversion of our Nation and people?

They are up there at the life-lines NOW, flashing their treachery to the enemy, poised and ready! Come top-side and, for the sake of your Country and your God, SEE what they are doing!

Then square your jaw as your forefathers did, steel your will, and tell these sneaks that America has TURNED AT LAST! Tell them that there are STILL iron men in the United States Navy who can not be bullied and frightened into dismissing a loyal and hard pressed brother officer for standing up to traitors!

In the best traditions of the Naval Service, Gentlemen, tell the bastards to go to hell!

Lincoln Rockwell, Commander
United States Naval Reserve

This was such a gross violation of all civil rights and justice - to throw a man out of the service after almost twenty years of honorable service in two wars - that I considered how best to dramatize the outrage. I decided to use the American Civil Liberties Union - an organization supposedly dedicated to protecting ANYBODY'S civil rights - but which often seems to fight mostly for Communists. By publicly asking their help, I put them in a tight spot, and insured publicity.

They also had an interest in helping me. They considered

me, at the time, a mere gad-fly, a nasty little mosquito on the body politic - and had something to gain by defending me and then pointing to the fact as evidence of their absolute dedication to the principles of civil rights, regardless of their hatred of the individual or his ideas.

It was while I was discussing the Navy situation with the ACLU that the struggle in the street occurred. So, on the next occasion, the matter naturally came up. The Jewish head of the Washington office, Lawrence Speiser, asked if I wanted counsel. When I said "Yes", he assigned me a particularly Jewy looking Jew, by the name of Shapiro.

The hanging jaws of the other Jews as we marched into the crowded prosecutor's offices that morning with Shapiro leading the way for his Nazi clients were worth the whole fight - just to see. And old Shapiro went to bat for us with a will and typical Jewish cleverness. He succeeded in having the charges against both parties dropped. Meanwhile, out in the corridor, I was explaining to the newspapers that it might be necessary later to gas Shapiro too, as he was suspiciously active with the Communists.

The whole thing was too much for the papers to suppress. Out it came, as we had calculated - and the Party had once again achieved a major victory without funds and with nothing but guts and brains.

Little by little, the publicity began to bring us more men, and we put these to work on the streets, too.

I had managed to promote a job in a little print shop under an assumed name, and worked like a mad-man for almost nothing, just to survive. But it didn't last long. I had brought my own photo and art gear to the shop, and one night hoods broke in and ripped and smashed it all. Somebody had found out I was in there. The next day fifty special policemen were assigned to watch the place. Needless to say I had to leave.

I worked for awhile in a sign shop, but again somebody learned of it and all hell broke loose.

However, our fighting exposures of Jewish treason were beginning to bring in a trickle of support again, and we redoubled our distributions and activities.

Finally, in December, Floyd Fleming, the most faithful of all American patriots, was inspired by our successes to make a down-payment for us on a new headquarters - even closer to the White House than before - in Arlington. We were BACK "on the banks of the Potomac".

Warner was doing a good job of organizing our mailing list and getting material to the sympathizers. The funds began to come in in a steady but small amount.

On official party stationery, which is extremely impressive, I now requested a permit from the Department of the Interior to speak on the grounds of the Washington Monument on April 3 - the earliest the weather would be warm enough.

They denied this, but did give me the information that I could speak without a permit on a ground almost as good on the Mall, between the U. S. Capitol and the Washington Monument - right beside the Smithsonian Institute. Millions of tourists pass by this spot, and we got the Interior Department to set up a roped-off area for us. We built a speaking stand, got a PA system on credit, and organized our men in a defense force.

The first attempt at speaking in the wide open as NAZIS was pretty terrifying. We kidded each other endlessly as to who would run first, etc., but prepared for April the third with iron determination.

When the great day arrived, we had Nazis from as far away as Detroit and Florida.

And then it rained!

I think our reaction is the proof that we will win our goal of power. Human ingenuity and will is, as we have stated before, the mightiest force on earth.

I knew the "silent-treatment" which had been prepared for our speeches on the Mall by the Jewish dominated press. The Jews endlessly reminded each other in their private sheets - which we got - that we were like all the other little rabble rousers and would dry up and disappear if denied publicity. So they were not going to mention it if we set fire to the White House or ran through the streets naked.

But they couldn't resist reporting our "failures". I remembered "Fiasco for a Fuehrer".

So I arranged a "failure" for them.

We went down in the rain without any of our shiny paraphernalia, stood in the downpour like drowned birds, and I gave a sad little talk to our tiny audience of troopers.

The Washington Evening Star took the bait hook, line and sinker!

They printed a three-column cut of my soaked speech and wet Nazis, and ran a supercilious little story on the big Nazi "flop". They even wrote up an editorial showing the good citizens what failures we Nazis were.

So the next week, when the sun shone, we went down there and showed them what Nazis really are. I had never made a real oration before, and was pretty lousy at first, mostly because of nervousness. It is bad enough to have to make one's first speech, but when it must be made in fear of one's life and fear of arrest or other catastrophe - it becomes quite a problem to stay cool and in command of the situation.

We played the Star Spangled Banner and the Horst Wessel song, then I launched into my speech. For two hours, I exposed the full villainy of the Jewish conspiracy, and documented fact after fact which have been hidden from our brain-washed people. At first the crowd was sullen and hostile, but as I drove home point after point, there was more interest, and I could feel the hostility melting in the warmth of wonder and amazement at the astounding facts which once amazed me too.

Our first rally was a huge success, even though we had less than a thousand people, and we went back to the headquarters to sing the Party song until our lungs fairly burst, and celebrate our entry into the speech-making business.

But in spite of the success and the fact that uniformed Nazis and storm troopers were making speeches in the Nation's Capital, the Jews clamped on their hooded censorship, and we remained unknown, except for the isolated rantings of Drew Pearson.

We had to FORCE the Jews to take notice of us, and on a national basis.

I had to come up with another publicity miracle somehow or other, since we were still relatively unknown outside of the East Coast. I applied the tested and excellent formula again, and decided to make the boldest possible move.

Union Square in New York City is the traditional stamping grounds of the Communists and Jew traitors. Hundreds of them scream filthy threats at our people and our government there every day, year in and year out. It is the pulsing heart of Marxism in the U.S.A.

So I demanded a permit from New York City to speak there too.

That was all that it took.

At first there was little reaction. The word went out as the Jews always try first, "Ignore Rockwell and his provocations!".

But Jews being Jews, and, as I have demonstrated, psychopathic paranoids, they are constitutionally incapable of ignoring anybody who brazenly defies them and their repulsive claims to be God's chosen people with the sole right to insult and wreck everybody else while they themselves are sacred and holy. And when one announces coldly that he intends to try those suspected of treason, and then kill them in the gas chamber when they are convicted - their psychotic personalities get the better of them and they become the ancient, hate-filled, vengeful Jews of the Old Testament - the same gang of "Pharisees" who got the Romans to crucify Jesus Christ.

The Communist worker launched a protest when they heard the Commissioner of Parks planned to give me a permit, in accordance with my plain rights.

Then the Jewish New York Post let go with a blast. The Jewish papers began to howl, and finally the dignified and disguised Jewish press, including the New York Times, began to mutter darkly about the matter. And all this time, Communists were openly preaching destruction of this Country in that same Union

Square, without a peep of protest - just as we knew would happen.

Within a few days, the full Hebrew chorus let loose, and New York made its Jewish character plain for all the world to see, as they went WILD. Jews ran to all the Jew judges and demanded everything from injunctions to electrocutions. The papers raged and argued. The Civil Liberties Union, caught in an impossible position had to stand for my rights to preach the trial and execution of such of their own members as might be convicted of treason. This enraged the Jews beyond all bounds, and they ranted and screamed at each other in a most satisfying and ludicrous manner. For the first time in history - exposing each other!

Finally a gang of these lovers of free speech and tolerance got a temporary injunction against my appearance in Union Square and there was to be a hearing on the matter in New York Supreme Court.

I decided to go up there and use my newly found legal abilities to fight for my rights.

When I arrived at the Court House, it was surrounded by herds of Jews, acres of them, howling and screaming and waving picket signs. They didn't recognize me as I walked past all of them and into the Court room, where I sat down quietly.

When the clerk announced the case, pandemonium broke loose. In all the courtrooms I have ever been in, I NEVER saw anything like that! At least FIFTY lawyers all ran up to the bench to demand I be run out of New York. They still didn't know I was there. But somehow the TV people had found out, and asked me to give an interview after Court. I agreed, and then stepped up to the bench among the pack of snarling Jewish lawyers. When the judge asked if anybody else wanted to be heard, after all the Jews had yelped their pieces, I spoke up - and the hot hate which then turned on me was something you could feel - and SMELL.

Immediately one of them demanded I be committed to the insane asylum. The judge pushed that outrage aside, and I got a chance to speak my piece. Then they lit into me. Who were my associates? Backers? Their addresses? How many troopers? Where? - They were making up their black lists. They read off selected excerpts from our "gas chamber" literature. They told sob stories of concentration camps, showed "tattoos" and "scars" and put on unbelievable exhibitions in a court room. The judge tried his best to keep order but it was almost impossible with that wild mob at the bench.

A rabbi in the audience fell on his back with his arms and legs sticking up like a dog playing dead - and actually FROTHED at the mouth! He was carried out.

Finally the judge called a short recess and the TV people asked me to step into the great marble rotunda of the Court House for an interview. As I emerged out there, I was blinded by the huge lights they had set up, and discovered I was solidly surrounded by Jews and Jews and more Jews.

The interviewer asked me if I intended to gas the Jews, and I told him that was ridiculous, we intended only to gas TRAITORS, Jews and anybody else who was convicted of treason - a Constitutional provision. Then he asked how many Jews I thought that might be, and I truthfully told him I could only GUESS from the number of Jew spies, etc. - but I thought it would probably be about eighty percent of the adult Jews we would have to gas.

That did it!

They began to scream, "Kill him! Kill him!" - a shout reminiscent of certain passages in the New Testament - and they closed in on me with insane rage. They got hold of me and knocked over the TV cameras and men, and I struggled to stay on my feet in the wild melee. Two husky New York City detectives forced their way through the mob and began to work me toward a dead-end hallway. We made it, and barricaded it off as we battled the bloodthirsty mob. They hustled me and Roger Foss, the trooper who had come with me, into a back room as more police and the riot squad arrived.

Finally sufficient order was restored to start the court hearing again, and I was guarded by squads of officers as we finished up. Then they asked me what I wanted to do, and if I planned to go to City Hall. The police were thoroughly respectful of my rights, courteous and courageous in the face of that murderous mob. They offered to enforce my rights anywhere in New York I wanted to go and for as long as I wanted to stay - even offering a police guard if I took a hotel room.

But I knew the Jews - and I was proved right in a very few days. They would use ANY pretext to lock me up for good and to hell with my rights, etc. My best bet was to get out of New York, and that's what I told them I wanted to do. They gave me a heavy escort out of the building, but even so it seemed impossible we could get through. I expected to have to battle - but the cops held back the mob except for one Jew who managed to spit into the car as we drove off.

We got on a plane at LaGuardia Airport - and the first great political battle was over. The Jewish-dominated press, of course, headlined that I was given the "bum's rush" by the cops - an outright lie!

We had won millions and millions of dollars of priceless publicity; we had demonstrated that it is possible to defy the Jews and survive; we had pointed up the glaring inconsistency of the Jewish hysteria about us in Union Square compared to their silence about the Communists; we had gotten the Jews fighting desperately among themselves as to how to handle us, and we had made the American Nazi Party the most dynamic, powerful name in the right wing in only a few months.

But I knew that we would have to pay the cost of the victory. We had yanked the tail of the tiger, and he would soon bare his yellow fangs at us. I warned my lads not to get overconfident and cocky, over and over again. We had learned to hold them at bay on the mall.

I had gained more and more skill as a speaker and had even learned to hold them with the power of voice and will alone. When they would scream and heckle and threaten to attack, I would point them out to the watching gentiles and embarrass even those brassy Jews so much they would subside. Once I had one of the boys put on a big plastic nose and eyeglasses, and come down and pretend to be a heckling Jew - which drove the long-nosed genuine variety almost out of their minds with helpless rage. They can't stand to be laughed at - and the nose bit is too much for them. They claim they are only a religion, so, of course, they can't take official offense at the phony beaks, without giving the game away.

After New York, however, I knew they HAD to get us, one way or the other. Sure enough, on the 3rd of July, they arrived in huge force, over two hundred and fifty of them - and the story of that riot is on the first pages of this book. I never got to say a single word, before they began their filthy howling and shrieking. And where the police had once been fair and square, they now retired, to allow these monsters full play. Even so it took them over an hour and a half to get up their courage to attack the nine of us!

All nine of us were arrested, along with a token sprinkling of three or four Jews, and offered the chance to forfeit ten dollars collateral. We demanded trial, and were released on posting our ten dollars each.

We went immediately out to Glenn Echo Amusement Park, where the Jews and Negroes were picketing for admission into the all-white park, and picketed NAACP and CORE troops. We were all torn, bruised, bleeding and bandaged - from the afternoon's battle - and our exhibition of courage and will won us a huge group of young men who came and saw and understood what it is to be WHITE MEN and FIGHT for survival.

The next day, our usual Sunday, the Jews, I am sure, were relaxing in the certain belief that we would not try to speak again. But to make doubly sure, the head of the department of Parks called me and advised me not to go down, lest we all be killed this time. He said they couldn't guarantee our safety - a travesty after the Park Police exhibition of the day before. I told him we were coming anyway. So then he told me there would be no speaking stand. I said OK. Then he said there would also be no ropes. No cops either, I presumed. He was dumbfounded when I said I would speak even if alone on the bare ground! The Jews are so sure anti-Semites are the craven cowards they always depict on their TV propaganda shows they couldn't imagine a man who would go down after a riot, beating and jailing, with no protection or police, and try it again! I told them I would be there at the usual time.

At two o'clock on the button we appeared with a red oil bucket for me to stand on. We set it up against a tree so they could attack from only three sides. Ten or twelve of our men gathered around me and I had just started to speak - when a delegation of police arrived with a paper still wet from a photocopy machine. They handed it to me and I read it while the mob watched.

George Lincoln Rockwell, leader of the American Nazi Party, addresses a sprinkling of his followers at a meeting near the Mall yesterday. He then called off the rally because of rain.—Star Staff Photo.

Rain Soaks Rockwell's Nazi Party

The American Nazi Party held a brief, rain-soaked meeting in the park at Ninth street and Constitution avenue N.W. yesterday.

The leader, George Lincoln Rockwell, made a short speech to a handful of his followers. He called off a scheduled rally because of the rain and promised to try again next Sunday.

T. Sutton Jett, associate director of National Capital Parks, said the meeting was held in one of the four park areas where political rallies of any kind may be conducted without permission.

This area, near the Mall, was the scene of rallies by racist John Kasper and demonstrations against the execution of atom spies Julius and Ethel Rosenberg.

The Nazi Party had asked permission to hold the rally in the Sylvan theater, but park authorities turned them down because the Monument area is crowded with tourists.

Yesterday's session was uneventful. Few passersby noticed what was taking place.

Clipping from "Washington Evening Star" - they took the bait!

Morning calisthenics for officers and troopers living at Headquarters

Getting picketting instructions from chief of Police, Democratic National Headquarters.

Photo of American Nazi Party rally in German equivalent of "Life"

It was a brand new order closing the park to speaking. I asked the officer what other areas were available for speaking, and they told me of a park near the municipal court. I told him we would proceed there and speak. He tried to dissuade me because of the "high feeling" - but I started to the new place.

When we arrived, it was already jammed and crammed with the same mob of murderous, screeching Jews! HOW they let us know this would be IT - we would get it for sure today!

The authorities showed me where I was to speak, and I stood up to begin with the circle of troopers around me. The Jews began the old tactic of howling "Sick! Sick! Sick!" and other endearments to drown me out, and began to move in closer and closer. The day before, there had been the claim that we had provoked these villians, so I determined that this time we would force them to be so obvious in their terrorism, if they dared, that no policeman could stomach it. I resolved to put the obedience and courage of my men to the acid test.

I ordered them to TURN AROUND - with their backs to the same raging mob of thugs and hoods which had attacked and injured them just the day before.

Every man obeyed, although there were many wondering glances up at me as I stood there on my bucket with my arms folded. I lit a cigar to dramatize the fact that I was not even TRYING to speak or provoke the Jews, and we stood thus for what seemed hours while the Jews howled and threatened and raved.

It worked!

The police moved in between the worst of the Jew attackers and our boys, and the Jews began to feel the full emotional wave of disgust everybody else there felt for their savage antics. Little by little they lost cohesion as a mob. Some Jews began to yell "Let him speak", as they realized THEY WERE DEMONSTRATING BY THEIR ACTIONS WHAT I WAS TRYING TO PROVE, BETTER THAN IF I HAD SAID IT! They began to quarrel among themselves like a pack of rats.

After an hour of this, I ordered my men to face forward once more. Silence spread as I took command of that mob with the force of will, even without saying a word.

I began to speak. There were sporadic outbreaks of hysterical yelling, but it was mostly by women and hangers-on. The brutal terrorists themselves were beaten and they knew it.

I made my speech successfully - with TV and movie cameras grinding away - and we marched out of that park victorious.

Our friends who were seeded in the Jew crowd told us afterward of the bitterness with which these lovers of free speech reproached each other for their cowardice in not attacking us as planned!

CHAPTER XV

On July sixth we went to have our "day in court" on the riot of July 3rd.

The imposing Municipal Court Room of the District of Columbia was jammed with Negroes and Negro policemen, as batch after batch of the dregs of humanity were dredged up from the drunk tanks below and herded into court for their one and two minute "trials". Judge Neilson on the bench was noted for his severe sentences and harsh judgments, and my men and I sat for hours watching him mete out two and three month sentences in jail to defendants on an assembly line schedule. We were waiting for our turn to face the old judge.

Now I stood in Court, charged with "Disorderly Conduct", and prepared with plenty of evidence to show WHO promoted the disorder and certain of acquittal.

But before I could begin my defense, I got one of the heaviest shocks of my life, although, as our friends will know, I had been expecting what happened. But I was so wrapped up in righteous indignation at the charges and my facts and arguments, that it very nearly caused me to lose my composure when the prosecutor stepped up and said, "Your Honor, I believe I have a prima facie showing here that this defendant may not be of sound mind and may not be competent to stand trial. Under the Federal Rules of Criminal Procedure and the District Code, I move that he be committed to the Psychiatric Ward of the D. C. General Hospital for a period of thirty days for observation"!!!!!

The murmur of joy from the horde of Jews and the ADL, who had filled up the Court Room, was audible. I realized immediately that, with no knowledge of the rules in insanity proceedings, I would never stand a chance against whatever devilish plans the ADL had cooked up with the prosecutor. In addition, I had had no opportunity to prepare any defense whatever. So I asked the Court for a lawyer and a continuance to get my balance and prepare a fight.

Since it was clearly my privilege to have an attorney in such serious proceedings, the Court granted my request, and gave me a man who was an experienced police-court lawyer, but who naturally had little knowledge of the kind of political battle involved and little imagination. Most of his practice consisted of drunk, disorderly and petty police-court cases, but he was honest and turned to with a will to help all he could.

We got a three week continuance and permission to hire our own psychiatrists to establish my sanity and competence.

Then we tried to find two Gentile psychiatrists to examine me - and learned once again why the White Man is being driven out of existence. Because of greed or cowardice or both, NOT A SINGLE PSYCHIATRIST IN THE AREA WOULD EXAMINE ME AND TESTIFY!! Finally I found one Irishman who would examine me and who gave me a letter as to my sanity, but that was not acceptable in Court, of course. Nevertheless, it was the best we could get, so we paid him, and got the letter.

Meanwhile we were getting hundreds of telephone calls from ugly-sounding Jews threatening us with death and destruction if we re-appeared again.

Since the police had ruled that the Jews could yell and heckle to their heart's content, and I had been attacked because we voluntarily agreed to the police request to remove our precautionary troops from the crowd (where they kept things broken up) - I decided to give the Jews a dose of their own medicine. I organized our rapidly growing troops into four squads in two ranks, and we practiced a new tactic out behind the headquarters on the drill field. On command, any ordered number of squads would march out and surround would-be "hecklers" who were working themselves up to attack (keeping their arms folded so as not to be accused of hitting anybody) and roar back at the Jews. We had already found that individual Jews were not so red-hot for combat when our men stayed out in the crowd right where fisticuffs might result in broken Jewish noses, and I knew that the would-be meeting-wreckers would not last long surrounded by MY men exercising their right to heckle the hecklers.

So, as we began to get the usual Jewish welcome the next Sunday, I ordered out the first two squads of men. One of my men, a monsterous individual named Al Wiengin, couldn't resist adding his own little fillip to my orders to keep his arms folded, and brought his folded arms up heavily under the chin of a big Jew as he came up to him.

Immediately, the police arrested all of us - even the man holding the flag, and packed us all off to jail. Incidentally, for those who are not familiar with such affairs, the jail is not half bad, compared to the police wagon on a hot day!

Ventillation is almost nil; the wagon is, of course, black; and, if you have ever gotten into your car after it has been in the hot sun - you know one-half of what it is like inside that wagon. And when you are in there an hour or so, packed together like sardines, sweating like pigs in a dark oven - the cool jail seems like heaven itself.

While we waited to get bailed out (most of the day) we roared the party song, squirted water at each other, and had such a ball in that jail, that several slow-witted Negroes asked who we were. When we told them they wanted to join and said it looked like fun.

But, as a result, before we had had a chance to find a psychiatrist who would testify, I found myself once again facing Judge Neilson. I could have forfeited ten dollars "collateral" and avoided it, but as a matter of principle, we had to establish our right to speak without being "convicted" for disorderly conduct each time, so I chose to face him again, come what may.

And come it did. Again the prosecutor brought up his charges of incompetence and insanity, and this time I could not get the Court to wait for my own psychiatrists. The D. A. presented three witnesses. One was a photographer who had been at our headquarters. He testified to the signs we have up telling about the Jews, etc., but admitted on cross-examination he considered me thoroughly competent. Another was a man who had joined us the year before to write a psychology paper. He acted most ashamed, as he had since learned how right we were, and did the prosecutor little good. Under cross-examination, he, too, admitted he believed I was sane and able to stand trial.

But then the prosecutor brought out the inevitable Jew.

Dr. Shultz, the head of the D.C. General Hospital, took the stand and showed dozens of photostats of cartoons I had done for the college humor magazine "Sir Brown" TWENTY YEARS AGO AT BROWN UNIVERSITY. Since then I had fought two wars for my country, risen from enlisted ranks to Commander in the Navy, commanded three Navy squadrons, established two successful businesses and a currently successful national magazine, U. S. LADY - and never been accused of being "sick". The photostats were kindly donated to the prosecutor by the Anti-Defamation League of B'nai B'rith - the inevitable Jew! Dr. Shultz also had some of our Party literature, and he testified he read it and it showed that I was "very probably very 'sick' " - "Paranoid"! Such hatred of "nice people" (i.e. Communist Jews) was evidence, he testified, that I was probably very dangerous! (There is a good bit of grim humor in that. To traitors, I AM dangerous.)

Under cross-examination, the great Doctor admitted he had never even seen me before in his life, and didn't even know if the stuff given the prosecutor by the ADL was my work!!!!!

But this seemed like a nice way to put an end to the Jewish pressure and agitation which was and is driving the public officials of D. C. to injustice and even perjury in some cases. So the judge ruled that I must be dragged off and locked up with the lunatics for a month to see if I could "understand the charges against me and assist my lawyer in my defense"!!!

For citizens who have never experienced the more brutal side of the law, it is something of a shock to discover how quickly the decorum and genteel atmosphere of the courtroom shifts to the naked force of the prison once the judge orders a commitment. As it becomes apparent that the verdict will be "guilty", three or four husky "marshals" slide in behind you, and, at the last word, hook a hammy hand in your belt and growl "Let's go!". You are lucky to hand your papers, etc., to a friend beside you before you are shoved out the side door and behind bars in a big cage which usually contains a herd of wretched looking criminals, mostly black, shuffling around, vomiting and spitting on the floor and all explaining how they were "railroaded".

Back into the filthy tank I went with the human scum until the patrol wagon came to trundle a load of us off to the jail and the insane ward. Those who have never ridden in a patrol wagon on a broiling summer day with a load of unwashed blacks will not be able to imagine the peculiar nature of this refined torture. There are only four little slits for air in the black wagon, which absorbs heat far worse than an ordinary auto in the hot sun, and it reaches well up above a hundred in only minutes. Jammed in with the reeking blacks for even a few moments is an olfactory experience never to be forgotten, to say nothing of the unbearable heat. And there is no rush to get the trip over. There are interminable waits for papers, for shifting prisoners, etc., so that the trip lasted a good hour, at the end of which even my socks were soaked with sweat and I feared I was permanently flavored with the stench of unwashed black bodies.

Finally, however, I was taken, under double guard to one of what they call the "units" at the D. C. General Hospital. After a check-in, in which even my wedding ring which has never been off was impounded, I was handed over to two Negroes and ordered to strip. My clothes were locked up, I was given a shower, and ordered to put on a degrading set of "safe" pajamas which could not be used for suicide, etc.

Then I was ushered out to the corridor and greeted by what the seedy looking herd of inmates told me was the "welcoming-committee". This group consisted of alcoholics and dope addicts, black and white, who had been locked up there for long enough to regain some composure, and who sought sincerely to ease the shock for the newcomers like myself. But there was no easing it for me. These people were so obviously nuts or seedy or horrible that it only served to double the impression on me of being locked up in a madhouse. One had only one tooth and insisted on keeping a grisly smile on his pock-marked face. Another, a dope-fiend, had runny eyes and nose, and clammy wet hands which made me cringe as we shook hands.

After welcoming, I was led to my "room", with a seeing eye at the top and an eternal light. Everything is done by the personnel there to pretend that the place is just like home - but no amount of make-believe can hide the nuts and the locks on the doors. EVERY door is locked everywhere, everytime you go anyplace - even the door to the place where they keep your toothbrush!!

In all fairness, I must admit that some of the Negro guards were kind and understanding, and to these I am very grateful. I was entirely at the mercy of and in the power of Negro guards, attendants, doctors and nurses. A white face was rare.

But, as might be expected, some of the guards and attendants took extreme advantage of their monstrous power over a white man, and did what they could to make life miserable. With my picture often appearing on TV, these sadists took especial delight in demonstrating their dictatorship over me.

Shining their infernal lights in my eyes all night was one of their tricks, making me take a shower in the middle of the night, locking my little barred window on unbearably hot nights, and giving arbitrary orders leading to my discomfort all day were some of the other methods used these boss Negroes.

In the meantime, my brave lads were out everywhere picketing and agitating for my release, even though many of them were convinced that I was a goner, and they might follow me. But they kept the light of publicity on the case, which is the only thing preventing the Jews from eliminating me by open and brutal direct bribery, legal skullduggery and even violence.

My own thoughts were often tinged with terror as I lay in my bare cell at night. It had been so easy for Shultz and the ADL to railroad me this far - it would be even easier for them, now that I was in Shultz's own hospital, to "discover" that I was crazier than a bedbug, and lock me up without communication for life. I was even more worried about the possibilities of frontal lobotomy, - where the thinking part of the mind is neatly severed from the brain by a simple operation, or injections which would make me appear genuinely insane at any hearings. It would be SO easy, it seemed.

But, as I thought and pondered the possibilities, I came to the conclusion (which proved to be true) that, while the Jews do indeed have a conspiracy going - it is not TOTAL. They can't possibly have everybody in on it - else it would soon be no conspiracy; everybody would know all about it. The conspirators are forced to rely on a few key Jews, a few stupid or scared shabez-goy who will do what they are told for money or because of fear, a larger group of brain-washed boobs who imagine themselves "progressive" and "enlightened" because they "understand" the twaddle put out by the "liberals" as deep thought. This whole apparatus works as well as it does mostly because of the ignorance, fear and cowardice of those who discover the truth about it.

The top Jews who operate the terror and tyranny machine can survive and manipulate us exactly as the lion tamer can manipulate a cage-ful of deadly lions and tigers because the animals are too stupid and afraid of the silly crack of his whip and his chair to see the situation as it is and use the enormous power they have but are afraid to use.

That I was not insane, nobody had any doubt. But proving my sanity under the circumstances was a terrifying prospect. Psychiatry, being notoriously Jewish, is so steeped in its own involuted concepts that anybody who "differs" in our regimented society is, by their definition, nuts. Since Negroes and Jews are obviously so lovable and valuable, failure to perceive and appreciate and worship the superior qualities of these marvels of Nature is ipso facto evidence that the subject is a lunatic. And here I was, not only a man who professed a dislike of many Jews and a refusal to mix socially with Negroes, but who openly and scientifically planned to put large numbers of Jewish traitors in gas chambers, and get millions of Negroes to go back to their African home! What chance had I to convince Dr. Shultz's herd of psychiatrists, whose jobs depended on the man who had already committed himself to the proposition that I was "probably insane" ? And what of Shultz himself?

The prospects were anything but bright. I am ashamed to admit that they were so bad, in fact, that two of my lads, men who had stuck with me through all sorts of fights and threats and jail cells now decided that the fight was over and ran off. One even went as far as Oregon, imagining that the whole Party would soon be in padded cells.

But I was convinced that I would not only get out of that hell-hole, but that history has come to the point where evil has reached its zenith, and our rise and triumph is as inevitable as the rise of the sun after the dark of the night.

To make things more difficult, however, my court-appointed lawyer came to see me and whispered that HE was convinced of the most monstrous plot to railroad me for life, and that my only hope lay in refusing to talk to ANYBODY, especially psychiatrists. Mr. Parker, the lawyer, had never heard of any of the facts of the Jewish conspiracy, but his short introduction to Jewish pressure, threats and tactics when he was handed my case convinced him that I was practically a goner. When I first mentioned the way the Jews work, he scoffed, but soon got panicky when he discovered that I had put it mildly. The pressure they bring on everybody and everything to get what they want in the most brutal way IS frightening the first time one is exposed to it.

But I was locked up and helpless under Dr. Shultz, and my only hope lay in THINKING my way out of the mess.

I had already discovered, in my battle to expose the Jewish traitors politically, that the conspiracy is not total - that only a very few top people were in on the illegal aims and plan, and these depend on fear, stupidity and brilliant tactics to achieve their goals in what always must appear to be legal ways.

The major weapon against this hard core of plotters is publicity, which I had already achieved with more than satisfying results. They can't slide one into a dungeon or padded cell quietly when you succeed in becoming sufficiently notorious and well-known.

And the other weapon I discovered and perfected in that mental lock-up is the technique of dividing the top plotters from their tools.

Here is the secret which is worth life itself to my fellow battlers for America and the White Race when the enemy attempts to lock you up and shut you up as a lunatic: MOST OF THE PEOPLE YOU FACE WILL BE <u>SINCERE</u>, EVEN IF MISGUIDED. The Jews cannot afford to let everybody in on what they are trying to do, and they depend on brainwashing TOOLS to do their dirty work. The tools imagine they are full of "modern", "progressive" ideas, etc., and SINCERELY accomplish exactly what the Jews want done for their own filthy purposes.

For instance, it is the Jews themselves who are, as a whole group, paranoiac. The major symptoms of paranoia are Delusions of Grandeur and Delusions of Persecution. For four thousand years these Jews have been ranting that they are "God's CHOSEN people (a delusion which would get a single individual committed in a minute if it were not made the fetish of a whole "religion") and, at the same time, we are endlessly reminded, with pitiful wails, that "Jews are persecuted," they are always "innocent scape-goats," anti-Semitism is "hate," etc., etc. These are clearcut and inescapable proofs of paranoiac tendencies.

Knowing this, we know that the psychiatrist, when he gets hold of you, is going to be looking for these "delusions of grandeur" and "delusions of persecutions". He is going to be waiting like a cat at a rat's hole for you to come out with the slightest hint that YOU (instead of the Jews) are chosen to fulfil an historical mission such as preserving the White Race, and the concomitant proposition that the Jews are "persecuting" you for trying to expose them. It makes no difference if the White Race IS being driven out of existence so far as it is in the power of a group of Jews, and that you MUST fight to defend yourself from the terroristic machinations of these "chosen" apostles of tolerance and brotherhood. Facts have nothing to do with the situation. Any attempt to convince the psychiatrist who is steeped in Jewish thinking will only snap the last lock on your padded cell.

But, at the same time, the psychiatrist, if he is not a Jew himself, is still human and subject to manipulation.

Knowing the rules of his game, if you have self control and plenty of courage, you can BEAT him at it and win his OK.

The first rule is to COOPERATE! Instead of obeying my lawyer, who said not to talk at all, I volunteered to be a social worker in my cell block for the insane blacks in need of therapy. I drew pictures for them, wrote letters for them, and talked to them, although their "conversation" was enough to send one halfway up the wall in some cases. They are looking for ANTI-SOCIAL BEHAVIOR - any indication that you can't "get along". So, repugnant as it may be, be friendly, popular with the coons, and make yourself liked by one and all, including the guards. Above all, don't get into a fight no matter what the provocation from the idiots, lunatics or guards. Any violence, and they can honestly testify that you "fight", are "dangerous", and must be committed.

The second rule is to be HONEST! When they sit you down with their little pads and tests and tricks, do not be afraid. They will be looking for NEGATIVE attitudes and fear itself. Take it easy and attack the tasks they give you with good will and a determination to accomplish them well and quickly. If they ask you what you see in their ink blots and smears, gear yourself to see POSITIVE things and pleasant things - and then tell them honestly. You will see in the blots what you are SET to look for, just as a woman notices another woman's dress while a man doesn't even see it, an artist sees the painting and skill of the artist in an advertisement which a layman never notices, and an architect sees principles, details and ideas in a building which may simply be a public comfort station to the ordinary person. Dc not see blood, bodies, wreckage, etc., but SET yourself to honestly see birds with handsome plumage, perhaps Japanese dancers with flowing robes, etc. If you do not thus set yourself, the gruesome atmosphere of the asylum, the guards, doctors, etc., will cause you to give DISHONEST reactions of doom and death, which will only drive you further into the horrors of the mental lock-up.

The third rule is to realize that, bad as is the Jewish conspiracy, it is NOT all-powerful, and it is NOT total. No matter how much most Jews cause us to feel like disliking all of them, there ARE "good Jews", honest men who hate the conspiracy which is going on as much as we do. I owe a lot to a Jewish psychiatrist from another hospital who volunteered to come over to D. C. General and examine me in spite of the pressure to rush me permanently and forever into the lunatic lock-up. I trusted this man, talked freely and honestly to him, and CONVINCED HIM I WAS ON THE LEVEL AND AS SANE AS HE WAS, EVEN THOUGH OUR POLITICS WERE 100% OPPOSITE! It was a long chance, but it paid off. He reasoned correctly that if I really were a paranoid nut, I would be totally hostile to a Jew who looked and talked like a Jew, regardless of my objective determination that he was not part of the undeniable plot to railroad me. When this Jewy-looking Jew asked me even the most embarrassing questions, I literally shocked him by telling the TRUTH without reservations. In spite of himself, this Jew got to LIKE me - and went out and wrote up an affidavit that I was of sound mind and capable of standing trial. He, along with another volunteer psychiatrist from St. Elizabeth's was on hand at the Habeus Corpus

The interview on radio and TV in New York Supreme Court,
just before the riot.

NEW YORK
Herald
A European Edition Is Published Daily in Paris

230 West 41st Street, New York 36, N. Y.
Telephone PEnnsylvania 6-4000

THURSDAY, JUNE 23, 1960

U. S. Nazi Mobbed, Mayor Bans Rally

Herald Tribune photo by Ira Rosenberg

NAZI GETS POLICE ESCORT—George Lincoln Rockwell (center), head of the American Nazi Party, leaving ide exit of the New York Supreme Court, in Foley Square, yesterday, accompanied by police squad and Capt. Jay ľ. Fox (right), of the court attendants' staff. A waiting taxicab whisked Mr. Rockwell away to avert near riot.

By Philip S. Cook

Mayor Wagner yesterday toed plans for a rally in nion Square on July 4 by eorge Lincoln Rockwell and s American Nazi party. A lf-hour before the Mayor sued his statement which arged Mr. Rockwell with tent to "incite a riot," a special detail of detectives hustled the self-styled Nazi leader aboard an air liner bound for Washington. The former Navy pilot, who lives in Arlington, Va., was placed in protective custody earlier in the day after he was threatened by an angry mob in the rotunda of the State Supreme Court building. Curses and threats echoed off the marble walls of the court building when Mr. Rockwell attempted to make a statement for television newsmen. Some persons pushed forward and tried to spit upon him while others shouted, "You want to gas all Jews." Police and court attendants quickly hurried Mr. Rockwell to safety in a rear office. Mayor Wagner denied Mr. Rockwell's request for a permit to use Union Square after a fifteen-minute conference with Parks Commissioner Newbold Morris and

Continued on page 10, column 2

Part of front page of N. Y. Herald Tribune

Into Alabama's riot-torn capital drives a cargo of political dynamite – the new American Nazis

Stormtroopers pose in front of famous "hate-bus".

Commander Rockwell is "booked" and jailed in New Orleans as an aftermath of the "hate bus" campaign through the South. Charges were thrown out in higher courts.

CHICAGO SUN-TIMES
10 Mon., July 4, 1960

NEW YORK MIRROR, TUESDAY, JULY 5, 1960

NEW YORK HERALD TRIBUNE, MONDAY. JULY

1 . . . . . July 1960 THE HOUSTON CHRONICLE

CHICAGO DAILY TRIBUNE: MONDAY, JULY 4, 1960

Tail-end of riot on July 3rd, 1960. We were setting up stand to speak again, even with fight still raging.

proceedings ready to stick his neck out for me, and which would have gotten me out if I had not gotten myself out first by winning over the staff of the hospital, particularly the psychiatrist directly in charge of my lock-up or "unit".

Dr. Shultz was head of the whole hospital, and the man who got me locked up sight-unseen by telling the court I was "probably insane". Under him was a liberal lady psychiatrist who was head of psychiatry. There was NO question of their position in the railroading scheme. And the Jews were sure that with the head of the hospital and the head of psychiatry determined to "get" me, I was a goner.

But even all this power won't work if you keep your head and remember that not too many people can be in on a plot, or it gives itself away.

If you are ever seized and locked up as a "nut" as I was, remember that the vast majority of the people you will meet are NOT in on the deal, and will try honestly to do their jobs as they do with the thousands of other inmates they see all the time. It is impossible for the schemers to take them all into their confidence and get them ALL to help "railroad" you. They depend on power and influence at the TOP to overwhelm all opposition.

Your job is to mobilize the entire body underneath in outrage at your incarceration, and the plotters at the top are helpless. Not all our courts (except possibly in New York Jewish Courts) are dishonest, and the villains know that you can summon as witnesses others beside themselves. They HAVE to give you some kind of a hearing before committing you for life, and if you don't get panicky and win over the entire staff of junior doctors, nurses, guards and spies on the ward, the senior schemers find themselves in the uncomfortable position of exposing their dishonesty to their own staff if they insist that you are crazy when all the others know you are not.

In my case, the doctor directly under the chief psychiatrist was educated almost entirely in Jewish hospitals and schools, but he was not a Jew and was, I believed sincere. I had every opportunity to howl persecution and "plot" but I DIDN'T! My lawyer had told me to "clam up", and the psychiatrist knew it, but I DIDN'T. I was supposed to be a wild hate monger, down on the world and crazy with hate of all Jews and Negroes. But I WASN'T! The Negroes liked me, the psychiatrists liked me - even the Jew, the patients liked me, and I was so obviously taking the injustice of the incarceration with a good will and calm assurance that they could NOT question my sanity or personality, especially after the dose of lies they had heard from the Jews before I arrived.

Rule four, if you are locked up as a mental case for trying to expose Jewish treason, is to remember that even the plotters are not courageous enough to resort to murder or outright Soviet-style injections, etc. What they try to do is frighten and goad you into ACTING like a nut, so they can honestly testify that you ARE a nut from their observations and the observations of the whole staff. If you are uncooperative, howl about persecution, sulk and curse the staff, they will class you with all the REAL nuts they see all the time who do exactly those things (without cause, however).

The major attack by the plotters could have been fatal to me if I had not steeled myself to a fanatical belief in my own reason. They burst into my cell one night with two Negro guards, a Chinese doctor, and a Negro nurse. The nurse held aloft a huge hypodermic filled with vile looking, brownish-black fluid, and ordered me to roll over for a "shot". I asked what it was, and they said it was "vitamins".

Ask yourself what you would have done under similar circumstances. I knew they were determined to put me away for good, Walter Winchell (Izzy Lipshitz) had stated this was the official line on what to do with me, and I knew there were plenty of ways to drive me out of my mind by shots, etc., while I was "under observation". Now here they come with "vitamins" in the middle of the night, tenderly thinking of my health, no doubt.

The temptation to fight, to scream, to struggle to the last ditch to avoid that "deadly" shot was overwhelming. But I didn't do it. I believed they would not dare use such methods, since getting caught would totally wreck their scheme for good. But if they got me to fight and scream and act insane and those WERE vitamins, any court in the world would commit me!

So I rolled over docilely and took the "shot".

And it WAS vitamins! I could TASTE them as they coursed into my blood stream.

That little scene in my cell with the vitamins is a capsule version of what the Jews are doing to our people who try to fight them all over the Country. They get US to act like madmen and get many of us to believe that they are so all-powerful that everything which happens to us is part of their plot.

The Jews have no such all-powerful plot. They DO have a deadly plot of the top Jew-Communist-Zionists, and it is taking over the world - but not because they are so brilliant or so daring. They have been winning because we have let them goad us into being stupid, weak and disorganized. As the Jews planned to show I was "nuts" in court because they were sure I would fight their innocent vitamin shot - they keep showing Americans how wild and crazy our side seems to be when it howls "plot" every time one of us is arrested for speeding or for violating a Court order. The law says, for instance, as it stands now, that schools must integrate. This is an ILLEGAL law, to be sure, but it does have the sanction of law at the moment - and the FBI, for instance, MUST enforce. When rabid "Southerners" join the Communist Worker in damning the FBI for enforcing that law - or the Constitutional Amendment which says Negroes are citizens and can vote, they are "fighting the vitamin shot" and convincing millions whom we must win that they are just what the Jews say we are - "hate mongers" and lawless terrorists. The proper remedy is to CHANGE the illegal law, not fight honest police and FBI for enforcing the laws WE ALLOW TO BE MADE by a cowardly Congress, and a trained-ape Supreme Court.

When you out-THINK them, and then back up your reason with GUTS - as I had to do with the vitamins and as we are doing with our Nazi Party - they are WHIPPED and dumbfounded!

By the exercise of REASON and GUTS instead of wild emotion and "righteous wrath" at the illegal incarceration, I won over the Dr's. under Shultz and the lady liberal psychiatrist, and these honest doctors had the courage to defy the two top bosses and declare I was sane in TEN DAYS, in spite of the hysteria of the Chief of Psychiatry, who was still shouting "You're SICK! SICK! SICK!", even as I left the lock-up.

I went back out to the park immediately to make a speech, and this time there were no more screams of "SICK! SICK! SICK!" ! The Jews now were subdued and baffled. They had been told by their leaders that this was "it", that I would be locked up and out of the way for good - as their good old Izzy Winchell had promised them.

It was a major victory - a total victory over the worst threat of the Jews. If an open Nazi, preaching the gas-chamber and power was not "nuts", it would be impossible for the conspirators to throw any more LITTLE anti-Semites into their "mental-health" lock-up as madmen SIMPLY because they tried to expose Jewish machinations.

CHAPTER XVII

The rest of the summer and through the fall, we continued speaking on a regular schedule until the Jews, by their helpless silence as they stood around at our rallies looking heart broken proved that we had utterly smashed their terrorism.

With our mastery in our home area thus established beyond dispute, I bent all my efforts toward the organization and indoctrination of the troopers and supporters we had won with our dramatic tactics.

Above all, I had to make sure that all of our people understood that Communism is not an economic plot and not even just part of the Jewish scheme for dominating the earth although it is both of these.

Communism is a mutiny of the world's inferiors against the elite.

Since man first fashioned a rude stone implement, he has fought a never-ending battle with the forces of nature which have overwhelmed him. Death in childbirth, death in earthquakes, volcanic eruptions, plagues, tidal waves, droughts, famines, and death at the claws and fangs of ferocious animals have been the lot of a great portion of humanity for tens of thousands of years.

In order to have one or two surviving children, parents had to have ten or twelve born. Only the strongest, wiliest and toughest survived human existence for unnumbered ages. This always seemed cruel and most unfortunate.

But the very severity of this unequal battle with nature insured that ONLY the smartest and strongest individuals rose to leadership; ONLY the best organized and most excellent families rose to leadership of the group; and ONLY the strongest, smartest and best organized of the groups rose to preeminence in a desperately struggling world.

Weaklings and fools did not last long. Especially, they could not swindle the strong and wise men who had survived the awful struggle of existence into accepting fools, demagogues and weaklings as "great leaders". Thus, from the dawn of human history, with rare exceptions (caused by inheritance of power, which did not last, relatively speaking) only leaders who could lead attained REAL, permanent leadership, and only races (groups) which were TRULY superior could dominate.

Under these conditions the group of humanity loosely called "Aryan white men" inevitably rose to complete domination of the civilized world, and civilized much of the savage world. And within this elite human group, or breed - Ceasars, Pericles, Fredericks and Washingtons rose to personal leadership.

The natural enemies of humanity, such as disease, wild beasts and brutal elements forced the naturally inferior groups to accept the domination and leadership of the superior white group. And the same cruel struggle within the white group forced the masses of inferiors to accept and even seek the leadership and domination of the naturally superior and elite minority. "People's Revolutions" were always relatively temporary, and power and leadership sooner or later was back in the hands of the biologically superior humans who had REAL capacity and force to LEAD.

As a result, the world was benefited by the civilizing drive of the exceptional whites of England, Germany, France, Spain, Portugal, Italy, etc. - but most of all by NORDICS.

While the "subjects" of colonization might have chafed and complained under the yoke, millions of inferior savages who had lived for thousands of years in prehistoric squalor, ignorance and savagery were relatively suddenly taught the rudimentary technical methods of controlling natural forces so that many more of them could survive and become, in their own way, more powerful than their savage, uncolonized brothers.

During all of these eons of history, it was highly advantageous to the subjects - inferior races and even to the inferior individuals among the white race, to seek and accept the leadership of the best races and best individuals even if this involved some tyranny. Nature herself was a still crueler tyrant and only with the leadership and organization supplied by the superior white race and the superior individuals within the white race could humanity hold its own or advance in the battle with nature.

The weapon of the superior white man and the superior individual who led the white men was never physical strength along but always the power of ORGANIZATION - which is the supreme form of THE HUMAN WILL in action.

In applying his intellect to the cruel forces of nature which tyrannized over him, the white man inevitably cast aside superstition, religious myths, old wives' tales and wishful thinking. He discovered what we now call the "scientific method" - the power of organized, scrupulously LOGICAL thinking.

With the full understanding and use of this intellectual tool MAN SUDDENLY GAINED TERRIFIC POWER TO CONTROL MANY OF THE WILD FORCES OF NATURE WHICH HAD BEEN BEATING HIM FOR THOUSANDS OF YEARS. With this method there is almost no thing or action which cannot be somehow dominated, controlled and used by mankind.

Man has penetrated outer space and the atom itself. He has controlled one natural killer and disease after another and even developed artificial human organs to replace those destroyed or decayed. He is, perhaps, on the verge of discovering the secrets of life itself.

Utterly astounded at his own genius and accomplishment through the use of the scientific method, MAN THEN MADE WHAT MAY YET BE HIS <u>FATAL</u> ERROR.

From the discovery that he could USE natural laws he jumped to the conclusion that he could CONQUER NATURE and FLAUNT HER IRON LAWS.

Bursting with conceit over his scientific and material accomplishments he forgot that HE, TOO, IS A PART OF NATURE, AN ANIMAL.

He proceeded to "conquer" EVOLUTION. He has now REVERSED it. THAT is the supreme danger of our chaotic times.

Where nature had for countless centuries culled humanity until the best individuals and the best group (speaking of the average) dominated humanity, he now applies scientific method to EVERYTHING ELSE BUT HIS OWN BREEDING. He allowed anthropomorphism - conceit - to enter the picture and control him just as it did his most savage and stupid ancestors 10, 000 years ago in the form of superstition. Science showed him the secrets of heredity and how to use these secrets to breed better cattle, dogs, horses and even bugs. But when it came to his own heredity man was loathe to admit the perhaps "unfair" but brutally true fact that there is no scientific reason why all individuals and groups of the species homo sapiens should be equally valuable and have equal natural abilities any more than that all horses or dogs should be of the same quality whether by breeds or by individuals.

As a matter of fact, during the 18th and 19th century MAN FELL IN LOVE WITH BOTH THE SCIENTIFIC METHOD AND HIS OWN INTELLECT. With his medical knowledge he largely conquered the natural forces which had so long SELECTED the best individuals and groups alone for survival, thus utterly reversing the process of evolution which produced the superior white man and the very brains of the geniuses among the white men who discovered these scientific wonders.

With this sort of worship of the intellect went a concomitant degradation of physical force. Where once the white man had not only out-thought and out-manoeuvred the savage races but also kept them in meek submission by naked force and even terror, when necessary, the white man now began to delude himself with the soothing "liberal" idea that force could be dispensed with and man could maintain and extend his accomplishments by sheer intellect alone. He laid down his knotty club, bent over his books and began to fancy himself as "above" the rest of the animal world which still had to copulate, deficate, urinate - and FIGHT to survive. And as he did this, there was one human group which had been schooled and especially selected in this super intellectualism for thousands of years: the Jews.

Naturally weak, unaggressive and lacking in creative force, this human group had survived solely by its wits as a sort of parasite and had even developed a "religion" which codified and even glorified intellectual paranoiaism and physical cowardice as the "way of God".

When the forceful, domineering and driving white man laid aside his club, forgot that he also was an animal, and allowed his scientific method and medical knowledge to reverse evolution, HE SET UP HUMANITY FOR DOMINATION BY THE JEW.

Instinctively the Jew perceived the white man's growing unwillingness to FIGHT, and realized that in a battle of words and mutual swindling his thousands of years of experience would be more than a match for the less subtle Aryan white man. The JEW THUS BECAME THE LEADING AND LOUDEST EXPONENT OF INTELLECTUALISM AND THE SCIENTIFIC METHOD. AND AT THE SAME TIME HE INSTINCTIVELY DEPRECATED ALL IDEAS OF HEREDITY, BREEDING, RACE OR INDIVIDUAL LEADERSHIP. It is the Jew who would be master in a mongrelized world.

A wolf pack is led by the strongest and smartest wolf by a sort of mutual consent based on force. This arrangement benefits the entire pack because the wise and tough old wolf leader is the best guarantee for the rest of the pack that they will be led in an organized and successful manner toward food and safety, etc.

Humanity until the seventeen and eighteen hundreds was much in the position of such a wolf pack, beset as it was with natural dangers and human enemies.

But with the rise of intellectualism and pacifism the Jew was able to approach the members of the "wolf pack" of humanity and say, in effect, "Why should we be bossed around by the leader, 'the tyrant' when we outnumber him so greatly? Let us set up a DEMOCRACY and we will VOTE him out of business".

If the "pack" can be sold on this swindle it will mutiny against its natural leader and the resulting "democracy" will actually be run by the smartest demagogue or smooth talker, usually a Jew, once the strong leader is eliminated by sheer numbers.

This is what we saw in the French Revolution, Oliver Cromwell's uprising, and a hundred other similar "people's revolutions" against the naturally superior leaders of humanity, the so-called "aristocrats", who had lost their FORCE and became decadent.

About 1850 the Jew, Karl Marx, organized and codified this

mutiny of the inferiors against their natural leaders in the name of intellectualism, science and democracy. Organized by the Jews in the form of COMMUNISM, this "mutiny" by the massed millions of the earth's inferiors against the naturally superior races and individuals threatens to overwhelm humanity.

Today, in the name of "humanitarianism" and "progress", man has selfishly and stupidly stopped or even reversed every one of the mechanisms by which Nature kept him vigorous and evolving as a species. Where he once had twelve or thirteen children, so that only the strongest and fittest survived, he now cruelly limits his offspring to one, two, three, or, at the most, four. Of these, he hamstrings the strong and vigorous with the frustrating doctrines of "pacifism" and brotherhood with human trash, while he mobilizes the entire forces of society and science to keep alive the sorriest kind of creatures - from drooling idiots down to two-headed monsters. Daily grows the number of high-powered appeals for contributions to this or that foundation for the preservation of the lives and therefore the ability to procreate of the most miserable and unhappy little human mistakes, whom Nature would mercifully put out of their suffering, were it not for the soft-headed "humanitarianism" of short-sighted men and women, of whom Eleanor Roosevelt is perhaps the most disgusting example.

While the white race is thus emasculating and extinguishing itself by severely limiting its offspring and then keeping the most unfit individuals alive at the expense of the species, it is also actively helping and even forcing the numberless hordes of colored humanity to proliferate at such a staggering rate that the result is nothing less than a population explosion of the lowest kind of human mongrels. There are already SEVEN colored people for every white person in the world, and the ratio is becoming more overwhelmingly black every day. If we really believe in "democracy", as our leaders would have us, then, with one vote per person, we are already only a tiny minority about to be washed away in a tidal wave of colored and black "equality". The United Nations is already giving even the stupidest whites an inkling of this development, as cannibals and the most improbable spear-toters from the Congo are treated as "statesmen" by our liberal toadies, even as these minstral "statesmen" are picking morsels of their late political opponents from their pointed teeth.

Even the diminishing number of high quality white human beings, if they are able to get born and then survive a world being increasingly rigged for the benefit of the unfit and lazy, are still not permitted to survive in our insane world. Twice in my own lifetime, the same vicious forces which promote the unlimited breeding of the poorest and darkest of humanity, in the name of "democracy", have promoted horrible mutual massacres called "World Wars", in which the BEST of the Whites on one side slaughter the BEST of the Whites on the other "side" - although neither of these "sides" ever "wins". Always it is the Jews, the colored races and the Marxists who "win" these nightmarish butcherings, while the cream of our people, the bravest, most idealistic, unselfish and self-sacrificing young men go off to murder each other as VOLUNTEERS. The 4-Fs and the mercantile princes stay home to provide the band-music, the bullets, the fine uniforms, and the rest of the machinery for inflaming "patriotic" youth to go and kill each other to "make the world safe for democracy", or to "put down tyranny", etc. - although these same lads are cautioned not to get excited about RED tyranny, or BLACK tyranny - which is really "democracy" at work. Every thirty years or so, it seems, the decreasing number of the white elite of the world are set at each other's throats, while they are taught to work and struggle to make the world a better place to breed more Jews and Negroes.

Our people NEVER see this cruel and suicidal process, and, even now, the BEST of our people, the most patriotic, are whooping and war dancing to go and murder the RUSSIANS - who are also White People - instead of realizing that it is the COMMUNISTS who are the enemies of humanity, not the miserable, uneducated and helpless Russian white men and women who are prisoners of these world-fiends, just as, in a sense, we are here in America.

And, in between these planet-wide butcheries of the biological cream of humanity, the Jews give the elite no respite. "Liberalism" castrates our intellectual youth, makes them actually LOVE their destroyers and every process of their own disintegration. The resulting moral depravity finally produces the ultimate disgrace of civilization - pansies - queers! The Jewish-dominated fields of medicine would have us look with compassion and tolerance on this abomination because the people are "sick". But then, so are mad killers in the street. The Jews say

Hitler was "sick" too, but there were no recommendations to let him work his poor, frustrated little will. They say I am sick, but they do not seem anxious to permit me my little pecadillos. It is always and ONLY for disintegrative moral depravity that they bring out the "let-him-alone-he's-just-sick" bit.

Our great-grandfathers would probably have risen in overpowering and natural wrath to slaughter, left and right, the unspeakable crawling, filthy things we excuse as "beats". Doped up with narcotics, physically dirty, ostentatiously anti-social and repulsive, "crazy" with the orgiastic rythyms of Africa's lowest cannibals, full of the phoniest imaginable Jewish "intellectualism", (Ginsberg) and sleeping interchangeably with male and female Negroes - these degraded and pitiful creatures are the inevitable result of putting "democracy" and "liberalism" into working practice.

In short, every force of "modern" society, scientific, cultural, moral and intellectual has short-sightedly forgotten the RACE, the GROUP - in the wild "liberal" scramble to pamper the INDIVIDUAL AT THE EXPENSE OF THE SPECIES. Every NATURAL process of selection and breeding has been violently REVERSED, and humanity is breeding itself back to the jungles and caves out of which our ancestors once battled in thousands and thousands of years of bitter struggle with a merciless but healthy environment.

The idiocy of despising their own hereditary genius and strength has been made the fashion among young college "intellectuals" all over the world and, unless the white man becomes aware that the intellectualism and scientific method he so much admires must be applied TO HIMSELF AND HIS BREEDING AS AN ANIMAL humanity will be destroyed by social chaos and the reversal of biological evolution. In fact this process is already far along, and, like hypnotized birds before snakes, the white men and nations all over the world are cringing in abject cowardice before mutinous gangs of inferior people and black savages, inflamed and led by Jews.

National Socialism is, above all things, the doctrine that it is not only for the good of humanity but absolutely essential for the survival of humanity that scientific method be applied not only to the breedings of animals and bugs but also to the breeding of

The kind of "argument" used by the Jews to discredit me with the kids. It does not work a bit.

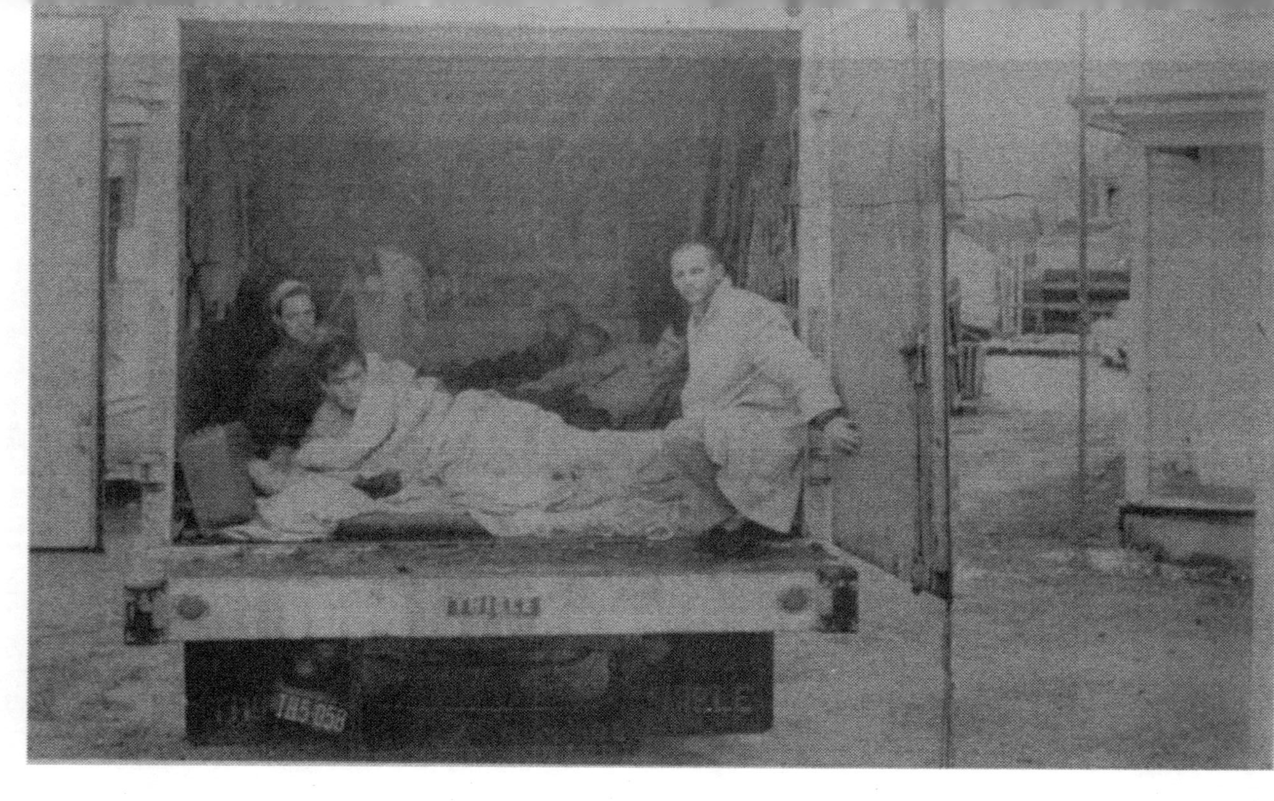

Truck-load of troopers arriving back in Arlington in a snow-storm after 36 hours of freezing and starving on the long, long road from Washington, D. C. to Boston and return. Lt. James in foreground.

Being rescued by Boston police from a mob of more than ten thousand screaming Jews!

The Stars and Stripes of America pass the banner of the White Man on our picket line against the scum who came to D. C. to abolish the House Committee.

human beings. National Socialism does not wish to destroy inferior races or individuals any more than a wolf leader wants to destroy the pack but only to organize them into a productive ORDER which alone can enable them to survive and enjoy some degree of human felicity.

National Socialism deplores the reversal of human evolution being accelerated by welfare-ism, brotherhood-ism, race-mixing and the unlimited breeding of the inferior races and individuals while the superior limit themselves to few offspring or none.

To accomplish these utterly fundamental and vital aims, National Socialism declares its goal to be nothing less than the absolute domination of the white, civilized areas of the earth by the Aryan white man and the leadership of the Aryan white man by the strongest and wisest individuals of the race rather than the largest number of weaklings, mediocrities and selfish private interests.

To achieve this goal National Socialism recognizes that power must be won legally, first in the strategic center of the world, the United States, and then in all the other white Aryan areas of the earth. National Socialism does not recognize the imaginary geographic boundaries of nations as being as important as the very real boundaries set by nature in RACE.

We therefore declare our intention eventually to incorporate all Nordic and Aryan white peoples into a single political entity so that never again will white men fight and kill each other on behalf of such silly things as imaginary geographic boundaries or such vicious things as Jewish economic swindles - either Communism or Capitalism.

We further declare that we do not seek to murder or destroy any race but only that we intend to establish separate areas within which each race will be at liberty to achieve its own destiny so long as it does not encroach upon or attack the areas or members of another race.

Finally, we declare our intention of utterly destroying all individuals, OF WHATEVER RACE, who are guilty of organizing, planning, or carrying out the criminal Communist conspiracy and mutiny against humanity and the laws of Nature. We recognize a great proportion of Jews have been, and are the leaders of this criminal Bolshevik mutiny and conspiracy against the race of humanity and will not shrink from the task of utterly destroying such poisonous human bacteria.

But this is only the negative part of our ideals and aims. The goal of National Socialism is and always will be a felicitous human ORDER in which each human being will be able to develop and express his contributions to humanity to the maximum possible extent and, by the application of scientific method to human breeding itself, to insure that this world is peopled, not with more and more negroid degenerates, but with human beings who increasingly approximate the lordly ideal expressed in the ancient Nordic sagas by the Gods and Goddesses of Valhalla.

CHAPTER XVII

(Note: The foregoing chapters of the book were written in September and October of 1960 for delivery to a publisher in Chicago in November. A full year was lost as the publisher and others were intimidated into abandoning publication by threats, mostly from the Anti Defamation League of B'nai B'rith and other Jewish organizations. Finally publication of the book was undertaken by Parliament House in New York in September of 1961. But this firm was not able to get the book printed and produced anyplace except on our own little Davidson 221 office duplicator.

Even then, the efforts to stop publication did not cease. "Volunteer typists" came to help set the book on our IBM - only to sabotage the work, as the typographical and spelling errors in the first chapters will show - in spite of all the diligence we could exercise. They actually set fire to the press room in the middle of the night, and disaster was saved only by the alert duty officer. My printer and layout man were manoeuvered into quitting at the crucial moment, so that I wound up producing almost all of the book myself, with unskilled help from loyal officers and troopers, except for IBM typing by a faithful woman member of the Party.

I have consequently re-written this last chapter in December of 1961, to bring the book up to date. The reader is again reminded that the book was written and produced under actual COMBAT conditions, with bullets, molotov cocktails, phosphorous bombs and rocks flying at the headquarters and print-shop, along with the more subtle attacks by Jewish agents. As I write, two of my lads are in prison, one just got out, and I am under sentence to prison in New Orleans and Arlington, pending appeal. The Jews in the Justice Department are combing every facet of my life, (including this book, copies of which were just picked up by the FBI yesterday, December 1, 1961) to find some grounds for a "prosecution" which would stick. Finally, our operating funds are so pitifully minute that we were printing and working in bone-chilling cold up until ten days ago - because we couldn't pay the gas bill since last April.

For all these reasons, we hope the reader will forgive technical failings in production of this work, and remember that CONTENT is here, regardless of the form, which is a temporary matter. Later editions will equal and surpass the tons of Jewish productions which fill our book shops now. In their case, the form is certainly there! : they have the millions to pay Gentile craftsmen to produce masterpieces of the book-maker's art - but the CONTENT is lacking - as with most things in our "modern" lives today - the age of plastic. We are already shifting from operation on sales of our PRODUCTION, and, with iron determination, we shall soon enough have the money to produce "THIS TIME THE WORLD" in the style to which it is entitled.)

With the victory in the Arlington Courts and the smashing victory over the "mental-health" attack in Washington, we were well launched into the first phase of our struggle to power. The world has read in the papers of our exploits since then.

That first phase was the fight to become KNOWN to the MASSES at all costs, as the fanatical champions of the White Man and enemy of the Jewish traitors.

There are many who think as we do, but who haughtily condemn our wild and wooly tactics as "undignified", etc. These know-it-alls cannot understand that being "dignified" or "refined" or "reasonable" has not helped any of the right-wing movements so far to SUCCESS.

The LEFT wing is not dignified or reasonable, but it is SUCCEEDING. It HAS POWER! It is winning because it understands the fundamental source of all political power, which is in the COMMON, ORDINARY MASSES of people.

Ultimate political power does not reside in "conservatives" or "liberals" or intellectuals or goon squads - but in the millions upon millions of plumbers, carpenters, laborers, taxi-drivers, bar-tenders, etc. And these millions are never won by argument, but always by the EXTREMES of emotion. They love and they hate. They play like kids, and they fight like animals. They despise weakness, especially in leaders, and love strength - even when it tyrannises over them. Roosevelt was a devilish example of that. They do not want to see an intellectual discussion between lofty political ideas, but the crushing victory of THEIR side and the utter annihilation of the enemy, whomever he may be.

The Jewish promotion of the idea of Democrary is a monstrous fraud to hide their OWN power over these masses, which consists of CONTROL of ALL media of mass communication and popular entertainment. An ordinary man cannot know personally the men and issues for which he is allowed to "vote". He gets to "know" these things, in a "free" democracy like America, ONLY AS THEY ARE SHOWN TO HIM ON TV, IN THE NEWSPAPERS, MAGAZINES, ETC. The candidates and issues upon which Americans, (and all citizens of democracies) vote are the IMAGES of men and issues painted with supreme cunning by the "hidden persuaders", the scientific mind-manipulators, who consciously and ruthlessly use emotional-engineering techniques to build "father-images" and all the rest of the tools of their POWER. "The other side" is simply not permitted to exist, let alone express itself.

Who ever heard of an anti-Semitic national TV show? - or a crime show with black criminals? -or even a John Birch TV program revealing, for instance, Ike's red record?

The result is that poor, ingenuous, ordinary and decent little John Doe, American, truly BELIEVES much of the crap poured into his head twenty-four hours a day from his press, TV, etc. The IMAGES he develops in his mind of "Jews", "agrarian reformers", "deprived Negroes", "sick criminals" - and all the rest of the liberal images - are not REAL - as anybody who has read a Jew paper or been mugged by a black criminal knows. But these synthetic images have immense power to INFLUENCE the masses EMOTIONALLY, so that they will vote for an insufferable spoiled popinjay like the millionaire Roosevelt, for instance, as a "man-of-the-people" !

The problem of building a political organization with the ability to MOVE these masses the OTHER way, in spite of the enemy's utter mastery of all means of communicating with the masses, is thus, FIRST, the problem of REACHING the masses - any way at ALL.

It does not matter HOW you reach them, at first - so long as they come to KNOW OF YOU, and the fact that you are at the opposite pole from those in power.

Our "Nazi" tactics force the Jews to blast us, in spite of their efforts at "silent treatment", as "monsters", "hate mongers", hoodlums, terrorists, etc., etc. In SPITE of themselves, the Jews must build, on their own TV, an IMAGE of us which is just as phony as the images they build of their own marionettes - but an image of us nevertheless, and an image of emotional impact which REACHES THE MASSES.

Ask the man in the street about Rockwell and the American Nazi Party, and he will probably tell you that this is the outfit which wants to "kill all the Jews and niggers".

That this is a foul Jewish-promoted lie does not matter. In fact, it is preferable that the image of us, at this stage, IS monstrous.

The masses think like an electronic calculator. They have no modulations, but only plus and minus, black and white, absolutely good, and absolutely bad. Pavlov proved with his dogs that fundamental behavior patterns are basically determined by PHYSICAL conditioning - and the Jews and Communists have proved with their "brain-washing", that human beings follow the same laws of mechanical psychology as Pavlov's dogs. With proper techniques, EVERY living being, including humans, can be MANIPULATED.

Only the hot-house intellectuals want their fiction to be "modulated" with "greys", as in real life. The common man wants HEROES and VILLAINS, and no mistake about it. He cannot fathom or sympathize with a "nice" villain or a "bad" hero. An examination of the pulp magazines and comic books he prefers will quickly establish the truth of that statement. If "Superman" got drunk and made an ass of himself, or turned coward once in a while - as real "heroes" do - he would be out of business in a trice.

The Jews, therefore, do exactly what we want them to do when they keep their Nazi atrocity lies pouring out over America in such oceanic floods. Right now, and for yet a while longer, they are the shining "heroes", and we are the 100% rotten "villains". Never mind, we have REACHED the masses with an image as the all-out opponents of what is going on. As long as John Doe is reasonably satisfied with what is going on and his own lot, he will continue to accept that image.

But the Jews and all their poisonous lot of liberals, queers, race-mixers, etc., CANNOT keep poor little John Doe happy for much longer with what they are doing to him. No amount of the most masterful TV brotherhood shows can keep a man whose wife is brutally raped by a gang of rampaging blacks from being rudely awakened to the PHONYNESS of the Jew-image of the "downtrodden" and "innocent" Negro. All the poetry of peace and co-existence can not keep Mr. Doe blind to the fact that Communism is CONQUERING THE EARTH, with one third of the world's people already enslaved, and the rest softened up, while it now HAS A BEACH-HEAD 90 MILES OFF FLORIDA!

At present, the "common man" is luxuriating in the products of a super-phony war scare and manipulated economy, and his ears are deaf to pleas that he examine the basis of this false "prosperity". But when the house-of-cards finally comes crashing down, as it inevitably will, in eight or nine years - John Doe will SUDDENLY WAKE UP! And he will be MAD!

With race riots all over America as hungry blacks and whites fight for non-existent jobs, all the pretty notions of brotherhood and sweet reasonableness will be gone in a few moments of agonized recognition that his "friends" have been his enemies all along; -------- and HIS ENEMIES HAVE THEREFORE BEEN HIS FRIENDS.

The liars are now convicting themselves before the jury of America, and the more they lie and swindle the jury, the more that jury will howl for the liars' blood when they discover how they have been taken. We are content - nay, HAPPY, to be advertised as the would-be murderers of all Jews, even though that is not true - since we thus (1) REACH the masses with SIMPLE IDEAS, and, (2) we stand forth as the uncompromising enemies of what we know the masses are growing to hate, and will hate with a passion in a very few years.

We have almost completed the first phase of our struggle to

power, now. Both our name and our fanatical opposition to Jewish Communism-Zionism and race-mixing are known all over the world, albeit with misunderstanding and burning hatred by many. That was our first aim.

The next phase of the struggle is to begin to drive into the brain-washed minds of the masses a few simple ideas of what we REALLY are - instead of what the Jews say we are. This book is the first major step in that direction, although the masses won't read it. But it will inevitably win over some intellectuals and fighters who will help us in the battle of propaganda. Most important, the book will stand as a crushing refutation of the Jew lies about our true nature and ideas, which can be judged in itself, - with fearful results for the liars. Even when I am railroaded to prison or another round of the bug-house, which is more than likely in spite of our scrupulous adherance to the law, as the Jews in the Justice Department get more and more desperate, the book will be preaching the truth and salvation silently to thousands, and perhaps millions.

We are still too weak to force our right to hire a hall and start public meetings. We couldn't rent the loft of a whore house for a meeting today. But that will not be for long. As income from the book begins to put blood into our veins at last, instead of the trickle of water from the contributions of a few hardy pioneers, we will go into court and FIGHT for our right to hire a hall like any other American - as we fought for the right to have a public park in New York - and won.

And when we can hire a respectable hall and hold a public meeting, we shall be well launched on the second phase of our struggle - the phase of EDUCATION by PROPAGANDA. We shall drill into the minds of the public a few simple, unforgettable slogans and ideas which will replace the disbolically clever slogans of the Jews now being driven into the minds of the people: "brotherhood", "you can't judge by groups, only as individuals", "tolerance" (for everything left, but hate for the "hate mongers"). When these lovers of free speech howl about Nazi "slogans", etc., let the thoughtful American consider the nature of the campaign being waged by the Jews and "liberals". And do they not also use slogans and the most monstrous of emotional propaganda?

With these scientific and powerful methods, we shall slowly

begin to make the masses understand what we REALLY are. And, again, the lies of the Jews will backfire on them, just as they do already in a small way when people come to interview me and find me intelligent, literate, courteous, reasonable and, many report, personally likable. The shock is apparent on their faces when they do not see the horns on my head nor smell fumes of the fire and brimstone. Over a period of five or seven years, we will convert thousands, tens of thousands, hundreds of thousands, and finally millions to our ideals and to belief in our masculine, straight-forward leadership toward the things Americans and White Men REALLY want.

In the meantime, we shall start running for every available political office, and insisting on our rights to buy TV time when we get on the ballot even for dog-catcher. The wild howls of the Jews as I appear before a swastika banner on TV and drive home the truths the people ache to hear will be music to our ears, and the death song of the sneaks and traitors. Sooner or later, we will start getting ELECTED, first to small offices, and then to large. As the Jews continue to drive and push and hound the honest people of Virginia with forced integration and subversion, pornography and communism, I will inevitably be able to win enough voters to be elected Governor.

And that will mark the start of the third phase in the fight to win back our American Heritage and enforce the Constitution for the benefit of the White Christian people who built the Country. With the prestige of public office, in spite of all the lies and terrorism of the Jews, we shall DEMONSTRATE what honest, fearless government is like - and ORGANIZE THE PEOPLE we have won. We will build our trained, hard-core of present Nazis into a nation-wide mass organization which will be inflamed with a holy zeal such as fired the American Revolutionists - and which has been lacking in our people since the civil war. By this time the "conservatives", with their stale-dish-water programs and their battle-cries of "back to the good old horse and buggy days!" - will be discredited and beaten by the Jews they now pretend not to notice. The enemies of America will be running wild over our liberties, our traditions, and most of all, over our white race. Goldwater is almost sure to follow Kennedy, when the latter has crammed four years more of insufferable betrayal down the throats of Americans. And Goldwater will be the last straw for the good and patient people who have tried so hard to believe the

Jews and their lies. When HE TOO betrays the people, there will be no place left for them to turn. The phony "contest" between the Republicrats and Demicans has already disgusted millions, who now hope to get something done as "conservatives" against the "liberals". And when these poor innocents find that the foxy Jews have once more pulled off their old trick of LEADING 'EM, when they couldn't beat 'em (as they did when they put Ike in) - they will be at the end of their sheep-like patience, and ready for ALL-OUT, uncompromising FIGHT with a deadly enemy they will finally see.

Especially the rich "conservatives" will flock to our banners after Goldwater has slipped them the final dose of brilliant betrayal. Just as the industrialists of the Ruhr finally backed Hitler, once they realized that there is no half-way method of beating the Communists who were reaching into their wallets, so the rich American reactionaries will back US, when they, too, learn that the Jews and Communists are about to seize their CASH.

With growing funds, not only from the people, but from scared reactionaries, by 1968 we will be able to start the fourth phase, the winning of POWER! We shall make the presidential race, which will, in turn, insure tremendous national TV coverage. We won't be able to beat Goldwater or any other Jew or Jew-stooge they put up, yet, but we will SMASH THEIR MACHINE OF INVINCIBLE TERROR at the top levels, even as we have done it down here in the gutter.

The key factor in our planned rise to power will be our solution to the Negro problem - a problem which has already become completely intolerable to both white and black.

The common working people of America are fed up with what they call "niggers", and are only prevented from taking violent action in the matter by the most extreme measures of brainwashing and the use of armed force, including the U. S. Army, as at Little Rock. This is not a Southern problem; the situation is even more explosive in Northern cities like Detroit and New York.

At the same time, the Blacks are understandably fed up too. Every human being on this earth MUST find some way to consider himself "valuable", and worthy of his own self respect. Otherwise he is forced by iron laws of psychology to (1) go insane (2) commit suicide (3) evade the problem by becoming a drunken, dazed bum.

Constantly being told he is "equal" by white hypocrites who pretend to love him (but who send their own kids to private schools so they won't have to mix with the blacks, etc.) the Negro in America is being increasingly frustrated in his search for the all-important feeling of worth-whileness.

A hundred years ago, when "equality" was unheard of, the situation of the blacks SEEMED less hopeful, but, in the respect being discussed, it was far, far better. The Negro lived and moved ONLY in his own exclusive black circle. Sure he was looked down upon, almost as an animal. But his psychological existence was 100% WITHIN his own group. He never even considered the possibility of a white wife, for instance, or even of association with whites. He gained his feeling or worth-whileness solely by his status WITHIN his own group - and here he could excel and become, perhaps, a "great man". The Negro who succeeded in being the best banjo-player or story-teller, perhaps, among the OTHER NEGROES, was a very real SUCCESS.

But with the rise of the modern hypocrisy of "equality", the Negro has constantly set before him the idea that he is NOT a success and is NOT worthwhile unless he succeeds in WHITE circles. He is no longer satisfied with a Negro woman, but, as is shown by the fact that almost every Negro who gets enough money and prestige marries a White - he dreams of getting white women, getting white jobs, and being accepted 100% as the same thing as Whites - which he can never be.

The "liberals" make light of the argument, of course, but it is the most fundamental part of the problem that even the most "liberal" whites are only talking with their mouths about equality, and only so long as it doesn't affect their PERSONAL lives. They have no intention whatsoever of mixing SEXUALLY for procreation with the Negro race - and, so long as this is denied the Negro, how can he really believe the slop that he is the SAME as white prople except for the color of his skin?

The honest Americans draw the color-line at their front door - and the dishonest "liberals" draw that same color-line at their daughter's bedroom door. But the line is THERE, and always will be. And it HURTS. You can be sure of that. Only a fishy-cold "liberal" prattling of "humanitarianism" could fail to realize the terrible hurt he is inflicting on the Blacks by giving them the false idea that 100% equality is only a matter of time, sit-ins and sleep-ins.

The common working white people of America, on the other hand, cannot be blamed for beginning to hate the black man who is becoming increasingly obnoxious in his pushing, as he is inflamed by the Jews behind the "Negro" organizations. Even if there may be a few scummy liberals who actually are prepared to offer their own daughters on the altar of Negro "equality", as did Sir Stafford Cripps, the unspoiled, healthy white working man will go all-out for naked violence before he will permit wholesale violation of his sacred instincts and Nature's laws.

The Jewish power of money is presently holding this army of irritated White Men in check through loss of jobs, as Fire and Police Departments are integrated and monsters like Sammy Davis, Jr. are paraded with their white wives in all our press and magazines, etc. But when the money and jobs are GONE, as they surely will be, as the phony economy collapses when it can no longer be patched up by Berlin "crisis" and similar frauds - then there will be nothing to stop the enraged millions of White Men.

The result is that all the makings of a nightmare of violence and bloodshed are in the works. The hypocrits and Jews keep telling the Negro he is equal, and that he should PUSH. And the Whites - in the North as well as the South - are kept from violence to stop the infernal pushing ONLY by the fact that they lose their jobs and perhaps go to jail. Calling them "bigots" will not stop them forever.

Most Americans who can't figure this all out intellectually know it by instinct. Everybody can FEEL the terrible, deadly tension as the Negro pushing continues.

It is by INTELLIGENTLY SOLVING this unspeakable situation that we shall win most of the votes to put us in office.

When economic catastrophe hits, race riots will be the inevitable result, all over the USA. The RACE problem, which is unanimously ignored or aggravated, by ALL our politicians, from Stevenson to Goldwater, MUST be solved by intelligence, honesty

Floyd Fleming taken as a member of the U.S.A. armed forces in Europe, while fighting anti-Communist White Christian Germans in WW I. Floyd resolved to find out the causes of the wars which are destroying our White Western Civilization. He finally got the truth from Father Charles Coughlin.

Commander Rockwell speaking at the
Black Muslim convention, Feb. 1962

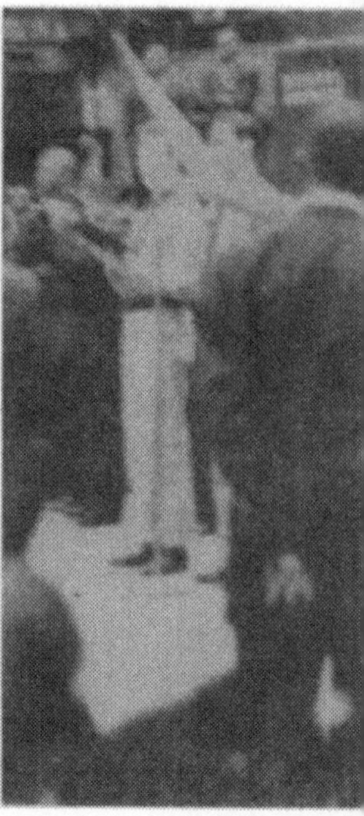

U.S. Stormtroopers picket the White House against race-mixing and Communism.

U.S. National Socialists remember Sen. Joe McCarthy.

Trooper Dawson Grant demonstrating our slogan, "Kike's for Kennedy!" with the rubber nose.

and goodwill, or it WILL be solved by massacre and bloodshed.

The American Nazi Party recognizes that the Negro can NEVER be happy in White Society, because he can NEVER gain that all-important feeling of worthwhileness and self-respect as long as he is constantly reminded of the color-line, whether it is at the honest-man's front door, or the bedroom door of the liberal's daughter.

Only on his OWN piece of geography, among his own people, can the Negro find the "status" he must have to exist as a contented human being.

Washington, Lincoln, Jefferson, Madison, Monroe and all of our early leaders recognized this fundamental truth, and helped set up Liberia in Africa for our Negroes whose capital was named Monrovia after our President Monroe.

Not too many years ago, Marcus Garvey, a Negro, led a Back-to-Africa movement which obtained FOUR MILLION NEGRO SIGNATURES on a petition seeking return to Africa. But this fact is not permitted to reach the public BECAUSE THE JEWS WANT THE NEGROES HERE FOR THREE ROTTEN PURPOSES.

(1) They USE the Negroes as a balance of power in politics. They have got the Whites almost evenly divided into two meaningless teams of Republicrats and Demicans, so that their votes neatly cancel each other out (the main reason for the huge Jew-led drives to "get out the vote", which keeps the suckers imagining they are participating in their government). Only by winning the BLACK vote, today, can a politician get elected, and the JEWS CONTROL THE BLACK VOTE. The Negroes, being relatively ignorant and simple-hearted, are easily led by the sly and foxy Jews like Marvin Rich and Arthur Spingarn. And these Jews of the NAACP, CORE, etc., peddle the votes of their black herds to whomever offers the Jews and Negroes the most, and to hell with the Country, the Constitution and the White Christian majority. It is an utterly VICIOUS scheme!

(2) The Jews prey on the economically helpless Negroes FINANCIALLY. One has only to visit the Negro section of any town and look at the names on the shops, or see who collects the huge rents on the roach and rat-ridden black tenements, to see

how the Jews milk their black cattle. See who is selling rot-gut wine and whiskey to the blacks. Or observe the municipal court records to see who is garnisheeing the Negroes' pitiful wages for "easy-payment" debts created in selling trash and plastic junk to the childish blacks.

The third reason the Jews keep the blacks here is more subtle. They, the Jews, use the Negroes as a BATTERING RAM to smash down White Gentile society for the benefit of JEWS, without making it obvious that it is a JEWISH operation. By preaching equality for BLACKS, and enlisting the soft-heads and fat-heads like Eleanor, who imagine they are intellectuals, but who won't think when they can FEEL, the Jews break down our society and our morale with NEGRO invasions, which are promptly exploited by the Jews who move in behind them.

In short, the NEGRO is as much the key to Jewish power in America as is the 100% Jewish run TV and movie business.

THAT is the reason why any effort toward a REAL solution to the Negro problem is hounded and driven out of existence by the Jews - as Marcus Garvey was thrown into jail and his movement broken up.

But, just as the Jewish outrages always produce a counterforce among the Whites, as they did in Germany, Italy, Spain, etc. - and as they are doing in the USA now, so they have at last produced a real LEADER among the Negro people, Elijah Muhammad, head of the "Black Muslims".

I am aware that Mr. Muhammad at one time preached massacre of the Whites. I can't say that I blame him. Were I a Negro, I would feel the same way. But Mr. Muhammad was and is faced with the same problems as we are - total hostility by the Jews and all their satelites, including the government. The Jewish press does its best to ignore him, while writing paeons of praise and adulation for the "black" organizations and activities led by Jews, such as CORE and NAACP. Under the circumstances and remembering the simple hearts, ignorance, and sorely oppressed status of most of the Negro people - he may be forgiven any kind of preaching necessary to gain the STRENGTH to do something constructive to solve the problem - just as we have to use some pretty powerful methods to outwit the Jew press liars ourselves.

But Elijah Muhammad has taken a million or more of the **LOWEST** kind of people on earth - lazy, drunken, dirty, filthy-mouthed, nasty-minded black bums and criminals - the repulsive creatures called "niggers", and turned them into disciplined, self-respecting, sober, hard-working, courteous, clean-talking and **CLEAN** people. Let the White Men who tax me with being a "nigger lover" for respecting Elijah Muhammad show me the White Leader today who has demonstrated any such masterful **ABILITY** to **LEAD** !

As Muhammad has grown in wisdom and stature, he had also become more moderate and statesmanlike in his program and demands. He knows how the Jews are using and abusing his people, and he does not fear to say so, like so many of the Southern Whites who damn me for praising Muhammad, and then whisper in the most cowardly manner about the "shhhhhh! 'j-e-w-s' ".

He used to demand American territory for his Negro nation. And I will say that, if there were NO other way of solving the Negro problem, and the alternative was the mongrelization of the White Race, which is inevitable if the present mix-pressures are continued, I would even be willing to give the Negroes an area of their own in America (New York City, perhaps, where they could enjoy the company of their Jew "friends") before I would see our White Race degraded to a nation of brown mongrels such as swarm in South America.

But that is not necessary.

When economic catastrophe hits, as it will in six to eight years when the phony war-scare economy runs out of Berlins and Laos, we will need no CCC camps or "PWA" to pump up or prime our economy. By ceasing our disgusting efforts to buy friendship and "neutrality" from our enemies with "foreign aid", and allocating that money and the money now wasted on civil rights and Negro crime, to our own Negroes to BUILD and CONSTRUCT a modern industrial nation in Africa, we can not only make the prospect of their own modern Nation so attractive that our Negroes will FLOCK to migrate, but we will pump eight or ten billion dollars a year into our own FREE economy - our contractors, technicians, service organizations, businessmen, banks, etc. And this will put millions more Americans to work on a CONSTRUCTIVE project to SOLVE a problem, not add to it.

Many people object that it would be impossible to MOVE fifteen million Negroes to Africa. These people forget that we moved many more people than that in World War II - under COMBAT CONDITIONS ! With the proper will and spirit, it will be easy.

As for winning the Negroes, it is truly child's play with modern methods of sales and public relations. The lot of most Negroes in America is incredibly rotten. The vision of glorious "equality" and a "little taste of honey" (i. e., intercourse with a white girl) held out by the Jews to the Negroes, is rapidly disillusioning the blacks, and will do so with increasing rapidity as the pushing continues. Only the rare "professional" Negroes really have anything, and they are in the overwhelming minority. The great mass of American Negroes are wretchedly poor, frustrated, exploited, given the bum's rush through our courts and prisons and generally have little to live for.

With any kind of funds for public relations work at all, we will sign up these downtrodden creatures by the millions for a GENUINE BREAK at long, long last. A man will charge the massed bayonets of the enemy on behalf of a VISION in which he REALLY believes, as every war proves on both sides. Our Negroes now HAVE no vision at all, except the hypocritical hope of "mixing", which bitterly frustrates them, especially the poor ones who can't afford a white prostitute, professional or amateur.

Savage Africa has almost NO skilled workers and leaders, so that our American Negroes would jump at once from the status of inferior and oppressed second-class citizens here to pioneering heroes and much sought-after experts in the new land. Attractive window displays in the Negro sections of all American towns, with literature and petitions inside, TV programs, public rallies, and all the rest of the tools of modern mass sales techniques will fire the imaginations and hearts of the frustrated millions of America's blacks, as the hopeless dream of 100% equality can never do.

And Elijah Muhammad is the obvious and proven leader to organize and direct this mighty movement - which is almost exactly the parallel of the way America itself was civilized by people who were persecuted and hounded in other lands.

In spite of the stupid howls of "nigger-lover" I must suffer, and the understandable fear of us in the heart of Mr. Muhammad, we have confidence that we will be able to reach a position of mutual trust and cooperation toward the great goal of a genuine solution to the Negro problem. His lieutenants have already made contact with us and assured us of any help they can give, and we have given them a similar assurance.

As we grow in power and influence, we will be able to work in dignity and separately, but in mutual helpfulness, toward the day when our American Negroes will at last have the REAL self-respect and decent environment we owe them after three hundred years of slavery and exploitation, and our White Men will have the pure white Christian civilization won for them with the blood of their ancestors.

And even the soft-heads and liberals will one day vote for us when we have solved this monstrous problem to the satisfaction of all honest people, black and white, except the Jew plotters.

In 1972, with Nazi Senators and Representatives in every state, and millions of Nazi voters, we will be able to sweep to power in the elections. And then will begin the fifth phase of the struggle--the CLEAN-UP! With an iron-broom (but always within the law and the Constitution) we shall sweep the hordes of traitors out of office and into the gas chambers--not because they are of any particular race or "religion"--but because they are proven in courts, before juries, to have been TRAITORS to the most wonderful people and system of government ever devised by the mind of man.

In one term in the White House, we will be able to finish the great mass movement of Negroes to Africa or to reservations here, so that our cities will be sparkling WHITE and relatively free of the rampaging criminals now making our own National Capital a vicious jungle of murder and rapine. The people, who have been endlessly told what tyrants we are and how we wish to murder and rob people, will have seen what we can REALLY do with power, and will know at first hand the pure white-fire of our idealism, just as courageous and honest Germans can tell you what a paradise Germany was in the "Great Days", even for honest Jews - but especially for Germans. Americans will once again REVEL in their wonderful, blessed AMERICA, spotlessly clean of the queers, pornography, hot-house sex atmosphere, hypocrites, false Christian pink preachers, and - most important of all, traitors and liars.

Then will begin the most dangerous of times for our Movement and our people.

The Jews pulling the strings in Moscow and Jerusalem and in the banking houses of the world (including the Vatican, where the Rothschilds have now got Pope John deleting passages of Holy Scripture which do not please the Jews who had Christ crucified!) - these international Jewish plotters will once again work with devilish ingenuity to plunge the world into another blood-bath to save their rotten secret empire of blood and gold, just as they plunged us into World War II to make the world safe for Marxism again, when Hitler had it on the run.

Hitler, never having travelled, was an incurable isolationist and chauvinist. He imagined he could create a spotless and clean little "bubble", disinfected of Jewish filth and phlegm, right in the middle of the filthy Jewish world empire. He managed the miracle for a time, but his task was as impossible as trying to create a hospital-clean and antiseptic little area in a sewer being flooded with roaring torrents of excrement. He was overwhelmed by the flood of Jewish hate and poison which surrounded tiny Germany.

Had he started from the beginning, not with a GERMAN movement, but with a WHITE MAN'S movement encompassing all White Men in the world, as the Jewish movement encompasses all Jews, without regard to nationality or even "religion", and as the Communist movement is international - he would have taken a lot longer to win - but he would have been sure of winning. You can't beat an INTERNATIONAL movement with a national movement, any more than you can create a nice clean place in a sewer.

We have not made that mistake. From the beginning, I have worked just as hard to build international solidarity of ALL White Men, regardless of religion or nationality, as I have to get the Party set up in the U. S. A.

The method is incredibly hard - I am banned from most Countries and can contact our people in other areas of the earth only by mail - but it is SURE. In England, Sweden, Norway, Iceland, Canada, Argentina, Germany, Denmark - even in Japan -

and dozens of other Countries, we are working to set up the World Union of National Socialists as the fight -to- the-death counterpart of the world Marxist Comintern and Zionist organizations. Today, the Nazi Parties in these countries operate with front names, just as I direct our Nazis in many American cities to operate under other names until they are strong enough to survive the Jewish terror attacks. But they are growing STRONG and PURE. Nothing can now stop them.

The Jews are now doing to the entire world what they did to Germany in the 1920's. The jewish moguls have even decreed that women's fashions must look like those of the insane '20's, as a look at the fashion ads will show. They monopolize everything, and they are spreading their filth and decay into every nook and cranny of this staggering planet. Their red United Nations is planned as the final grave-yard of all National liberty, and, as it becomes increasingly colored and black, the ultimate grave-yard of the White Race.

As we grow and win power here in the U. S. A., there is the terrible danger that the Jews will decide on the ultimate insanity of another World War to stop us - a threat they use now to drive the world crazy with their interminable alternating threats and handshakes, just as Pavlov's dogs were driven to such states of anxiety by mechanical alternations of torture and care that they became living zombies willing to do anything commanded by their manipulator, exactly as our people are beginning to do en masse. The Jews have no intention whatsoever of blowing themselves up in the hydrogen-bomb war they keep depicting for us in frightening full-color articles and on TV, etc. The "cold-war" is strictly to make money in the war-scare economy and keep the suckers busy watching with horror "over there", while the dirty work is being done over HERE - and to keep us spending ourselves to death, as Lenin commanded.

If, however, it appeared that the Jews were on the verge of total exposure - and the consequent punishment they have so diligently earned, they would try at the last minute to pull everything down about everyone's ears, in the hopes of escaping retribution in the catastrophic confusion and misery.

This we have guarded against by the fundamental idea of our movement, which is the UNITY OF THE WHITE ARYAN RACE - regardless of the location on the globe of the members of that race. THIS UNITY INCLUDES THE WHITE ARYAN RUSSIAN PEOPLE - who are as much victims of Jewish Communism as WE are - even the Russians who go along with the thing, like our own fat-headed "liberals", not knowing the nature of the fiends who are using them.

At the same time we are working and growing here in the U.S.A., and our fellow Nazis are working in the other Western nations, we are doing what we legally can to prepare a Nazi movement in RUSSIA TOO. We have no desire to go and murder Russian White Men, as we once went forth to murder our German brothers because we were told they were "enemies". We DO have a burning desire to massacre the Bolshevik traitors to humanity, who have turned the earth into a slaughter house in World War II for their own rotten and selfish ends, and who now openly boast that they will "Bury us"! We are not ashamed to HATE them, whether they speak Russian, Yiddish, or English with a British accent like Mr. Acheson. And the way to see that they meet the fate they have earned, is to HELP THE RUSSIAN WHITE MEN THROW OFF THE TYRANTS - not HATE the Russian people, as we are being taught. Sure they are ignorant and perhaps hateful to us, now - but so are many sincere "liberals" right here in this Country. They are like poisoned children who vomit on the living room rug. Who can curse and hate them for being poisoned, knowing the cunning and infinitely devilish genius of the poisoners?

In the 1920's, the Jews thought they had everything going their way - and they did. The Western world was burning itself up in a wild and immoral orgy of speculation, sex, jazz, crazy fashions, idiot pastimes, poisonous negroid "culture" and all the rest of the Jewish arsenal of destruction of the racial will to survive. Our intellectuals flocked to the red banners, and our literature for the time is almost openly communist. In Germany, the Jews were arrogantly and openly Communist with seven million red hoodlums marching and beating people up in the streets of Germany, and figured they had it made. Germany was to be the hub of their world revolution, and they almost succeeded. But, as is happening in the U.S.A. now, their vicious attack forced the rise of a counterforce from among the people itself - Adolf Hitler. At the very last minute, the despised and persecuted Nazis rose up and smote the traitors down.

Today, the Jews are doing all over this earth exactly what

they did in Germany. The same wild orgy, the same mad speculation and spending, the same build-up of Communism, the same immorality and pornography, the same wild crime-waves, even the same fashions. We are fast approaching the point of TOTAL decadence and confusion, which is the planned prelude to red revolution.

Perhaps most deadly of all, this time the Jews, with their Communism and "democracy", have inflamed almost the whole of Africa, South America, India and Asia with savage and mutinous rebellion by the colored swarms of the planet against the White Man --and therefore against civilization which is the product of White ideals and genius. If this frightful mutiny were eventually to succeed, as it is doing by leaps and bounds, the result would not be paradise for the colored races who would overwhelm and run riot over the Whites. The result would be the same regression to savagery and squalor which has taken place every time the White Man has been driven out of negroid areas such as Haiti.

The reason that America is mecca for the world is not that it is richer in resources and wealth. South America is infinitely richer in natural wealth, but is nevertheless sunk in squallor and typical, unstable, tyrannical "latin-American"-style revolutions and mustacioed musical-comedy type "leaders". Only as the population becomes WHITER, as in Argentina and Uruguay, does the civilization become more idealistic and orderly.

The soft-headed "liberals" who are so hell-bent to hand civilization on a platter to pygmies and cannibals fail to comprehend that the very ideals which motivate them, and which they worship --depend for their existance in this world on the WHITE RACE, and that their efforts at equality will not only not help the inferior races, but will operate exactly like taking the parents away from helpless and innocent children. The results of withdrawing White Domination in savage Africa are already apparent, and will soon become catastrophic. As the colored mutiny is spread by the Jewish "democrats" and Marxists, the White Man will not find the colored races raised up to HIS level of civilization and the ideals which can maintain civilization, but rather HIS OWN civilization and ideals will be PULLED DOWN toward the level of the savages, and finally obliterated in a roaring black flood, as we are witnessing in bloody Africa - and New York's Harlem -today!

But, again, just as in Germany in the '20's - these villains have driven into existence a COUNTERFORCE. In the '20's it was local - in Germany, Italy and Spain.

But today, as they again approach the same crucial moment of their seizure of world power - they are not faced by only one little isolated nation which woke up. Like the sorcerer's apprentice, they have chopped the "broom" which they couldn't stop all to pieces - and now the PIECES are coming to life.

An almost imperceptable quiver here . . . A little movement there. . . A few swastikas smeared on a Jew wall. . . A high-school group in Kansas meeting by candle-light underneath the Leader's picture! The Horst Wessel song in hoarse, choked voices in a tavern in Berlin! The British Spearhead fighters rushing the platform and smashing up a meeting of red traitors in London! The fighters of the Rikspartiet in Sweden and Norway attacking Jewish Communist traitors in Stockholm and Oslo! The Prime Minister of South Africa warning the Jews publicly that he will not tolerate any more of their open and infamous revolutionary racial agitation! . . . A police official in a great city privately confiding that most of the Department understands at last what we are trying to do, and is all for us! . . . Japanese Nazis fighting bloody battles with the arrogant, snake-dancing reds set up with the encouragement of our own State Department! . . . . . A swastika flag flying from a fraternity house in Maryland! . . . . The sound of Nazi drums and marching boots in Cologne, before the brave ones and their swastika banners are thrown into the Jew dungeons. . . The holy light reflected in the candle's gleam from the shining eyes of a boy from Texas as he is sworn in at Headquarters as a new storm-trooper for the White Race! . . . . . The little swastika pennants fluttering from the taxicabs in Mexico City! . . . The reverent, secret meeting of the faithful in Argentina! . . . The sacred "Blutfahne" ("Blood-flag") of Adolf Hitler, lovingly folded in a safe-deposit box in Chile, awaiting the Great Day! . . The young Icelandic Nazis, marching in the grey and drizzling streets of Reykjavik to the graves of Nazi pilots with their swastika banners flying bravely! . . . The roaring, defiant voices of forty young American Nazis marching under the Swastika to speak in Washington, D. C.! . . . "WE MARCH AND FIGHT, TO DEATH OR ON TO VICTORY! OUR MIGHT IS RIGHT! NO TRAITOR SHALL PREVAIL!" . . .the glorious red-white-and-black banner of the WHITE MAN whipping and snapping in the wind beside the Stars and Stripes as we march in defiance of the screaming hate-contorted Jew terrorists!

From all over this planet the little movements are gathering, the courageous little bands of persecuted heroes are joining up! The defiant ones of the Hitler Jugend lift their bloodied heads again and again under the blows of the Jews and their toadies. A Nazi WILL not die! Die Fahne HOCH! Die Reihen Fest Geschlossen! The sound of their brave singing is HEARD! We are COMING, brave comrades! Your White Aryan brothers in England, Sweden, Nigeria, Iceland, America, South Africa, Italy, France, Demark, Argentina -----EVERYWHERE --hear you! We are COMING! MARCHING! FIGHTING! The Great Day of JUSTICE DRAWS NIGH!

THIS TIME the traitors will not be able to find any group of White Men anywhere who will listen to their lies and go and murder the Jews' enemies for them. There will be no place to hide -no place to start their eternal game of friendly subversion of their unsuspecting hosts -no place to generate their infernal hates and fratricidal wars, no place to set up their anvil of Capitalist exploitation and their hammer of Communist revolution and slaughter.

THIS TIME the traitors will have only one place left in which they can at last find respite from the insane hate-monster which has been eating out their diseased hearts for six thousand years! . . . And we shall provide that final solace.

With deadly, incredible irony, Fate is now repeating what happened in Germany, on a world-wide scale!

THIS TIME we shall not be soft-hearted and gentle like the Great Man who refused to use his tanks to slaughter the helpless British at Dunkirk because he believed even Churchill had some honor and loyalty to Britian and the White Race left.

THIS TIME we shall not be content with "minding our own business" here while the Jews stir up another World War to wash us away in oceans of irreplaceable White Blood!

THIS TIME we shall not permit traitors to "escape" so that they can move in on some other innocent people to organize and betray them as the German Communist Jews did to America. None shall pass or escape retribution, not one!

THIS TIME we shall not put our faith in anything or anybody

but ourselves and our unshakeable WILL, impelled onward by an inscrutable Destiny Which has already demonstrated Its determination to resurrect the Good whenever it is crucified by evil, as it is now all over the wretched planet.

THIS TIME we shall not rest nor lower our arm until the very last human rat and red snake is beaten to death, no matter how they squirm and crawl from pole to pole or from mountain top to jungle swamp!

THE LAST TIME our Leader showed the way to victory in one single area of the earth. "Today Germany!" he predicted --"TOMORROW THE WORLD!!"

Now it is TOMORROW! Now is the time, White Men!

THIS TIME THE WORLD!!!!!

HEIL HITLER!!!!

Matt Koehl, Commander of the National Socialist White People's Party in a 1978 Photo

EPILOGUE

On August 25, 1967, Lincoln Rockwell fell. The man who had raised the immortal standard of the Swastika out of the ashes of defeat and degradation the man who led the postwar revival of Adolf Hitler's National Socialist movement - was foully struck down by an assassin's bullet.

The Jews and their henchmen gloated. They assumed that when they had a cowardly traitor murder Lincoln Rockwell, the National Socialist movement and the party he had formed would automatically collapse, and the only real threat to them since 1945 would forever be removed from the face of the earth.

But they failed to reckon with the loyalty and steadfastness of those faithful comrades whom Commander Rockwell had gathered around him, and who in that fateful moment refused to give the Jews and their stooges the satisfaction they had counted on. Not only did these loyal ones pick up the torch and keep alive the bright flame of National Socialism during an extremely crucial time, but by their dedication and faithfulness they succeeded in building Lincoln Rockwell's party stronger than it had ever been.

Over a seven-year period, it was my distinct privilege and good fortune to serve under and work closely with Lincoln Rockwell in varous phases of National Socialist activity. During this time, I was able to observe at first Hand the incredible genius, the mettle, the iron WILL of this man in battling against some of the most formidable odds a human being can face. Not only did he have to contend with vicious external enemies, but most heartbreakingly with so-called White men and pseudo types claiming to be National Socialists who, by the foulest means, would contrive to stab him in the back and destroy his work. Never can anyone who was close to Commander Rockwell forget the grief and needless agony that these treacherous creatures caused him.

Ultimately, Commander Rockwell knew that he would one day face an assassin's bullet. With an uncanny premonition, he had uttered these prophetic words at the very beginning of his struggle:

"1 knew I would not live to see the victory which I would make possible. But I would not die before I bad made that victory certain."

Much as his enemies had hoped, the fateful shot which ended the earthly mission of Commander Rockwell did not destroy the immortal Cause for which he fought. For he had built a movement capable of superseding his own human existence — a movement which is now in the process of securing that great victory which he foretold.

Lincoln Rockwell's great work, his whole life and soul, was the party — not just any party, but that entity which he eventually chose to call the *National Socialist White People's Party.* He left that party to us as a legacy.

Today I can think of no finer tribute to this great hero than to build even stronger the party which he founded and the movement which he led, as a monument to his eternal memory and a bastion of hope for an embattled White race everywhere. I know Commander Rockwell would have wanted no other tribute.

Matt Koehl, Commander
National Socialist White People's
Party Arlington, Virginia, January
1979

DIE FAHNE HOCH! RAISE THE BANNER HIGH!

www.ingramcontent.com/pod-product-compliance
Lightning Source LLC
Chambersburg PA
CBHW030418310726
48979CB00007B/1098

* 9 7 8 1 5 9 3 6 4 0 1 5 6 *